"Promise me you'll never again do anything as foolish as this," Bandit whispered.

"I can't make promises," Tori replied.

She refused to open her eyes, and she could feel every sensitive place where her body touched his.

"Promise me," Bandit said, more demanding than before.

"I don't promise that which I can't be sure of."

Bandit's hand cupped her chin. His eyes glittered behind the black mask.

"Promise me," he repeated.

Tori shook her head, despite his holding her chin. "I'll never stop until Jonathon Krey gets what he deserves," she whispered, her anger rising. "What's wrong? Can't the infamous Midnight Bandit take the competition?"

"If you're not careful, *you'll* get what *you* deserve."

"And what might that be?" Tori demanded angrily. She would not be intimidated by anyone—not even the Midnight Bandit.

"This," Bandit replied.

She wasn't sure what to expect, but it wasn't Bandit's kiss. And once his mouth was pressed against her own, his lips firm and commanding, she certainly didn't expect the response of her body to the kiss. It was as though he were kissing her everywhere simultaneously. Every fiber of her body came alive, and Tori surprised herself by not resisting but slipping her arms up around Bandit's chest.

# TODAY'S HOTTEST READS
# ARE TOMORROW'S SUPERSTARS

**VICTORY'S WOMAN** (4484, $4.50)
by Gretchen Genet

Andrew—the carefree soldier who sought glory on the battlefield, and returned a shattered man . . . Niall—the legendary frontiersman and a former Shawnee captive, tormented by his past . . . Roger—the troubled youth, who would rise up to claim a shocking legacy . . . and Clarice—the passionate beauty bound by one man, and hopelessly in love with another. Set against the backdrop of the American revolution, three men fight for their heritage—and one woman is destined to change all their lives forever!

**FORBIDDEN** (4488, $4.99)
by Jo Beverley

While fleeing from her brothers, who are attempting to sell her into a loveless marriage, Serena Riverton accepts a carriage ride from a stranger—who is the handsomest man she is ever seen. Lord Middlethorpe, himself, is actually contemplating marriage to a dull daughter of the aristocracy, when he encounters the breathtaking Serena. She arouses him as no woman ever has. And after a night of thrilling intimacy—a forbidden liaison—Serena must choose between a lady's place and a woman's passion!

**WINDS OF DESTINY** (4489, $4.99)
by Victoria Thompson

Becky Tate is a half-breed outcast—branded by her Comanche heritage. Then she meets a rugged stranger who awakens her heart to the magic and mystery of passion. Hiding a desperate past, Texas Ranger Clint Masterson has ridden into cattle country to bring peace to a divided land. But a greater battle rages inside him when he dares to desire the beautiful Becky!

**WILDEST HEART** (4456, $4.99)
by Virginia Brown

Maggie Malone had come to cattle country to forge her future as a healer. Now she was faced by Devon Conrad, an outlaw wounded body and soul by his shadowy past . . . whose eyes blazed with fury even as his burning caress sent her spiraling with desire. They came together in a Texas town about to explode in sin and scandal. Danger was their destiny—and there was nothing they wouldn't dare for love!

*Available wherever paperbacks are sold, or order direct from the Publisher. Send cover price plus 50¢ per copy for mailing and handling to Penguin USA, P.O. Box 999, c/o Dept. 17109, Bergenfield, NJ 07621. Residents of New York and Tennessee must include sales tax. DO NOT SEND CASH.*

# ROBIN GIDEON

# PASSION'S BANDIT

**ZEBRA BOOKS**
**KENSINGTON PUBLISHING CORP.**

*To Hannah Lee*
*10/22/93*
*Welcome to the world darling,*
*Mommy and Daddy love you.*

ZEBRA BOOKS are published by

Kensington Publishing Corp.
475 Park Avenue South
New York, NY 10016

Zebra and the Z logo Reg. U.S. Pat. & TM Off. The Lovegram logo is a trademark of Kensington Publishing Corp.

First Printing: May, 1994

Printed in the United States of America

# One

Tori Singer stood in the dark, her back pressed against the high brick wall surrounding one of the finest mansions in all of Santa Fe. Her heart pounded in her chest, and her palms were moist with fear. What she was about to do was illegal, and if she was caught, she knew she hadn't a prayer of getting a fair trial.

She could hear laughter from inside the mansion. Gathered in the enormous, lavishly appointed ballroom, the cream of Santa Fe society probably sipped chilled champagne. Making deals to expand their already considerable personal fortunes, the gentlemen undoubtedly laughed among themselves and pretended that life for everyone was as deliciously satisfying as it was for themselves.

Easing cautiously along the wall, Tori felt a loathing for the people in the ballroom. She resented their wealth and their smug condescension as she imagined them standing with cool, champagne glasses in manicured hands, congratulating each other on how magnanimous they were to have planned, then financed, the charity hospital for those less fortunate.

But these folks didn't fool Tori for a second. She knew

the charity hospital was just a ruse to promote themselves. Worse, the journalists who chronicled the event were willing pawns duping the public into believing that the wealthy weren't simply manipulators of society's good nature.

Another carriage rattled down the street. Tori moved to her left, stepping into the darkest part of the shadows. She could hear a woman laughing inside the carriage. Who was having such a wonderful time on this sultry summer evening?

Tori forced the question from her mind. She didn't care who occupied the equipage. The only person she was interested in was the mansion's owner, who was already partying inside. And that man Tori Singer would destroy.

Jonathon Krey.

A bitter smile compressed Tori's lips. Krey and his family had been linked to every major criminal enterprise in the territory for the past thirty years, from bribery of elected officials to cattle rustling and extortion. Tori and the authorities knew of Krey's involvement, yet he'd never spent so much as a single day in jail.

Tonight Tori would even the score, however. Tonight, Jonathon Krey and his thieving family would be the victims, not the villains. They would finally get a taste of their own medicine.

Inhaling deeply, filling her lungs with the night air scented with wild flowers, Tori jumped up to reach the top of the stone wall with her right hand. Strong and agile, she quickly pulled herself atop the two-foot-thick barrier, paused to reassure herself that she hadn't been seen, then leaped soundlessly to the thick green grass below.

The mansion was surrounded by two hundred and fifty

feet of lawn on all sides. Crouching, Tori covered the gap in less then a minute, her light green eyes darting right and left, searching for the multitude of gunmen parading as guards who always surrounded the Krey residence. Whenever Jonathon Krey left his fortress, some of these men served as his bodyguards.

Tori pressed herself against the mansion wall, waiting, forcing herself to be patient, willing her erratic heartbeat to become steady and slow, her breathing normal. To her left, the darkness was heavy, though she'd spotted two guards walking slowly back and forth along the perimeter of the wall. She would avoid that area. To her right was the main entrance to the mansion, which, though well lit, lacked the armed guards who were the greatest threat.

As more people moved in and out of the huge, double, front doors, Tori was glad that she had spent the money to purchase new Levi's for herself. They were dark blue, and they helped to conceal her in the shadows. She didn't care that the so-called good people of Santa Fe scoffed at her because she wore men's denim trousers, and she didn't care that the local preacher once gave a sermon using her as an example of the moral decay infecting womanhood, citing the fact that she was never seen without a Colt revolver in the holster strapped around her hips.

The metal grid placed along the south wall of the mansion to encourage the vines to grow upward was suited for a makeshift ladder, so within seconds, Tori was scaling the wall and pulling herself onto the balcony of a second-floor bedroom.

Dropping to one knee, she then crouched low, her eyes narrowing as she looked in the window to search the interior darkness. Her ears were now attuned to the slightest sound that did not belong. Several times she resisted the urge to pull her revolver from the holster. She feared that, tense and nervous as she was, she might shoot too quickly or inaccurately, and could not chance that.

This war—her personal, private war against Jonathon Krey and the evil he represented—would be one fought intelligently. And in the end, when Tori failed—she had no doubt that she would fail, because the Davids of this world defeat the Goliaths only in the Bible—she would be able to say honestly that she'd never hurt an innocent person.

Satisfied at last that no one was in the dark room, she stepped inside, easing her way past the immaculate white curtains.

An eerie sensation overcame Tori the moment she was inside the Krey mansion. She'd dreamed of this moment for so long that she'd expected the air would smell different, foul in some way, as though the greed ingrained in all the Kreys had an odor to it. The room, in fact, had the pleasant aroma of cleanliness and freshly cut flowers.

Tori was a little disappointed. She had, in her mind, imbued Jonathon Krey with so many foul traits that it disturbed her to discover, in even a small way, that he was really just a man—though perhaps more clever than most, certainly more treacherous and greedy. Just the same, Jonathon Krey was only a man, and as such, he could be defeated, even by a frightened but determined young woman like Tori.

She looked over the room, wishing she could light a candle but not daring to. It was pleasantly, though certainly not elaborately, appointed, with a few feminine touches. Tori suspected the room belonged to one of the servants, perhaps an upstairs maid. Having made this determination, she moved to the door. She had nothing against the servants working for the Kreys, only the Kreys themselves—and those who willingly were involved in the Kreys' criminality.

She slipped out of the room and peered left and right down the hallway. Two lamps, one at either end, lit low, gave off pale yellow light. Tori could hear music filtering up from downstairs. She smiled. The twelve-piece orchestra Jonathon Krey had hired for the evening would help cover any sounds she might make.

She checked the next room down the hall, pressing her ear to the door briefly to listen for sounds from inside. Opening the door slowly, she found this room, also dark, was clearly a man's. Much larger than the first bedroom Tori had entered, it contained, along one wall, an enormous glass-walled gun case.

She paused a moment to look at the weapons, hating the fact that she herself found it necessary to constantly keep the Colt with her. But the Kreys did not keep guns to provide needed food for their table. They were so-called sport hunters, which meant that they killed indiscriminately and, after decapitating their quarry for display, left the carcass behind.

To Tori's thinking, it was a sinful waste of an animal's life not to eat it or use its hide.

She walked over to the dressing table and sat on the small bench seat. The brushes and combs she saw were inlaid with the gold initials *JK*. Although it could be either Jeremy Krey or Jonathon, Tori suspected it would be the son, Jeremy.

Absurdly proud of himself, the elder Krey would have a much more elaborate bedroom, she suspected.

Her hands shook slightly as she searched through the chest of drawers. Countless fine shirts, snowy white and made of the finest silks and cottons, neatly filled the drawers. Tori found a small box containing cuff links, and for several seconds she thought of stealing it. She replaced the box. The cuff links were probably one of a kind and, as such, would be difficult to sell. Most likely if she did sell them to reimburse victims of Krey's greed. the sale would be traced back to her.

She closed the last drawer, careful that everything appeared exactly as it had when she entered the bedroom. Tori looked around. She was surrounded by wealth, from the exquisite silver candle holder to the gold-plated Remington revolver on the nightstand behind the bed.

Another bitter smile pulled at Tori's lips. Why on earth would Jeremy sleep with a revolver at his nightstand table? Did he really need it for defense? The mansion was protected by a high stone wall, and there were always guards on duty. Could it be that the Kreys, understanding how much pain and suffering they had caused over the past thirty years, knew that sooner or later someone would try to even the score?

Tori hoped, in fact, that Jeremy Krey did sleep fitfully, always worrying whether some honest soul would decide that enough was enough and enter his bedroom with gun in hand, intent on murder—not theft, as Tori was now.

She thumbed through a small book on the bedstand, hoping that she might find something of value there. The book contained the names of women—apparently those Jeremy was intimate with, or hoped to be.

"What a swine," Tori murmured aloud when she read the name of a young woman she knew and saw beside the name Jeremy's notation that the woman's father was having financial difficulties. It didn't take a genius to figure out that Jeremy was hoping to exploit the father's unfortunate situation and coerce the woman into his bedroom.

On a writing table in the corner of the room, Tori found a small leather pouch, with fifteen or twenty gold coins inside. Without determining exactly the value of the coins, she stuffed the pouch into her back pocket. Not a fortune, but a start, she told herself, moving on, glad that she had been able to strike out at Jeremy. But it wasn't the son who was the evil heart of the Krey family, it was the father, and Tori wasn't going to stop until she had metaphorically drawn blood straight from the heart of the Krey criminal dynasty.

*Too bad it won't be first blood,* she thought angrily as she slipped out of the bedroom, moving down the hall to the next door. *Jonathon Krey drew first blood with me, and he'll probably draw last blood . . . but before that happens, before his guns silence me forever, I'm going to make him bleed, I'm going to attack him right where he'll feel it most—in his wallet!*

Mack Randolph took an obligatory sip of champagne and was able to stifle his grimace. The wine had gone warm because he'd held the same glass so long, and he loathed champagne that wasn't icy cold and the finest money could buy. He pulled the heavy gold watch from his pocket and touched the stem, opening the protective case. It was still too early, he decided, reminding himself that tonight patience was not only a virtue . . . it was a necessity.

A portly old journalist with a ring of frizzy hair on his skull, his notebook and pencil at the ready, approached.

"Mr. Randolph, do you have just a moment more? I'd like to ask you a few more questions, if I might?" he asked.

Mack smiled, even though he did not feel like answering any more insipid questions. "A few more, then I think we should concentrate on having a good time. After all, that's what the celebration is all about, isn't it?"

The two men exchanged a laugh, both knowing that this event was designed to get Jonathon Krey's name in the newspaper in association with the charity hospital.

"It seems an unlikely alliance, your working so closely with Jonathon Krey on the hospital," the journalist began. "Everyone knows that you and Mr. Krey have been on opposite sides in several controversies over the past few years. Can you tell me how it came about that the Randolphs and the Kreys got together to build the hospital?"

"First off, let's get the record straight. *I* didn't get together with Jonathon Krey. I had started organizing the charity hospital almost four years ago, when I first realized the great need for it. It wasn't until last year that Jonathon Krey got involved. By that time, most of the work was completed."

Mack looked away, forcing himself to be calm. He resented the fact that the public might think the Kreys benevolent. But no matter how much he hated Krey, he wasn't going to turn down Krey's money—not when it was needed to complete the construction of the hospital.

"Aside from the hospital, there's your political career to consider," the journalist continued, hoping for a juicy morsel of news that his competition hadn't gotten. "When are you planning to run for elected office, and what's the first office you'll seek?"

Mack smiled at the journalist, pleased that the conversation had turned from Jonathon Krey, a subject that always spoiled Mack's mood.

"For now, I am quite content to practice law. As you know, the Circle R ranch—run by me and my brother—has just recently signed a contract with the Army to provide beef for the troops. That'll keep all of us more than busy for quite some time."

"Yes, of course," the journalist said, but his old eyes indicated to Mack that he did not entirely believe everything that he'd just heard. After a brief pause, he asked, "What will be the first office you seek? Give a hardworking man like me a little leg up on the competition, Mr. Randolph. I'm getting along in years, and the editors all think you've got to be a young buck to be any good in this business."

Mack laughed softly, enjoying the man's honesty, but still not willing to answer such a question.

The journalist pressed on, taking a new tack. "What's your opinion on the Midnight Bandit? The story has it he's out to destroy Jonathon Krey. Do you believe that?"

"No, I don't," Mack said, answering just a bit too quickly for his own peace of mind. "If the Midnight Bandit is out to destroy Krey, why did he break into the Colville Saloon and burn it down?"

"Everyone knows Jonathon Krey was a silent partner in that saloon," the journalist replied.

"Oh? Not everyone. *I* didn't know that."

"Well, it's true."

Mack decided to change their topic of conversation.

"I can't speak about the Midnight Bandit. How can I talk about something I really know nothing about. What I can tell you is that the first office I'll be going for is mayor of Santa Fe. I'm only twenty-eight, and though my father pretty much had it in his head all along that I was going to be the politician in the family, there's an awful lot I need to learn."

"So you'll start as mayor of Santa Fe, then move on to . . . ?"

Mack smiled. "I repeat, I'm only twenty-eight. I'll keep the job of mayor for at least two terms. When my second term is over, I should have learned what I set out to absorb. Obviously, the next step would be territorial governor."

"Or governor, if we're a state by then."

"That's right," Mack said.

At that moment Jena Krey joined them, moving slowly, her steps as fluid as the silk she wore. She'd always looked to Mack like a house cat that was still a wildcat in her soul. Even though a person could keep this little kitty in his lap and scratch her behind the ears to make her purr, in this animal's heart was a feral creature that had never given up the thrill of the hunt or lost the taste for a fresh kill.

"Territorial governor right from the beginning," Jena declared, her moist red lips curling into an all-knowing smile. "Why not start right at the top?"

"The top of the political ladder is the presidency," Mack commented.

"Darling, you don't want to go that high," Jena said,

her tone soft, smooth, and unmistakably sensual. "If you were president, then you would be much too busy to do anything except lead this great nation of ours, and it would be such a shame if you had no time to just enjoy yourself." She turned to the old journalist and gave him the full impact of her startling blue eyes. "Don't you agree?"

The journalist had seen countless gold diggers and dangerous and ambitious women, but they couldn't compare to Jena Krey. Stunned nonetheless by the blatant sensuality in the woman's unwavering look, he mumbled, "Yes, you're quite right." He excused himself quietly and walked away, looking for a glass of rye whiskey to calm his nerves.

"I'm afraid I've frightened the poor dear away," Jena smiled, casting Mack a sideways glance that other men would kill to get. It plainly said if he was interested, Jena was more than willing. "I do hope the interview was over."

"No, you don't, Jena. You ended it. You're not the type to share the stage with anyone. It's either all of you or nothing."

Jena laughed softly, sipping champagne. "You're right, darling. But then, you're almost always right, aren't you? I do appreciate your honesty."

Mack looked away from her; wishing he could hate her, knowing in his heart he couldn't. With all her annoying and infuriating traits—her rampant vanity, her heartless ability to use people and then cast them aside when they were no longer necessary to her—he could never trust her. But her candor, her *joi de vivre*, her refusal to live life by anyone's rules other than her own, made her fascinating to him.

"You know, you'll never get elected without a wife. The voters just don't trust a bachelor," Jena reminded him, her tone businesslike now.

"I'm aware of that."

"And everyone knows you've slept with more than just a few fine women in Santa Fe."

"Not everyone knows that," Mack said, an edge to his tone. "In any case, you're hardly one to talk about the number of lovers a person may have had."

"I'm not criticizing you, darling, I'm merely pointing out certain salient facts that you should be aware of."

"What exactly are you getting at, Jena?"

She moved just a little closer to Mack, close enough now so that he could feel the heat of her body. Though she was beautiful, Mack knew she was treacherous, traitorous; and if there was anything he could not accept, it was a traitor within his ranks. That—and that alone—was what had kept Jena from working her way into his arms, despite her continued efforts.

"I'm telling you that a marriage of a Krey and a Randolph would be wonderful for everyone. Think of it. The power of your family combining with the power of mine! Who could stand in our way? Who'd dare? We could crush all opposition!"

"But Jena, I don't love you. Frankly, I'm not even sure I like you. And you don't love me. Besides, your father would go right out of his mind at the mere mention of such a preposterous notion."

Jena's luscious mouth curled into something akin to a smile. "You let me worry about my father. He's a businessman, and he'll do what makes money. And as for love . . . what difference could that possibly make? I am the one woman who can tame you, Mack Randolph—the one who can satisfy you like no other woman ever has, or ever will. Once you've been with me, you'll never again want to sleep with any other. Isn't that something to think about?"

"Yes, but not for long." Mack smiled to soften the impact of his words. "Really, Jena, you must be more careful about how much champagne you drink. It makes you say the silliest things."

Perhaps another woman would have been offended and stormed away. Not Jena Krey. She smiled sweetly at Mack and raised her glass in a subtle, silent toast.

"We'll talk about this again . . . later," she said, then turned on her heel and walked into the crowd of guests.

Though she appeared perfectly calm and poised, Jena was seething inside. Mack Randolph was going to be the next mayor of Santa Fe and, after that, the territorial governor. She wanted to be at his side. To marry Mack Randolph would give her a prestige she could not have while she still carried the Krey name. Being Mrs. Mack Randolph would give her the power of elected office, too. And perhaps best of all, it would infuriate her father to no end.

Jena knew she had lost this battle, but the war was a long way from over. If there was anything in this world that she knew about, it was men—and sex. Mack was handsome, virile, and sexy—and she would bring him under her control, if it was the last thing she did.

Mack, freed from Jena's presence, breathed a small sigh of relief. He had known her for years, and though she was no longer a little girl, the savagery of a child was still within her. She had never really learned the difference between right and wrong, and whenever Mack was witness to that, he was chilled to the marrow of his bones.

He noted several people standing discreetly aside, waiting for the chance to talk to him. On another night, he would have given them the chance, but not tonight. There was too much to do, and this time was a perfect one to make his exit.

He saw Jonathon Krey standing with the mayor of some tiny town near Santa Fe. The appropriate move would have been to say good-bye to Jonathon, then leave, giving the guests the impression that he and the elder Krey were not the enemies rumor made them out to be.

Mack just didn't feel up to forcing an insincere smile on his face. He had a passion for justice; it was the reason he had become an attorney in the first place, and the reason he devoted so much of his time to protecting the rights of people who lacked the financial clout to stand up to a man like Jonathon Krey. Tonight, Mack was going to see if justice could be served. Only this time, he wasn't seeking to find justice in a courtroom.

He eased his way through the crowd, smiling and shaking hands whenever necessary, delivering comments such as "Too much work to do at home yet tonight," "Is everyone having a good time?," and "I'll be right back as soon as I get my glass refilled." He wanted at least a dozen people to have stories to tell of exactly when and why Mack Randolph had left the celebration, all of them just different enough to make absolute verification impossible.

He ordered his carriage to be brought around. When it appeared, Mack slipped inside, after giving a final wave to an elderly, potbellied banker who'd requested "just one more minute" of his time.

Though it was a warm evening, Mack kept the carriage completely closed up. The instant the horses began to pull away from the curb, he reached into the pocket of his jacket and extracted a firecracker with an especially long fuse. He pulled a match from his pocket, and a second later, opened the window and tossed the lighted firecracker out of the carriage.

"Six . . . five . . . four . . ." Mack counted aloud, as he rushed to tie the midnight black cape around his shoulders and to wrap the black mask over his eyes. From beneath the leather-covered cushion he withdrew a black holster containing a well-oiled Colt revolver and strapped it around his lean hips.

When the firecracker exploded on the north side of the carriage, all eyes turned in that direction. At precisely that moment Mack, dressed now as the notorious Midnight Bandit, slipped silently out of the south-side door of the carriage, melting into the shadows, unseen, even by the coachman.

As Bandit moved toward the mansion, keeping to the shadows, putting distance between himself and the carriage he'd just left, he heard one of the guards near the front doors curse, "Damn kids are at it again! You'd think they'd all be in their beds by now!"

# Two

*Crack!* Tori thought for certain that her heart had stopped beating. Was that sharp noise the report of a small-caliber pistol? Within a few seconds she was convinced that the sound was that of a firecracker, not a handgun.

She rose and went to the bedroom door, her heart still pounding against her ribs. Instinctively, she kept expecting to hear a gunshot, then to feel the numbing effect of a lead slug striking her. So, each second that passed without her being struck, she considered a small victory both for herself and for all the people who had been damaged in one way or another by Jonathon Krey.

She opened the door just an inch and peered out into the dimly lit hallway. The celebration downstairs was even more raucous than earlier. The effects of alcohol, Tori decided, would help to cover up any noise she might inadvertently make.

The hallway was still empty. Why? Perhaps security guards weren't allowed on the second floor. If that was so, her chances for success were considerably greater.

She moved into the hallway and tried the next door in line. Sooner or later, she would find Jonathon Krey's bedroom, and when she did, she would undoubtedly come upon some of the riches she was seeking, riches that would help the poor souls in no position to help themselves.

The instant she closed the door, Tori knew she had at last found Krey's bedroom. It was twice the size of any other she had been in, and over the bed was a portrait of Jonathon's first wife, the one he'd called, simply, the Sainted One. Tori had heard that wives Number Two and Number Three had been unable to live with the ghost of the original Mrs. Krey and had left the mansion without a trace.

Though the rest of the estate had been adorned with the trappings of wealth, Jonathon's bedroom was crowded with them. Against one wall was a couch of burgundy leather. It was the longest couch Tori had ever seen, about ten feet in length.

The bed, too, was vastly oversized. And against the north wall stood a massive fireplace, with two wing-backed chairs angled toward it.

The room would be warm and comfortable when the cold winter winds came howling, and in the summer, with the balcony doors opened wide, a gentle breeze would keep it cool.

Every item within the room seemed created for the single purpose of making Jonathon Krey as comfortable as possible.

Tori forced this awareness aside. This was not the time to dwell on the comforts others were able to enjoy.

She went first to the table at one side of the bed, and opened the slender drawer. Though this was her first experience as an avenger, she already knew that nightstands, tables, or desks near a person's bed usually contained valuable items.

Inside the drawer was a small ledger, new and completely unused. Tori made a mental note that on her next visit she would check it, certain that then it would be filled with information capable of destroying Jonathon Krey. She put the ledger back where she'd found it, checked a few slips of paper in the drawer, and was disappointed to learn that they contained random ideas Jonathon perused while trying to get to sleep.

She went around the huge bed to inspect the desk on the other side. That, too, proved fruitless.

"Where do you keep your money, then, Krey? Where would a thief like you keep . . . ?"

Tori caught her lower lip between her teeth. Talking aloud was a habit of hers whenever she was deep in thought. Never before had it been something she was worried about, but never before had she slipped quietly into the mansion of her most hated and powerful enemy.

She checked a larger desk in one corner of the room. Clearly this was where Jonathon worked when he wanted complete privacy, it contained plenty of papers and files, but nothing Tori could use to destroy Jonathon Krey. Furthermore, there was nothing in or on it a hungry man could sell to feed his children.

Frustrated and angry, Tori looked around the room. When she had first planned to steal from Jonathon Krey, she had believed getting inside his mansion, inside his *sanctum sanctorum*, would enable her to destroy him easily. In her mind's eye, she had pictured money and gold piled up high in a closet, there for the taking. Foolish woman!

Yes, reality was considerably different.

"Damn you, Jonathon," she murmured. At least it

would infuriate him to have her, a commoner, call him by his first name! The thought brought a smile to her lips once more.

She placed her hands on her hips and looked around the bedroom, imagining what it would be like to have Jonathon Krey's status. How did he think?

The portrait of the "sainted" Mrs. Krey seemed to be eyeing Tori, keeping a careful watch on her, no matter where in the room she moved. Was it guarding the skeletons safely locked away in the Krey closet?

"So where's the money?" Tori asked the portrait. "Where does your husband keep . . ."

Pausing, she approached the portrait slowly, as though the woman in the painting were alive and might call out to the guards. Kneeling on the bed to touch the ornately carved frame of the portrait, Tori was shocked when she inadvertently tripped the hidden spring of a latch, causing the painting to swing out smoothly on well-oiled hinges, revealing a wall safe.

As she was looking up at the safe, wondering how she could get past the thick steel door to the valuables nestled inside, a hand clamped tightly over her mouth! An instant later an arm, strong as steel, wrapped around her waist, squeezing her so tightly that she could hardly breathe.

She was hoisted off the bed, and though she kicked and flailed, her own grasping hands could not loosen the hand over her mouth or the one around her waist.

As she was carried quickly across the room and through the curtained balcony doors, a thousand chaotic ideas raced through her brain. Once on the balcony, she was lowered enough so that her feet at last touched the marble floor.

She felt the warmth of a man's breath against her cheek, heard a flinty whisper, "Don't make a sound! Don't move!"

A second later, Tori heard conversation, as the door to Jonathon Krey's bedroom opened. In walked Krey, along with the man she recognized as Andy Fields, the businessman who had tried and failed to be elected territorial governor during the last election, and the well-known Judge Robert Ringer.

The hand was still clamped tightly over Tori's mouth. She grabbed the stranger's wrist with both of her hands, trying to free herself without moving too much. The strength of the man who had taken her from her mission was astonishing.

"Stop fighting me, or we'll both get caught," the stranger whispered. "Just stop."

What could she do? She relaxed finally, and when she did, she began thinking more lucidly. This man couldn't be one of Krey's bodyguards because if he were, he wouldn't be hiding on the balcony.

Tori released her hold on the stranger's wrist and let her hands fall loosely to her sides. She was facing the bedroom, able to look inside through a slight parting of the balcony curtain. The stranger, directly behind her, kept his hand over her mouth, though not clamped as tightly as earlier. His left arm was around her middle, resting easily against her, though still forcing the full length of her body to press against him. The stranger looked over her head into the bedroom.

Who was he? Though she tried to pay attention to what was happening inside the bedroom, the presence of the man was so overpowering that she could think of nothing else. She realized, as she stood there feeling the heat of his body seeping into her own, that he had saved her from being caught by Jonathon Krey. *She* hadn't heard Krey approach with the judge and Andy Fields, but the stranger had, and he'd carried her out onto the balcony—lifting her as though she weighed nothing at all, though Tori was most definitely not a small woman—so that she wouldn't be discovered.

The Colt .44 was still in its holster at her right hip, close to her right hand. Tori knew she could try to draw the weapon . . . but what good would that do? She could not possibly shoot her way out of the mansion. There were far too many armed guards. Even if she *could* make it to the grounds, she'd still have to get over the stone wall. Once the shooting started, she wouldn't be able to climb over unnoticed, as she had when she'd entered earlier.

As disturbing as those questions were, Tori could not ignore the fact that a man she did not know—one she had not really seen—was holding her closely pressed to his body. She felt the heat of his left palm against her ribs, touching her just beneath the rise of her breast, the solidity of his frame. Because her back was pressed into him, she could tell that his stomach was flat and hard, his chest broad and powerful. From the beginning she'd realized her captor was a tall man.

"Just be calm!" the stranger whispered, bending slightly so that his lips were against Tori's ear.

When he straightened again, Tori felt his pelvis against her backside. Was it intentional? She could not tell, though the touch of him was most disturbing.

Again, she grabbed the stranger's left wrist, and pushed down on it. But he pushed against her, pressing her even more tightly against him. His hand came up even higher on her ribs, now pressing against the taut lower curve of her breast.

"Don't fight me or we'll both swing from a rope," the stranger whispered, his lips brushing Tori's ear as he spoke. "I'm not going to hurt you, but you mustn't fight me."

Tori closed her eyes and released his wrist. He was right, of course. There wasn't anything to be gained by fighting him—with the exception of putting some distance between her body and his.

*Ignore him,* she thought, struggling mightily to convince herself that it was possible. *Listen to what Jonathon Krey is saying. He's your real enemy.*

Inside the bedroom, Jonathon Krey sat at his desk, the judge and Andy Fields seated on the oversized sofa. Each man held a drink from the bottle of fine cognac sitting on the table. Krey was saying something about how good it was that they were finally able to get away from the festivities long enough to be able to talk privately for a few moments.

As Tori struggled to concentrate on what was going on in the bedroom, something behind her caught her attention. A faint breeze had swirled over the balcony, bringing the edge of a midnight black cape into her peripheral vision. Her gasp of surprise was silenced by the hand still clamped over her mouth.

The Midnight Bandit!

She tried to turn in Bandit's arms, but he held her tightly. She tilted her head, trying to look over her shoulder, not wanting to believe that her worst fears were true. At first the hand over her mouth prevented her from looking back, then her captor relaxed his hold and allowed her to turn just enough to look up at him.

"Yes, it's me," he said, smiling.

He wore a flat-crowned black Stetson, pulled low, and beneath that, a black mask over his eyes and nose. In the pale moonlight, when he smiled, Tori could see that his teeth were strong, even, and very white. There was a dimple in his left cheek, in his chin a faint cleft. He wore a black cape that apparently came down to his ankles, and beneath that, though she could not see it, she was certain he was garbed all in black.

Tori had not really believed the Midnight Bandit existed. She'd thought him a story created by bored journalists who had nothing better to write about, and who were hoping to increase newspaper circulation. Now, seeing him, she could understand how the popular legend had taken the shape it had.

No wonder he was called the Midnight Bandit. Legend had it he could transform himself into smoke and then disappear into the night without leaving a trace or making a sound.

She turned away from him, her heart now beating faster than ever. The Midnight Bandit existed! He held her, at this very moment, captive . . . and all Tori could think about was whether the greatest threat to her safety was in front of her in the form of Jonathon Krey and the evil that he represented or behind her in the form of the mysterious Midnight Bandit.

Now that she knew who held her in his arms, Tori felt his touch even more acutely than before. The strength of Bandit had become fused with another element—the mystery of his manliness. An odd sensation passed through

Tori as she reflected on the power that compelled this man to do things even brave men did not dare.

Very gently, Tori touched the back of Bandit's hand, the one covering her mouth. The hand did not move.

"You mustn't make a sound," Bandit whispered, his lips brushing against her ear as he spoke. "Promise me that."

She nodded. She would bide her time.

The hand covering her mouth released its pressure, hesitated a moment, then moved lower to rest very lightly upon her shoulder. But Tori knew he could silence her again in a heartbeat if he wanted to.

The sense of powerlessness that Tori felt, trapped between dangerous men, was both overwhelming and infuriating. She wanted to strike out, to attack these men who frightened her, but to do that would only put her in even greater jeopardy.

"I won't hurt you," Bandit whispered. "But you must remain very quiet. Jail cells are smelly, vile places, and I don't intend on spending any time in them."

Tori could feel his lips against her ear, and she wondered if he was leaning into her a little more than he absolutely had to, letting them caress her ear more than was necessary.

Could she draw the Colt from its holster before he could stop her?

Tori had heard the stories of Bandit being lightning quick on the draw, but she'd really never given anything concerned with the Midnight Bandit credence. Whenever a so-called badman surfaced in Santa Fe, the gossipmongers always made the scoundrel out to be the fastest gun anyone had ever seen. And, almost without exception, there wasn't a shred of truth to the story.

Badmen—criminals of one stripe or another—tended to be cowardly, Tori believed. She'd heard enough stories of senseless murders, of violence, of rape, for her to know that criminals were not the types of men who fought face-to-face. They ambushed their prey, just as Bandit had silently ambushed her, grabbing her from behind.

The difference was, he had grabbed her so that she would not be caught by Jonathon Krey's untimely, unexpected entrance into his own bedroom. But if his intention had been to save her, why hadn't he released her? Why was he still holding her so close that she could feel the heat of his body, his great strength, the life-force that coursed through his veins?

In the bedroom, Jonathon Krey laughed, drawing Tori's attention.

"You're a wicked one," Krey said to Judge Robert Ringer. "I never knew you had that kind of mind."

The judge leaned back on the sofa, smiling coyly. He sipped the cognac and glanced at the businessman, Andy Fields. "When Andy found out it was Mexicans who had stolen the horses, it was pretty much fair game on all Mexicans, as far as I was concerned. Before the whole thing was over, there'd been nearly a dozen lynchings."

Andy Fields laughed, and Tori thought he'd had too much to drink. "We lynched a Mex for every horse that was stolen."

"You got involved in it yourself?" Krey, leaning back in his chair, asked Fields.

Tori noticed that Krey brought the cognac to his mouth often, but sips were extremely small. He wasn't as casual about this meeting as he tried to appear.

"Me? Naw! I don't get into the lynchings myself, just

in case somebody'd see me. There's gonna be another election coming up, you know. I just let the voters know where I stand and urge them to do what they think is best."

Judge Ringer was shaking his head slowly, as though he found the businessman-as-politician a buffoon, but a valuable one. Like Krey, the judge was taking very small sips of his cognac, careful not to let his intellect become dulled with liquor.

"This talk is all fine and good," Ringer said, his tone changing slightly to indicate a man of considerable power, a man accustomed to giving orders and having them followed. "But it doesn't get me what I came here for, now does it?"

Jonathon Krey smiled. A crooked smile, Tori thought. "No, judge, it doesn't. I like a man who cuts the fat and serves only the prime."

Suddenly, Tori could hardly believe her eyes and ears as she watched Jonathon Krey move over to his bed, swing aside the portrait of his deceased wife, then spin the dial on his safe. A few seconds later he turned the handle and opened the thick, heavy steel door of the safe.

On the couch, Andy Fields was subtly craning his neck to see into the safe without actually changing his position; Judge Ringer was leaning back on the couch, his legs nonchalantly crossed, his demeanor one of a man in complete control of his life and his future.

"No wonder we can't get any justice in this territory," Tori murmured.

She regretted saying anything instantly because the Midnight Bandit once again placed his hand over her mouth. This time, however, he did not clamp his palm as tightly over it, and for some reason, he lightly ran his thumb over her cheek. She closed her eyes for an instant, damning herself for speaking, wanting to push her captor's hands from her body, but not daring to do anything more to anger the man who now, quite literally, held her life in his hands.

When she opened her eyes again, she saw Jonathon Krey hand the judge a small envelope he had taken from the safe. The judge removed three paper bills from the envelope, folded them in half, and handed them over to the would-be politician.

"Don't spend it all tonight at Lulu's," Judge Ringer said sternly. "You show that much money at one time, right after you and I have been seen together, and people might start talking."

"Don't you worry about people talking, Judge," Andy Fields said, draining the last of the liquor in his glass. "Anybody opens his mouth, I know just how to shut it for him."

"None of that," Judge Ringer snapped. His eyes became hard and unforgiving, his jaw was thrust forward commandingly. This was a pose he'd used countless times to instill fear in the hearts of those men who stood before him in court. "Don't draw any attention to yourself—not if you want me to back you in the next election."

Fields frowned drunkenly, looking like a spoiled child who'd just been scolded. "Don't worry 'bout me, Judge. I'll go to Lulu's and stay the night there. Won't see any-body but my special gal."

Judge Ringer nodded toward the door, and Andy rose a bit unsteadily to his feet. "Guess I'll be moseying on," he decided, making his way toward the door. "I'll see me ownself out."

Alone now, Judge Ringer and Jonathon Krey exchanged smiles. They were, after all, competent, capable thieves no longer needing to deal directly with one of the inferior, though essential, elements of their enterprise.

"Do you trust him?" Jonathon asked.

"I don't trust anyone. Not completely, anyway. But he's a good man for what we need done, and he has the gift of gab that the common voters like," the judge replied. "Andy Fields is a fool, but he knows his place, and when we make him territorial governor, he'll listen to us and know who pulls his strings."

Jonathon nodded. Tori guessed his thoughts about Fields: such men, though displeasing to be near, were necessary to carry out profitable deals, and still keep one's hands unstained by the blood spilled.

A moment of silence passed as the two men simply looked at each other. There were many things that had to be said, Tori sensed, and though these two were willing to smile at each other, they weren't willing to trust each other.

Finally, it was Jonathon Krey who broke the silence. "Do we know any more than last week?" he asked.

The judge shrugged. "Nothing definite. I've asked my questions when I'm at the courthouse. Nothing unusual about a judge asking questions of the marshals and sheriffs in courts now, is there?"

"What have you learned?"

There was an edge to Jonathon Krey's voice that hadn't been there before, Tori noted. She didn't know him well enough to determine whether impatience was wearing at his nerves, whether he simply did not like the judge, or whether it was something else entirely.

"Like I said, nothing definite. If he makes a move, I'll hear about it though, and when I do, I'll let you know."

"Do that," Jonathon said, the edge to his voice this time more pronounced, dangerous, and undisguised. "We're in this together."

"I know that, Jonathon. I've never forgotten that."

"Don't forget how much of my money has gone straight from that safe"—Jonathon nodded toward the portrait of his deceased wife—"to your pocket."

For several seconds the judge, his eyes hard and cold, stared straight at Krey. Tori thought if she were in the judge's courtroom and he stared at her that way, she would shiver in her boots.

"Yes, Jonathon, I've profited by our association, but never forgot that you do not pay me out of the goodness of your heart, you pay me because I earn my money. If it were not for me, Jeremy would be spending his days and nights in a cell in Yuma instead of living here, fat and comfortable. And if it were not for the strings I pulled on your behalf just this spring, you wouldn't have been allowed to reroute that creek near the Dahlberg range. When you rerouted the water, you destroyed Dahlberg's pasture, didn't you?"

"Yes, I did. But I had no choice. I needed the water."

"So did Dahlberg." Judge Ringer rose to his feet, setting his nearly full glass of cognac aside. "I only say this to illustrate the fact that our association has been profitable for both of us. We're experiencing a little trouble right now, but it is minor trouble. As soon as I get more information, either you or I can assign men to it, and the problem will disappear as completely as if the Midnight Bandit had never been born."

Tori's breath caught in her throat as the Midnight Bandit's arm tightened unconsciously around her. A moment later the grip loosened, but she understood that he wasn't as fearless as she'd thought. He had a healthy respect for the power of Jonathon Krey.

Krey nodded, still leaning back in his chair. It was rude of him not to rise with the judge leaving, but he had just been given a lecture and this was his way of showing that he was still the man in control, still the boss.

Moments after the judge left the room, there was a soft knock at the door, and a dangerous-looking man in his early twenties entered. Though he had a long, ugly scar on one cheek, which he seemed to bear with pride, he looked like a man who enjoyed inflicting pain. Tori trembled in Bandit's arms.

At precisely that moment, from the room next to Jonathon Krey's, a young woman's high-pitched laughter cut through the night air. A moment later, Tori could see from their position on the balcony that a lamp had been lit in that room, and the sounds of laughter soon became more pronounced.

"Get down," Bandit hissed in Tori's ear. "Get down on your knees."

She was relieved when he took his hand from her mouth, but the relief was short-lived. In the next moment he pulled her down, and removed her trusted Colt from the holster at her right hip.

Hearing the soft, distinct metallic sound of the Colt's hammer being thumbed back to firing position, she thought frantically, *I never should have expected I could get away with this!*

# *Three*

Cursing silently, Mack got down on his knees, keeping the young blond woman close to him. He tossed his black cape around her to conceal their position as Jena Krey's laughter continued.

For several weighty seconds, Mack was afraid that Jena would step out onto her bedroom's balcony, dangerously near them. If he were seen, then what? Shoot it out with the men guarding the mansion? Mack could picture the headlines in next week's paper. MIDNIGHT BANDIT UNMASKED! LOCAL LAWYER CAUGHT BREAKING INTO CHARITY HOSPITAL CELEBRATION HE CO-SPONSORED!

The laughter suddenly died away, and Mack didn't have to look into Jena's bedroom to guess what she was doing so quietly.

He eased the Colt's hammer down, shifting his position just enough so that he could tuck the weapon into his belt.

Keeping a grip on his captive, he turned his attention back to Jonathon Krey's bedroom. Though the name escaped him, Mack recognized the man who'd entered as a hired killer. The scar-faced gunman was sitting quietly on the sofa while Jonathon read some papers at his desk.

Mack turned his attention to the young woman kneeling

on the hard balcony. Tall and broad-shouldered for a female, she was strong. He shifted his position slightly to
get a better look at her honey-blond hair, her classic profile with the rather Romanesque nose, her wide, sensual
mouth. He remembered the woman's name.

"Tori," he whispered.

She turned her face to him, her pale green eyes wide
with shock, but she said nothing. In the moonlight, Mack
found her strikingly beautiful, and this rather surprised
him, since his taste in women tended to run toward petite
brunettes rather than tall blondes with a propensity for
wearing Levi's and carrying a Colt.

"You know me?"

"Not really," Mack replied quietly. "Just stay quiet and
I'll get you out of this." He used the flinty tone often
written about in the *Santa Fe Journal,* and which so ef-
fectively masked his own voice.

"I can get out of this myself," Tori replied. She
squirmed on her knees, not at all liking the fact that her
waist was surrounded by the Midnight Bandit's thighs,
and that his arm was still around her. "Give me back my
gun."

"No. And be quiet. I want to hear what Krey's saying."

When Tori turned toward the open window again, Mack
tried to pay attention to the people inside the room. But
that wasn't possible. Not when he had Tori so close to
him, and he could feel the heat and strength of her body;
not when he could see her striking profile, definitely aris-
tocratic, which was ironic, since he knew she came from
a family that had never been able to get two dimes together
at the same time.

Her unexpected presence added a dimension to his plan

to strike at the heart of Jonathon Krey. As the Midnight Bandit, Mack found her a nuisance, reducing his odds of success and jeopardizing him needlessly; as Mack Randolph, the lawyer, he thought Tori's presence terribly sad, since he was certain that sooner or later she would get caught stealing, and then he would have to defend her in court—possibly before the corrupt Judge Robert Ringer.

Suddenly both Jonathon Krey and the scarred gunman left the room. At almost the same time, Mack heard Jena's voice, low and authoritative, telling someone to take his hands off her that instant or she was going to change him from a stallion to a gelding.

Mack smiled as he adjusted his mask. Obviously, Jena's evening wasn't turning out the way she'd wanted, and Mack knew her well enough to realize that tomorrow she was going to be impossible to be around.

Mack rose silently to his feet, reaching down to take Tori's hand to help her up. She refused his aid. Smiling in the moonlight, he pulled aside the curtain and bowed theatrically. Tori scowled at him as she stepped into the bedroom of the man she considered the most dangerous one in the Southwestern United States.

"You want to tell me what you're doing here?" Mack asked, his voice still low, though not as low as it had been before.

"I could ask you the same thing. Who are you anyway?" Tori shot back.

"The Midnight Bandit."

"I know that much. I mean behind the mask."

With the mask over his eyes, his hat pulled low, and the ebony cape draped over his shoulders and hanging nearly to the floor, the Midnight Bandit looked dangerous as sin. But Tori couldn't help noticing that his smile was devastating and put the dimple in his cheek on display. The shimmer of moonlight off his white teeth was dazzling, and despite his clipped manner, Tori could tell that he was disguising his voice. He seemed—she was going on instinct here—like an educated man. But why would an educated man become the Midnight Bandit?

"If you think you can steal from Jonathon Krey and live to spend whatever you get, you're taking one hell of a gamble. There are easier ways of making money," the Bandit said, sounding rather disgusted with Tori.

"I'm not looking for easy money for myself," she replied.

"Then what are you looking for?"

"Justice. Revenge."

Mack had never really thought he would sympathize with a thief, but Tori's terse answer had set him back on his heels. Was it possible that she, like the Midnight Bandit, was fed up with the lawlessness rampant in Santa Fe, and had decided to do something about it?

For several seconds Mack pondered the question before casting it aside. As the Midnight Bandit, he could not afford to have friends or allies.

He had to keep his identity secret. He believed that if two people knew his secret, it would only be a matter of time before three people knew, and shortly after that, everyone would know that Mack Randolph, firebrand attorney for the downtrodden, was also the Midnight Bandit.

"You won't find justice in Jonathon Krey's bedroom," Mack said finally. "But you will find money. Let's have a look in that safe."

"It's locked. You'll never get it open without dynamite."

Mack smiled. "Never underestimate the skills of the Midnight Bandit."

He went to the portrait, kneeling on Jonathon Krey's bed, and swung it open. When he thought of how furious Jonathon would be when he discovered that the Midnight Bandit had been traipsing through his bedroom, Mack's smile broadened.

"It's a combination lock," Tori whispered, kneeling on the bed beside Bandit. "I already looked at it."

The safe was a Barns & Bradley Model 6, but Mack had known this even before he'd first set eyes on it. When he'd first begun practicing law, he had defended a bank robber who'd specialized in banks using Barns & Bradley safes. When the client was finally apprehended, it was discovered that he had worked for the company. One of the man's last official acts as an employee of the Barns & Bradley Safe & Lock Company was to install a wall safe in the residence of Jonathon Krey.

In exchange for his legal services for the bank robber, Mack had received lessons of a most peculiar and helpful nature for a defense attorney.

He now spun the dial four times around in a clockwise direction, then did the same thing counterclockwise. Finally, very slowly, he began turning the dial, listening carefully to the clicks as the internal tumblers turned, only his fingertips touching the metal.

On number thirty-eight, he felt the unlocking handle register ever so faintly the tumbler falling into place. Mack smiled. The only flaw with Barns & Bradley safes was that when the tumblers fell into place, they tapped lightly against the unlocking handle, and if a person's touch was sensitive enough, it could be felt.

It took Bandit nine minutes and four tries, but he eventually got all four numbers correctly, and swung open the safe door.

"Amazing," Tori whispered.

She was suddenly aware of how ill-equipped, both intellectually and emotionally, she was to be a thief. She had no idea how Bandit had managed to open the safe. To her, it was magic, pure and simple.

Mack smiled at Tori, and let his eyes touch her for just a moment longer than necessary as they knelt side by side on the bed. He'd never really cared much for tomboys, for women who did not ride sidesaddle, for those who acted, he felt, like men. But Tori possibly could change his attitude. Daring and brave, even wearing Levi's and a cotton shirt, she was all woman. Her breasts were large and round, pressing against her shirt front. Though this wasn't the time for Mack to be wondering exactly how feminine Tori Singer really was, the memory of holding her close against him came back with startling intensity.

He forced himself to look away from her and into the safe. There were a number of bound stacks of paper money, which Mack counted, surprised that the bundles contained varying sums.

"Bribery money?" Tori asked, breaking the silence.

"They're not marked." Mack counted all the bills, which came to nearly two thousand dollars. He split the sum approximately in half, handing some bundles to Tori. "Be careful how you spend it. You don't have the cash to get showy with it and not draw Krey's suspicion."

"It's not for me," Tori said, folding the money in half and stuffing it into the back pocket of her Levi's. "I told you, I'm not in this for the money, I'm in it for justice."

In the darkness, Mack looked at Tori, realizing that he'd never before met a woman like her. Though he didn't entirely believe she was not out for personal gain, he *did* believe she would not steal from an innocent person. As a lawyer, Mack had been lied to too many times for him not to understand the power and allure of stolen cash.

"Sure," he said, deliberately letting Tori hear his skepticism. He turned back to the safe and began inspecting the papers still inside, hoping for some damning document that would put Jonathon Krey in prison where he belonged.

Privately, silently, Tori fumed with rage. The Midnight Bandit thought she was just another thief—as though he wasn't one himself! Even though she'd told him otherwise; he'd refused to believe her. She was glad that he'd at least divided the stolen booty. The money would go a long way toward making the Dahlbergs solvent once again, and might even be enough to relocate them so they could start a new herd.

Mack was disappointed with what he found in the safe. The rest of the legal documents were mostly deeds to property that Jonathon Krey controlled. Although this let Mack know that, among his other criminal activities, Jonathon Krey was also loaning money to ranchers at usurious rates, it accomplished little else.

He closed the safe, spun the dial, and returned the portrait to its place. Easing off the bed, he waited until Tori got off, then smoothed out the wrinkles on the bed linen.

"How had you planned to get out of here?" Bandit asked.

"The same way I got in—over the front wall. But I'm not leaving yet," Tori replied.

She took a step away from him, wanting to put more distance between herself and him. There was a dangerously appealing quality to him, even though he wore the mask over his eyes. Maybe it was the way he smiled, though she couldn't be sure; it could also be his unshakable confidence. Whatever it was, it touched something within Tori that she instinctively realized was best left ignored.

When she was near him, the surface of her skin was electrified and her flesh tingled as if she were hot and cold at the same time. Because she'd grown aware of her body in a new way, she didn't know whether to hate Bandit or to search deeper to find out why he affected her so.

"You're leaving now," he said, moving a half-step closer so that his broad chest nearly touched her. "If you're going to be a thief, you're going to have to know when you've stolen enough."

"I'm not a thief," Tori replied, looking up into his eyes. It was eerie how, with his broad-brimmed hat and his mask, he could keep himself in shadow and darkness, yet his eyes could gleam in the moonlight. She wanted to step backward, but she didn't want to appear willing to follow his orders. "And you've still got my gun. I'd like it back now, if you please."

The Midnight Bandit smiled, saying, "I don't please."

Tori wanted to slap the smile from his face.

"Give . . . me . . . my . . . gun," she whispered through clenched teeth, refusing to be intimidated, taunted, or aroused by him.

"Little girls shouldn't play with guns. You'll only get yourself hurt."

"I'm *not* a little girl!" Tori snapped.

"Shhh! You've got to keep your voice down," Mack replied.

At that moment, he thought himself the most foolish man in the world for standing in Jonathon Krey's bedroom and taunting a woman into an argument. She was, without doubt, the most—what was the appropriate word for her?—*different* woman he'd ever spoken to. Her determination and feistiness were unheard of in the wealthy social circles Mack frequented.

"Keep the damn gun then," Tori whispered, hating the arrogant masked man.

Stabbing him with angry eyes, she turned on her heel and headed toward the bedroom door, but he caught her wrist.

"Don't try to stop me," she whispered. "After tonight, Krey's going to have a thousand men watching this house. I'll never have the chance to get in here again, so I'm going for it all tonight."

Mack nodded after a moment, realizing the logic of her statement. He really hadn't intended on making any money by breaking into the mansion as the Midnight Bandit, had been hoping instead to find documents that would put Jonathon Krey and his sons in prison. He wasn't in it for cash. Just the same, if the Midnight Bandit could cause Jonathon to lose a night's sleep, then the evening would be successful.

"Just do what I tell you," he whispered in his flinty tone, the one that brooked no opposition.

Tori was stubborn and proud, but she was also intelligent, and she knew that the Midnight Bandit was considerably more skilled at this sort of thing than she was. After all, hadn't he been tormenting Jonathon Krey for nearly two months, intentionally leaving behind a series of tantalizing clues that seemingly led nowhere?

"Just don't slow me down," Tori whispered, realizing it was nothing but stubbornness that made her say the words.

They made their way down the hall to Michael Krey's room. Mack walked over to the window. He quickly noted all the latest little gadgets—among them a new alarm clock with small soldiers that circled on a battlefield when the alarm rang, and a cigarette-rolling machine—that the youngest male Krey found so fascinating.

Tori found a small wooden box, intricately carved and held closed with a small gold lock, beneath the bed. She smiled broadly as she placed the box on the bed.

She looked up, about to inform him of what she'd found, and for an instant she lost her breath. To see the Midnight Bandit moving in the shadows of the bedroom, half-illuminated by the moonlight streaming through the balcony windows, touched Tori in a secret, primordial place.

He was tall, perhaps six feet, with broad, powerful shoulders and a thick chest, yet his waist was narrow. He moved with the supple grace of a stalking cat. With each move, the long cape fluttered lightly, streaming over his shoulders and down his back. Tho mask over his eyes, though it continued to conceal his true identity, no longer was frightening to Tori. Rather, not knowing his true identity, knowing him only as the Midnight Bandit, added something inexplicable to his allure.

He was, she thought then, absurdly handsome. In reality she could not see very much of his face—just his eyes and his beautiful smile—so she certainly couldn't say that he was handsome. But her intuitive self knew that he was . . . and it was her intuition that her body was listening to.

His hands were beautiful in the moonlight as he handled the letters on the small writing table near the windows. She'd watched them masterfully work the dial of the wall safe, and had guessed them to be extraordinarily dexterous. And she had felt his firm right hand over her mouth, holding back her scream of protest.

*He's an outcast, just like me.* It came to Tori somehow. She flinched at the thought. Never before had she thought there was anyone like her, with the singular exception of her brother, Jedediah, the bounty hunter.

From the corner of his eye, Mack caught Tori flinching, and he wondered why, but grinned when she saw the carved jewelry box on the bed.

"It's locked," she whispered.

As he approached her, his ebony silk cape billowing around him, she flushed. She thought he looked like a gigantic bird of prey. Would he devour her?

He knelt on the floor beside her, inspecting the locked box. For the first time, with moonlight shining upon his face, Tori saw him closely.

*He* is *handsome,* she thought.

"This doesn't look like much trouble," the Midnight Bandit said, reaching inside his cape. "Where did you find it?"

"Under the bed."

"That's where the best secrets always are."

*And what's that supposed to mean?* Tori wondered.

Bandit removed a slender leather case from an inside pocket. He opened it to display a series of small, silver instruments that, to Tori, looked like those a dental surgeon would use. He extracted one of the long, slender instruments and inserted it into the gold lock. A moment later Tori heard a soft *click* and then the lock opened.

"As I said, no trouble."

"You're arrogant," Tori whispered, though her tone revealed she was clearly impressed with the skill she had just witnessed.

"I'm confident. There's a difference."

"Not with you," Tori said, trying hard to convince herself that Bandit wasn't the least bit interesting to her.

The locked box contained letters from a woman working in a bordello that, from what Tori and Bandit could glean during their brief perusal, Michael Krey either owned or frequented.

The box was returned to its place beneath the bed, and for an instant, Tori and Bandit were both on their knees, their faces close together.

"I . . . I'm sure there's more here . . . somewhere," Tori whispered, her throat feeling tight with the closeness of the Bandit.

"We've already gotten quite a bit. How much is enough?"

Tori looked into his eyes, realizing for the first time that they were dark brown, and in them was a hint of playfulness that told her the Midnight Bandit had a boyish side to him that, perhaps under other circumstances, she might find it entertaining to bring out.

"I don't know how much is enough," she said finally.

Bandit took a lock of her hair and curled it around his index finger. "It varies with each person," the Bandit explained, and Tori suspected he was not talking about stolen cash. "For myself, I can, on occasion and when truly inspired, become quite greedy—never get enough. But even in the midst of my greed, I never forget to share." He released her hair. "You see, sharing is very important—vital, even. Because, when you share, then you actually get more in return, which makes you want to give more, which makes you get more . . . and so on, and so forth. It makes life much more gratifying."

Tori watched Bandit's lips moving as he spoke. They looked to her, at that moment and in the eerie glow of the moonlight, delicious.

Delicious?

She'd never before thought of a man's mouth as delicious, but that was how his lips appeared to her at that moment . . . and she wanted to taste them.

Jena Krey's voice sounded in the hallway outside Michael's bedroom, shattering Tori's thought. She crouched lower, hiding herself behind the bed. The Bandit, however, did not flinch.

"That's Jena. She's still complaining to the man she brought up here to the second floor. She won't come in."

Tori felt a prickly sensation running through her system. She looked at Bandit and thought, *He recognizes the voices of the Kreys, and knows where their bedrooms are. Who the devil is he?*

"How did you get in?" Bandit whispered, his hand resting lightly on her shoulder.

"I jumped over the wall, then climbed the ivy brace to the second floor," she answered as softly as she could.

"And nobody saw you?" Bandit sounded surprised.

Tori shook her head.

"Follow me. I've got a better way out."

He took Tori's hand in his and led her out to the balcony.

Her fingers laced with his, her own hand dampened with fear and a little trembly, his dry and strong. She wished his confidence could seep through his palm into her.

*Where's he leading me?* she wondered, not really caring so long as Bandit was with her.

# Four

They slipped through the drapes onto the balcony. The Bandit climbed onto the surrounding railing, grabbed hold of a drain pipe and climbed onto the roof of the mansion. On his stomach, he stretched out, leaned over the edge of the roof, and reached down for Tori.

"Come on, you can make it," he whispered.

She climbed onto the balcony railing, then, grasping the drainpipe, started climbing, just as she had seen Bandit do. Mack's respect for her increased as he watched her struggling, awkwardly inching her way higher.

He knew that she was scared, but her fear did not paralyze her. Instead she overcame it through sheer force of will, through determination and desire.

"You can make it," he encouraged in a whisper when Tori paused a second to catch her breath. She needed to climb only another foot before Bandit's outstretched hand could help her the remainder of the way. "Just a little bit more."

The toes of Tori's boots were jammed between the bricks of the wall. She stretched her right hand out, reaching for Bandit.

"I can't make it," she said, feeling the strength in her fingers going.

"Just a little more and I'll have you."

She began to look over her shoulder. If her fingers gave out, she would hit the railing and might fall onto the balcony or over the edge to shatter on the ground far below.

"Don't look down!" Bandit hissed, and this time there was urgency in his tone. "Just look at me, Tori. Look only at me, and I'll help you."

It was the first time he had used her first name since he'd surprised her by recognizing her, and the sound of it galvanized Tori's spirit. With a final contraction of the muscles in her arms, she was able to raise herself just enough for Bandit to catch her wrist. Moments later he pulled her onto the roof of the mansion, folding her body protectively into the safety of his arms.

"That's harder than it looks," she whispered, feeling a little guilty about having had so much difficulty in reaching the roof.

"You just haven't had much practice at it," Bandit replied. He took her hand in his once again. "Come on, we're vulnerable here."

It surprised Tori that she made no effort to get out of Bandit's arms, and when he'd pulled her to her feet; she had not tried to remove her hand from his grasp.

He led her to the highest point of the roof, where there were several chimneys and ventilation ports. Far below, the celebration continued. Tori wondered what time it was, how long it had been since she first entered the Krey mansion. From the moment Bandit had come into her life, she had had more questions than answers.

From the ground came a loud exclamation, and one man asked another to look up at the roof. At first Tori did not understand what exactly was happening; then it dawned on her that they had been seen by one of the many armed guards, now gathering below.

Bandit's reaction was instantaneous. He grabbed Tori by the arm and pulled her tightly against him, at the same time wrapping his cape around her, pulling her head down against his chest.

"Don't move," he whispered, pushing her so that her back was against the brick chimney. "It's that beautiful blond hair of yours, darling. It catches the moonlight."

Tori's heart pounded in her chest. Were the bullets about to fly? Her holster was still empty. Bandit hadn't returned her revolver.

*What difference would that make?* she asked herself angrily. The guards would be armed with rifles, which were infinitely more accurate than pistols.

She inhaled deeply, trying to control her fear as each agonizing second ticked by. She caught the smell of Bandit's body, and in a strange way she couldn't have anticipated, the scent of him pleased her. He smelled of a fresh bath and expensive soap, yet also of male exertion. She felt the heat of him through his shirt, the strong beating of his heart against her cheek.

*Bandit will get us out of this,* she thought. *He's never been caught before, and he won't get caught now.*

"Stay very still," Bandit whispered.

From the ground, Tori could now hear the guards arguing among themselves, one saying that he'd seen someone on the roof, the other saying it was probably just an owl hunting.

Bandit eased Tori a little to her left, hiding her more completely from view. He pulled away just enough so that he could look down into her face, keeping her in the curve of his arm, his cape hiding her long blond hair.

"You're trembling, " he said in that low, flinty, confident tone of his that Tori had learned to appreciate, even though she knew it wasn't his natural tone.

"I'm scared. I never thought it would be like this," she replied, shocking herself by speaking so honestly.

"You mustn't be," Bandit said softly. He touched the tip of Tori's chin, turning her face up to his own. "I won't let anything bad happen to you."

She looked up at him. He now had the moon at his back so that while her own face was visible in the moonlight, his features were completely hidden in shadows.

"I don't even know who you are. Why are you helping me?"

"Because you need it."

She wanted to be angry with him, but she just couldn't. All Bandit had done was speak the truth, the painful truth. She *did* need help, but she was far from helpless.

Tori moistened her lips with the tip of her tongue, unaware of how intriguing she looked when she did this. "Will you let me see your face?" she asked. "I want to know who you are."

"It's better for you if you don't know." Bandit looked away a moment, uncomfortable with the conversation. "There are people who would pay a lot of money to find out my identity."

"I would never betray you."

"Perhaps not. But I also know that Jonathon Krey is an evil man, and if he thought you knew my identity, he would torture you until you told him everything."

"I wouldn't break," Tori said with quiet, forceful determination.

"Everyone has a breaking point. Even me."

Below, the guards continued to argue, at least one still convinced he'd seen someone on the roof.

"As long as we don't move, they'll never see us. The cape doesn't reflect light," Bandit explained.

Tori leaned her head back against Bandit's forearm and looked up at him. He'd been totally prepared to break into the Krey mansion, and despite the time she'd spent plotting and planning this evening, she had not been.

"I thought I would be better at being a thief than I am," Tori admitted.

"It's not a skill to be proud of," Bandit replied.

She closed her eyes. There was nothing to do now except wait until the guards finally convinced themselves there was nobody on the roof. Just remain still, stay hidden beneath Bandit's cape, and wait.

With her eyes closed, she became very aware of Bandit's forearm against the back of her head, his body touching hers, his chest pressed lightly against her breasts. She felt warm all over, and though she tried to convince herself that it was the sultry evening air affecting her, she suspected it was something more than that . . . or *someone*.

"Promise me you'll never again do anything as foolish as this," Bandit whispered.

"I can't make promises," Tori replied.

She refused to open her eyes, painfully conscious of every sensitive place where her body touched Bandit's—their knees pushing together, the inside of her thigh rubbing against the outside of his, her breasts against his chest.

"Promise me," Bandit said, more demanding than before.

"I don't promise that which I can't."

Bandit's hand cupped her chin. His eyes glittered behind the black mask.

"Promise me," he repeated.

Tori recalled all the people she knew who had been hurt by Jonathon Krey and his family, and she shook her head, despite Bandit's hold on her chin. His fingers tightened.

"I'll never stop until Jonathon Krey gets what he deserves," she whispered, her anger rising. "What's wrong, can't the infamous Midnight Bandit take the competition?"

"If you're not careful, *you'll* get what *you* deserve."

"And what might that be?" Tori demanded angrily. She would not be intimidated by anyone—not even the Midnight Bandit.

"This," Bandit replied.

Tori wasn't sure what she'd expected, but it wasn't Bandit's kiss. And once his mouth was pressed against her own, his lips firm and commanding, she certainly didn't expect the response of her body to the kiss.

As though he were kissing her everywhere simultaneously, every fiber of her body came alive. The Bandit turned her head, angling her so that he could more completely dominate her mouth, and Tori surprised herself once again by not resisting.

Her arms had been resting loosely at her sides, but now she slipped them up around Bandit's chest, sliding her palms lightly over his silk shirt and over his jacket, under his cape. When she did this, he leaned into her, forcing her more firmly against the brick chimney.

The tip of his tongue teased her lips. Tori knew what he wanted, and she resisted him for the first time. She kept her lips closed, turning her face away at last to end the kiss.

But Bandit was undeterred. He kissed her cheek, then bent lower to kiss the smooth arch of her throat. To feel his lips, then the sharpness of his teeth, against her sensitive neck was perhaps even more stimulating to Tori than being kissed on the mouth.

"The guards . . . they might see us," she whispered, not knowing what else to say.

She wanted to push the cape off her head, to put some distance between herself and the enigmatic masked thief who could artfully steal away her better judgment. But a step in any direction, even uncovering her blond hair, would put her in jeopardy, and that she could not afford.

She felt trapped between the armed guards three stories below, at that moment still inspecting the rooftop, and Bandit, showing her the irresistible allure of a dangerous man in a dangerous setting.

*I shouldn't let him do this,* she thought. She could not, however, put the notion into words.

*It's only a kiss . . . just a harmless kiss,* she told herself as his lips, warm and gentle, coaxed a little more response from her.

When the tip of his tongue touched her lips ever so lightly a second time Tori fully realized what Bandit expected of her. Expected or wanted? She could not really tell, but she did know that his kisses were unbearably pleasing and stripped away her anger at the injustices in her life—an anger she had carried in her for so long it was now a part of her.

"Relax . . . your body is so tight," Bandit whispered, his lips brushing Tori's as he spoke.

"We're standing on the roof of Jonathon Krey's mansion. If we fall off, we'll die; if the guards see us, we'll die. I have good reason to be tense."

"The guards can't see us as long as we stay right where we are," Bandit said.

And then, as though to prove his point, he pushed Tori just a little more to her left, so that she was even more trapped between the three chimneys that rose up from the slanted rooftop. He leaned into her, and this time she had no doubt at all that he was intentionally crushing her breasts with his chest.

"Don't," she whispered, a strange, weak, one-word protest.

Hearing the single word seemed odd to her then, as though someone else had spoken it. Could that really be her, sounding that . . . aroused? What had happened to her conviction, her heartfelt belief that she had been made a victim by society too many times already and would never again allow *anyone* to take advantage of her?

When she felt Bandit's hand against her stomach, she involuntarily sucked in her breath. Wherever he touched her her pleasure was heightened.

*He's going to touch my breasts,* Tori thought.

She pulled her arm from around Bandit's neck, quickly, stabbing her elbow straight down to knock the masked man's hand from her. She would not let him touch her so intimately. She would be in control of her own body, and would respond only when and how she allowed herself to!

"Don't, I told you," Tori whispered with only a fraction

of the angry conviction she'd hoped for. She searched the darkness to look into Bandit's dark brown eyes. Once again, he'd maneuvered himself so that his face was deeply buried in shadow.

Raising his hands, Bandit placed them upon Tori's shoulders. He pushed himself away slightly, releasing the pressure of his chest against her breasts. Very slowly, he sighed and nodded his head.

Looking up into his face, Tori found herself a little disappointed that he had stopped, that he had chosen to be the gentleman without protesting more.

Why couldn't he, just once, be like all the other men she had known—and hated?

The Midnight Bandit wasn't the first man to have kissed her, though his kisses were the first to make her body respond so quickly, so completely from head to toe. But before, when Tori had been in a man's arms and he was kissing her and she was trying hard to pretend to herself that it really wasn't as bad as she believed and she'd told the man to stop, he hadn't done so.

Actually, there had been three such occasions in her life. Two of the men had persisted until Tori had at last demanded that they leave.

When the third had begun to force himself upon her, she had brought a candleholder down on his skull, then had began screaming for her brother, Jedediah.

That man, though he'd lived through the beating Jedediah Singer gave him, later told everyone in town who would listen that he'd taken Tori Singer's virginity and that he now wanted nothing to do with her because he was much too concerned with his reputation to be seen in public with such trash.

He left town before Jedediah could kill him, and from that point forward, Tori always carried the Colt in the holster at her right hip.

She had promised herself that the next man who kissed her would end up looking down the muzzle of her revolver, and if he could do that without going pasty-faced with fear, then maybe he'd be man enough for her to consider kissing.

"After tonight, you must never do this again," Bandit chided again, his voice suddenly stern and commanding.

He had managed to completely shut down his passion, Tori could tell. She wished she had such an ability. She could still feel the muscles of his chest, strong and warm, pressing firmly against her breasts. Her nipples were still hard and erect—achingly so. Her lips tingled from kisses that had been warm and exciting, not wet and defiling.

"Do what again?" Tori asked softly, not at all certain she wanted to know the answer.

"Strike out at Jonathon Krey," Bandit replied. There was a fleeting hint of a smile on his sensual lips, letting Tori know that he was not as immune to feelings, or as solidly in control of them, as he wanted her to believe. "Did you think I was talking about you and me? That you must never do this again?"

Before Tori could respond, he leaned down. Cursing herself silently, she closed her eyes to receive yet another kiss.

As his tongue pressed against her lips once more, she opened her mouth just slightly, very hesitantly. Kissing this way was something she had only done once before, and then it hadn't been entirely voluntary, the experience having been repugnant. She'd always shuddered when thinking about that awful kiss forced upon her so long ago.

But the shudder going through her now as Bandit's tongue eased between her lips and entered her mouth was not one of revulsion. A low, tremulous moan of desire purred from her throat, shocking Tori.

Cautiously, she put her tongue against his, and instinctively, the kiss deepened even more. Tori pressed closer to Bandit, her body responding spontaneously to this new and deliciously evocative kiss. A heat, mysteriously low and deep within her, escalated from an ember to a glowing core of passion.

And just as quickly as it had started, it ended. The Bandit stood upright again, a faint smile curling his lips.

"I wasn't talking about our kisses," he said then, much too calmly for Tori's liking. "I was talking about breaking into Jonathon Krey's home. If he'd caught you, he wouldn't have had you arrested. You'd have been found in an alley somewhere in Santa Fe, or maybe you wouldn't have been found at all."

Tori's head was spinning. How could he go from kissing her at one second to lecturing her on her life style in the next? Didn't the kisses mean anything to him at all, affect him in any way? And if they didn't, then why did he bother kissing her in the first place? And why, since it appeared that the kisses were as unemotional as a handshake to Bandit, was he so good at it?

"I wouldn't have gotten caught," Tori said defiantly.

A warm breeze passed across the rooftop. The sky held a million stars. She found it nearly impossible to think about the things he was saying, or to make any sense of what she was feeling.

Trying to forget the new sensations she'd discovered in Bandit's arms, she tried to pay attention to the guards on the ground. They were mostly laughing and having a good time, no doubt having picked up a drink or two, but one kept looking stubbornly to the roof. While her body tingled with passionate excitement, however, the guards barely existed for her.

Suddenly, Bandit grinned at Tori condescendingly, and the anger that evoked was an emotion she embraced. Anger was familiar to her; intense sexual arousal wasn't.

"We're not out of here yet," Tori said sharply, for a moment forgetting where she was. "What makes you think you wouldn't—*won't*—get caught?"

"I trust my own abilities. I test them all the time. I know precisely who and what I am, and what I am capable of accomplishing."

"You're absurdly conceited. People don't know themselves that well."

"It's a mistake to assume that your limitations are my limitations," Bandit explained, speaking as though he was declaring an irrefutable fact.

Tori wanted to slap him, and she would have if they weren't hiding from the guards.

She glowered at him. "I don't want to talk to you anymore. You always twist my words around. I don't trust you." She tried to position herself so that her body wasn't touching his.

Then turning away from Bandit, she peered around the edge of the brick chimney. All she could see of the guards below was shadow, so she knew that they couldn't see anything at all of her. Now she felt safe from them, but not from the infuriating stranger in the black mask and cape who had already saved her life once that night and had shown her that her body wasn't as unfeeling and unresponsive as she'd always assumed.

"Is it me that you don't trust, or yourself and how you behave when you're in my arms?"

Tori glared at Bandit. Why did everything he said make her want to slap the smile from his lips or kiss them?

"I don't think you're one to talk about trust. You don't trust me enough to give me my revolver back."

"Oh?"

Tori held her hand out. "Then give it to me. If we get in a fight with those men down there, you'll need my help."

"I can't give you back your pistol again."

"What do you mean, you can't? Did you leave it in the bedroom?" Tori exclaimed, her voice rising dangerously. She wasn't certain the gun could be identified as hers, but the risk of it was enough to send a chill through her.

Then, seeing the half-smile curling Bandit's much too tempting lips, she thought about his words, paying a bit more attention to them this time.

"What do you mean, *again?*"

Without looking, Tori placed her right hand down to her holster. The hard, smooth, reassuringly familiar walnut grip of the Colt greeted her palm. Somehow, Bandit had slipped the revolver back into the holster without her ever becoming aware of it.

"When did you . . . ? How?"

"I had tucked it into my waistband. When we were kissing, I didn't want anything separating us, so I gave it back to you," Bandit explained. "You see, I trust you more than you think."

He reached out to brush his fingertips against Tori's soft cheek. His gaze dipped down briefly to her heavy breasts, which rose and fell with her deep, ragged breathing. It was not easy for him to keep from taking them into his hands to feel their weight, their firmness, their response to his touch.

"Now it is time for you to trust me a little," Bandit continued, his throat tight with sexual tension as his fingertips passed along her cheek and throat. "I've got a plan to get away from here without anyone seeing us. Follow me, and you'll get out as well. Continue to fight me, and you can take your chances with Krey's bodyguards. Incidentally, most have a price on their head in one territory or another. That's the kind of man Jonathon Krey likes to hire to carry a gun for him."

Tori had known that the men working for Krey were dangerous, though she hadn't known exactly how dangerous until this moment. Studying Bandit, she wondered how he could have learned so much about the Krey mansion and the men on the Krey bankroll. The Midnight Bandit was, beyond doubt, a most enigmatic man. He'd opened the safe in Jonathon Krey's bedroom quickly, without knowing the combination; he'd returned a revolver to her holster without her being aware of it; he'd kissed her and made her enjoy it, as well as want more.

"I'll go with you," Tori heard herself say.

"All the way?" Bandit asked, reaching out to take Tori's hand in his own, his fingers curling around hers.

Tori nodded her head, quite certain that she was getting herself into something she couldn't back out of, but she knew a strange sense of freedom at having someone else make the decisions for her.

## Five

Tori was surprised at Bandit's ingenuousness in the choice of an escape route. Holding her hand, he led her along the roof to the rear of the mansion and there, where the servants' quarters were, he slipped them both down from one balcony to the next until they were on the ground.

"All the servants are working," Bandit observed, "so this whole area of the mansion is completely deserted."

"How did you know this side of the mansion contains only servants' quarters?" Tori asked, kneeling on the ground beside Bandit to search the shadows for guards that might still be around.

When he did not reply, she did not press the point. There was only so much information Bandit would allow her, she decided, and it would be in her best interests not to push him beyond that limit.

"Here, put this on," Bandit said, taking off his black Stetson and handing it to Tori. "Tuck your hair up inside. You've got beautiful hair, but it shines in the moonlight like a beacon."

Tori smiled, despite her fear, now that she was on the ground. The voices of the security guards and of the guests at the celebration in the ballroom were clearly audible.

Still . . . he thought she had beautiful hair? Tori wasn't certain how she should respond to the statement, so she said nothing at all.

As she tucked her long blond tresses up beneath the Stetson's headband, she looked at Bandit. His hair was jet black, perfectly parted on the left side, not overly long. Though he was once again in shadow—wasn't he always?—it seemed to her that his haircut was an excellent one. Did that mean he was a man of wealth? Poor men, she had noted, tended to have poor grooming habits, and the Midnight Bandit was impeccably groomed.

"Come on, and stay low," he instructed, once Tori had his hat in place.

This time Tori reached out for his hand. For an instant, they stood motionless in the moonlight, looking into each other's eyes, their fingers laced together, their hearts racing with excitement.

"Don't be afraid," he whispered. "I'll get you out of this."

"I won't be afraid if you hold my hand," Tori said.

She immediately wished she hadn't said a word. The last thing in the world the arrogant bandit needed was someone else having confidence in his abilities—and letting him know it.

They moved away from the mansion, racing across the lawn until they reached the high surrounding wall. Here, at the rear of the estate where security was most likely to be breached, the wall was almost twice as high as it was on the street side. Tori's heart sank. How in the world could she scale such a high wall? She doubted that even Bandit could.

But instead of stopping at the wall, he banked sharply

left, following the wall to the livery stable. Tori's heart was pounding and her mouth felt bone-dry as she and he pressed their backs to the livery's side and listened to the conversations of the hired men within.

She could hear laughing and arguing. The coachmen of the wealthy guests at the celebration were responsible for getting their employers back into their respective carriages and home.

"This way," Bandit said, placing his hand at the small of Tori's back and urging her along the stable's exterior wall. Across from them stood the security wall.

His hand warmed Tori's shirt, then her chemise, and as her skin responded, it was as if she were in his arms again, feasting upon his probing, intimate kisses.

They'd taken only three steps when the sound of a woman's laugh stopped them in their tracks. A second later, a man and woman appeared in the shadows. They were in their forties, were well dressed and jovial; both had drunk more than a glass or two of champagne.

"Walter, what has gotten into you tonight?" the woman asked, laughing softly as she tried to sound annoyed.

"Give me half a chance, and I'll show you," Walter replied.

The woman's laughter was suddenly silenced as he kissed her.

Tori stood less than twenty feet away. Horrified at the thought of being caught, but astonished at what she was seeing, she recognized the couple now: Walter and Margarite English. Citizens of Santa Fe, they'd made a fortune by bringing lumber and building materials to the territory. Both had earned prominence by spending time and money with local church and charitable organizations. Three summers earlier, when Tori had sprained her ankle—Jedediah was off hunting desperadoes—it was Margarite English who'd appeared unexpectedly at the Singer house with a large kettle of stew and three hearty loaves of bread. It was a simple act of kindness, and Tori had never forgotten it.

Now Tori was on the verge of being caught by that very same altruistic woman, and the thought of it distressed her.

"Stop it now," Margarite continued, making only a half-hearted attempt to scramble out of her husband's ardent embrace. "This champagne has turned you into a wolf."

"A wolf that wants to eat you alive!" Walter replied, pulling his wife of more than two decades back into his arms and firmly placing a hand over her breast.

Tori was shocked that the Englishes were still so passionate. For reasons she did not at all understand, she had believed them too old and much too genteel to still be involved with something as tawdry as sexuality.

The moan of passion from Margarite told Tori the woman's feelings were not those of a long-suffering wife who had to bear up under her husband's ardent demands.

Suddenly, Bandit took Tori by the elbow, spinning her so that she faced him. He pulled her tightly into his arms and kissed her hard on the mouth.

Tori balled her hands into fists and jabbed them into his chest. How dare he—at a time like this!

The commotion drew the attention Bandit had planned. His back was to Margarite and Walter as he said in a growl, "Go find your own love nest! This one's spoken for!"

"Sorry, good fellow, didn't know," Walter said, snickering. Margarite pulled frantically at her bodice, trying to get her dress properly arranged and buttoned.

After the couple had stepped out of the darkness and moved back toward the ballroom, Tori heard Margarite say, "I'm so embarrassed! I hope they didn't recognize us! I'll never have another glass of champagne again—and I'll never go for a midnight stroll with you, not as long as I live, Walter English!"

Alone once more, Tori breathed a sigh of relief. Bandit's quick thinking had saved them from discovery once again. How truly unprepared she was for this attack on Jonathon Krey and his criminal empire!

"That was close," she whispered. "You think fast."

"I was going to kiss you anyway. Margarite and Walter just gave me the excuse," he said with a boyish smile that was very seductive. He was apparently unfazed by how near they'd come to being discovered.

Once again with no idea of what kind of response she should make to his devilish teasing, Tori said nothing.

They went to a ladder built into the rear wall of the livery stables, and climbed up into the hay loft, where Bandit unlatched the small door and eased himself inside. Tori followed him, crawling on hands and knees to peer down over the edge at the men below.

There were nine of them, five playing cards and four throwing dice. All were drinking heavily. This was a night when liquor was provided for everyone, and these men were determined to drink all they could.

The Bandit tapped Tori on the shoulder, then moved away from the edge of the hay loft. She followed him toward the rear of the loft, then knelt in the darkness, facing him. The loft was dusty, but she sensed that they were safe in it. None of the hired hands would be feeding the horses this late at night, and there was no other reason for coming up here.

"Now what?" she asked in a whisper, distinctly aware of her proximity to Bandit. She doubted that she needed to work so hard at whispering, for she was very close to Bandit, but she figured it was best to be safe.

"Now we wait. It's nearly one o'clock. By about three o'clock, Tyler Napki will be drunk as a skunk, and his coachman will toss him into his carriage and take him home. Mrs. Napki and the children were already taken home, at eight-thirty."

"What's that got to do with us?"

"We'll be riding on the roof of the carriage. Once we're outside the gates, we'll jump off. Napki and his coachman are both notorious drinkers on Saturday night. Neither one will hear a thing."

"You've planned everything, haven't you?"

"I didn't plan on you," he replied, looking deep into her soft green eyes.

Tori looked away. When Bandit looked into her eyes, it seemed he could see right through the defenses that she had erected to keep herself safe from the world, but when she looked at him, she saw nothing but shadows, both literally and metaphorically. He was all light and darkness, part of him revealed, part of him concealed, his identity and his essential, intrinsic self elusive and enigmatic and tantalizingly seductive to the responsive female Tori had never before suspected she was.

"I'm sorry," she whispered. "I didn't mean to cause you any bother. I just wanted . . . I *had* to strike out at Jonathon Krey, don't you see? Somebody has to. He's gotten away with everything, absolutely everything . . . and the law never touches him. He *owns* the law."

Mack listened carefully to Tori and wondered how many people shared her sentiments. He also wondered what Jonathon Krey had done to her to make her hate him so much. Her contempt for Krey was based on more than principle. Mack hated Jonathon Krey because he'd witnessed the havoc left in the wake of Krey's greed, but Tori hated the man for personal reasons.

Though Mack Randolph's legal expertise told him not to get involved, Tori's unexpected intrusion into his life had delighted him too much for him not to pursue the answer.

"He owns a judge, and a businessman who one day might be the governor of this territory, but he doesn't own the law, Tori. Nobody can own the law," Bandit said quietly.

She looked at him, shaking her head. "You just don't understand."

Mack reached out, removing his Stetson from her head. Her long, honey-blond hair tumbled down around her shoulders in waves of satin. He smoothed some of it over her shoulders, wanting to touch both her hair and her body. She did not move away from his touch.

"How did Jonathon hurt you?"

Tori looked away, shrugging her shoulders, unaware that the move caused her heavy breasts to rise and fall beneath the well-washed blue cotton shirt. This was not something she wanted to think about, much less talk about, with a masked man—albeit one who could kiss her fears away.

"It doesn't matter," she answered quietly after a long

pause, sensing that she had to say something. "It happened a long time ago. It really doesn't matter anymore."

"I think it does," Bandit observed softly. He reached out to brush the backs of his knuckles lightly against Tori's soft cheek. When she turned her gentle green eyes upon him, he felt a strange tightness in his chest, a reaction that mystified him, since he'd known the gazes of many a beautiful woman in the past and had never before reacted quite this way. "Jonathon Krey has done something to you that he shouldn't have, but I won't force you to talk about it, if you don't want to."

"Thank you," Tori replied, the words coming out so softly they could barely be heard, even though Bandit was kneeling very close to her.

She closed her eyes and rolled her head back on her shoulders, suddenly feeling very tired. It wasn't a sleepy kind of fatigue, though, since she was still far too energized by excitement to even consider sleep. She had spent days thinking about how she would break into Jonathon Krey's mansion during the charity hospital ceremonies, and as it turned out, she had done almost everything wrong. If it hadn't been for the Midnight Bandit, she would now be in the custody of some sheriff, sitting in a jail cell, or be the captive of Jonathan Krey, being tortured.

The thought made Tori shiver.

"What's wrong," Bandit asked.

"Nothing." She shifted positions in the hay, curling her legs beneath her. Sometimes she wished he wasn't quite so perceptive.

Bandit unknotted the tie at his throat, and then removed his cape and spread it out on the hay. Tori ran her hand lightly over the black silk, enjoying its texture. She thought it a shame that he would put such exquisite material upon hay.

"Sit on it," Bandit prodded, taking Tori by the upper arm and urging her onto the cape. "We've got a couple hours yet to kill, so you might just as well get comfortable."

Tori knelt on the cape, though she was careful to keep her boots off the fabric as she sat with legs curled beneath her and to the side.

"Why is it *you* hate Jonathon Krey?" Tori asked then, at last feeling a certain sense of safety after so many hours of unremitting emotional strain. "You seem to know an awful lot about him, his house, and all the people in it."

Beneath the mask that covered his eyes, Bandit's mouth curled into a smile that touched Tori deep inside.

"I like your dimple," she whispered.

In a bold gesture for her, she touched his face lightly with her fingertips. That night he had reached out to her, but she'd never been the one to bridge the chasm that separated them physically.

"You won't tell me why you want to destroy Jonathon Krey," Tori continued. "You're embarrassed about your dimple. If I didn't know you better, I'd say you're the kind of man who has one set of standards for himself, and one set for the women in his life."

The Bandit tossed his Stetson aside. He'd had women tease him flirtatiously before, to be sure, but he'd never had anyone accuse him of having a double standard, and he frankly didn't like the accusation, though he couldn't blame Tori in the least for voicing it.

"I don't mean to," he said quietly, his deeply melodic voice still disguised though not as greatly altered. "For reasons that are crucial to me, I must keep my identity a secret. And because I must, I am in a position where I might be able to help you, but you can do nothing for me."

Tori looked away, thinking of Bandit's words, wondering how many of them were true and how many deliberately tantalizing lies meant to please the ear.

Bandit looked at Tori's profile, and another surge of emotion went through him, this one heated, sensual, irrepressible. Tori was so different from the women he usually associated with, yet the differences delighted him. She was independent and brave. And from her long blond hair, which she left free and unbound, to the full breasts pressing against her cheap cotton shirt that had obviously seen countless washings, to the men's Levi's which hugged her hips tightly and seemed brand new, to her full mouth that was absolute heaven to kiss—she excited him. Even the holster and Colt strapped to her hips pleased Bandit, even though, despite his considerable skill with firearms, he had always had an aversion to them. The gun was just one more symbol of Tori's independence, and that was why it pleased him.

The thought of what would happen to Tori when Jonathon Krey caught her stealing from him bore into Bandit's consciousness, hitting him with a painful clarity.

"You must never try to steal from the Kreys again," he whispered. "If you need help—money, whatever—I'll give it to you. But if you—"

"I don't want your charity," Tori hissed quickly, angrily. "I don't need anything from you, or from anyone else!"

From the livery stable below, a drunken male voice asked, "Charlie, did you hear that? I thought I heard a lady up in the hay loft."

There was a general commotion as the card players argued the merits of checking out the possibility of a woman's presence. Most thought it just a ploy to separate the players from the money on the table.

Tori and Bandit immediately moved closer together, each instinctively drawing a revolver. They waited, neither breathing, listening to the men arguing below them. It wasn't until the card game resumed that Tori breathed again.

"I'm sorry," she whispered into Bandit's ear. "I didn't mean to get so angry with you. In the past, the only time men have ever wanted to help me was if they . . . if they thought . . ."

"If they thought they could get something in return?"

Tori nodded her head and holstered her revolver. She didn't know why she was telling him the truth. It certainly wasn't like he'd ever done anything to warrant her opening her heart to him. When she looked at him again, she thought of how strange it was she had become accustomed to the mask he wore, so that now she hardly noticed it.

"I want to help you, and I want to keep you safe," Bandit whispered, his face inches from Tori's. "But I'll never expect anything from you in return."

Tori looked at his mouth and thought, *I want his kisses.*

A sudden burst of drunken laughter from the card-playing coachmen intruded on the moment, and Tori closed her eyes, wishing the drunken men would miraculously disappear. In the moment her eyes closed she felt Bandit's lips, warm and pleasing, lightly touch her own.

"I thought you wouldn't expect anything from me," Tori whispered when the brief kiss ended.

"I don't. But you're much too beautiful for me not to want you."

He kissed her again, pressing his mouth more firmly against hers. She gave herself over to the sensations his kisses drew from her. When he leaned into her, his powerful hands taking her by the shoulders to press her back into the hay, she did not resist, ignoring the little warning bell clanging in the back of her mind.

"You are so exciting," Bandit whispered between kisses. He caught Tori's lower lip between his teeth and bit gently, surprising her with both the act and the sensation it caused.

Tori tumbled backward, her back cushioned by the hay, but separated from it by the silk cape. She parted her lips in invitation and quickly received Bandit's tongue.

She moaned, her tongue dancing against his, shocked at the force of the pleasure she derived from this new way of kissing. She wrapped her arms loosely around Bandit's broad shoulders as she stretched out her long legs.

The kiss lasted an eternity, and when it finally ended, Tori turned her face away from Bandit, needing to catch her breath and see what shred of cooler judgment still remained to her. When she did so, she felt Bandit's lips against her cheek, then her neck. The wet warmth of his tongue and lips on her sensitive flesh sent a surge of excitement pulsing through her.

*I have to stop this insanity now,* Tori thought. *I don't even know who he is.*

She opened her eyes and saw, in the darkness, the dusty arched beams of the hay loft overhead. She could hear the laughter and arguments of the coarse men so incredibly near. Bandit's body pressed against hers while his lips worked their own special brand of seductive magic.

The threat of discovery mingled with her passion, escalating its intensity, heightening its force.

Why did it have to be Bandit who made her body come alive? Previous experience in kissing had taught her that there was nothing pleasurable in the act, but even the first of Bandit's kisses was addictive.

A particularly loud and vulgar laugh from one of the poker players made Tori flinch in Bandit's arms.

"Don't think about them," he whispered into her ear, his body pressing into hers. The tip of his tongue traced the circumference of her ear briefly. "They mean nothing to us. They're no danger at all."

"I can't help thinking of them," Tori replied softly. She stifled the moan that threatened to escape her when Bandit caught her earlobe between his teeth and bit gently. "They're so close."

"They're a world away from where we are now," Bandit replied.

Why did his words make sense to her passion-addled brain? Those dangerous men below, all bearing pistols beneath the fine clothes their employers had bought for them, were not a world away—they were very close. Dangerously close! That was why she and Bandit had to whisper, so that they wouldn't be heard—which was why Tori was at that very moment in Bandit's arms.

No, it wasn't.

She was in his arms because that was right where she wanted to be, even if she couldn't quite admit that damning little fact to herself.

"Forget about them," Bandit repeated, his lips now at

Tori's throat, warm and moist, touching her flesh yet touching her deeper than that.

His right hand was at her hip, pulling her toward him so that the fit of their bodies would be more secure. She parted her knees just enough to capture his thigh between her own. Bandit moved closer still—close enough to slide his hard-muscled thigh up to the juncture of her thighs.

The pressure of him pushing against her so intimately drew an immediate and surprising response from Tori. Though layers of clothing actually separated them, she could feel the heat of him, and even more, the heat of her own passion, escalating now at a furious pace.

The dewy moisture of Tori's desire was centered down low yet traveled throughout her body. She tried to clamp her thighs together, to prevent his thigh from rubbing even more intimately against her, but all she really accomplished was trapping Bandit's leg against her.

"It's not wrong to give in to your feelings," he whispered.

There was a half-smile on his lips that was at once seductive and thoroughly infuriating. As Tori looked into Bandit's dark brown eyes, she realized that to him, this encounter—this stolen moment of eroticism—was nothing more than a diverting way to pass the time while waiting to escape from the well-guarded Krey estate.

With a forceful shove, Tori put her hand on his hip and pushed away with all her strength. At the same time she unclamped her thighs and slid her hips away. That kind of contact had been much too pleasurable to be allowed to continue, especially with a man as devilishly seductive as Bandit.

"It *is* wrong," Tori hissed through clenched teeth, as angry at herself as at him.

"Why?" Bandit asked, his half-smile still tauntingly in place.

Tori opened her mouth as though to speak, though no words came out. The answer was obvious, yet when she came to put words to it, she could find none. Why, indeed, was it wrong to give in to one's feelings? Society, she knew, considered it to be perfectly acceptable for *men* to let their passions run free. Why was that freedom not accorded to women?

"Well . . . ?" Bandit chided, sliding closer to Tori once again. He eased his hand from her hip, running it around to the small of her back, very subtly pulling her to him again.

"I d-don't know why," Tori at last confessed, her mind in a whirl.

# *Six*

The hypocrisy shocked her for a thousand reasons, but mostly because she'd never thought of it before. How many other injustices were there that she'd never given a second thought?

Unconsciously, she eased her arm around Bandit's neck.

She felt his lips upon her own and turned her face aside, exposing it even more, the most delightful tingles going through her. Bandit's teeth nipped at her flesh, the sensation almost painful yet very stimulating. The soft gasp never escaped her lips because before it could be expelled in a rush of breath, Bandit soothed her fevered flesh with his tongue. He knew exactly where to draw the line.

*Why is it wrong to do what feels so good?* Tori asked herself. She angled her head slightly more to the left to allow Bandit to kiss her collarbone. Everywhere he kissed her he left behind a trail of tingling, aroused flesh that wanted more of his attention.

"It's not wrong."

It took a moment for Tori to realize that she had spoken, answering the question that had been dancing in her mind. Anything that felt this good simply couldn't be wrong, she reasoned.

"That's right," Bandit gently growled. His touch, precise and light, went unnoticed by the woman in his arms as he unfastened yet another button of her blue cotton shirt. "It's not wrong at all."

He continued to hold Tori in his arms, his weight lightly upon her. She was bold and brave, he realized, but she was also relatively inexperienced in the ways of the flesh. He could tell from the way she kissed, moved in his arms, and reacted to his kisses.

Something made him stop.

If Bandit had unfastened just one more button, the view exposed to him would have taken his breath away. But he realized with a shock that he had gotten much more aroused by this enigmatic, poor young woman from the outskirts of Santa Fe than he'd thought he would.

She was femininity to the nth degree, Bandit realized, to his surprise. Broad-shouldered, wide-hipped, strong in the arms and legs, yet curvaceous. Her firm breasts drew a man's eye, and her soft lips begged to be kissed. She was that rare combination of softness and strength . . . and everything about her excited Bandit.

Shhh!" he hissed, placing a finger to his lips. "I think I hear something."

He rolled away from her, turning his back to Tori. Actually, he hadn't heard anything from the men down in the main area of the stables. Bandit quickly rearranged himself within his clothing so that he would be more comfortable and his passion would be less visible. He had responded to Tori's beauty, his manhood throbbing to life and straining against the fabric of his exquisitely tailored trousers.

If she had been another woman, if the confusion that went along with her passion had not been genuine, then perhaps he would have continued with her, using his charm to seduce her so they could both experience the release they needed.

But she was not one of the coy, wealthy debutantes who played at innocence, throwing themselves at the wealthy Mack Randolph and then pushing him away and pretending to be shocked at his passionate ardor, only to succumb to his desire in the end.

Tori wasn't playing that silly game of cat and mouse, and because she wasn't, Mack wanted her all the more, and knew he couldn't have her.

He breathed deeply several times, trying hard to compose himself, wishing he had as much control over certain parts of himself as he did of his thoughts. His mind said he had to stop; his manhood was still pulsating with need.

What in hell did he think he was doing with Tori Singer? He knew her brother and had even helped the bounty hunter with legal problems on occasion. In theory, there was absolutely nothing he, Mack Randolph, and she, Tori Singer, had in common. But Bandit *did* have something in common with her. Though a lawyer with political aspirations might never look twice at a woman from Tori's background, Bandit, who had held the young blonde in his arms, had tasted the sweetness of her kisses and felt the lushly feminine graces of that curvaceous body hidden in man's clothes, he could accept her as an ally in the war against Jonathon Krey, for she was a woman of courage and passion.

"What is it? Did they hear us? I'm sorry," Tori whispered, crawling on hands and knees until she was behind him, her hands light on his shoulders.

Together they looked down at the men throwing dice

against the wall, Tori peering over Bandit's shoulder, quite unaware of the warmth of her breasts lightly touching his back. When he looked at her, their faces close together, he realized that if he would seduce her, his name—albeit, as the Midnight Bandit—would be added to the list of men who had at some time taken advantage of her, abused her in one way or another.

It was not a list either Mack Randolph or Bandit wanted to be on. No matter how aroused he'd become because of Tori's unique, ineffable allure, he had honor.

"I'll get you safely out of here," he whispered, feeling the need to say something, yet not quite knowing what the appropriate words were.

The far door to the livery opened, and a uniformed maid from the mansion stuck her head inside. She was immediately greeted with whistles and catcalls from the men. Tori and Bandit ducked low, keeping hidden.

"Bugger you all!" the maid said, disgusted with the behavior of the coachmen. "It's time to get Mr. Napki. He's passed out stone cold in the game room." She slammed the door quickly, before the loutish men could say anything more to her.

"It's time," Bandit whispered, turning to Tori.

For several seconds, they looked into each other's eyes, knowing they were parting company.

Did Tori want to leave him? Even she wasn't sure of that answer. In his arms, she had discovered something about herself that she'd never known, something mysterious and frightening, beautiful and inspiring. But he hadn't trusted her enough to reveal himself, keeping his mask over his eyes. And she felt that without mutual trust, she could never allow herself to accept anything more intimate than his kisses.

"What now . . . for us?" Tori asked, unsure whether she was questioning their next move or their relationship.

Bandit took Tori's hand and helped her to her feet. He knew words needed to be spoken, thoughts and feelings needed to be expressed. He also knew that he could not do that now. Chaotic emotions collided with beliefs he'd held deep within himself for a long time. He could not speak.

He led Tori to the rear of the stables where they had entered. After a quick inspection of the shadows to see if guards were nearby, he slipped down the ladder with Tori close behind.

On the west side, where the carriages were all lined up waiting to be occupied, Tori saw the largest private carriage she'd ever viewed. It took six horses to move it, and it was Tyler Napki's. Enormous and ornate, it was the fitting symbol for a family man with a wife and eight children. When Tyler Napki went to church on Sunday morning, his entire family surrounding him, his hangover from his Saturday night binge howling in his ears, everyone knew he was a successful man—and penitent for his behavior of the night before. That, anyway, was what Tyler Napki hoped the good people of Santa Fe thought.

Tori and Bandit climbed onto the roof of the carriage and, lying flat on their stomachs, waited breathlessly in the dark. Very soon, they could hear the coachman grunting drunkenly with exertion as he assisted his employer, the wealthy and even more intoxicated Tyler Napki, to the carriage.

"In you go, sir, and we'll get you right home," the

coachman groaned, pushing his employer into the plush confines.

"I'll be fine," Tyler said, one foot still outside the carriage door. "All I need is forty winks, an' I'll be back in the game fresh as a daisy."

"The daisy's done wilted, sir. Get some sleep and I'll wake you when we get home."

Tori caught her lower lip between her teeth and bit hard, causing pain. She needed the pain to keep laughter from bubbling out. In her mind's eye, she could picture the two men, Saturday night after Saturday night, going through the same ritual.

She looked over at Bandit. Behind his black mask, his dark eyes were shining like wet onyx, with mischief, twinkling with the *joi de vivre* that seemed as much a part of him as the color of his hair or the dimple in his cheek.

*He's such a handsome man,* Tori thought, smiling at the mysterious stranger who had changed so many of the beliefs she'd had about herself. *Even with the mask, he's so handsome . . . too handsome for my own good.*

The carriage rattled under the high stone archway at the gate and onto the street beyond. Glancing over her shoulder, Tori looked at the massive mansion that hours earlier she had broken into, and the exciting events of the past hours came back to her. She breathed a sigh of relief, suddenly realizing how tense she had been, even if she hadn't been totally aware of it.

The horses settled into a leisurely pace as soon as the coachman fell asleep. They knew the way home, and would take their own time returning.

When the carriage had traveled several hundred yards, Bandit rose to his knees and motioned for Tori to follow him. Soon they'd jumped to the ground, as the carriage continued into the night, neither of its occupants having been aware of the additional passengers.

"Over here," Bandit said, his hand on Tori's elbow, leading her off the street, moving between several houses so they wouldn't be seen.

Tori leaned back against a small, freshly painted smokehouse. The air, now that she was no longer surrounded by the Kreys' high stone wall, seemed fresher, cleaner. She inhaled deeply just to reassure herself that this was true.

Bandit stepped back into the street, looking in all directions until he was convinced that their escape had gone completely unnoticed. As he returned to Tori, his hat, mask, and cape still in place, she watched him practically dissolve into the shadows next to her, and she understood once again why the stories concerning the Midnight Bandit had always sounded so fantastic.

"We made it," Tori said in a whisper.

Her heart accelerated as Bandit stepped closer. She tried to remind herself that he was an outlaw, that she should have nothing but contempt for him. After all, didn't she hate the Kreys because *they* were outlaws?

"Yes. Despite the odds and a few unforeseen obstacles, we made it, Tori."

He was still disguising his voice, adding the hard, flinty edge to it, but she could tell there wasn't the anger in it that she'd heard before.

"Was I one of the 'unforeseen obstacles'?" she asked.

When he nodded, Tori wished desperately that he would take off his mask. Who was this handsome stranger?

"A delightful one, to be sure, but an obstacle just the same."

Bandit took his hat off, letting it hang from the neck cord down against his back. Then he placed his hands against the smokehouse wall on either side of her, trapping her between his arms without ever touching her.

"What are you going to do now?" he asked softly. "You know if you ever try anything like that again, you'll get caught. You would have gotten caught tonight, if it were not for me."

"I owe you for that," Tori whispered, her mouth dry.

When she inhaled deeply to compose her erratic thinking, her breasts rose and strained against her shirt. She saw Bandit's gaze touch her there tenderly. She realized then that she hadn't refastened the buttons he had undone in the livery's hay loft.

As though he had touched her physically with his gaze, her nipples instantly hardened, denting the much-washed fabric, an undeniable incrimination of her body's responsiveness to him.

"T-thank you for the money," Tori said, her voice sounding strained. She couldn't think of anything else to say, and silence with Bandit so near was intolerable.

He was very close now, his lips tempting her. For one second, Tori thought of crossing her arms to hide her breasts from his view; in the next, she thought of unfastening another button or two so that he could see even more.

Bandit saw her pale white flesh glowing erotically in the moonlight.

"It should be enough for you to live on for a long time, provided you don't get extravagant. And don't spend the money too quickly, or Jonathon Krey will be on to you."

"I told you before, the money's not for me. There are

others who need it more than I do. Like Mr. Beaumont. Krey has almost ruined him."

"You're really going to give the money to people who have been hurt by Krey?"

"I told you that before."

Tori didn't know what to think, what to feel. As much as she hated not being believed, she detested even more having to explain all over again her reasons for behaving like a common criminal.

Through the darkness, Bandit looked deep into her eyes. She did not look away. She didn't even blink. She sensed that he was challenging her in some way, waiting for her to back down or perhaps suddenly admit that she was lying and that the money was really for her own needs.

He reached into his pocket, extracting the remainder of the money he'd taken from Jonathon Krey's safe. Tori breathed a sigh of relief, finding it easier to breathe now that his arms were no longer surrounding her.

"In that case, as long as you're an angel of mercy, you should have this as well."

He handed her the money. Despite her surprise, Tori calmly folded the money in half and tucked it into her back pocket. When she did this, bending her arms behind her back, her shirt opened even more, exposing her breasts and chemise briefly to Bandit. She immediately brought her hands forward, beginning to work the buttons with trembling fingers.

"Don't." His long fingers curled around Tori's wrists. "Don't do that," he added softly. "You're so beautiful. I like being able to look at you."

Tori didn't know what to say. She felt naughty and daring, especially knowing that she was displaying cleavage because Bandit had worked the buttons free so smoothly that she'd been completely unaware of it.

"Who are you?" she asked quietly. "What are you? You seem to know all about me, and I know nothing about you at all."

"That's not quite true . . . on either count."

Bandit pulled Tori's hands apart, and she did not resist when he pinned them lightly against the smokehouse wall. His gaze went down to her cleavage and her pebble-hard nipples.

"We are strangers," he whispered. He leaned forward and kissed her lightly on the forehead, his lips brushing against satiny tendrils of blond hair. "The only thing we really know about each other is that we excite each other."

He kissed the tip of Tori's nose, then placed a firm, demanding kiss on her lips to silence her protest to the truth he'd spoken. "Don't try to deny it. You know it's so. I can feel it in you. *You* can feel it in you."

Tori knew that with very little effort she could pull her wrists out of his grasp. He was hardly using any pressure at all to pin her hands to the smokehouse wall. But she did not want to be free from him. She did not want to button her shirt, as she knew she should to be proper.

Then Bandit made love to her mouth with his tongue, teaching Tori as he aroused her. She sighed, opening her mouth wider, hungrily taking him in, playing her tongue against his. When he moved a fraction closer, she arched her back, her shoulders still against the solid wooden wall behind her, but her breasts now against the solid muscled wall of Bandit's chest.

Her nipples throbbed with tension, aching to be touched and caressed. She wanted it all and more, with as great an intensity as she wanted to be free from his intoxicating kisses and allure.

*This mustn't go on,* Tori thought.

Again, her body did not listen to her better judgment. She turned her shoulders just slightly so that the tips of her breasts rubbed against his chest. Hot tingles of pleasure raced through her, and she moaned deeply, soulfully against Bandit's mouth.

Very slowly, he inched his hands from Tori's wrists, his palms sliding over her forearms, then biceps. She did not move her arms away from the wall, leaving them bent, hands near her shoulders.

"Tell me not to touch you, and I won't," he whispered, his lips at Tori's ear. "Tell me not to kiss you, and I won't."

*I can stop this madness now,* Tori thought. She could not, however, make her lips form the words that would put an end to it all.

She turned her face away from Bandit. Undeterred, he kissed the velvety arch of her throat, sending fresh waves of pleasure coursing through her. She squirmed against the smokehouse wall.

His hands moved from her shoulders, sliding over the full, taut curves of her breasts. When he captured her passion-peaked nipples between his fingers and thumbs and pinched softly, a tiny cry of ecstasy escaped her.

"You can't tell me to stop, can you?" he whispered, his lips at her collarbone. "You can't say the words because if you did, you know they'd be lies . . . all lies."

He squeezed her breasts more firmly, filling his hands with warm, firm flesh, his own passion racing now at a fever pitch that nearly matched Tori's.

"You don't want me to stop because we both know

we're each other's destiny. That's why we met tonight; that's why we're here now."

Tori's eyes closed tightly, her expression carried a grimace of passion and confusion. Why couldn't Bandit touch her the way she'd been touched by that other man, so that she felt she was being pawed, not caressed? Instead of making crude comments about her being big and strong enough to make a "good bucking horse" for a man in bed, he treated her body as though it were a shrine to femininity, to be worshipped.

In short, why did the Midnight Bandit—damn him!—have to be everything she wanted when he was the one man in the entire world she simply couldn't have?

"Tell me to stop," he murmured, his lips now at Tori's chest, near the top button still fastened.

Quickly three more buttons of her shirt were undone, and Bandit's tongue, warm and enticing, was sliding back and forth over the valley of her breasts, above the top bow of her chemise. His fingers curled into the cotton shirt and pulled the tail out of her Levi's, exposing a chemise that was even older than the shirt.

Suddenly, Tori was embarrassed by the age and condition of her undergarments, though logic told her that it shouldn't mean anything at a time like this.

Her breasts, full and tight, hurt from the tension. Not wanting to position her arms anywhere that might prevent his caresses from pleasing her, she placed her hands lightly upon Bandit's shoulders.

Looking down, she saw her breasts inside the thin chemise. To her embarrassment, her body was responding with absolute honesty.

Only three ties held the chemise closed. Three simple

knots to be pulled loose, so Bandit could feast upon Tori's bosom. But he would not untie the chemise himself. He'd already gone much further into the sensual realm with her than he'd ever thought he would, and before he at last exposed her golden body to his passion's hunger, he wanted—his conscience *needed*—her complete and un-equivocating acceptance.

Tori's knees were shaking. Her spine seemed to have melted. Her breath came in deep, ragged gulps. Her skin was burning. She was certain that everywhere Bandit touched her, the flesh was seared from her bones.

"Untie them," he whispered. "Untie your chemise for me. Let me kiss you. Let me taste your breasts."

*Just do it, Bandit!* Tori thought feverishly. *Don't make me help you! Don't stop! Don't be a damned gentleman now that you've made me so excited!*

"Give them to me, Tori," Bandit whispered, his voice passion-hoarse.

Tori looked down, and when she did, it was very nearly her undoing. She watched as he kissed her between her breasts, just above the top tie of her chemise, then he moved to the side, opened his mouth wide, and took her cloth-covered breast between his lips. Even through the material of the chemise, the sensation of wetness and warmth was all pervading.

For only a second, Tori's knees buckled, and she sagged against the smokehouse wall as Bandit's lips tugged her nipple into even greater arousal.

"Oh, God!" she gasped, unable to believe that anything could feel so good, that the sensations coming from her breast could arouse the rest of her body so completely.

He bared his teeth, nipping the tip of Tori's breast

She shivered, her legs straightening so that she stood upright once more, though she leaned heavily against the smokehouse wall and would surely have fallen without its support.

"Do it for me, Tori!" Bandit urged. He turned his attention to her other breast, taking the tip into his mouth, moistening the nipple through her chemise. "Open it. Let me taste you."

His request intoxicated Tori, who knew that to do as he asked meant her passion would reach yet another, even higher, plateau. But how high was too high? Could she ascend so far that she never came down? And when she did come down, how fast and brutal would the descent be? With Bandit's kisses, so warm and intimate even through the cotton, it seemed entirely possible that her passion would never cease, that she would never again know a moment's peace from the longings of her body.

She felt his hands slide slowly down her sides, then curl around her hips to cup her buttocks. She groaned as his long, strong fingers kneaded her buttocks, squeezing and caressing her through the Levi's, tight across the backside because they'd been cut for a man's narrower hips.

Bandit's heart nearly burst right out of his chest as he cupped Tori's backside in his hands and nipped the crest of her trembling breast with his teeth. He hungered for the taste of her nipples without the distracting cotton chemise, but he would not strip that last barrier from her. That was something she had to do.

His arousal ached from being trapped inside his trousers for so long. He wanted to free it, but he knew that Tori would never understand. She was still holding back, still unwilling to completely explore the senses, and he honored her reticence, even if he was disappointed with it.

"Untie your chemise," Bandit whispered, his lips warm and wet in the deep valley of her breasts. He'd hoped to remain more in control than he now felt. "Untie your chemise . . . *for me.*"

Tori's hands were still at Bandit's shoulders. The pleasure that she anticipated was almost unimaginable to her, but she believed there were more important things in the world than simply giving free rein to one's desire for gratification.

Each time his strong hands squeezed her backside, a fresh burst of pleasure coursed through her, emanating from down low. When his right hand eased around her hip to slide up high between her thighs, Tori's breath caught in her throat.

"Oh, God! Bandit! Bandit!" she gasped as his hand cupped her, the heel of his palm rubbing back and forth to spread the inferno of her passion through her limbs in heated waves.

She wanted to push him away. She needed to if she was ever to think of herself in the same way again.

But she could not. Her body could not do the bidding of her mind. Her sense of propriety was no match against the passion that Bandit had ignited within her.

His hand moved back and forth, pushing firmly against her, touching her through her Levi's. He felt the heat of her desire, the wetness of her readiness. Bandit caught her breast between his lips again, tugging at the small, aroused bud through the moist cotton.

Tori spread her feet farther apart, shocking herself with her wanton behavior.

*What is happening to me?* She tried to think, but was wildly confused.

Bandit's hand moved more quickly between her thighs, his palm and fingers putting just the right amount of pressure, the right amount of friction, against Tori's secret place to draw out her pleasure. Still, his teeth tugged at her nipple, sending yet additional waves of excitement rippling through her curvaceous body.

For Tori, it was as though she had become possessed, her body taken over by a demon. She spread her feet even wider apart, her shoulders against the smokehouse wall, her hips churning madly in response to the motions of Bandit's hand between her thighs.

The tension was agony. It was as though there was a knot being wound tighter and tighter within her. That tension was now sheer pain. There was, she thought, absolutely nothing pleasurable about this, yet she could not stop the motion of her hips.

And then, when the pressure could build no more, when it had reached it peak, the release came.

She cried out, sobbing her joy, as the passion still surged through her. She clutched onto Bandit, grabbing him so that she would not fall to the ground, her knees buckling, her legs no longer strong enough to support her weight.

Her breath came in deep gulps. Once she'd reached her release, once the waves of white-hot ecstasy had subsided, clear, lucid thinking returned with frightening speed. Quite suddenly, Tori was all too aware of what she had been doing . . . and she didn't like it at all.

She pushed out of Bandit's arms and turned her back to him. Crazy little tingles, aftershocks of the ecstasy she'd just experienced, continued to shiver through her, but she did her best to ignore them.

"Don't touch me," she whispered. She tried to button her shirt, but her hands were trembling too much to accomplish that simple task. She shoved the tails of her shirt back into her Levi's. "Go . . . please go . . . please leave me. This is all wrong."

The sun would be up soon. Tori wanted to turn around to look at Bandit. At last she would be able to see him clearly, without the darkness and shadows that he kept to maintain his secret identity. She wanted to look at him, but she didn't dare because whenever she looked into his eyes, she ended up in his arms, doing things that she'd never before even thought of . . . things that certainly were terribly, sinfully wrong.

"You want me to leave?" he asked.

Without turning, Tori nodded her head.

"Remember what I said about Jonathon Krey. Don't go after him. If he catches you, he'll kill you," Bandit warned.

Tori said nothing. She couldn't think of Krey at a time like this.

She waited, wanting him to speak, wanting to make some sense out of what she'd just done.

"Bandit, will I ever see you again?" she asked.

Silence greeted her.

Tori waited. Still she received no answer. Finally, she turned around. Bandit was gone, disappearing from her life just as quickly and mysteriously as he'd entered it.

# Seven

It was midafternoon when Tori awoke. She sat bolt upright in bed, instantly awake yet thoroughly and completely confused.

She recognized her familiar surroundings, the same four walls that had constituted her bedroom for the past six years. She was home, waking up in her own bedroom, so everything should be just the same as it always had been.

Except everything had changed.

No, that wasn't quite right, and Tori knew it. Everything hadn't changed . . . only *she* had.

"Oh, no," she said in a soft, defeated voice. She put her hands to her face and fell back prone on the bed.

The Midnight Bandit.

It hadn't been just a wildly exciting erotic dream, it was reality . . . and now she had to live with the consequences of what she'd done—or at least allowed to happen.

But what consequences were there?

Tori removed her hands from her face and stared at the rough-hewn timber ceiling of her bedroom. Only two people in all of Santa Fe knew what had happened the previous night. It wasn't likely that the Midnight Bandit would tell anyone, and she most certainly wasn't going to breathe a word concerning that exchange. So what possible consequences could there be?

Tori closed her eyes, shutting troubling questions out of her mind as she went backward in time to just before dawn, when she'd been in Bandit's arms.

He had called it destiny. He'd explained everything they'd done with one another as destiny, a preordained event that could not be avoided any more than a person could change the arrangement of the stars in the night sky.

A slow, sensual smile spread across Tori's mouth. She had surprised herself. Rather, her body had surprised her by reacting the way it had—so readily, almost greedily accepting the pleasure Bandit was willing to provide.

And maybe—just maybe the best part of all—was the fact that nobody would ever know what had happened in that shadow-shrouded alley in Santa Fe. Tori knew the damage done to the reputations of girls who let men have their way. These unfortunates were ruined. They were called scarlet women—and worse. Ironically, the reputations of the men involved rarely were damaged. In fact sometimes they were enhanced, as though these men had achieved some great victory.

To the high society crowd of Santa Fe, Tori Singer, if known at all, was just the tomboy sister of a local shootist who made his living as a bounty hunter. Although a tomboy and often disliked as a trouble-maker, she did not have the reputation of being loose with men. Despite her behavior of last night and very early this morning, that would remain unchanged, no better—certainly not good but at least no worse.

What time was it? Tori looked at the small clock ticking

on the bedside table and groaned. It was nearly three in the afternoon. She never stayed in bed this long.

But then, she'd never before spent the evening with the Midnight Bandit!

She got out of bed, determined to put Bandit out of her mind, at least until she got her chores done. The horses had to be fed and, with any luck, she might be able to scare up a jackrabbit along the windbreak trees. Her stomach was grumbling. It had been many hours since she'd eaten.

At the foot of her bed were the clothes she'd worn the night before. Exhausted, she'd quickly removed them before falling immediately to sleep. Now, she picked up the chemise and looked at it, a little surprised that the places where Bandit's mouth had been were not still damp. The chemise, old and very thin, was the only one she owned, and she wasn't going to put it on until she'd washed it.

When she looked at her Levi's, memories, luscious and embarrassing, made her blush crimson. She would wash her denims, too, she decided, symbolically ridding herself of any evidence that she'd ever been near the Midnight Bandit.

Feeling a little scandalous because she wore nothing underneath, Tori pulled on her old blue dress. She hadn't planned on today being laundry day, but she'd make it one. She smiled to herself, aware that she was trying to pretend that she'd intended on washing the clothes anyway.

She was glad now that her brother wasn't home. If he had been, then she'd have to go about pretending that nothing had changed. In fact, she'd never been very good at lying to Jedediah—or at hiding the truth from him.

Once Tori had the big kettle of laundry water boiling outside, she checked the pockets of her Levi's. In the back right pocket she found nearly a thousand dollars; in the left, she found an identical sum.

Never before had she come anywhere near having so much money at one time. Tori counted the money three times, just to be sure it was all really there, right in her hands . . . placed there by the Midnight Bandit, who could just as easily have kept every dollar for himself.

So why had he given her all the money? In payment for their time together? That didn't seem very likely. Nothing about the Midnight Bandit made her think he would have difficulty finding willing women. Though she was a long way from being experienced in such matters, she knew that she'd had a much better time than he had. With very few exceptions, she'd never really touched him—at least not like he'd touched her.

The more she thought about it, the more confused she became. After all the hours she'd spent with Bandit, she'd learned a great deal about his skills and abilities—that he could open a locked safe or unbutton a woman's shift with the same ease—but almost nothing about why he'd chosen to become the mysterious Midnight Bandit.

She tucked the money into the pocket of her faded dress and, as she began washing her clothes, wondered who she should give the money to. Who of all his victims was the most deserving of Jonathon Krey's money? Her mind filled with appreciation for the Midnight Bandit who had helped her plan to redistribute Krey's wealth to his victims come true.

\* \* \*

"Good Lord, Mack, would you mind concentrating?" Paul Randolph asked, his brows furrowed in anger.

Mack shot his older brother an angry look, but kept his rebuttal silent. As a skilled attorney, part of Mack's training informed him that when guilt was irrefutable, it was sometimes best to throw oneself on the mercy of the court. In this case that court was the always-impressive head of the Randolph ranch, Paul.

"Where were we?" Mack asked, not even making an effort to lie.

His thoughts had been wandering from the lengthy government contract he held in his hands, and it was useless to pretend otherwise.

"Page four, paragraph six," Paul answered, his tone a little softer now. "Mack, is something wrong?"

His brother shook his head. "Not really. Just a woman," he said with glib indifference, never once taking his eyes off the contracts.

Paul looked at his younger brother, the concern he felt evident in his expression. It wasn't like Mack to let a woman play on his mind for very long, and certainly not enough to interfere with his work.

"You haven't gotten a girl in trouble, have you?" Paul asked.

Mack looked up from the contract. He smiled at Paul, hearing the honest concern in his brother's words. "No, nothing so drastic as that. It's just that a slip of a girl slipped right through my fingers, I'm afraid. She made it quite clear that she wanted no part of me."

Paul made a face. Though he sympathized with his younger brother, he didn't consider this reason enough for thoughts to stray when work was at hand.

Hours later, after every sentence of every paragraph had been read, reread, and analyzed carefully, Mack at last allowed himself the comfort of a glass of whiskey. It felt good to sip the liquor and relax—a luxury he hadn't had time for since he'd created his alter ego, the Midnight Bandit, and accepted all the responsibilities that went along with fighting Jonathon Krey.

"Will she hurt you down the road, come election time?" Paul asked, stretching out on the leather couch, his own whiskey glass in hand. "We don't need some dalliance coming back to haunt you when you run for territorial governor. Hell, there are some folks in town who think you'll only be wasting your time with taking on the job of mayor of Santa Fe. They think you should shoot straight for governor, go for it now while its still a territory and not a state."

Mack issued a weary smile. "I haven't run for *any* office yet, and already your friends are trying to push me up the ladder. How much am I going to owe these men once I become mayor, or governor or whatever the hell else I think about running for."

"Not a thing, little brother. I wouldn't sell you out like that. You just be the best politician you can. That's all they can expect of you, and that's all I expect of you."

"Good, because that's all I expect of myself."

There was a pause as each brother settled on his own thoughts. Then, with a sly, boyish grin, Paul asked, "So what's her name?"

"Don't press on this one," Mack said with mild censure, though he immediately realized that would only whet Paul's curiosity and make it that much more difficult to get off the subject.

"The sun was up before you got home. Now if a woman gave you the slip, and you still don't get home until Gretchen was making breakfast, it seems to me you must have found another woman to soothe your bruised heart." His grin was wider now. "I'm your brother. You can tell me."

Mack smiled then, though his heart was still heavy. "Being my brother makes you the *last* person I'd tell. She was nothing special, so just worry about your own love life."

"I enjoy thinking about yours. . . ."

Paul continued talking, but Mack had stopped listening. He was thinking about Tori, reliving all the moments they'd shared in their too-brief time together. Was she thinking about him? What was her opinion of him after what he'd done to her? Rather, what was her opinion of the Midnight Bandit after his attempted seduction?

Mack sipped his whiskey, enjoying the burn of the amber liquid. He had given Tori every single dollar he'd taken from Jonathon Krey's safe. Why had he done that? Had he been buying her good graces?

That ludicrous thought nearly made Mack laugh out loud. He barely knew Tori, but the notion that her sexual favors might be for sale stretched the boundaries of everything he'd learned about human behavior.

Paul rose from his chair, deposited his empty glass on the sterling-silver serving tray in the corner and, exiting the office, said, "Get her out from under your skin quick, little brother, so we can get back to work."

Alone at last and happy for it, Mack closed his eyes. He recalled vividly how Tori had responded to his kisses.

She was not a woman who had been kissed often. He'd been able to tell that almost the first time their lips met.

Certainly he'd realized it the first time he explored her mouth with his tongue. She'd been shocked initially. Then, once she had a better understanding of what was happening, she'd blossomed, coming to life under his deeply probing kisses.

And when at last she'd found the curiosity or courage or passion to thrust her tongue between his lips and deep into his mouth, Mack's hunger for her had turned ravenous.

Even thinking about Tori caused Mack's manhood to awaken from its slumber. Immediately, he cursed himself—and Tori as well—damning himself for wanting her as much as he did, and her for leaving his passion unrequited. She was a thief, after all. Certainly not much time would go by before she was arrested or caught by Jonathon Krey, and then her corpse would be found in the New Mexico desert.

Any lawyer with political aspirations would be a mindless fool to spend more than two seconds thinking about the future of a thief, no matter how gorgeous she happened to be, no matter how statuesque her body, no matter how firm her breasts.

To prove to himself that Tori Singer was just a thief, he would ride out at night and watch her house. He doubted she really intended to give the stolen money away, but he'd give her the opportunity to prove her innocence. If he uncovered her guilt, however, then he could turn his back on her without feeling that he'd abandoned her.

With savage determination, he pushed Tori out of his thoughts, to concentrate on problems he had some control over.

How much longer could the Midnight Bandit continue to fight Jonathon Krey?

Mack had spent countless hours planning every move in each raid on one of Jonathon Krey's business operations in Santa Fe. Such care had enabled him to continue his raids. But clearly Tori hadn't planned her moves. Mack was astonished that she'd been able to crawl over the stone wall without being seen, and he was certain it would have been impossible for her to elude the guards on leaving the Krey compound.

He was thinking about her again.

"Damn her!" he hissed through clenched teeth, bolting to his feet.

He wasn't exactly sure how he was going to get her out of his mind, but he was going to—and soon.

As he straightened his tie, he went through a mental list of women who were more than willing to attract his attention and keep it through a long and passionate night. As he thought about them, it surprised him that none seemed particularly enticing. In one way or another, all of Mack's lovers paled when compared to Tori Singer.

He left the room, angry with himself.


"What the hell do you mean you thought somebody was on the roof?" Jonathon Krey asked, contempt icing each word.

The guard's eyes were shifting right and left, apparently too afraid to look into Jonathon Krey's chilly, lifeless eyes.

"Well?" Krey demanded, still sitting in a chair behind his desk.

"I can't be sure. I thought I saw something . . . in the

shadows. It was dark, though, and when me and the boys gave the roof a real good look, we didn't see nothin'."

Krey's cold gaze went from the guard to his son, Michael. The head guard had already been fired, then tossed into the street with a broken nose and several cracked ribs so that everyone would know the price paid for failing to carry out Jonathon Krey's orders.

"What do you think, Michael? Should we keep him on, or give him the same treatment we gave his boss?"

The gunman blanched, but he did not back down, nor did he beg for mercy. His courage, not easy to find in those of his element, turned the winds of fate in his direction.

"Let's keep him around," Michael decided. "He's the only one who saw anything at all, and he knows what happens when hired guns allow thieves to steal from us."

Jonathon nodded slowly, pleased with his son's decision. He had been grooming Michael to one day take over the reins of the family's legal and illegal business ventures. Lately he was pleased with the leadership qualities Michael had been demonstrating. Earlier that day, his son had personally supervised the beating given to the head guard. He had even been the one whose fist had shattered the hog-tied man's nose.

When the gunman left the room, Jonathon looked at his son, shaking his head slowly. "The Midnight Bandit had to have gone through all our bedrooms last night. He opened my safe, took the cash, then closed it up again as pretty as you please."

A muscle twitched in his jaw, the only outward sign of the rage boiling inside him. "He entered my home during a huge celebration, went here, there, and everywhere. After he'd gotten what he came for, he left without ever being

seen. The newspaper calls him the Midnight Bandit, but
I want to call him a dead man."

He picked up an expensive, ivory-handled pen from his
desk and snapped it in half.

"I want him done away with, Michael. Now. Tonight.
Tomorrow at the latest. I don't care about the money. I
can make more. What I can't afford to lose is my well-
earned reputation. Everyone must know that to cross
Jonathon Krey is to commit suicide. I don't want anyone
thinking for even a second that I'm vulnerable, that I can
be robbed." His tone was calm, almost reserved. Only the
seething hatred in his eyes showed his true feelings. "The
newspapers make that damn Midnight Bandit sound like
a phantom, a ghost."

Michael said quietly, "I own one of the writers for *The
Santa Fe Star*. I'll get him to pen some stories about Bandit
that'll change the way people think of him. I'll have him
painted as an atheist—or a drunkard—or maybe a rapist."

Jonathon nodded, liking the way Michael's mind
worked.

"Do that. And double the guards here. The thought of
that bandit touching your mother's portrait makes me ill,
I tell you. *The Midnight Bandit must die!*"

By sundown Tori had decided to whom the two thousand dollars stolen from Jonathon Krey's safe should go.
All she had to do now was ride out and place the money
where the beneficiaries would find it. Her anonymity
would remain intact.

Three families—all injured by Krey's greed—would receive the money. Five hundred dollars for the Sanders

family, and the same for the Beaumonts. And that left a
thousand dollars for the Dahlbergs. They would receive
more because they had been most damaged by Jonathon
Krey—and because they had the largest family. The thousand dollars would give them a new start in life, a chance
to pick up stakes and move somewhere far away from
Krey and his conniving offspring.

The difficult decision having been made, Tori should
have been ready to ride. After all, it would take a fifteen-
mile circuit to deliver the money to these families in one
night. That meant she'd have to take advantage of all the
dark hours, if she wanted to get some sleep eventually.

But she wasn't dressed for riding. She was still in the
same old thin cotton dress she'd put on that afternoon,
when she'd awakened from a fitful slumber.

On the bed were her Levi's, fresh and clean from the
laundering she'd given them that day. Beside them was
the single white cotton nightgown she owned, but seldom
wore. The lovely gown had been a gift from her brother
the previous summer, when, wistfully, she had remarked
that she didn't own anything that was pretty and feminine.

And it was pretty and feminine. No getting around that.
Jedediah wasn't much of a romantic, so he'd had the
woman at the seamstress shop pick out the gown. Ankle
length, with lace trim at the wrists and cuffs and a scooped
neckline, it was soft and white and beautiful.

How many times had she worn it in the past year?
Three? Her birthday. New Year's Eve. Wasn't there one
other time? She couldn't remember exactly when.

Why should she wear something so pretty when there
was no man to see her in it? At least, not the right man.
Her brother didn't count, though she loved him dearly. It

didn't seem right that she should have received such a gift from a brother instead of from a husband or beau.

These thoughts, so strange for her to ponder, had kept her in the small cabin and had delayed her preparations for her philanthropic mission.

What if the Midnight Bandit decided to visit? He'd arrive at midnight, true to his name, wouldn't he? He knew Tori's identity, she'd discovered. When he'd caught her in Jonathon Krey's bedroom, it had taken him a second or two, but then he'd recognized her. At some time or other, she *had* to have been introduced to him when he wasn't wearing the mask over his eyes. But no matter how long she thought about it, she couldn't picture any man she knew disguised as the mysterious—and much too attractive—Midnight Bandit.

"He won't come for me. He got what he wanted last night," she whispered, looking at the nightgown spread out upon her bed. The sound of her own voice was not very reassuring, and inside her head another voice whispered, *No, Bandit didn't get what he wanted, Tori! You got what you wanted, but he didn't!*

For a moment, standing in her small, spartan bedroom illuminated only by the glow of a single candle, Tori closed her eyes and thought about whether or not she wanted to be home—alone—when Bandit showed up.

She did.

She wanted to be waiting for him in her pretty white nightgown with nothing on beneath it. She knew she shouldn't want Bandit's arms around her, but she did. She wanted that more than anything she'd ever wanted in her entire life. More than a big, beautiful home to live in.

More than pretty dresses filling a huge closet. More than a stable of the finest horses in all of New Mexico.

She wanted Bandit's body against her, his hands upon her, his kisses taking her breath away. He wasn't her husband. She didn't even know his real name . . . and none of it mattered.

Tori trembled deep inside, as though she were reacting to invisible caresses from Bandit's skillful hands. He'd begun to teach her something about herself, but he hadn't shown her all the mysteries of sensuality. He had pleasured her beyond measure and made her feel sensations she'd never known, but he hadn't taken her virginity. And for that, Tori did not know whether she should be grateful or sad.

*He'll come for me,* she thought then as she began pulling the tattered old dress over her head. *He'll come for me because I did not touch him, and he's a man, and men are selfish about their own pleasures.*

The pure white nightgown slid down over the womanly curves of her body, touching her like a caress. Tori smiled. The gown wasn't caressing her, but thoughts of Bandit had so heightened her to the possibilities of sensuality that everything, every touch against her flesh, was pleasing somehow, infinitely sensual and exciting.

Barefooted, she walked out of her bedroom, taking the candle with her. She placed it near the front window. It was a beacon for Bandit. If he was coming to her, he'd see the candle, and not even a moonless night would prevent him from finding her cabin in the dark.


Mack lifted the small flask from his hip pocket and took a sip of brandy. The liquor tasted good. He was particularly happy that on this evening he did not wear his mask and cape, or the black Stetson pulled low over his eyes. At this particular time he was just Mack Randolph, out late at night, ostensibly checking to see that the sentries hired to watch over the cattle on the west range were doing their jobs. That, anyway, was the story he intended to tell Paul in the morning, and the story he would tell anyone he ran into this evening.

In the distance, he watched the candle burning in the window, then looked away. In his attorney's heart, he knew he shouldn't be disappointed. After all, hadn't he talked to a dozen criminals before, all of whom promised never again to steal?

But it was different with Tori Singer. She had seemed so sincere when she'd said the money she was stealing was for other people who'd been damaged in one way or another by Jonathon Krey. Had she really been sincere, or had Mack simply wanted to believe her?

It didn't matter now. He had been at his post, hidden behind a copse of trees a hundred yards from the small cabin that Tori shared with her brother. He had been there since before sundown, watching the cabin with his binoculars, wanting to believe that soon she would be riding out to give away the money, as she had promised.

But she was still at home. For reasons that were baffling to him, she had placed a candle in the window. Perhaps Jedediah was scheduled to return that night, though he wouldn't need a light to find his way. Mack knew the bounty hunter was an accomplished tracker who could follow any criminal over any terrain, which meant that he certainly could find his own cabin, even in the dead of night.

The candle either burned itself out or was extinguished. For a few tense minutes, Mack watched the cabin carefully through his binoculars, the moonlight illuminating the shack just enough for him to see anyone coming or going. Finally, deeply saddened, he put the binoculars down, then pulled the heavy gold watch from his pocket. He touched the stem with his thumb and the protective case flipped open, revealing the dial. He angled the watch against the moon until he read the time: two-thirty.

She wouldn't be going anywhere tonight.

Damn her.

He'd handed her nearly two thousand dollars, believing that she'd give the money to those people who would need it most. In his mind, he could picture Tori laughing about the Midnight Bandit's gullibility.

# Eight

Tori ran the brush through her long blond hair once more, then tied her tresses back with a ribbon. She'd learned from Bandit that her hair was too visible at night, and she was determined to learn from her mistakes. She put on an old felt hat to help hide her hair.

Next she wrapped the old leather holster around her curving hips, tying it down snugly to her right thigh. She tested to see that the Colt could be drawn easily from the leather and hoped she wouldn't need to draw the weapon.

Lastly, she picked up the three small leather pouches she'd made from antelope hide. They contained the money stolen from Jonathon Krey, along with rocks to add weight, so she could throw a pouch if she couldn't get close enough to a house to actually set it down carefully. Within each pouch was a single sheet of paper with the statement *TELL NO ONE!!!* written in ink.

Tonight, she would begin again her campaign to attack Jonathon Krey and help those people he'd victimized.

Her plan had gone exactly as Tori had hoped. Neither the Sanderses or the Beaumonts had a dog, so she'd been able to hitch her horse a safe distance from their homes, then walk silently to the house and drop the money-stuffed pouch near the front door, where it would be found at sunrise.

The Dahlbergs, the last family Tori intended to help that evening, had a small dwelling just a stone's throw from the Krey Cattle #3 office.

Tori found it strange to be so close to one of Jonathon Krey's offices so late at night, especially when it contained the payroll money to be distributed on the following morning.

Everybody in and around Santa Fe knew what Krey's cowboys did once they got their pay for the month. Lulu's bordello was busy for three or four days before the men had spent all they could, and half the saloons in town had to hire men to keep the drunks from tearing the walls down.

Tori set a hard pace for her mare, Daisy, who kept to it, even though it was difficult. Short-legged but deep-chested, the mare had astonishing stamina, though she was not fast at a dead run. For Tori's needs, Daisy was perfect.

From a ridge, Tori saw the Dahlbergs' ranch in the Tula Valley. The barn had remained half-finished for nearly two years. There simply hadn't been the resources to buy the lumber to complete it. Tori smiled. Very soon there would be enough money for that—and for a couple of breeding heifers to get the Dahlbergs' ranch up and running once again, if that was what they wanted.

She tied Daisy's reins to a dead cactus, patted her mare's neck, then headed out on foot to the Dahlbergs' ranch. The moon, a sliver in the night sky, cast little light. For this, Tori was thankful, since it concealed her presence, but it made travel difficult, particularly when she was walking rather than riding on her sure-footed mare.

Tori approached slowly, pausing to listen for sounds inside the house. A lamp burned in the living area, and in one of the bedrooms. It wasn't the ideal situation for Tori, and she briefly considered coming back another time.

Suddenly, she heard a woman weeping. Were the Dahlbergs fighting? It wouldn't surprise her if they were, considering all the troubles they'd been through recently. Still, Mr. and Mrs. Dahlberg had always seemed like a loving couple to Tori. Though she didn't know them well, she saw them as a husband and wife who would draw closer together in times of strife and conflict.

Curious, Tori crept closer to the house than necessary, approaching it from the south, where there was only one dark window. She flattened herself against the outside wall and stopped breathing for a moment so that she could hear better the words softly spoken within.

"Now, Mother, don't you worry about a thing," Mr. Dahlberg was saying to his wife. "I'm a strong man with good hands and a good back. I can find a job in town, or maybe I can even hire on with Krey. He's always needing men to watch his herds."

"That monster! I'd rather we lose everything than have you riding with his shootists! They're murderers, every one, and you know it, too! I won't have it! I won't have my husband riding with those men! It's Jonathon Krey that's put us in this mess, and we won't look to him to get us out!"

Fresh tears cut off Mrs. Dahlbergs' words. Tori was struck by contempt for Jonathon Krey. She wanted to alert the Dahlbergs to the money, but she knew that would not be wise. Best to leave the antelope pouch on the porch near the front door, where Mr. Dahlberg would find it first thing in the morning. The distressed husband and wife had a troubling evening ahead of them, but Tori knew that in the morning, with the money she'd provided, their lives would be much, much better.

She tossed the pouch onto the porch. It landed with a dull *thud!* Then she made her way quickly from the house, heading back to Daisy. Krey Cattle #3 would be her next stop, and after what Tori had heard, she was more determined than ever to steal every penny she possibly could from Jonathon Krey.

The Midnight Bandit stood motionless, all but invisible in the night. His ebony cape was wrapped around him, his face shrouded by a cape-covered arm to keep even that from showing in the moonlight.

Though he stood motionless, his mind was spinning from what he had just witnessed.

Could that really be Tori slinking away in the night after tossing something onto the porch of the Dahlbergs' home?

Mack hadn't gotten a good look at the fleeing figure, but as it moved away from the house, he'd caught a glimpse of pale blond hair, brushed back into a ponytail, streaming down its back.

For a week, Mack had cursed Tori mentally. Watching her every day had reaffirmed his cynicism concerning the motives of people. When he had learned of the dire trouble the Dahlbergs were in, he'd decided that the Midnight Bandit would do what Tori had only pretended she meant to do—he would give them money anonymously. But she'd beaten him to the Dahlberg porch by only a few minutes.

Why had she waited a week? Was her guilty conscience getting the better of her?

Mack cast the suspicious thoughts aside. She was now proving to him that her word was good, that she was neither a common thief nor a common woman. There could be a thousand perfectly good reasons for her waiting an entire week before giving the money to victims of Krey greed.

Mack waited until Tori was nearly out of sight before he headed after her. With a smile on his face, he thought of being able to taste her kisses and quickened his pace.

Looking through the binoculars, Bandit scanned the horizon. Seeing nothing, a tickle of fear stirred in the pit of his stomach, a premonition of something going wrong. But what? He knew he shouldn't believe in such things as gut instinct. Trained as a lawyer, he should consider only the facts. Still he couldn't keep a cold dread out of his veins . . . and he couldn't find Tori.

He'd spotted her twice that night since he'd first seen her leaving the Dahlbergs'. He'd needed to make a dash to his horse after he'd seen where she'd left her mount. By the time Bandit had returned to his lookout, she'd already put plenty of distance behind her.

So where had she gone? At last look, he'd thought she was moving toward a specific destination, but twice she had stopped and looked behind her, as though she'd heard something suspicious. After that, she must have taken a more circuitous route, causing Bandit to lose her.

Squinting through the binoculars, he peered along the Fugina Bluff area southeast of Santa Fe. The tightly spaced buildings that constituted Krey Cattle #3 were there, illuminated by moonlight. Built into the side of the bluff, they remained protected from bitter winter winds and the occasional torrential rain that came in the spring. Only a few kerosene lamps were lighted in the bunkhouses.

The buildings were nearly empty now, but soon, starting at sunrise, cowboys would be coming in from the range to receive their pay, then drink and gamble in the bunkhouses with the other hands. Later, they'd ride hellbent for leather to Santa Fe, where there'd be drinking, gambling, and whoring of appalling dimensions.

Bandit noticed movement outside the camp. A man was hiding in the darkness, no doubt a guard assigned by Jonathon Krey. Moonlight glinted off a well-oiled rifle barrel. Bandit turned his binoculars to the other side of camp, and after a few minutes found another guard kneeling in the darkness.

And seventy yards from the second guard, Bandit saw yet another figure moving in the shadows of the night— only this one had a blond ponytail streaming down her back!

He jumped from his horse and headed toward Tori. Krey had set a trap for the Midnight Bandit, but she was about to walk right into it, and when she did, those guards with their Winchesters could cut her to ribbons.

He ran, stumbling occasionally, his Colt revolver clutched in his right hand. His own footsteps echoed in his ears, loud as a stampede. Didn't the guards hear him coming? Any second now he expected to feel the burn of the bullet.

*No, it won't happen that way,* he told himself; perhaps thinking to avoid precipitating such a happening, though logic insisted that thoughts and actions were entirely different things.

Tori was barely thirty yards from him when he heard a soft exclamation from the guard on his left. Alerted by the sound, she immediately dropped to her knees. But Bandit continued moving forward, his boots crunching against the sun-baked earth, his heart racing.

"Jack, is that you?" the guard asked.

Tori heard Bandit a split second before he reached her. Once again, he grabbed her from behind, one hand clamping down tight over her mouth, the other grabbing her right wrist so that she couldn't level her pistol at him.

"Jack, damn it, is that you out there?" the guard asked, louder than before.

Bandit tossed his cape over Tori, his face close to hers. He had holstered his pistol, needing both hands free to silence her and keep from getting shot by her; now he wasn't so sure he'd done the right thing by leaving himself temporarily unarmed.

From his right, the sentry Jack said, "What are you jabbering about? I ain't moved!"

"I heard somethin'," the first guard snapped back, clearly angry at Jack's lack of concern.

"If you heard it, then you find it," Jack shot back. "I didn't hear nothin'. Probably just a coyote, out and about at this time o' night."

Tori closed her eyes for no more than a second and

silently issued a prayer of thanks for Bandit. Once again, he had arrived just in time to save her. She had spent nearly an hour looking into the shadows, searching for the guards, and she hadn't seen them. Now she was between two of them, and only Bandit, with his cape that absorbed them into the night, prevented her from being seen. If she'd walked another fifteen or twenty yards in the direction she'd chosen her presence would have undoubtedly been discovered.

The seconds ticked by slowly, Bandit and Tori remaining on their knees, huddled together, motionless, fearful. The guard whose suspicions had been aroused moved on several yards in a rambling fashion, scanning the shadowed sage brush, muttering under his breath at the laziness of Jack. The man was unaware that every move he made was being watched, that should he spot the kneeling man and woman hidden beneath the ebony cape, he'd die by gunshot before he could raise his rifle.

After what seemed to Tori to be an eternity—one in which she was quite certain she had aged considerably, and badly—both guards returned, bored, to their seated positions.

"Follow me," Bandit whispered, moving so that he could look into Tori's eyes.

Grateful that he had once again saved her from certain discovery, she was not yet ready to abandon the money inside Krey Cattle #3. Fortunately, Jack and his more alert colleague would now, as likely as not, dismiss any sound made as coming from coyotes.

She tugged at Bandit's hand. Even in the darkness of the night, and with the black mask across his nose and eyes, the look he shot at her was chilling. For one of the very few times in her life, Tori simply, quietly followed the orders of a man without complaint or open confrontation.

Tori's near capture had frightened Bandit almost as much as the infuriating reality that she was still determined to strike out against Jonathon Krey. Hadn't he explicitly told her the last time they'd been together that she simply must not ever do that again?

She didn't say a word until they had scrambled to Bandit's horse. When he looked at her, she was smiling as though she'd just been through another grand adventure. Bandit wasn't sure whether he should slap the smile from her lips or kiss it away.

"I thought we agreed that you weren't going to try any more of this nonsense," he said through clenched teeth.

Up close, Tori looked even more attractive than he remembered, and her beauty was playing havoc with the anger he was struggling to maintain.

Tori knew he was furious. But having escaped twice from Jonathon Krey's vicious minions, she was feeling charmed, as though the fates were surely looking out for her.

"*We* didn't have any agreement at all," she said, not in the least bit intimidated by Bandit's anger. "That was a conclusion you came to all on your own. It was erroneous, I might add."

"I should have let you get caught. I nearly got caught myself just trying to save you." Bandit turned away from Tori, finding it infinitely easier to maintain his anger at the beautiful young woman still smiling at him when he didn't have to look at her. "Next time, I'll just let you fend for yourself."

"No, you won't."

"Yes, I will."

"You won't."

"What makes you so damn sure?" he demanded.

"The knowledge that you want me," Tori explained, shocking herself, not only for having the thought but for voicing it.

The smile left Tori's face the moment Bandit reached out and placed large hands upon her shoulders. Very slowly, he brought his hands together until, for just a moment, he held her throat. Then one of his hands moved upward to knock her hat off so that it hung by the neck strap. His fingers slipped beneath the heavy fall of her hair, moving slowly in a circular pattern at the base of her neck, massaging her scalp and sending warm, sensual tingles through her brain. He didn't like her hair tied back in the ponytail, preferring it to flow freely.

"Yes, I want you," he whispered in his flinty, hard-edged, disguised voice. "I want you because you're probably the only person besides myself in all of New Mexico who is crazy enough to think Jonathon Krey can be hurt, can be taken down a notch, can even be destroyed."

Tori closed her eyes and rolled her head back a little on her shoulders. She loved Bandit's firm touch upon the nape of her neck and her scalp. She closed her eyes so that all she had to think about was how it felt to be touched by him. The liquid gold of desire heated her body, seeping into her pores.

She could feel Bandit's eyes upon her body, could almost feel him mentally taking off her clothes. This thought was exciting, though she was not at all certain she should entertain it, much less actively pursue it. Still, with Bandit touching her this way, his caresses skilled as a practiced thief's . . .

Bandit inhaled deeply, forcing himself to remain calm. He was still furious with Tori for being foolish enough to think she could break into Krey Cattle #3. But anger was not uppermost in his heart. Not when he watched her close her eyes and roll her head back on her shoulders, like a cat being scratched and loving it. Not when he could watch the rise and fall of exquisite breasts, large and firm and round, pressing against the soft cotton of her shirt and chemise. Not when the memories of how her body had come to life beneath his touch a week earlier were still vividly exciting.

He wanted to kiss her, but this was not the place for it. Once before he had tasted Tori's kisses while danger lurked about them in the darkness. Though it had been exciting, on this evening he wanted to slowly peruse all her charms without having to look over his shoulder for armed guards who would love nothing more than to be known as the men who shot the Midnight Bandit. Bandit had already learned that one kiss from Tori's full mouth was not nearly enough to satisfy his thirst, and he was ready to run any risk to get another immediately.

"What did you think you were going to do?" he asked then, more than a trace of condescension in his tone. Lucid thinking when Tori was near was no easier now than on the first night he'd spent with her.

Both his tone and words irked Tori. She opened her eyes, coming back to reality instantly, leaving her fantasy world where nothing existed but her body and Bandit's hands.

"Tomorrow, Krey starts paying his men for the month. I thought I'd take his money."

Bandit's lips curled below the mask. "Just like that— you thought you'd take the gold, eh? Well, Jonathon Krey thought the same thing. That's why he hired those two men out there—the ones who very nearly caught you."

This was not the conversation she wanted to have with him. She felt invincible, daring, and terribly sexy. She did not want to be made to feel like a fool.

"It was you they heard, not me."

"You would have walked right into them if it weren't for me."

Tori turned her back to Bandit. "I'm not going to argue with you," she said over her shoulder, continuing to keep her voice down. She knew full well that voices carry across the desert at night. How far was she from where she'd tethered her horse?

"No, you're not going to argue with me, you're going to go home . . . and wait for me there."

The words kept Tori in place. So he wasn't as immune to her as he tried to make her think! She was proud that she could effect him so strongly—though she wasn't at all certain it was something she should take pride in. She sensed that Bandit had no difficulty getting women to go to bed with him, and that he wasn't terribly pleased with himself for wanting her as much as he did.

She turned very slowly to face him. "Are you telling me what to do?"

"Yes."

As much as she wanted to be in Bandit's arms again, something inside her simply could not comply with any order given by a man—even if he was dangerous and terribly attractive and the best kisser she could imagine.

"You've got me confused with some other woman," Tori said flatly, the passion he had sparked moments earlier extinguished in an instant. "I don't take orders. Not from you. Not from any man."

She turned and began walking.

"Where are you going?" Bandit asked.

"To get my horse. If this isn't the right way to get into the payroll office, there must be some other way."

"Wait, we'll take my horse."

Bandit got in the saddle and, Tori, watching the way he moved, admired his grace and power. Clearly, he was a man who'd spent much time on horseback. Suddenly, she remembered that he had told her to go home and wait for him there. He knew where she lived?

Who was he?

Tossing his cape to the side, he extended a hand down to her. She took it, slipped her foot into the stirrup, then mounted his horse. Her arms eased around Bandit's waist, though she knew that it was dangerous for her to touch him.

"My mare is over there about a half mile," Tori said, pointing.

They traveled in silence, each dealing with personal thoughts and private demons. Tori was distinctly aware of the heat of his body. Touching her, it warmed her blood.

Was he angry with her for having cast him aside when they had been in Santa Fe? she wondered.

He had given her extraordinary pleasure with his hands and his kisses, and she had not reciprocated in kind. He had asked her to untie her chemise so that he might kiss her breasts, and she had refused him that, too. But why had he insisted *she* be the one to untie the chemise? His hands had proved sufficiently skilled to accomplish such a mundane task . . . why had he insisted that she do it?

"Stop thinking about it," Bandit said then.

A hot flush of embarrassment went through Tori. Could he actually read her thoughts? Did he really know she recalled every second of the excitement that had been hers when he'd kissed her too-responsive, traitorous body?

"Thinking about what?" she asked, trying to sound innocent, sounding guilty as sin.

"About stealing the payroll. You'll never get away with it."

Tori breathed a sigh of relief. The Midnight Bandit wasn't as perceptive as he thought he was. She was grateful for that, for she now was able to think of him as fallible and far more human, which prompted her to once again consider her original goal for the evening—hitting Jonathon Krey where he would feel it the most, by stealing his money.

"We'll see," she said after a moment.

When they reached Tori's mare, she quickly dismounted from Bandit's stallion. She needed to think more clearly than she could when he was close to her. Whenever silence had stretched out between them, her thoughts had headed in a decidedly sensual direction—a situation she did not appreciate.

"Go home," Bandit said softly, the two words tinged with anger. "You'll only get yourself in trouble if you try to break in there. Let me do it. I'll get the payroll, and I'll bring it to you."

Tori sensed that in his true identity, Bandit was a man accustomed to giving orders and having them followed.

"Why do that?" she asked, her hands on her hips, oblivious to how the stance dramatized her womanly curves. "If you steal the money, you should keep it for yourself."

"You gave the money to the Dahlbergs tonight, didn't you?"

Tori was shocked. "Y-Yes," she said after a moment. "But how did you know?"

"I know more than you think." Bandit grinned then beneath his mask, and confessed to how he knew.

"So you were going to help them, too," Tori muttered softly. "We seem to be working toward the same goal. Wouldn't we be helping each other if we worked together?"

The statement was a shocking one for Tori to make. She'd always been taught by her brother that the only person she should trust was herself, that if she took a partner, she'd end up getting cheated in one way or another. Jedediah always worked alone, and in whatever endeavors Tori pursued, he warned that she would do well to follow his example.

"No."

The single-word denial shocked and irritated Tori. Didn't Bandit realize how unusual it was for her to propose such cooperation? Didn't he realize that he should be flattered?

True to her nature, Tori changed tactics instantly.

"Fine. I'll work alone." She tossed a leg over the back of her mare, Daisy, and eased into the saddle, muttering, "I work best alone anyway."

"You're *not* going after Krey, *damn it!*"

"You're *not* going to tell me what to do . . . *damn it!*"

Bandit gritted his teeth. Surely, no woman more infuriating or with poorer judgment ever walked the earth. As Tori angled her horse around, Bandit looked at her, contemplating what her next moves would be and exactly how little control he actually had over her behavior. Clearly, if he was to have any hope at all of keeping her out of trouble, he had to stick with her.

"Wait, let's find a compromise," he said through clenched teeth.

Hearing the words coming from his own mouth was surprising. He'd always felt that compromise, at the very least, was partial failure.

Tori smiled at him. "Perfect. Now how are we going to break into Krey Cattle #3? There's a lot of money in there that's just waiting for us."

# Nine

The more Bandit thought about it, the worse it seemed. Having Tori with him was bad enough; having Krey's guards on duty made it even worse.

And what if the payroll money wasn't in that office, as Tori had predicted it would be?

"You've got doubts," Tori said softly. "I can see it in the set of your mouth."

Bandit smiled wryly. She was an extraordinarily perceptive woman in some ways, but in others she seemed so daft it was confounding.

"Of course I've got doubts," he at last replied in the cold, flinty tone he used when his mask was in place and he'd assumed the persona of the Midnight Bandit. "I like to plan my moves in advance. Mistakes are made when you're forced to act in a hurry, without knowing all the facts. In case you've forgotten, what we're thinking of doing—"

"What we *are going to* do!"

"—is anything but well thought out."

They were moving into position on the bluff, so that they would be looking down on Krey Cattle #3. Tori had been in favor of simply moving in a crescent direction around the guards posted on the flatland, then going straight into the payroll office, entering through a window. A little voice inside Bandit's head, however, had warned him that danger waited at the end of that particular trail.

So they had circled wide around the payroll office and its surrounding buildings. Tethering their horses far from the encampment, now they were standing at the treacherous Fugina Bluff, looking down at the buildings.

"What do you think?" Tori asked, looking at the roofs of the buildings. She couldn't see any guards positioned on them, but then she hadn't spotted the two sentries stationed in the scrub grass either. So now she sought Bandit's opinion.

He remained silent. He didn't know what he thought. The payroll office was down to his left, and it would be easy enough to move slowly and quietly down the bluff. Once inside the building, there was the safe to open. Krey had chosen a Barns & Bradley safe for the mansion, and he probably had one here, too. Bandit was reasonably certain he could open it, knowing the single flaw in the safe's design.

So why, when he should feel confident, was that little voice of warning refusing to quiet down?

He squinted into the darkness, searching the shadows and moonlight below, struggling to see the danger his instincts and intuition told him was there. The pale yellow light that came from the few lamps glowing within the bunkhouses offered little help. The faint, warm evening breeze carried the occasional sounds of laughter and revelry coming from those cowhands who had already made it to the bunkhouse and were waiting sunrise to get their pay.

In addition to the two sentries hidden in the scrub grass

outside of camp, Bandit could see two more—one on the roof and one on the ground—outside what looked like an auxiliary bunkhouse. No guards stood outside the payroll office . . . and that just didn't make any sense, not if that was where Krey was keeping the money until it could be distributed the following day.

"The money's not in the safe," Bandit said aloud.

Tori moved a little closer to him, looking into his dark eyes. "How do you know?" she asked quietly.

Bandit looked at her, stunned once again by her allure, especially when she was making no effort at all to be appealing. He immediately cast the thought aside, forcing himself to concentrate on the gun-toting guards below.

"Krey wants us to think the money is in the payroll office."

"Right," Tori replied, her tone indicating that anyone who thought Jonathon Krey wouldn't keep the payroll in the safe was irrational.

"But he also knows that I opened his safe at home, doesn't he? And he's got no reason to believe I couldn't get into his safe here."

"Right. I still don't see what you're getting at."

"So if he's got the payroll in the payroll office, why is there a guard on that rooftop over there, and another guard on the ground, when that building itself seems to be un-used?"

Tori looked at the building he'd pointed out. After a moment, she was able to spot the guards he'd indicated. Then, slowly, a smile spread across her mouth, and her respect for Bandit took another giant leap forward.

"The payroll office is a decoy. The money's in that building, isn't it?" she asked. She found it difficult to whisper because of the burst of excitement going through her.

"That's my guess. He tried to trick us, and it would have worked if he hadn't hedged his bets. That'll cost him the payroll." He looked into Tori's eyes, and at that moment wanted very much to kiss her. His throat felt tight as he said, "That's my guess. What do you think?"

"I think you're a genius," Tori replied.

Bandit looked away, not wanting her to see how greatly the comment pleased him.

*She's just a girl,* he thought. *She's very young, very impressionable.*

They made their way down the bluff slowly, careful not to dislodge any rocks that would roll down and announce their presence. The sliver of moon cast only a little light, but this helped them. The guards were alert, but they were anticipating that the Midnight Bandit would approach from the south and would head for the payroll office.

It wasn't long before Tori and Bandit were pressed against the side of the darkened bunkhouse. Listening to the footsteps of the guard on the ground as he walked slowly back and forth, Bandit motioned for Tori to stay where she was. Then he moved away from her, his boots silently touching the ground. He disappeared around the corner of the building, and Tori quietly thumbed back the hammer of her Colt, her heart racing. She was now more afraid for Bandit's safety than for her own.

In the darkness, she heard a dull *thump!* It sounded like flesh striking flesh. Just that sound, then nothing else. Overhead, she continued to hear the soft tapping of the guard there; the man was absentmindedly tapping his boots against the roof. The cadence of the tapping didn't change at all, and Tori breathed a sigh of relief, confident that she alone had heard the *thump!*

A moment later Bandit returned, a too-confident grin on his too-kissable lips. On the tip of his finger dangled a large key ring. Without saying a word, he went to the side door, tried several keys, then swung the door open. With a bow and a theatrical sweep of his arm, he indicated that he wanted Tori to enter first.

She waited until he'd closed the door behind them before she hissed, "You're absolutely incorrigible! Aren't you afraid of anything?"

"Of course I am. Only a madman knows no fear. I just don't let my fear stop me."

Tori wanted to be more angry with Bandit than she was. But when he smiled like that—and his words, in some strange way, made a certain amount of sense—she just couldn't maintain her anger toward him.

Within the building, Tori couldn't see her hands in front of her face, and under the circumstances she didn't dare strike a match. Apparently intended to be used only once a month, the shed was poorly built, with holes in the walls that let glimmers of moonlight in.

Bandit managed to make his way around, though she did hear the telltale *thunk* of a shinbone striking a wooden chair and the muffled curse which immediately followed it.

"Over here," Bandit said.

Tori followed the sound of his voice, her hands groping before her in the darkness. She still couldn't see a thing, and when strong fingers closed around her calf, just beneath the knee, she nearly jumped out of her skin. She was glad that she'd put her Colt back in the holster, or she might have accidentally pulled the trigger.

Bandit was on his knees on the floor, and as soon as Tori composed herself, she got down beside him.

"What is it?" she asked, feeling something on the floor in front of him.

"A strongbox. The payroll's in here."

"How do you know?"

"The room's almost empty. Who would put a locked box in a vacant building, then station armed guards outside, if there wasn't something very valuable in that box?"

Tori was beginning to realize she still did not have the ability to think like a thief. Inexperienced as she'd proven, she realized that she would have to learn very quickly to think like a thief or she would have to *stop* being one.

It was as simple as that.

"Here. Light one of these when I tell you," Bandit whispered.

His hands surrounded hers. He had shoved a handful of sulphur-tipped wooden matches into her palm, and now their fingers touched for a moment longer than was necessary. Once again the now-familiar tingles went through Tori.

Wasn't she ever immune to the thrill of Bandit's touch, not even when danger was all around? Or did the danger heighten her pleasure? Before she could give this much thought, Bandit asked her to light a match.

The flare of the burning sulphur was blindingly bright in the dark bunkhouse. Bandit had closed his eyes tightly until the sulphur had burned away and only the wood was aflame. This prevented the momentary blindness Tori suffered for about thirty seconds.

She kept blinking her eyes until she could focus. When at last she could see clearly again, she noted that he had out his little leather kit—the one that looked so much like a cigar case. The strongbox was sturdily built, its lid secured with an enormous lock. Bandit was deciding which particular instrument he should use to pick that lock.

When the match burned down almost to her fingers, it was Bandit who blew out the flame before it singed her fingertips.

"You have beautiful hands," he whispered in the dark. "When the match burns away, just blow it out and light a new one. Whatever is inside the strongbox isn't worth burning your lovely fingertips for."

Tori lit another match, but her thoughts were not centered on what she was doing. Rather, she was thinking about Bandit's comments. He had the most peculiar way of making her feel absolutely precious and feminine.

At least thirty to forty cowboys would come to this station to receive their monthly pay which, as Tori had heard, ranged from twenty to thirty-five dollars a month. For *that* kind of money, she'd gladly singe her fingertips by holding a match too long.

Several matches later, Bandit opened the old, heavy lock, and raised the lid of the strongbox.

"Oh, my God!" Tori exclaimed when she saw the thick stacks of paper money.

Bandit was not so easily impressed. He picked up one of the stacks and fanned it with his thumb, scanning the denominations. The bills were all small ones, designed to appear hefty to an illiterate cowboy and to feel good in his pocket. The strongbox *looked* as if it contained a fortune, but Bandit guessed there was no more than fifteen-hundred dollars in it.

Jonathon Krey had not become a wealthy man by paying his employees any more than he absolutely had to.

"We'll split it up later," Bandit said, shoving several more matches into Tori's palm.

She watched as he took the bundles of money and began stuffing them into the pockets of his trousers, and inside his boots. He opened his cape to reveal several more pockets into which he stuffed stacks of money.

"It's not nearly as much as it looks," he said, his pockets now bulging, as Tori lit yet another match.

"I can carry some," Tori volunteered.

Bandit grabbed a stack of money and reached for her, about to shove the bills into the breast pocket of her shirt. Had she been a man, the move would have been perfectly innocent. But she wasn't, and the powerful response each had to the other could never be denied. For several seconds, Bandit's hands hovered near Tori's breast pocket . . . so very near the breasts he had kissed through her chemise a week earlier, the breasts she had refused to reveal to him by untying her chemise as he'd requested—as he'd *demanded*.

As they looked at each other for what seemed an eternity, the match burned down to Tori's fingers. She gasped softly, shook it out and lit another. But the gap in time had destroyed the moment of sexual tension between them.

"Hurry," Tori whispered, cupping the match in her hands to allow the light to be seen by Bandit, yet shielding it from the many cracks in the rickety building.

Bandit carefully dipped a single finger into Tori's breast pocket, then with his other hand stuffed a stack of money into it. It didn't take long before all the money had been removed from the strongbox. And though it shouldn't have pleased or aroused him as much as it did, he was glad that she had trusted him enough to allow the money to be placed in her pockets, and had allowed him to feel the warmth of her breasts, however fleetingly, against the backs of his fingers.

"Let's go," Bandit whispered.

Tori blew out the match. She sensed rather than heard him stand and, for an instant, tried to see him but could not. Only inches from her, in his dark clothes, ankle-length black cape, black mask, and black Stetson, the Midnight Bandit was absolutely invisible.

As she got to her feet, Tori wondered whether she could make just such a cape for herself and melt into the night like a mythological creature of no more substance than smoke.

She reached for him blindly, yet in that total darkness their hands met as though Bandit knew that she needed him then.

It felt so natural to have her hand in his, Tori realized, though she knew she should never voice this thought. He was the Midnight Bandit, a man who did not trust her enough to reveal his true identity to her; and she was Tori Singer, a poor woman—a tomboy, some said—out to destroy Jonathon Krey, a man who would in all likelihood destroy her for her efforts.

"What's wrong?" Bandit asked.

"Nothing. Let's go."

"Are you sure? I thought I felt something."

"It was nothing. Let's go," Tori replied. But she was already wondering if Bandit could somehow read her thoughts through her touch, and if he could, what other thoughts—thoughts of an infinitely more intimate nature—had he been able to sense?

Though she couldn't see a thing, she followed Bandit without hesitation, trusting him to lead her in the direction they should go. When he stopped, Tori was amazed that through the total darkness he'd brought them back to the door by which they'd entered. Only the memory of Bandit hitting his shin on something earlier convinced her that he really couldn't see in the dark like a cat.

For a single moment, Tori thought of kissing him. This was the perfect time for a stolen kiss. It was so dark she couldn't see him. She could look straight at him and *know* that he was handsome without being reminded of the mask he wore over his eyes. She could taste his lips and enjoy all those feelings she'd had when in his arms, without once having to be reminded that he was an outlaw who didn't trust her.

*I don't want his kisses.* Tori told herself as Bandit opened the door and peered out.

*And if I think that's the truth, then I'm a damned liar and a fool!* she thought a moment later, when Bandit released her hand and stepped through the doorway.

A deep male voice boomed out, "Take one more step and I'll put a bullet in yer back, mister!"

Tori's heart stopped beating at that moment. Bandit had not taken more than two steps out of the door and into the moonlight, when she saw him raise his hands in surrender.

"Where's Carl?" the armed guard asked.

The Midnight Bandit said nothing. He raised his hands higher and turned until he faced his accuser.

"I asked you a question, damn you!" the guard said, much louder than before.

Tori acted instinctively, with a response she had previously not thought in her nature. In a single, fluid move, she drew the heavy revolver from her holster, raised it high over her head, then leaped out the doorway, bringing the butt of her pistol down upon the guard's head.

He grunted, crumpled, and fell to the ground. Tori looked at him, shaken at what she had just done.

"Did I kill him?" she asked, her voice quavering.

Bandit knelt and felt for a pulse. He smiled up at her. "No, you didn't, but you did save my life."

He took Tori's hand and began pulling her along, forcing her to step over the unconscious man she'd just struck. He was the guard who had been stationed on the roof. As they moved on, Tori soon had to step over another prone form, that of the guard who'd been stationed on the ground outside the bunkhouse. She didn't have to check to know that he was still alive. From what she knew about Bandit, he would not kill unless it was absolutely unavoidable.

Three-quarters of the way back up the bluff, they heard cries of alarm sound below. Bandit, leading the way, muttered over his shoulder, "Just keep going," and that was exactly what Tori did.

They were nearly to the top when, "Up! Look up there!" was shouted from far below.

A gunshot echoed through the night, causing more noise than fear. The men below could either climb the bluff or they could get on their horses and ride far to the east, then take the gentle slope back to the west, the same route Tori and Bandit had taken. Either way, Tori and Bandit would have gotten to their horses and would be long gone.

"We made it," Bandit said when they reached their horses. "I can't believe we made it."

"You're a pessimist," Tori replied. She felt buoyant, thoroughly invincible. "That's your weakness."

Bandit leaped into the saddle. "You're my weakness."

Tori replied without a beat, "Without me, you'd still be down there, trying to explain to those men why you've got their money in your pockets."

She turned Daisy around and put her heels to her flank, feeling more alive than she'd ever felt—with the singular exception of when she was in Bandit's arms.

# Ten

Tori stood alone on the desert in the darkness, holding the reins to Bandit's horse. When the gunshot echoed through the night, she hunched her shoulders and squeezed her eyes tightly shut.

*She was just a horse.* Tori tried to believe that, only Daisy hadn't been just a horse, she'd been a companion as well, and no amount of self-delusion would change that.

But it didn't help. Her mare was dead now, mercifully put out of her misery by the Midnight Bandit. The death had been made necessary by an incredibly lucky shot from one of Jonathon Krey's men, who, though far out of accurate rifle range, had lobbed a bullet into the rump of Tori's mare as she'd run away.

There was no doubt in Tori's mind that she had been the only one who had been seen, and that it was because Bandit was dressed in his cape and other garments of concealment that the bullets had not been directed at him. Tori's error had cost Daisy's life. The mistake, she promised herself, would not be repeated.

Bandit returned carrying Tori's saddle, blanket, and bridle. The tight line to his mouth said the mercy killing, though something he realized needed to be done, was an ugly business just the same. Death, even the death of a horse, affected Bandit, and Tori was grateful that was so. He hid Tori's saddle beneath some scrub for later retrieval.

"She's out of her misery now," he said softly, taking the reins of his stallion from Tori. "She won't suffer anymore."

"She won't be found?" Tori asked.

Bandit was about to step into the stirrup, but he stopped to look at Tori. With only his eyes, because words would be much too cruel, he reminded her that her mare would be found. She would first be discovered by coyotes, then by wolves, and finally by buzzards. By the time the men pursuing them found the carcass of the mare, there would be no way of identifying the animal with Tori Singer.

"Let's go," Bandit said, mounting and easing into the saddle.

He took his foot out of the stirrup so Tori could use it, then reached down for her. She slipped easily onto the rump of his stallion, and both of them were vividly aware of the brief but unmistakable contact as firm, lush breasts pressed momentarily against well-muscled shoulders.

They moved off into the night at a canter.

"There's a place I want to show you," Bandit said, breaking the silence that had developed between them.

Tori was curious, but she said nothing. Guilt over the death of her mare had put a pall over the happiness she felt at having once again successfully raided Jonathon Krey's coffers.

They had been riding steadily for over two hours. Wondering where he could be taking her, Tori was distracted by her body touching Bandit's. The insides of her thighs rubbed the outsides of his, and with each stride the horse took, she was unable to prevent the sensitive tips of her breasts from brushing against Bandit's broad, strong back.

He'd brought her to a high, rocky area where, in the very middle, a low spot in the rocks trapped water from an underground source. Around this small oasis were trees and vegetation of indeterminate health and species. Tori had seen other exotic places in the desert surrounding Santa Fe, though she had never before heard about this one.

"Who knows about this place?" she asked. She quickly slipped off Bandit's horse, wanting to put some distance between herself and him so that she could keep her thoughts clear, lucid, logical.

"Just myself and the animals, as far as I know," Bandit replied, also dismounting. He led his mount to the small pond at the epicenter of this strangely tropical area of the desert, and let the animal drink. "I've been coming here for years, but I've never once come across any other human, or even seen a trace of one."

Been coming here for years? Tori looked at Bandit, aware that he knew her, and expecting should somehow know him—that is, know the identity *behind* the mask. If he'd been coming to this secret spot for years, then he'd probably always lived in Santa Fe or, like her, near enough to be known to the people in town.

But she'd seen Bandit's uncanny ability to keep himself shrouded in shadow, and though the mask over his eyes really did not conceal much of him, it obscured his features enough so that she couldn't determine what he truly looked like.

"We'll rest here for a bit," he said, keeping an eye on his horse. "This ol' boy's in need of water and a rest."

At first Tori thought he was talking about himself, but when she looked at him, she realized he was referring to his stallion. Was her additional weight a great burden? Tori suspected so, though she hated to admit it, loathing the feeling that she was incompetent, not quite as capable of taking care of herself or of attacking Jonathon Krey as the masked man had proven to be.

She watched as Bandit rubbed down his stallion, allowing him to drink, praising the animal quietly for his stamina, strength, and courage. The tenderness Tori saw him show the horse touched her deeply, and for the hundredth time she wondered exactly what kind of man the mysterious Midnight Bandit really was.

Where were they headed next? She was curious, but she was in no hurry to part company with Bandit. She turned away from him, moving down near the cool water. Now what? she kept wondering, not really knowing whether she really wanted an answer.

"We'll stay here an hour or so," he said. His deep voice carried easily on the still night air. "Then we'll head out again."

Tori watched him approach. His movements were all grace and power, smooth and yet loose-limbed despite the considerable strength in his chest and biceps. And the black cape, flowing over his shoulders and moving gently with his steps, gave him an appearance of flight, as though he were a gigantic eagle about to take off.

"What time is it?" she asked, not really curious but feeling she should say something.

Bandit withdrew a heavy gold watch from his pocket,

flipped open the case, and angled the timepiece so he could read it in the thin moonlight.

"A little after three. I'll have you home before the sun comes up," he answered.

When he was close enough to touch, Tori felt the nearness of him, felt it deep within herself, and though she understood the sensation and even took a certain pleasure in it, she also realized with crystal clarity that it was something she would do well to avoid.

She took off her hat and placed it on the ground beside her as she knelt, then cupped her hands and tasted the water. It was from an artesian well, bubbling up naturally from deep beneath the earth's surface.

Out of the corner of her eye, she looked at Bandit's boots. They were made of high-quality leather, the craftsmanship showing the stitching. They were the kind of boots she had promised herself she would one day own.

She tasted the water again, aware that Bandit was almost hovering over her. She felt intimidated, but couldn't tell whether there was any logical reason for this or not.

"Now what?" she asked, not looking up. The cool water in her hands would cool her blood, she hoped.

When Bandit did not answer, Tori got to her feet. She would not be intimidated by him, she told herself.

"Here," he said, taking her right wrist.

She had been just about to dry her hands on her Levi's, but Bandit gently took her hand in his and wrapped his black cape around it. Slowly, very sensually, he dried each finger one at a time, blotting off the water.

*He's just drying my hands,* Tori told herself. *It's not like he's caressing me.*

But a caress was exactly what it felt like.

"What are you doing?" she asked softly. She thought, *I'm babbling like an idiot!*

"Just drying your hand for you," he replied, false innocence ringing in every word.

Tori pulled her hand out of his grasp. She finished drying her hands on her Levi's. "It felt like much more than that," she accused softly. "And don't talk to me in that I'm-as-innocent-as-the-night-is-long tone. I know you too well to believe that."

"Too well?" He moved a half-step closer, his masculine senses fine-tuned to her nearness, her allure. "I'm not so sure that's true. In fact, I suspect you hardly know yourself, much less me."

Tori had been watching Bandit's mouth as he spoke, and though his words had piqued her anger—a reaction she was certain he'd intended to provoke—she remembered the pleasure she had known from his lips, and questioned why she had denied herself even greater pleasure from them.

Why had she denied Bandit his passionate request when they had stood so close together in the darkness a week earlier? At the time, denying him had seemed absolutely critical. Since then, the why of that particular action had become obscured, leaving her with the hazy realization that she could not deny Bandit without denying herself as well.

"By not responding, I'll have to assume that you agree with what I have to say," he said in a whisper, raising his hands to place them very lightly upon Tori's shoulders.

*I don't agree with you! You assume too much, Mr. Midnight Bandit!* Tori thought, though she could not get herself to speak the words.

The heat of his hands upon her shoulders seemed to burn her flesh. The weight of them, though actually light, threatened to push her to her knees, or perhaps merely to coax her to them.

She moistened her lips with the tip of her tongue and fought the tightness in her throat.

"You shouldn't touch me," she managed to say at last in a soft, thin voice.

"Does that mean that you don't want me to touch you?"

They were not the same things, and Tori just didn't know what the proper answer was.

"You're so good at all the wrong things," she said with a kind of quiet resignation that she wished carried more criticism of Bandit.

"I don't want to want you to touch me," she said at last.

The truth of her statement surprised her. This was one of the few times she had been with Bandit that she had spoken the complete truth, and it was shocking that she hadn't realized it until after the words were out of her mouth.

"I'm not really as bad as you make me out to be," he said, and now his whisper was most definitely seductive. "In fact, I'm not a bad man at all."

Tori pulled her eyes away from his mouth, from those too-enticing lips that could mesmerize her with their touch, with tantalizing words that played havoc with her senses and with everything she had believed about herself.

"Please . . . I'm not really the woman you think I am either," Tori said, her eyes upon Bandit's chest. She felt his fingertips moving slowly against the tension-tightened muscles in her neck and shoulders, loosening the pressure.

"The last time we were together . . . the way I be-haved . . . that wasn't—"

"Wasn't something that you normally do? Yes, Tori, I know that." His thumbs slipped under her chin to gently but insistently tilt her head back so that she was forced to look into his face. "I also know that you are much more beautiful than you realize, and I fully intend to show you how beautiful you are until you believe it. Believe it deep down in your heart."

*I mustn't listen to him,* Tori thought.

Bandit exerted his will to keep from taking Tori into his arms, crushing her voluptuous body against his, feel-ing the heat and firmness of her lush breasts pressing against him. He knew himself, and was certain that the next time he tasted her kisses, he could not satisfy *her* passion alone.

"We should leave," she said, looking into his masked face, trying hard to convince herself that she was unaf-fected by the way he looked, by the things he said, by his touch.

"Not yet."

"Why?"

"Because you haven't kissed me yet."

The tingling inside her became stronger at those words. "What would you do if I said I don't want your kisses?"

"I would say you're lying, and kiss you anyway."

She stood there, looking at him, wanting him to kiss her, wanting him to take her into his arms. How could she be so brash, so wanton and bold, as to ask for his kisses or, worse, to initiate them? So she waited, hungry for his touch, thirsty for his kiss.

Bandit took off his Stetson and cast it aside, then very

slowly he bent down, his fingers sliding around the back of Tori's neck to angle her face up toward him.

"Kiss me," Tori whispered, a moment before his mouth came over hers.

It had been important for her to say those words. She was a strong and forceful woman, and she would flaunt convention if need be to get what she wanted. At that very moment, more than anything else in the world, she wanted Bandit's kisses, wanted them to be intimate, so she parted her lips invitingly and received his enticing tongue.

She melted against him, her arms slipping around his body beneath his cape. When that first long, deep kiss finally ended, Tori sighed, leaning against Bandit, her heart thrumming, her body alive.

"I love your kisses," she whispered. She leaned forward, pressing her cheek against his chest. His black silk shirt was soft and smooth against her lips as she spoke, in contrast to the firm, warm pectoral muscles beneath it. "I know I shouldn't—I know that women aren't really supposed to enjoy such things, but I do . . . with you."

These were words Bandit wanted to hear. He pushed Tori away from his chest just far enough so that he could kiss her again, and when he did, it was a fiercely aroused, almost bruising kiss.

She could feel the passion in it, sense the burning desire that flowed in his veins. As the kiss deepened, his tongue filled her mouth and danced with her own, every part of her responding, coming alive, opening like the petals of a flower to the warmth of Bandit's desire.

She felt his hand at her shoulder, sliding between their bodies. And when at last he cupped her breast, catching the nipple between his fingers to pinch it firmly, she sighed against his mouth.

"My God, what breasts!" Bandit gasped, his lips against Tori's as he fondled her nipple into a state of erect, fevered excitement.

She turned her face away, ending the kiss, knowing this was the time for her to put an end to their lustful madness. As Bandit touched her, his hands strong and demanding— one on her breast, the other at her buttocks—she shivered with rapidly escalating excitement. It was time to tell him to stop . . . but she couldn't.

One and then two buttons on her shirt were unfastened. Then a third one inexplicably refused to release under Bandit's experienced fingers. For several seconds Tori feared that he would stop, that the stubborn button on her old cotton shirt would deny her and Bandit that which they both desired.

The sound of the button being ripped from her shirt was both shocking and exciting. She hadn't expected him to be so brash and bold. Certainly not after he'd simply walked away from her a week earlier, when she'd refused to untie her chemise for him. Though there was something disturbing about his tearing a button off her shirt, it was also exciting to know that she could arouse him so that he would follow his instincts.

"Beautiful, beautiful, beautiful!" Bandit whispered in a litany of passion as he opened Tori's shirt, pulling the tails out of her Levi's, kissing the satiny flesh of her throat.

Tori was consumed by the desire going through her. His hands were everywhere, strong, forceful, touching her, giving her no choice but to respond. Her shirt was soon unbuttoned down to her Levi's, and a moment later the three ties closing her chemise were unknotted.

"So beautiful," Bandit whispered.

She expected him to finally touch her breasts now that they were exposed, but instead he took her by the shoulders and pushed her to arm's length.

"I've got to look at you," he whispered hotly. "I've imagined you a thousand times . . . I must look . . . I must see the beauty of you!"

Tori felt on display, but, strangely, she was not self-conscious. Rather, she was proud of the way she looked, and when Bandit eased his hands within her shirt and chemise, opening the garments to bare her breasts in the moonlight, she squared her shoulders and subtly thrust her chest toward him.

The deep groan that came from Bandit shocked him. In the back of his mind, he tried to remind himself that he was a man of considerable experience in such matters, and that he should be more in control of his emotions, though at this moment control meant nothing to the man known as the Midnight Bandit and as Mack Randolph. Pulling Tori to him, he bent his knees and buried his face between her plush breasts, inhaling deeply to savor their scent.

She held his head between her hands. The silk of his mask was against her fingers, and for an instant, she thought of ripping it from his face. Then she watched, as though she were more an observer than a participant, as she turned her shoulders and guided her pink-tipped breast to Bandit's mouth.

"Ohhh!" she wailed when he captured her nipple in his

mouth, putting his tongue and lips in motion against the throbbing bud.

She had anticipated what it would feel like to have him kiss her there, but that was nothing compared to the reality. The pleasure of feeling his mouth against her bare breast was a thousand-fold what she had experienced when she'd felt the heat and moisture of his mouth *through* her chemise.

Tori's knees trembled, her breath coming in uneven gulps as she guided Bandit's mouth to her other breast. She wanted to feel him everywhere, to know the ecstasy of his tongue, slick and yet raspy, touching her, electrifying her flesh. It seemed she was being devoured by Bandit, but miraculously, rather than being smaller because of it, she was expanding, becoming greater, more powerful.

His hands were everywhere on her, running along the backs of her legs, her thighs, moving close to the core of her moist hunger without ever touching her there. Shivering with ever-escalating passion, Tori thought that her Levi's most certainly would be scorched from her body's heat at Bandit's touch. He was just too exciting to be with; his kisses and caresses stripped her of all common sense and propriety as surely as his hands stripped her of her clothes.

Tori clutched Bandit, her fingers digging into the powerful muscles of his shoulders as he feasted upon the passion-hardened tips of her breasts. Wantonly, she spread her feet far apart, trembling from head to toe as a need, a ravenous desire that she was quite certain could never be fully vanquished, went through her, consuming her, burning like a forest fire out of control, devouring everything flammable.

Deep within her, she felt superheated, moist, desperate. This was too much pleasure, she told herself. Much too much . . . but even as she thought this, she knew it was not so, because Bandit's hands had once before brought her to a passionate fulfillment that was at a more mystical plane than the one she was on now. She knew from experience—the experience that Bandit had given her—that there was greater satisfaction in the future. Primordial in scope, and soul-shattering in intensity, Tori knew in her heart that unless she felt that great, liquid, surging release of passionate tension on this evening, she would surely lose her mind.

"Bandit! Oh, Bandit!" she gasped, helpless against the excitement that had taken over her judgment, that consumed and controlled all her thoughts. "I must have you! Here! Tonight!" Her legs were shaking and she wasn't certain she could remain standing, so when Bandit stood upright, releasing her throbbing nipples from his mouth's loving attention, she leaned into him, holding onto his shoulders, needing him for support and guidance. "Make love to me," she sobbed. "I've never let any man touch me the way you have. I've never wanted a man to touch me before!"

Tori knew Bandit was not the type of man who would stay with her, and she accepted that without remorse. This masked man with the kisses that seared her soul was the Midnight Bandit, and he had stolen her better judgment from her. When this night was over, when the harsh light of day shone, Tori would live with the fact that she had given her virginity to a man who would not stay with her, much less marry her . . . and though she'd always thought she would never give herself so intimately and so completely to any man but her husband, she took Bandit's hand, raised it to her mouth, and kissed the back of it tenderly.

"Make love to me, Bandit," Tori said softly, looking into the masked man's eyes. "You can leave me later. I know you will. I'm not asking for a lifetime with you, only this one night. Make love to me, and then you can set me free."

# Eleven

She'd needed a moment to think. Just a second, that was all. And thinking—at least clear, lucid thinking—was absolutely impossible when she was in Bandit's arms, so she had insisted that he step away from her. The look he'd given her then had said he didn't believe her, that he figured she would once again leave his passion unfulfilled.

"Just a moment of distance . . . I promise, you won't be sorry," she said, rising on tiptoe to kiss his mouth before pushing him away.

This was not the most romantic place for a woman to make love for the first time in her life, Tori decided. On the other hand, she was about to make love to the most exciting man in the world—possibly the most romantic man ever to walk the earth.

*Calm down, Tori!* she thought, angry with herself for her own passionate exaggeration. *This demigod you're creating doesn't trust you enough to take off his mask. Tomorrow, after he's had his fun, all you'll be is a memory to him.*

Bandit removed his cape and spread it out on the ground near the water. The earth was sun-baked, hard as rock. He gave Tori a faltering smile beneath his mask, as though to say his cape was as much comfort as he could provide.

She wanted to speak, but she did not entirely trust her own voice. Still, it was easier to know what she should do, what she wanted to do, when she was not in Bandit's arms.

She shrugged out of her shirt, then removed her chemise, her gaze cast down in embarrassment, bared to Bandit's avaricious look, her taut-tipped breasts glowing pale and seductive in the moonlight. She heard his sudden intake of breath, then his long, slow exhalation, and she knew that he enjoyed looking at her. Her confidence expanded just when she needed it most, and she lifted her chin to look straight at him.

"Don't stop," Bandit said, a bit too quickly.

The strain in his voice pleased Tori. He wasn't as collected as he wanted to appear, and she greatly enjoyed the power she had over him.

"If you're going to look at me, then it's only fair that I get to look at you," Tori said, shocking herself with her own boldness.

She removed her boots, and when she was standing erect once again, she looked at Bandit. This time she was the one to suddenly suck in her breath and unconsciously hold it. He had already removed his shirt, and she saw the strength in his large biceps, broad chest, and exquisite shoulders. She watched as he removed his boots one at a time; then, when he was naked from the waist up as she was, she looked into his face and thought: *I wish I believed in my own beauty as you believe in yours.*

Bandit took only a single step toward her before she motioned for him to stop. She had never before looked at a man—not really. At least, not the way she was now looking at the Midnight Bandit, and most certainly not with the same feelings going through her.

"Let me look at you," she whispered, once again shocking herself with behavior that seemed much too wanton. "I've never thought there was anything"—words almost failed her—"interesting to look at in a man."

Bandit removed the holster from around his lean hips. There was a confident half-smile upon his mouth as he set pistol and holster aside, and his fingers hovered near his belt buckle.

"And now you find something interesting?" he asked facetiously.

"You would be an easy man to hate," Tori murmured. To herself, she thought, *And an easier man to love!*

He turned sideways to her as he removed his trousers. At first Tori thought he was only being modest, though this thought was soon amended when she decided that a more likely explanation was that he wanted to show himself off in profile. When he stepped out of his trousers and underclothes and turned toward her again, her mouth went dry.

"You are beautiful," she whispered. She had to hear her own voice to know she'd just spoken.

He was standing with his feet spread to shoulder's width, his hands hanging loose at his sides. Every muscle in his body was revealed, and at the sight of the naked strength that stood ready for her, Tori's insides melted.

She let her gaze caress his chest and shoulders, move down to the rippled muscles of his stomach. Then, forcing herself, she looked down at his feet and allowed her gaze to work its way slowly upward over strong calves and even more powerful thighs.

Finally, she let herself look at Bandit's arousal.

Once again, her breath caught in her throat. Tori bit her bottom lip and forced her breathing to become rhythmic, regular.

He was beautiful from head to toe. Even that part of him that was rather intimidating—his thrusting arousal, which stood almost straight out from his body and throbbed visibly with passion for Tori—was beautiful to her.

When she finally pulled her gaze away from his nakedness and looked into his face, she saw that he was smiling slightly.

"You're much too confident," she said a bit resentfully.

Bandit shrugged, took one step toward Tori, then stopped himself. His smile broadened, and if Tori didn't know better, she would have sworn that it was an absolutely wicked grin.

"What is it?" she asked.

Her own confidence had vanished, and now she realized how tenuous it was, especially at a time like this, and in contrast to Bandit's rock-solid confidence.

Suddenly, he'd stretched out on his cape, clasping his hands behind his head. In this position, his arousal stood up as though it were an offering of some divine kind, and the muscles in his chest and stomach looked to be a delectable treat for Tori to nibble on at her leisure.

"The last time I asked you, you refused. I'll ask you again, Tori . . . take your clothes off for me . . . then come to me."

"You really are much too confident and far too demanding," she whispered, though in truth she was glad that he was giving her another chance to show courage under exactly the same circumstances as when her courage had failed her.

Feeling on display and yet enjoying the sensation of having Bandit watching her every move, Tori unfastened her belt, then very slowly undid the buttons of her Levi's. As she worked the denim material past the curves of her hips, she wondered if Bandit thought it hideously manly of her to wear trousers. She'd heard most men thought it terrible that she wore them, though none dared say as much to her face.

When she stepped out of her Levi's and the old cotton pantalets, washed so many times they were thin as paper and frayed at the edges, Tori was suddenly aware of two entirely different and conflicting emotions. Naked, outside at night under the desert stars, she felt free, completely natural and at ease in her environment; and at the same time, she felt utterly vulnerable and exposed to Bandit.

She desperately wanted to look into his eyes and see the desire he had for her, but at that moment, she could not find the courage to do so. What if he thought her shoulders were too wide, as some men did? What if he thought her thighs were too well developed and muscular from the hours she'd spent on horseback? What if—

"If you do not come to me immediately, I will be forced to come to you," Bandit said in a voice hoarse with passion. "My darling Tori, I have been exercising as much control over my desire for you as I am capable of. Do not tempt me further, or I'll not be able to answer for my actions!"

Tori looked at him. Now, he was on his side, his long, muscular body knotted with suppressed desire, his arousal jutting forth intimidatingly—an entity, a part of Bandit yet independent of him. She knew she should go to him, but her feet seemed rooted in place.

He had not been joking. When Tori hesitated, he suddenly exploded to his feet and rushed across the brief span that separated them.

"Temptress!" he hissed, taking her into his arms, crushing her naked body against his own as his mouth slanted down hard over hers.

The impact upon her senses was stunning. Bandit's naked chest against her breasts was supremely exciting, warming her blood, electrifying her in a thousand different ways.

She leaned into him, forcing her breasts to flatten slightly and become more round as she pressed them hard against him. His hands cupped her buttocks, squeezing her, very nearly lifting her. When his tongue ceased its exploration of her mouth, she explored his mouth, kissing him deeply, thrusting her tongue between his lips just as he had taught her to.

She began to wind her arms around his shoulders, but Bandit suddenly took her wrists, then moved a half-step away so that their bodies were no longer pressed tightly together.

He then brought Tori's hands down, guiding them to his arousal. She felt the heat of it against her fingertips, and though she was wildly curious, she could not look down at it.

"Touch me," Bandit whispered, still holding lightly onto her wrists, as though cautious that she might suddenly become so fearful she would leap away.

Very tentatively, Tori curled her fingers around the broad shaft of his manhood. She squeezed him lightly at first, then more firmly as she gained confidence. When Bandit sighed, his lips parting slightly, she knew that she was pleasing him. But could she please him as thoroughly as he had pleased her? She doubted it. He was simply much too experienced, she decided. He knew exactly what he was doing with a woman when he wanted to arouse her; Tori Singer didn't know what was expected of her.

She looked down at that which filled her hands. He was warm, solid, pulsing with virility, trembling with desire. As she moved a fist over him, Bandit sighed his approval.

"I've never . . . before," she said in a whisper so soft Bandit barely heard her.

"It will be beautiful," he replied.

"I've heard that it hurts."

She looked into his eyes, expecting him to lie to her, to deny what she knew was true.

"Sometimes it does. I'll be careful, but sometimes . . ."

Part of her wished that he'd lied. She knew it was not good for her to think too highly of this man. Had he lied, had he told her that losing her virginity to him couldn't possibly cause her any pain, she would have been able to think less of him, to see him as an opportunist, a seductive liar.

Tori whispered, "I know you will."

Bandit removed her hands from him, then he brought her to his cape on the ground. He sat on it, turning so that he faced Tori, a hand raised to her. She looked down at him, not entirely certain what he expected. She had always thought a woman would be on the bottom, pinned against the ground, helpless against a man's greater strength. But the light in Bandit's eyes suggested something else entirely as the moonlight played over his naked body.

She took his hand and let him pull her down so that she knelt near his hip. Her pale green gaze was filled with questions.

"The ground is hard," he said, reading Tori's look. "If you're on top, you can move as you want. This time . . . this first time . . . perhaps it is best if you're in control of our . . . movements."

Tori took a lock of Bandit's ebony hair and smoothed it back, tucking it into the top of his mask, near his temple.

"You are a mystery to me," she whispered, feeling a warm evening breeze playing over her naked body. "You tear a button off my shirt to get my clothes off, then you worry about my comfort so much you're willing to sacrifice your own pleasure."

Tori kissed Bandit's mouth softly, closing her eyes, letting her senses feast upon the moment. She felt his hands upon her naked body, and she allowed him to guide her until she slipped a knee over his thighs to straddle his prone body.

"Mmmm!" she purred as she kissed him, half-sitting upon him now, still rather uncertain of what precisely was expected of her.

Bandit placed his hands on her hips and pulled her down so that her weight was upon him, the firmness of her buttocks warm and exciting against his lower abdomen. Then he played his hands over her buttocks, touching and squeezing, feeling her responding to his caresses hesitantly. He could tell that despite the pleasure she felt and the hunger for completion that compelled her to go forward, Tori was still afraid that the consummation would cause her pain.

"Take your time," he whispered when their tender kiss

had finally ended. "I'll let you do everything yourself. Just take your time and it will be perfect."

"A woman could fall in love with you," Tori whispered.

It surprised her that she'd said the words, but she had already said so many things to Bandit, done so many things with him, that her openness was no longer shocking to her.

Bandit had no idea of how to respond to what she had just said. He brought his right hand to her mouth, brushing the pad of his thumb over her lips. He could kiss those full, sensual lips forever without ever completely satisfying his hunger for them. When she kissed his thumb, then let the tip of her tongue dart out briefly, he groaned with desire, and his expanding manhood throbbed.

As he brought his moist thumb to Tori's nipple and pinched her softly, she tossed her head back and issued a soft, tremulous sigh. Every place Bandit touched her seemed to burn with desire. Even her hair, spread out over her shoulders and down her back, seemed to be caressing her skin. Her breasts were tight, full, aching with tension. And down low, she was moist, swollen with passion, neglected and needy.

"I love how you touch me," Tori whispered, her hands on Bandit's chest, her body trembling softly as he played with her nipples. "I love everything you do to me."

She leaned forward, inching higher on his body so that her pink-tipped breasts hung above his face. Arching her back, she lowered herself, feeding one throbbing nipple to him as his hands once again slipped around her hips.

It seemed to her that Bandit was not just one man, but many men. Surely, no one man could touch her the way he did in as many places as he did. With his lips tugging at her nipple and one strong hand manipulating her buttocks, the fingertips of the other touching the moist, pink petals of her femininity. He managed to caress her in every area that hungered for his loving attention.

"Yes, yes, yes!" Tori whispered, her hands kneading the solid muscles in his shoulders as his lips tugged at her nipple.

She felt the tip of his finger enter her. It was just the very tip, but she felt it throughout her body. And when his fingertip found the small, erect nub that lay hidden between the velvety folds of her femininity, she cried out even louder than before.

How long she stayed in that position, hovering over Bandit, moving just enough to shift her shoulders so that each breast received his attention, Tori could not say. His long-fingered hands touched her skillfully, heightening her readiness, until at last she knew that the moment of truth had come. She was as ready for Bandit as she would ever—could ever—be.

"I want you now," she whispered huskily, looking down at the masked man who held her tingling nipple lightly between pearl white teeth. "I can't wait another second to have you."

"Then take me," Bandit said, moving his hands to Tori's hips, holding her without in any way restricting her mobility.

Tori slid down his body, pressing herself intimately against him as she moved. When the long, throbbing length of his arousal, hard and hot, was against her, she issued a tremulous sigh. Raising her hips, she moved lower still until his arousal was trapped between their bodies, and his powerful shaft was throbbing lustily against her femininity.

"Go ahead," Bandit whispered, looking down at her. With hair streaming down the sides of her face, her features cast in light and shadow, he was certain that no woman could ever be quite as beautiful or as desirable as she was at that moment.

Tori wanted him to help her, to take command; but as before, he insisted that she allow her own boldness to come to the fore. Reaching between their bodies, she tentatively grasped his manhood, positioning it as she raised her hips even further until at last the crown of his desire was pressed tightly against her moist entrance.

"It will hurt," she said.

She waited for Bandit to say something, to lie to her or give her encouragement. He did neither. He just looked at her, his body tense, his passion flagrantly ready for her, his self-control indisputable, astonishing.

Tori leaned forward and kissed his mouth very lightly. "You amaze me," she whispered . . . and then began lowering herself upon him, feeling the fiery length of his manhood pushing into her, opening her, filling her deeply, completely.

Her fears proved to be unfounded. For only a fleeting moment did Tori feel any pain. But it mingled with so much pleasure that when at last her body melded with Bandit's, his towering manhood throbbing and pulsing deep within her, she laughed with pleasure.

"What's so funny?" he asked. His hands rested lightly upon her buttocks, his turgid desire was engulfed in the warmth of the most amazing woman he'd ever known.

"You amaze me!" Tori said, having absolutely no idea at all of why she felt it important to say that.

She began moving, very slowly at first, then with increasing confidence and a quickening tempo. Up and down, just a little bit at first, then further and further, she moved her pelvis. The friction was slick and arousing, heightening her passion, as did the strange sensation of having Bandit *inside her,* moving, filling her completely with his great strength. And then, when she raised her hips, he was released almost completely from her honeyed embrace.

On two occasions, in her inexperience and haste, she raised herself too far, so that Bandit slipped completely from her. Hurriedly, with a trembling hand, she brought the flared crown of his passion to her entrance once more, then descended upon him, in one sense impaling herself upon him, in another capturing Bandit and holding him hostage for her own pleasure.

She was aware of the smoothness of his silk cape beneath her knees, and under that the hard ground. In a disconnected way, she wondered if she would find bruises on her knees in the morning. She didn't care. She wasn't going to stop or change anything she was doing.

She was conscious of the motion of her breasts as she raised and lowered her hips. In the past, when she had ridden Daisy, she'd been annoyed by the movements of her breasts. They moved too much, she'd always thought. But now, with Bandit buried so deep inside her and his powerful hands behind her, guiding her undulations, the movements of her breasts were deliciously exciting, almost as though they were being caressed by Bandit.

She leaned forward just enough so that the aroused tips

of her breasts brushed against his chest each time she impaled herself completely upon him, and her excitement became just a little hotter, her passion slightly more intense and demanding.

She knew the feeling. She'd experienced it once before, only that time it had been caused by Bandit's hands and her clothes were still on. The seductive thief who had stolen her better judgment wasn't buried deep within her most secret place that first time. Only now, with the experience to make a comparison, was she aware of what she had denied herself before.

Even though she'd understood what was about to happen, the intensity of it, the runaway-train force of it, was a thousand times more powerful and jarring to the senses than Tori had expected. At one moment she'd been in control of herself, raising and lowering her hips smoothly to draw the most amount of pleasure from Bandit's invading manhood as she could.

And then, quite suddenly, her body was going mad, completely out of control. She dropped onto him, taking every pulsating inch of his desire into her; then her hips began jerking crazily back and forth. With her knees pulled up and squeezing his ribs, and her body doubled forward, she shivered and shook, a silent gasp opening her mouth wide.

And then it hit her. Powerfully. Shatteringly. It seemed the top of her head was going to explode. The pressure within her grew and grew; then at last it was released in a series of constricting spasms that shuddered through her.

When the spasms had subsided, Tori blinked her eyes to clear her vision. She was gulping in air, her knees pressed tight against Bandit's ribs, her cheek against his, her breasts against his warm chest, her femininity pulsing around his solid flesh which filled her.

"My . . . oh, my!" Tori whispered when at last reality eked back into her consciousness.

She felt Bandit's fingertips running along her curved spine, touching her lightly from the nape of her neck down to her buttocks. She raised her face just enough to look into his eyes. What was he thinking? Was she too passionate? Was it wrong for a woman to be that . . . excitable? She did not know, and there was nothing in her background to give her even the slightest hint of what was right and wrong, or of what Bandit might think of her now.

His hands were at her hips, and he raised her. She did as he silently commanded, but then when she was about to drop down upon him again, he held her solidly in place, still joined, poised above him. At last, she looked into his eyes questioningly. Bandit smiled, and Tori could not resist kissing his mouth quickly one more time.

"What?" she asked.

"My turn," he replied.

He held her up and away from him, then began moving beneath her, filling her with his desire before moving down so that she nearly released him. Each time she thought she had his rhythm down, he changed it slightly, and occasionally he seemed to enter her from a different angle, adding to the friction that heightened her sensitivity to him.

She'd thought her passion had been fulfilled, that she could not be brought to such heights of ecstasy again, but Bandit, moving smoothly, mysteriously, was proving that she'd been wrong.

"Ohhh!" she moaned when he grabbed her breasts, filling his hands with them as his hips churned beneath her at a constantly increasing tempo.

She could see the tension in his face, feel it in his hands as he grasped her breasts. She wanted it all. She wanted to take Bandit to that mysterious land of pure ecstasy he had introduced her to.

"Go," she whispered, urging him on as he thrust up into her, harder and deeper than before. "Go, my darling!"

Her words shocked and delighted Bandit. With a groan he arched, raising her, embedding himself as deeply into her as was possible. Then, with his back arched, carrying Tori's weight, he released his passion in a torrent, feeling it rush through the throbbing length of him.

# Twelve

Bandit was laughing, and it scared the daylights out of Tori.

Was he laughing at her? She didn't want to believe such a thing was possible. Could any man be so cold and heartless that he would laugh at a woman just moments after he'd taken her virginity? While he was still within her?

He reached up to cup Tori's face in his hands, the light in his eyes shining brilliantly.

"I know that was your first time, but my darling Tori, you are a natural lover," Bandit said softly, his thumbs lightly brushing Tori's soft cheeks. "You are exquisite."

She was elated then. It probably wasn't right for a woman to be exquisite at such a thing, but she was—Bandit had told her she was, and he certainly seemed to be a man who knew what he was talking about when it came to lovemaking. His laughter, she now realized, was just at his release of passion.

Before long, Tori was smiling, too, and then she was laughing. Yes, it had been exquisite, everything she'd ever dreamed it would be and more.

Playfully, she slapped him on the chest, and he groaned theatrically. The sound of her palm smacking naked flesh was a wet one, and Tori only then realized how much exertion both she and Bandit had put into their loving.

"Was it really exquisite?" she asked, her soft green eyes now glittering with mischief. She could still feel him inside her, but she didn't move. She wanted to keep him there as long as possible, suspecting that she would never again have this experience with him.

"Yes," Bandit said. Then he grinned wickedly. "You're sure this was your first—"

Tori slapped him on the chest again before he could finish the sentence.

"You know that's true!" she shot back, not liking the implication behind his words.

Immediately sensing the tenderness of the subject, the smile vanished from Bandit's face. He touched her face very lightly, then let his hands glide down her throat to her breasts to circle her nipples, hardly touching her flesh.

"Yes," he confirmed in a whisper. "I know that's true. And I can't say what this has meant to you, but I can say what it has meant to me, Tori. It's meant more than you know. You've been on my mind and in my thoughts constantly since I rescued you from Jonathon Krey's bedroom."

She smiled, her confidence returning. "You've rescued me, but I've rescued you. Let's not forget what happened tonight," she replied, thinking about the guard who'd had his gun trained at Bandit's back.

"No, I'll never forget that," Bandit replied, and from his tone it was clear that he wasn't talking about anything but their lovemaking.

For several seconds they looked into each other's eyes.

Then Tori moved slightly, and he slipped out of her. They both groaned, and the moment of tenderness evaporated.

"I've got to get up," Bandit said. "My back is killing me."

Tori tossed a leg over him. Her knees hurt somewhat, but other than that, she felt beautiful and healthy in a dozen different ways. The pleasure she had hoped for was fulfilling, spiritually satisfying; the pain, brief, minor, insignificant.

As Bandit got to his feet, she sat on his cape, pulling her knees up to her chest, then wrapping her arms around her legs. She watched him in all his naked, natural splendor as he went to the pool, cupped the cool, clear water in his hands, then drank it.

*He's so beautiful, she* thought, then blushed. How many times had she thought that since she'd seen him without any clothes on? A dozen? A hundred? Too many times, to be sure.

Tori didn't care. She had him with her, and as long as she did, she would gladly accept every bit of pleasure offered by the evening and the masked thief who'd stolen her heart.

Had he really done that?

Tori was not inclined to dwell too long on this question. She knew her time with him was limited. She didn't even know his name, so how on earth could she possibly have allowed him to steal her heart?

But she hadn't *allowed* him to do that. He was a thief, the most charming and exciting man she'd ever known, and he'd simply stolen her heart, easily and effortlessly.

*It's a good thing he did, otherwise I'd have to face the*

*humiliation of offering it to him and having the offering
refused.*

Tori immediately banished this disquieting thought
from her mind. There would be plenty of time later for
doubts and recrimination. Plenty of time for remorse and
regret. Tonight, she was going to make the most of it, and
be damned with whatever anyone else thought was im-
proper!

Bandit walked back to her, his stride easy and loose,
and Tori could tell he was completely at ease with his own
nudity. She hoped one day she, too, could be so free with
her own body.

"How do you feel?" he asked, kneeling near her hip.

The tenderness in his voice touched Tori's heart. "I feel
wonderful."

"It wasn't painful? You're not sore?"

Tori just smiled.

"The only lingering effect of making love with you is
an inability to stop smiling, and an overall sense of well-
being that goes to the marrow of my bones." Tori ran a
hand over her leg and grimaced. She had perspired during
the energetic lovemaking. "And I need a bath."

Bandit leaped to his feet so quickly that Tori at first
thought Krey's gunmen had found them. But Bandit never
lost his grin, so when he extended his hand down to her,
she just looked at the offer questioningly. She wasn't feeling at all energetic, preferring to sit quietly in the after-
glow of their lovemaking, in a quiet conversation with
him a rather than frolic about this desert oasis with him.

"You need a bath, and a bath awaits you," he said, his
smile still in place, though fading.

She looked at the long-fingered hand extended to her,

then up into Bandit's face. Tori sensed that by taking his hand, she would once again be submitting her will to his and there might be ramifications to that which at present she could not see.

"You'll feel most refreshed afterward," Bandit said, his hand still extended. "I always take a dip when I come here."

Tori wasn't certain exactly why she took his hand. Before long the light of a new day would be upon them. She wasn't sure what she actually felt now about having made love with him.

"Sooner or later, I'm going to have to learn to say no to you," Tori said with a self-deprecating smile, taking his hand and allowing him to pull her to her feet.

She was glad that he had turned to lead the way on the short distance to the small pool of artesian water. Now that her passion had been more than satisfied, she felt terribly self-conscious about her nudity, especially when she was up and walking around rather than sitting in the dark with her knees pulled up to her chest.

Bandit made a production out of dipping a toe into the water to test its temperature. "Yes, the maid has gotten the temperature just right this time." He stepped into the pool, still holding Tori's hand. "Trust me . . . you'll feel better after a bath."

In a sudden rush of uncertain feeling, Tori wondered if Bandit had taken other women to this oasis to make love to them. Was she just one of a string of those to have an assignation with the virile Midnight Bandit here in his purportedly secret place?

She tugged against his hand, resisting the pull that had taken her to the water's edge.

"What's wrong?" he asked. He released her hand, walking into the pool until the water was up to his waist, then dropping down until the water was up to his chin. He began rubbing his chest and shoulders vigorously.

"Who else have you brought here?" Tori asked, fervently hating the jealousy in her voice. Still, she was impelled to discover whether she was the only woman to have cooled her love-heated body in the pool after passionate lovemaking with Bandit.

Clouds had diminished the scant moonlight, but with Bandit now facing her from the pool, Tori placed one hand at the juncture of her thighs and the other across her breasts.

"Are you jealous?" He sounded amused at the prospect. His attitude did nothing to assuage Tori's newborn fears, or to bridge the distance that now separated them when only a few minutes earlier they had been as one.

"Of course not!" Tori shot back, sounding as haughty as possible under the circumstances. "I just want to know if there are spirits of past lovers lurking around, that's all."

"Spirits!" Bandit exclaimed.

He realized Tori was open, tender, and much too vulnerable for further jokes.

"Well?" she demanded.

"No, Tori, I've never taken anyone here but you," he said with absolute solemnity. "And to ensure that your spirit retains its privacy, you can rest assured in knowing that I will never again bring anyone here but you."

"That's a promise?"

"With all my heart." Bandit offered her a dazzling smile that made her want to trust him.

*My weakness for this man will be my undoing,* she

thought, though at that happy moment, she had no desire to be anything but "undone" by Bandit.

With her hands still strategically placed, Tori walked into the pool, then knelt in the water to conceal herself. The bed was solid rock, somewhat slippery with plant life, the water's temperature was cool enough to be refreshing and cleansing, but not so cold as to be uncomfortable.

They bathed in silence. He at one end of the pool, she at the other. Tori ran her hands over herself, washing away her own perspiration and Bandit's. After their lovemaking, the scents of their bodies had hovered about her, continually reminding her of what they'd done with each other, of what she'd felt. Tori had never before experienced that peculiar, unmistakable aroma—that of man and woman fresh from energetic loving. She filed it away in her memories.

She turned at last toward Bandit, shocked to see that while she'd been bathing, he'd taken off his mask to wash his face. But he had turned away from her, and was just now tying the black silk over his eyes once more. Tori had been lucky enough to get a glimpse of him without his mask, though for such a brief time and in such poor light that she still could not guess his identity.

"Doesn't the mask make it difficult to swim?" she teased, feeling more refreshed now that she'd spent ten minutes splashing about in the cool water. Bandit, it seemed, had again been right.

"I haven't gotten it wet," he replied, and Tori could hear a bit of tension in his voice. "I keep it on for your protection, not my own. I explained that to you already."

"I can protect myself," Tori replied softly. Trying to convince herself that it didn't matter whether he revealed himself to her or not hadn't worked. More than ever she wanted to know who he was . . . after all she'd shared with him.

"Sure you can," Bandit teased, moving closer to where she knelt, concealed in the shallow water.

"I can!" she replied petulantly, disliking her strength or courage questioned after having had to prove herself for much of her life.

"Even against me?" he asked, gliding toward her, only his head and those much-too-broad shoulders visible, his smile wolfish.

Now it was Tori's turn to smile. She retreated in the water, trying without much success to move away from the advancing Bandit while at the same time staying low enough to remain concealed.

When he closed in, reaching for her, she giggled playfully, trying to move faster. Her feet lost traction against the hard, slick bed of the pond, and she went under the surface.

"Oh, you!" she sputtered, bobbing up, without any of the anger she really wanted to display. "I didn't want to get my hair all wet!"

Tori raised her hands and, twisting her thick blond tresses into a roll, piled them atop her head. With her arms raised, her breasts were elevated above the surface of the water, where they glistened and glowed in the moonlight, the areolas soft pink, the nipples peaked from the cool water.

The sight of them froze Bandit. He knew he should not respond so forcefully to the sight of a woman's breasts; Tori's most certainly were not the first he had seen. But experience did not matter. Tori's breasts were the most beautiful he'd seen, big and round, riding high on her body, and in perfect proportion to the width of her shoulders, the narrowness of her waist, the erotic curve of her hips.

For several weighty seconds, Tori and Bandit remained motionless, looking into each other's eyes. She wanted to dip beneath the surface of the water to hide herself once more, but she also wanted to stand up so that he could see all of her. Torn between what was right and what was wrong, she stood absolutely still, her hands holding her hair above her head.

"Tori . . ." Bandit whispered breathlessly, closing the distance that separated them.

He moved close enough so that beneath the water his knees surrounded her hips. His gaze went down just briefly to her exposed breasts, and he felt himself coming to life in the water, expanding in response to Tori's un-practiced sensuality.

As she felt his thighs against her own, she saw the hunger for her in his dark eyes. So soon to make love again? she asked herself. She looked at his mouth, wanting his kisses once more, though not certain she could accept lovemaking once more. Contrary to her earlier denial, she felt a little sore now.

"So beautiful," Bandit whispered.

He raised his hands to her face. Tori closed her eyes, still keeping her arms over her head. She felt him touching her, starting at her forehead and trailing his hands down over her face, the contact of his fingertips barely more than a whisper of feeling yet shattering in their impact upon her senses.

A warbling sigh was emitted from Tori's throat as he circled her lips with a fingertip. The touch was so light

and soft, yet it aroused her deeply and made her feel she
was being kissed. When his hands moved lower, she angled her chin upward, exposing her throat to receive his
strange, feather-soft caresses.

Over her throat, chest, and shoulders Bandit's fingers
moved, and then lower still, into the valley of her breasts,
at first stroking in large circles, circles which became
tighter and tighter until at last he used only the tips of his
forefingers to follow the outline of her areolas.

He watched as her nipples elongated, and knew that her
passion had been reborn, as had his own.

On her knees in the cool, clear water, her hands above
her head and every nerve in her body fine-tuned and waiting for the ecstatic moment when Bandit would once again
touch the crests of her breasts in that manner she found
so exquisite, Tori could hardly breathe. Any second now,
she told herself . . . any second now. . . . And even though
she had very little experience in these matters, she knew
in her heart that he could make sweet love to her once
again, and that she could receive his passion.

The sound of loose rocks disturbed at the water's edge
jarred them from the moment.

Instantly, Bandit was on his feet, high-stepping it to
shore where his Colt rested in its black holster. He drew
the weapon and pulled back the hammer, his eyes searching the darkness for the enemy he was certain was upon
them.

When Tori had heard the rocks moving, scraping
against stone, she had not reacted as swiftly. To her left,
she saw what had caused the sound—a jackrabbit, having
come to get a drink from the oasis, had become on evening
meal for a desert fox. The struggle was short, and the fox

quickly carried her meal off into the darkness of the night with nothing more than a backward glance at the two unusually large creatures in the water.

Sadness struck Tori at the jackrabbit's fate. Though she knew that tonight the fox and her babies would eat well, the laws of nature could be tragic.

Why was it impossible for all living things to have what they needed? wondered Tori.

Bandit turned toward her after realizing what had caused the brief commotion.

"I guess I don't need this," he said, presenting his Colt as an object of humor. He tucked the pistol back into the black, form-fitting holster.

*Even when he is embarrassed, his movements are so smooth, so graceful,* Tori thought, watching him.

She loved looking at his body, with all its dormant power. Only the mask marred this picture of the American male at his finest. She never could ignore its significance.

Did he trust her? And where exactly in Bandit's life would Tori Singer fit? She tried to elude the question, but it hung with her.

It was time to get out of the water. Tori took a deep breath for courage, silently cursing herself for being a prude because she wished Bandit was not watching her. Then she straightened up.

He had seen her body before, of course. He'd seen her, touched her, tasted her . . . but that didn't stop him from staring at her as though he'd never before viewed a naked woman. Her voluptuous curves made her quintessentially feminine, dramatically so. Even though she was uncomfortable with her nudity, he could not obliged her modesty by taking his eyes from her.

The water running down her body drew Bandit's eyes. All he could think about as she walked slowly toward him was that he wanted her again, then and there. He'd throw her down on the hard rocks if necessary.

But that last thought told Bandit—and Mack Randolph as well—that he'd already gone much too far with Tori. He'd taken more from her than he had any right to. Something in the way she walked out of the water with her shoulders squared and her head held high, despite her pained modesty, told Bandit that. She was only being brave because of the things he'd done to her.

"Let me dry you," he offered, feeling the sexual tension evaporating. Picking up his cape, he shook off the dust, then held it up for Tori.

"It's so beautiful though," she said, looking at it, fighting hard not to cross her arms over herself to answer in some small measure the call to modesty.

"And so are you. Take the cape."

Tori took it gratefully. Then Bandit turned his back to her and started wiping the water from his arms and legs with his bare hands. Turning away also, Tori ran the silk cape over herself, and when she did, caught the lingering aroma of passion once more. Fresh memories were awakened in her, memories she immediately tamped down. There would be time enough later, when she was alone with her thoughts, to put this evening into proper perspective. Right now, with sunrise a few hours away, and standing so near Bandit without a stitch of clothing on, other matters needed her attention.

"Tori," he said, stepping up behind her, touching her lightly on the shoulder.

"We'd better get going." She held his cape against her. "Your stallion has to carry both of us, and we can't be sure those men won't pick up our trail."

"Of course," Bandit replied.

He dressed in silence, and so did Tori. When she got onto his horse, seated behind him, a tension, a nebulous emotional distance, had come between them.

Dawn was lighting the horizon when Bandit let Tori off his horse.

"Save a little of that money for yourself to buy a new horse," he said, getting out of the saddle so that he could look into her eyes. "I think Jonathon Krey can buy you that much."

"I told you before, I'm not in this for the money."

"I know you're not. I'm just suggesting that you use a little of it to help you with . . . expenses incurred doing business."

Tori smiled. Such an odd way of putting it. "What is it you do, Bandit?"

"What do I do? I steal from Jonathon Krey, just like you," he replied, showing the dimple in his cheek.

"No, I mean in real life, when you're not wearing that mask."

The question caught Bandit by surprise. He looked away, fully aware that she had a right to more honesty than he'd shown her, and knowing if he *were* to be honest with her, he would regret it. She was safer not knowing his identity.

"I'm sorry," Tori said quietly, bridging the silence. "I shouldn't have asked. I know that's not allowed."

"It's not really like that."

"Of course it is. It's exactly like that," Tori said.

Strong fingers seemed to grip her heart. She did not want to leave Bandit; she didn't want him to leave her. She had opened herself to him physically and emotionally, and now, with a painful separation at hand, she was getting the terrible, empty feeling that the evening had been memorable only for her. For him, it was just another night of adventure and seduction, entertaining, to be sure, but in no measure unique.

With any other man she could ask if she would see him again, but with Bandit, she couldn't even ask who he really was.

"Be careful about what you do with the money," Bandit said as he removed his Stetson. "Krey is going to be furious about what happened tonight."

"I'll be very careful. There are lots of people around here who need the money. I'll give it all away."

Hearing recrimination in Tori's voice, Bandit looked away. She deserved much more from him than he'd given her this evening.

"Be good to yourself," he said softly, touching her chin to turn her face toward him.

They kissed, softly and with sorrow. She gave him a quivering smile.

"Good-bye, Bandit. You be careful, too." Tori smiled, holding back tears.

She turned away and began walking the last hundred yards to her cabin, stepping out of the tree line while Bandit remained hidden. She felt him watching her, and though tears burned in her eyes, she would not let them fall.

Nothing that had happened on this night was anything she should be ashamed of or regret. That was what she needed to believe. But how could she when the only man who'd ever made her feel totally alive and beautiful was known to her only by his alias, the Midnight Bandit?

# Thirteen

"I want that bastard dead, do you hear me? Dead! Dead! Dead!" Jonathon Krey screamed, slamming a fist down on his desk.

Jeremy and Michael Krey knew better than to say anything at all whenever their father got into one of these murderous moods. There was no telling exactly which of them might suffer the brunt of Jonathon Krey's anger at a time like this, so it was best to just sit quietly and wait until his volcanic fury had spent itself and rational thought had returned to him.

"I thought we'd protected the payroll!" Jonathon shouted, still glaring at his sons. "Some smart guys you two are! You didn't even put the money in the safe!"

Michael thought, *We had money in the safe in your bedroom, and that didn't stop the Midnight Bandit.* His father's favored son, he knew that to say such words might well be a grave mistake.

"I want the Midnight Bandit dead right now!" Jonathon continued, throwing himself into his plush leather chair. Continuing to glower at his sons, he ordered: "If you haven't got the men to catch him, then find the men who can."

"The best man for the job would be Jedediah Singer,"

Michael suggested, spotting his chance to please his father and make his brother Jeremy look inadequate in the process.

"The bounty hunter?"

"The very one. He's the best tracker in the territory by far, and he's got a reputation for bringing corpses rather than prisoners back to town," Michael continued. "The Randolphs hired him last year when rustlers were making off with their northwest herd. He caught every one of the rustlers."

Jonathon nodded approvingly. "Yes, I remember that. But I thought he wouldn't work for anyone but himself. He's got a reputation for being a lone wolf."

"He only goes for men with dead or alive printed on their wanted posters," Michael explained. "And though what we're asking is a little different, I'm sure if he gets a few hundred dollars up front, he'll be happy to go after the Midnight Bandit. The reward won't even have to be that extravagant."

"I don't care what the reward is," Jonathon said quickly. "Money's not the issue. Make sure he gets enough to make this worth his while. I want him hungry for the Midnight Bandit. This isn't the time to try to save a few pennies." He looked from Michael to Jeremy and asked, "And why didn't *you* think of this? Why is it you always sit there like a deaf mute?"

Jeremy's face colored, his hatred for his father and brother increasing as it always did in these situations. He couldn't think of a single thing to say in his own defense, and that, too, infuriated him.

"Now, Father," a sweet feminine voice wheedled from the doorway.

Jena Krey glided into the room. Though it was nearly noon, she was still in a nightgown and robe, the robe untied to reveal an immodest amount of her slender, firm body. She walked around her father's desk, slipping her arms around him to kiss him first on the top of the head, then on the cheek.

"You know it isn't good to let your temper get the best of you," she continued, occasionally kissing her father's cheek or ear as she spoke. "Now try to calm down, and don't be so hard on Jeremy. He tries very hard to please you."

There wasn't another person in the world who could talk to Jonathon Krey that way. Jena alone had the power to calm him, just as she alone could tease him or occasionally talk down to him. She was her father's little girl, and it didn't matter that she was reputed to be a loose woman, or that everyone knew she had the blackest heart in the entire New Mexico territory. To Jonathon Krey, Jena was his beautiful child—and anyone who said otherwise was courting death.

"Close your robe," Jonathon said quietly when Jena was gliding out of the office. "You shouldn't walk around the house that way."

"Yes, Father," Jena replied over her shoulder, making no effort to pretend to comply.

When the men were again alone in the room, Jonathon said with deadly calm, "Hire Jedediah Singer. Pay whatever it takes. And tell him I'll pay double if the Midnight Bandit dies a slow and painful death."

"Yes, Father," Michael and Jeremy said in unison, each rising from his chair to leave.

\* \* \*

Mack was edgy. He had a problem with no easy solution.

How could he give Tori Singer a horse without her figuring out he was the Midnight Bandit?

She'd said she wouldn't use the stolen payroll money to buy a new mount for herself. She hated Jonathon Krey so much she just wouldn't do that. And Mack doubted that she had enough money of her own to buy a decent horse. She might be able to afford a forty-dollar nag, but she deserved much better than that.

She also deserved much better than the miserable treatment she'd received from the Midnight Bandit.

Mack tried to convince himself that their lovemaking had been mutually satisfying and mutually acceptable. But he knew he'd seduced her, a virgin with very little money and no experience with men.

He felt like a cretin. He'd known far too many rich young men who used exactly the same reasoning to excuse their seduction of household maids or young women from the outskirts of town. Certainly it was not rape; still these wealthy men used every social and economic advantage they had to get the pantalets off disadvantaged, naive women.

"Hell," Mack muttered aloud, sipping his cold coffee. He added some hot liquid from the silver pot on the tray.

Now what to do? he kept asking himself.

He had Jonathon Krey to imprison, Tori Singer to set free . . . and he wasn't at all certain he could accomplish either of his goals.

The butler knocked softly on the bedroom door and announced that the mail had arrived.

"Thank you, Juan. Leave it on the bed, and I'll see to it in a moment."

"Yes, sir," Juan, confused, placed an assortment of letters and packages on the bed, his brow furrowed with consternation. Since mail was always a priority for Señor Randolph, why was he making it await his attention? Whatever was playing upon Señor Randolph's mind, was evidently very important.

Mack stared out the bedroom window, sipping the rest of his coffee, seeking a believable excuse for giving Tori a good riding horse. He told himself he just had to think long enough on it and he'd come up with the answer.

He left his chair by the window and walked over to the bed. Running a finger across the envelopes there, he decided some were important, others not. All needed his attention, yet he didn't feel like giving any of them more than a minute of his time.

Any except one.

The handwriting was clearly that of his friend in Taos, the sheriff. Mack ripped open the envelope and read the letter quickly, allowing the enclosed bank draft to wait until he was finished. As he read, a smile stretched across his face.

The letter concerned a simple legal matter, one having more to do with a town's prejudice against bounty hunters than legality. Jedediah Singer had brought the corpse of a wanted murderer in to Taos, then had demanded the reward money. Several of the town's more fanatically religious men decided that Jedediah simply wasn't spiritual enough to warrant the bounty, so they refused to give him the money. The outlaw, they decided, had been struck down by a vengeful God, and therefore, Jedediah, the bounty hunter, wasn't due the reward.

Jedediah pointed out that the corpse had three bullet holes in his chest of exactly the same caliber as the gun currently in his own holster. This argument was conveniently and self-righteously ignored by the town's leaders.

Rather than getting into a gunfight when he was drastically outnumbered and outgunned, Jedediah returned to Santa Fe and hired an attorney, Mack Randolph, to see what he could do to right the wrong.

Several snappy letters from Mack to the town leaders in Taos convinced them that they would be ahead financially if they simply did the legal, proper thing, and paid Jedediah Singer the money owed him. The sheriff's letter accompanying the bank draft for one thousand dollars strongly suggested that neither Jedediah Singer nor Mack Randolph be seen in Taos in the near future.

Mack picked up the draft. He could either ride into town and deposit it into his own account, holding the money in escrow until he saw Jedediah next, or he could ride to the Singer cabin and deliver it in person.

There was no question of what he would do. Worth much more than the three thousand dollars he'd paid out was the excuse to see Tori.

As Juan knocked again on his bedroom door, Mack groaned with impatience. Delays were intolerable now that he knew his destination: Tori.

"There's a young woman here to see you, sir." Juan stuck his head inside the room.

"Who?" Mack asked excitedly, thinking his luck might be getting better and Tori had come to him.

"Señorita Krey, sir. She said it was very important she speak to you privately. She's waiting for you in the library."

Mack's training as a lawyer helped him keep his disappointment from showing, but as soon as Juan had closed the door, he shook his head angrily. He didn't want to deal with Jena Krey now, and he wasn't pleased with himself for momentarily overlooking the fact that Tori Singer did not know he was the Midnight Bandit.

Jena, wearing an amazingly low-cut gown inappropriate for morning wear, was lounging on the sofa when he arrived in the library. Her pose, the position she intended to be "caught" in when Mack arrived, was one of indolent boredom and smoldering sensuality. She had the look of a woman who had either spent the last few hours making love or who intended to spend the next few hours in that pursuit.

"You've kept me waiting," she pouted. "I'll have you know, there aren't many men who dare do that without facing my wrath."

Mack smiled. As annoying as Jena was, she was a one-of-a-kind woman.

"Not many men?" Mack asked with a faintly mocking arched brow. "I'm not in a category by myself?"

"Darling Mack, you know I like to keep my options open. It's good business, and if Father's taught me anything, it's that business always comes first," Jena said with absolute honesty. Her blue gaze was slowly peeling off Mack's clothes. When he decided to sit in the wingbacked chair instead of beside her on the sofa, she pouted in annoyance.

"What did you come to see me for, Jena? You obviously want something."

"Something? No, darling, I want *someone*. You, for instance." She smiled and nibbled on her lower lip, favoring him with a practiced look combining sensuality and little-girl innocence. "But you've known that all along, haven't you?"

"Jena, I've a very busy day ahead of me, and I really haven't got time for this. Please, can we get to the point of your coming here?"

She drew a knee up and hugged it to her chest, allowing her other leg to remain stretched out. Her gown was pulled up, displaying a stocking-sheathed leg to well above the knee.

Mack looked at her display, and once again only his legal training prevented his thoughts from showing in his expression. Jena Krey was definitely beautiful, and her skill in the sensual realm could not be denied. If Mack hadn't spent the early morning hours in Tori's arms, he would have been mightily tempted to taste her blatant offering. But as it was, the memory of Tori fresh and clear in his consciousness, Jena appeared to be an attractive trollop, much too open about what it was she wanted to be truly seductive. The more he looked at her, the less tempted he was.

"Nobody can be *that* busy, darling," Jena purred. "Haven't you time to take a little nourishment?"

Mack smiled at that. "Nourishment? What an interesting way to put it."

"And I am the interesting woman to give you that nourishment." Jena slid just a little lower on the sofa, just enough to make the hem of her gown rise higher still to reveal the top of her stocking, and an inch of creamy white flesh between that and the bottom of her pantalets. "But then, you already know that, don't you?"

"Yes, Jena, I do," Mack said, not denying truths he

couldn't rationally dispute. "I also know that you want something more than just . . . nourishment. Now, once again, I'm very busy, so unless you get to the point of your visit, I'll have to leave you to your own devices."

Jena laughed softly. "I've been left to my own devices before, my darling, and I've managed to have an absolutely wonderful time. Actually, it's a guaranteed wonderful time. Not quite the same as having a good man with me, but wonderful nevertheless."

Her openness shocked even Mack, who'd believed Jena was no longer capable of shocking him.

"As long as you're being such a prig about this," she continued, "I suppose I must go along with it—for now. I'm here to discuss with you a union."

"Marriage?"

"Call it what you want. You're going to be an important man in the territory, and I want to be there at your side when you become territorial governor."

"We've already talked about this, Jena, and you know what my answer is."

"Mack darling, you'll find that I can be a wonderful companion . . . or I can be an enemy with the power to keep you from office." Jena's expression evolved from coy seduction to steely resolve. "Think about that. You can't make governor without me, and I can't live in the governor's mansion without you. It's a good deal for both of us."

"You're assuming I want the governorship that much, Jena. You're also assuming that I can't get the votes without your help. You could be wrong on both counts."

Jena got up from the sofa. She would not get to sample Mack's sensual skills on this afternoon, but she was not defeated. This was merely a minor setback, one that would be righted later on, after Mack realized the truth of her offer.

She went to him and placed her hands on the arms of his chair. She bent low, bringing her face close to his, giving him an unimpeded view down the bodice of her gown.

"Just think about it, Mack," she said, then kissed his cheek when he turned his mouth away from her.

She was out of the library moments later, leaving him smiling and shaking his head. Jena Krey was the most audacious woman ever to walk the planet. He was certain of it. And though he couldn't hate her with the vehemence he felt she deserved, neither could he allow himself to touch her again. Now that he'd touched Tori, Jena looked pale, frail, and only remotely feminine by comparison.

He went to his bedroom, deciding to change clothes for his ride to the Singer ranch. He wanted to present just the right appearance, for with any luck at all, Jedediah wouldn't be home and he'd have Tori all to himself. He hoped Tori would not make the connection between Mack Randolph and the Midnight Bandit.

Though Jena was fanning herself constantly, she was still perspiring. Perspiring was such a low-class thing to do, even if it was hot and all of this had happened because she'd tried to talk reasonably to Mack about a perfectly acceptable arrangement.

He'd refused her once again.

Jena gritted her teeth in anger as she thought about the open invitation she'd given him and how he'd turned her down. Getting turned down was not something Jena was accustomed to; it infuriated her. More annoying than anticipating physical pleasure with Mack and not getting it was his attitude of indifference toward the office of territorial governor.

Jena thought with certainty, *I can stonewall him politically, or I can buy him the office.*

How could she make Mack realize that he needed her? She wanted all the privileges that went along with being the wife of the territorial governor. She lusted for them and for power with even greater ardor than she lusted for Mack's body. Mack was great in bed. Positively heaven. But sex only went so far. It wasn't as good as buying new gowns or having round-the-clock servants to tend to her every whim.

Somehow, some way, Jena had to convince Mack that his life and his ambitions would be destroyed unless he took her as his wife.

Maybe she could get Jeremy to assist her. Her brother was essentially very stupid, Jena decided, and she had always been able to get him to do whatever she wanted.

She smiled and leaned back in the carriage, stifling an urge to yell at the coachman. She would be home soon enough, and then she could strip off all her clothes, take a cool bath, and sip mint juleps until she no longer minded the heat of the day.

She'd find an answer to getting Mack Randolph under her control. Jena was certain of it.

# Fourteen

Mack pulled his mount, a long-legged white gelding that ran like the wind, to a halt at the edge of the tree line. Actually, he was very near the spot where, in the persona of the Midnight Bandit, he had said good-bye to Tori Singer on the previous day before dawn.

He wanted to give both his horse and himself a breather so he'd look professional when he arrived at the Singer cabin. After all, no attorney rode at a full gallop just to deliver a bank draft to a bounty hunter.

"Easy, boy," Mack said, patting the gelding's neck as the powerful young animal pranced beneath him. The horse loved to run, and Mack had given him free rein. So easily recognized by its size and its unusual white coat, the gelding could not be ridden by the Midnight Bandit.

The cabin was a hundred yards away, one of any number of dwellings in the area, all built pretty much the same. A single large room cordoned off into smaller rooms by walls that didn't reach the ceiling, which allowed the heat to move from room to room in the winter, or more simply by blankets hanging from strategically placed ropes.

Suddenly, Mack felt like a teenager again, and the sensation brought a boyish smile to his lips. How long had it been since he'd felt giddy about a woman? That was how Tori made him feel. She didn't know it, of course. In fact, as attorney Mack Randolph, he had had very little association with Tori; but as the Midnight Bandit, they had become closer than he'd ever dreamed possible.

Could he ever tell her that he was the Midnight Bandit? The question had plagued him since he'd last left her.

For this meeting, Mack had dressed carefully, choosing one of his finer charcoal gray suits, a simple white shirt, shiny black boots polished just that morning by Juan to a mirror finish, and a gray Stetson with a rattlesnake leather hatband. Gone were the cape and mask, the black clothing from head to toe, the low-slung Colt at his hips. Gone, too, would be the flinty tone of voice so difficult to maintain, especially with Tori when his thoughts and emotions were anything but hard edged.

"Come on, boy," Mack said, tapping his heels against his horse's ribs. "Let's go find out what the Fates have in store for us."

He rode slowly toward the house, taking his time so that he would be noticed long before he actually got there. A leisurely approach was proper out here, where thieves and desperadoes killed without reason, possessing not a drop of compassion. He wanted to give Tori a good long look at him so she would not feel threatened.

Surprisingly, he was quite close to the cabin before she stepped out onto the dusty porch. Mack's heart did a crazy little flip at the sight of her. Her unbound hair cascaded over her shoulders in a profusion of silken blond waves; she filled out a blue cotton shirt, washed countless times, and faded blue denim trousers that displayed the now-familiar curves of her hips.

Mack was already lost in her presence.

"Evening," he said, remaining on his gelding, waiting—in the custom of the area—to be asked to dismount.

Tori looked at him, suspicion shining strong and clear in her pale green eyes. "Evening," she said, as noncomittally as possible. "There a reason you're here?" She didn't much care for lawyers, especially rich ones.

Mack suppressed a grin. Clearly, she didn't recognize him as the Midnight Bandit, for which he was thankful. But her contempt for the wealthy was evident, as was her distrust of him.

"I've come to see your brother." Then, in an effort to get into Tori's good graces, he said, "I've got some money for him."

Tori continued to look at Mack as though trying to judge whether or not he was an immediate threat. Finally she turned away, and only then did he see that she'd been holding a sawed-off double-barreled shotgun just behind her leg, ready to use it at a moment's notice.

"Come on in," she said over her shoulder, apparently as friendly as she intended to be. "I was just making a cup of coffee for myself. You can have a cup if you want."

Mack dismounted and tied his horse to the hitching post, then stepped onto the porch and into the cabin. It was stark and austere as Mack remembered it. He had an urge to take Tori out of here and put her in a house where there were more comforts—the comforts he knew.

"It's not the Randolph ranch, but it suits Jedediah and myself," Tori said, moving over to the stove.

Mack wasn't certain what to say to this sarcastic remark. He pulled out one of two chairs at the rectangular table and sat down, watching her back, wondering what she'd really think of him if she knew who his alter ego was.

She placed an enameled tin cup on the table, then filled it. The rich aroma was pleasing to Mack, and he suspected that Tori was a good cook.

*Stop thinking that way!* he chided himself. *Next you'll be wondering if she'll be a good mother to your children!*

"What are you looking at?" Tori asked, her green eyes narrowing.

"I'm sorry," Mack said sheepishly, unaware of how he'd been looking at her. "I was just thinking of something."

"I'll bet you were," she shot back contemptuously.

Mack leaned back in his chair, giving Tori as much of a scrutiny as she'd given him.

"Why do you get so angry with me?" he asked. "I haven't done anything or said anything to displease you. At least, nothing that I can think of. But every time I've seen you, you've made no effort at all to hide the fact that you dislike me intensely."

Tori was shocked by his bluntness, and it took her a moment to compose herself. Then she shrugged her shoulders, unconscious of how the gesture made her breasts move beneath the overwashed cotton shirt.

"It's nothing against you personally," she said finally. "I just don't like rich people. They're always looking down their noses at Jedediah and me. They cause all sorts of problems and do whatever they please and the law doesn't touch them. It's nothing personal, but I think you and rich people like you simply cause more trouble in a person's life than you're worth."

"What would happen if you became rich? Would you hate yourself then?"

Tori laughed, a rich, amused laugh that pleased Mack enormously. Her rare laughter was a special pleasure he'd learned to savor because it was so delightfully spontaneous.

"Me? Now how would I get rich? No, that's not likely at all!" She laughed again, poured a cup of coffee for herself, then sat down at the table and faced Mack. "Mr. Randolph, you are a funny man."

"Call me Mack. We've been on a first-name basis before."

He looked at Tori, wondering what she really thought of him. Did she hate him, or was it just anger toward people like the Kreys coming out in her? What if she never got over her prejudice against successful people? Would she always have to be the Midnight Bandit, just so he could be with Tori without her hating him? What if she thought of him for all time as a "funny man," someone not to be taken seriously?

"Jedediah will be back soon, if that's what you're wondering," Tori said. "He returned from a trip just a little while ago and headed off to the stream to clean up. He wants to go into town." Tori shook her head slowly, a fragment of a smile tickling her mouth. "He thinks I don't know about the gal he's got there. He can't hide anything from me."

"But can you hide what you do from him?"

Mack watched Tori's cheeks color slightly. There was anger, fresh and new and spiteful, shining in her eyes as she looked at him. "I don't see as how that's any of your business, Mr. Lawyer."

"I didn't mean anything by it."

Her mouth twisted into a sneer. "You lawyers always mean something by everything."

He was not a man given to apologizing needlessly or insincerely, but he said, "I am sorry, Tori. I didn't mean to offend you, and I hope you believe me when I say that."

She looked at him in silence, weighing the truth and sincerity of his words. Finally, very slowly, the anger faded from her eyes. "Apology accepted, Mack. I've had plenty of trouble with rich folks in the past. I just wanted you to know from the very beginning that you weren't going to come here to my house and start telling me what to do."

"I wouldn't do that anywhere; certainly not in your own house." Mack sipped his coffee. It was delicious, though it didn't please him nearly as much as the fact that Tori's attitude toward him had taken a marked turn toward the positive. "There's a dance coming up in Santa Fe," he commented.

"There's always some dance or other coming up in Santa Fe," she replied caustically. Her anger obviously wasn't ever far from the surface.

"Yes, it seems so. Just the same, there's a special dance coming up the sixteenth." Mack looked away briefly, thinking himself a silly fool for feeling so nervous. "Would you like to go to the dance with me? I would be honored if you would."

Before Tori could respond, a shout came from outside, followed immediately by the pounding of hooves.

"Mack! Mack, is that you?" Jedediah called out.

Randolph rose from his chair and went to the open doorway. Jedediah was just reining his horse to a dusty halt. His hair was wet, his face freshly shaven, his clothes clean.

"Evening, Jedediah," Mack said.

They clasped hands and the smile Jedediah gave him was exuberant.

"It's good to see you again. I've been on the hunt for the past three weeks."

"Catch who you were looking for?"

"Yep. They won't be robbing no more banks, neither." Jedediah stepped into the cabin and kissed his sister on the cheek. "Thanks for keeping my friend company while I was gone," he said to her.

"He wasn't much trouble," Tori said. She rose and walked through the kitchen area toward the back of the cabin. "Good to see you again, Mack," she said before disappearing.

Mack watched her retreating figure, wanting desperately to get an answer from her yet not wanting Jedediah to get involved. He knew how protective of her Tori's brother was, and he was healthily cautious of how Jedediah would react to learning of what he, in the guise of the Midnight Bandit, had done with Tori.

The business with Jedediah was conducted, Mack explaining that it really hadn't been any trouble to ride to the cabin to deliver the bank draft to his client. Jedediah Singer had little formal education, but he suspected there was something more behind this act than a business courtesy.

"Who's the gal you've got in town?" Mack asked. There was a finger's worth of fine Kentucky sour mash whiskey in his cup now instead of coffee.

Jedediah grinned. "Can't understand at all what she sees in me, but she sees something. We've got to keep it all quiet though. You know what the folks in Santa Fe think of bounty hunters."

"To tell you the truth, they don't think much of lawyers, either."

Jedediah grinned even more. "Maybe not. But mothers tell their daughters to marry a lawyer. They don't tell them to run off and marry some bounty hunter, now, do they?"

They laughed again and raised their cups in a silent toast. Mack decided he liked Jedediah more than he'd previously thought, and he hoped that whatever happened between himself and Tori wouldn't change his relationship with him.

"I don't mean to rush you along. . . ." Jedediah left the sentence unfinished.

"I've got to be running," Mack said, taking the hint, annoyed that he'd have to leave without getting the answer he wanted from Tori. In truth, he wanted much more from her than just her consent to go to the dance with him, but that was an issue he hadn't yet completely resolved.

An instinct told Mack that he should be seen in public with Tori. He couldn't say why he felt this way. Maybe to balance their secret relationship, hidden in shadows and darkness, behind masks and separate identities . . . he just didn't know. But he wanted the whole world to see him with Tori Singer at his side, and he was willing to move heaven and earth, to thumb his nose at Santa Fe society to accomplish this feat.

Mack and Jedediah shook hands once more. As Mack stepped out the door, Jedediah rushed to his bedroom where the small gold necklace he'd bought for his sweetheart rested, wrapped in three layers of tissue and tucked under his mattress so that Tori wouldn't find it.

"Mack . . ."

Mack turned quickly toward the sound. Tori was standing at the edge of the cabin, leaning against it with apparent nonchalance, though the set of her mouth and the look in her jade green eyes suggested she was not feeling casual.

"Hello," he replied, suddenly unable to think of anything to say.

"I can't go to the dance with you."

His heart sank. "Why not? It's just a dance."

He saw the anger—that damnable anger always so near the surface with her—spring forth again. "It's just another dance to you, Mack, but not to me. I don't have the fancy clothes to go to your kind of dance."

Tori turned and walked away, disappearing around the corner of the cabin. Mack rushed after her, reaching out to take her arm. She pulled out of his grasp, spinning to face him.

"I'm sorry," he said, looking down into her lovely face, wanting to take her into his arms, knowing that she'd fight him like a wildcat if he tried. "I didn't understand. I just didn't think—"

"That's right!" Tori cut in fiercely. "You just didn't think!"

These weren't easy words to swallow, not for a man who had graduated second in his law class and who was considered by friends and enemies alike as extremely intelligent. But they were true.

"We don't have to be enemies," he said.

"Of course we do!" Tori raised her hands in protest, then brought them down to slap her thighs. "Don't you understand anything at all? You're a man and I'm a woman; you're rich and I'm poor. Good Lord! We're *natural* enemies!"

Now it was Mack's turn to shake his head slowly in disgust, and to look upon Tori with something less than respect in his eyes. "We're not natural enemies. What makes us enemies is your narrow sense of right and wrong, your bias."

"Me? Biased? It's your 'society' that won't accept me!"

"And you won't accept me!" Mack shot back, his anger rising. "The knife cuts both ways. You're the monster you hate, railing against biases of others, then letting your own thoughtless resentments rule your life and dictate your actions."

He turned on his heel, heading toward his horse before he said any more to the young woman who'd infuriated him so.

But she rushed after him, taking his arm and forcing him to face her. When he looked down at her, a rush went through Mack. How lovely she was, faintly flushed, young and vibrantly alive! Powerful memories came over him as he recalled the subtle expressions that had played across her face while they'd made love.

"I'm sorry," Tori said. An apology from her, strong-willed and stubborn as she was, was even more rare than one from Mack.

He acted without thinking. The sincerity in her voice made him forget their differences. He bent low and kissed her lips, softly at first and then with a bit more pressure, a little more desire. His arms wound round her waist and he pulled her closer to once again feel the firm, tantalizing warmth of her breasts pressing against his chest. And when the tip of his tongue touched her lips and they parted just slightly to allow partial entrance, Mack's passion burst into flame within his heart.

Tori was stunned that Mack Randolph had kissed her. She closed her eyes . . . and at that moment, with her eyes closed, her body and her senses told her what her eyes had not seen. The society lawyer in the exquisitely fashionable charcoal gray suit was also the enigmatic Midnight Bandit, who wore a Colt at his hip, a mask over his eyes, and a black cape to keep him hidden in shadow.

When the kiss finally ended, Tori took a step away, a hand over her mouth, her eyes wide with shock. Mack Randolph was the Midnight Bandit! Her head was spinning. Everything she'd ever thought she knew about humanity, about society, was now in question. Her eyes studied Mack. This was the Midnight Bandit—the mysterious masked man she'd shared her passion with!

Jedediah stepped around the corner of the cabin, a strange look on his face. "What are you two doing over here? Mack, I thought you'd be gone by now."

"I'm just leaving," he said coldly.

After kissing Tori, he'd looked into her eyes, and the horror and shock he'd seen in their green depths was unmistakable. He didn't choose to wait around to hear what she thought of him—it was written in that look. She was disgusted that he, a rich lawyer, had kissed her.

He rushed to his big white gelding and climbed into the saddle. "Jedediah, you stay out of trouble now," he said, turning his horse around to ride off.

"Mack, wait!" Tori called out. She walked over and placed a hand lightly on the toe of Mack's boot as he sat in the saddle. She tried to smile up at him. "I'd go to the dance with you, but I just don't have the proper clothes. And even if I did, those people would never accept me. That's the way it is. I'm sorry. I'd feel out of place."

"Sure," Mack said. He wanted to ask Tori how she could be brave enough to sneak into Jonathon Krey's bedroom to steal his money, but not brave enough to go to a dance where some privileged young women might look down their noses at her.

Mack rode off, wondering whether the differences that separated him from Tori would always be as insurmountable as they now seemed.

# Fifteen

As Mack rode off in one direction, another rider was approaching from the south, his horse moving at an easy pace. Tori welcomed the newcomer at first because he drew Jedediah's attention away from her. She didn't want her brother asking what she and Mack had been talking about at the side of the cabin.

A subtle smile played across the lush fullness of Tori's mouth. Her brother had never considered the possibility that she and the sophisticated lawyer, Mack Randolph, might be kissing, that a man of Mack's wealth and style would be physically drawn to her. Jedediah had always been very protective of his younger sister, especially after the murders of their parents and siblings. Jedediah and Tori being the only family left, they had developed a bond that had grown and strengthened over the years . . . though there was still much about her that he knew nothing of.

"What's *he* doing here?" Jedediah murmured, squinting at the rider heading their way.

Tori looked at the man. She could make out a figure, but it was still too far away to recognize.

"Who is it?" she asked finally, curiosity getting the better of her. Her brother's superior eyesight annoyed her.

"Jeremy Krey."

Cold, raw fear jolted Tori, painful as a bucket of ice water poured over her after a steaming bath.

*He's coming to have me arrested,* she thought. She struggled against the impulse to rush into the cabin to retrieve her double-barreled shotgun; Jedediah had shortened the barrels on it. It could stop man or beast at a range of thirty yards.

But if Jeremy Krey was coming to arrest her, where was the sheriff? Jeremy certainly wouldn't come alone, knowing how protective and dangerous Jedediah was.

"Are you all right?" her brother asked then. He'd been looking at his sister's profile, watching the blood draining from her face.

"Me? Sure, I'm fine," Tori replied glibly. She stepped onto the porch, turning her back to her brother. "I haven't got time to stand around here doing nothing. I'll have some good jackrabbit stew going in no time."

"I don't know if I'll be around long enough to eat. There's something in town I've got to do."

Tori turned and grinned at her brother. "I'll just bet there's something in Santa Fe you've got to do . . . and I'll be polite enough to not ask her name."

She went inside, leaving her brother to meet Jeremy. She did not want a face-to-face meeting with any Krey unless it was absolutely necessary, and since Jeremy was riding alone, his visit couldn't possibly have anything to do with the break-in at the Krey mansion.

Still, curiosity was killing her. From the kitchen, she could hear Jeremy and Jedediah talking in low tones on the porch . . . but what were they saying? Neither raised his voice, yet neither whispered, indicating that Jeremy wasn't angry, or trying to keep a secret.

So what was it all about?

From the cupboard, Tori pulled out her brother's bottle of homemade rye whiskey—the cheap stuff made by Jack Bowden, not the special Kentucky sipping whiskey—and two clean glasses. Though every cell in her body rebelled at the thought of pleasing any Krey in any way, she stepped out onto the porch, a smile on her face.

"With all that talking, I thought you two might need something to wet your throats," she said.

Jeremy Krey put the stopper back into the gold, engraved flask that he and Jedediah had been passing back and forth, and put it back into the inside pocket of his jacket.

"This may be a bit strong for your taste," Jedediah said to Jeremy as he took the glass from Tori. He waited until his sister had poured three fingers' worth of whiskey into each glass before nodding his approval to her. "It's not as smooth as what you've got in that flask."

"I'm sure it's got character," Jeremy said before sipping the whiskey.

The liquor burned going down his throat, very nearly bringing tears to his eyes, but he kept his contempt for the harsh brew to himself. He couldn't afford to insult Jedediah. The bounty hunter's reputation with a gun was unequaled, and Jeremy needed Jedediah's services to catch the Midnight Bandit.

Casting a sideways glance at Tori, Jeremy was pleased with what he saw. He'd long thought she had the potential to be beautiful if only she'd make the effort. But how could any woman be beautiful when she insisted upon wearing blue denim trousers, like a man, and spent her time tending to cattle and riding the range? And no woman could expect to draw and hold Jeremy Krey's attention long enough for him to take her to bed if she insisted on wearing a Colt at her hip.

He wondered what she would look like without any clothes on. At that thought, a smile ever so faintly creased Jeremy's mouth. Dressed, she was a curvaceous tomboy; without clothes, Tori would be just another woman for him to have his fun with.

"A little more?" Jedediah asked, breaking into Jeremy's reverie.

"What?" He looked at the bounty hunter uncomprehendingly. Mental images of a naked Tori Singer had really gripped him. "Oh, whiskey! No, no more for me, thanks." When Tori turned to go back into the cabin, Jeremy felt compelled to ask her to stay. Even with trousers on, she was something to look at. "Stick around, Tori. Maybe you can offer your brother some advice on a proposition I've just presented to him."

She stopped, a quizzical look on her face. Jeremy wondered if he could get her into bed, and what she'd be like once he got her there.

"You've been reading about the Midnight Bandit in the newspaper, haven't you?" Jedediah asked. Tori nodded. "Jeremy wants me to hunt him down. He's offering ten thousand dollars, if I can bring him in."

"No questions asked. Just bring me his corpse and the money's all yours. Of course, you'll have to prove that the body is really the Midnight Bandit's," Jeremy explained.

"Of course," Jedediah replied. He thought of the bounty from Taos that had been so difficult to collect, but he'd heard no rumor that Jonathon Krey was a man who didn't pay his debts.

A wave of nausea swept over Tori. Her own brother hunting the Midnight Bandit . . . hunting Mack Randolph, her lover! How could the Fates be so cruel as to set her own brother against the one man who had shown her any pleasure, given her any happiness?

"W-Why? Why you?" Tori asked her brother, trying to keep the emotion from her voice, though not doing a very good job of it. "I thought you only went after murderers. The Midnight Bandit has never murdered anyone. I'm *sure* he hasn't."

"How can you be so sure?" Jeremy asked with a dismissive sneer. "He's a thief. He's probably a murderer as well."

"You don't know that," Tori snapped back. "The newspapers have never said that he's fired a gun against anyone. He's only been seen a couple times, from what I've read, and then it was from a great distance."

Jeremy, his face stern, turned toward Jedediah. "See, this is exactly why the Midnight Bandit has to be brought to justice. The newspapers have turned a common thief into some kind of hero! This kind of reaction to the Midnight Bandit has got to be crushed, I tell you!"

Jedediah nodded his head slowly, but he could not completely dismiss what his sister had said. As a bounty hunter, he read the wanted posters and decided for himself who he'd go after, made his own judgment as to who most needed to be brought to justice, who presented the greatest danger to decent people. The reward for the capture of the Midnight Bandit would be five hundred dollars from the businessmen of Santa Fe—Jedediah knew that the

Kreys had spearheaded the drive to make the Midnight Bandit a wanted man with a price on his head—and the ten thousand dollars was an additional inducement put up by Krey. There really was no good reason for a "Dead or Alive" tag on the wanted poster, since the Midnight Bandit hadn't killed anyone. He hadn't even stolen a cent from the general public, only from Jonathon Krey.

"You see what I'm talking about, I trust," Jeremy said, forcing the last of the cheap whiskey down his throat. He hated the taste of it, and he didn't really like being in such close proximity to men like Jedediah Singer, but he needed the bounty hunter's services, and until he had them, he would continue to pretend to be enjoying the companionship. "What about giving you an advance against the bounty?"

"Advance against the bounty?" Jedediah was puzzled. He'd never heard of getting paid for a job not yet begun.

"Call it working expenses. Say . . . two hundred dollars . . ." He reached into his pocket, extracted a wad of bills folded in half, and began counting them out in front of Jedediah, making sure the bounty hunter could see each bill as it flipped forward.

"I don't know about that," Jedediah said quietly, distracted by anticipation of the delights he could have that very evening with a pocket full of money. The young lady he had been seeing would be enormously impressed. Still, he couldn't quite shake the notion of a trap, and if he accepted the money, he'd be stepping into it. "Somehow, it doesn't seem quite right to get paid for something that isn't done yet."

"Don't you worry about that. I have every confidence in you."

"Still . . ."

"Perhaps five hundred would be more in keeping with your expectations," Jeremy said, sensing Jedediah's weakening state. He flipped several more bills over in his hand. Five hundred dollars was every penny he'd taken with him from his home, so he counted the money out slowly realizing the effect it had on a man like Jedediah.

"I don't think you should do it," Tori said, a witness to the scene, her fears galloping unchecked. No matter how skilled the Midnight Bandit was, she was certain her brother could track him down and capture him . . . or kill him.

"This is business for men," Jeremy said crisply, no longer finding the voluptuous blonde's companionship so appealing. "Why not leave the decision up to your brother?"

"Jedediah, I just—"

"Shut up, woman!" Jeremy snapped. He positively loathed women who didn't know their place.

He saw the dangerous glint in Jedediah's eyes, and knew instantly that he'd made a terrible mistake. In a flash of precognizance, he pictured himself in a duel with Jedediah Singer, and that was horrifying. Jeremy had never been particularly good with guns. The two men he'd shot had been hit in the back, one from ambush and the other as he was running away. He wouldn't have a similar advantage with Jedediah.

"I'm terribly sorry," Jeremy said, not to Tori but to Jedediah. He hated apologizing to people of inferior station. "This business with the Midnight Bandit has gotten my family—and me—terribly upset. I apologize for what I said to Tori. I'm sure she's only trying to do what's best.

Jedediah, what about you taking this five hundred, and considering it just half of your advance? You can ride into town and I'll have another five hundred in cash waiting for you." Jeremy saw the stony anger in the bounty hunter's eyes. "Well, as soon as I get back home, I'll draw out another five hundred and have a rider bring it straight here to you. How would that suit you?"

Tori wanted to scream at her brother, to tell him not to take the money, but her personal involvement shouldn't be too obvious. She didn't need more problems than those she already faced.

"Rather than making a decision now, why don't you sleep on it?" she suggested softly, her hand resting on her brother's forearm. "You were going into town tonight, right? Why let this ruin your fun?"

Jedediah looked first at Tori, then at Jeremy Krey. "My sister's got a point. This kind of job—it's real different for me. Bank robbers that murder folks, rapists and those kinds of varmint—they're no more than animals. That's why I hunt them down like animals. But this Midnight Bandit, he's never killed anyone. Sure, he's stolen from you and your family, but it doesn't seem to me that he's exactly taken your last penny. I don't have to be a lawman to know that you Kreys haven't exactly been on the right side of the law in all you do."

"Neither have you," Jeremy said, grinning falsely. "Perhaps we've bent a rule here and there, Jedediah. I won't insult your intelligence by pretending otherwise. But you can't say that the Kreys have ever had anyone murdered, now can you?"

Actually, the Krey name had been linked to several

murders, though nothing had been proven; but Jedediah kept this to himself.

"Sometimes you've got to bend the rules to make money," Jeremy continued, his tone friendly, man to man. He didn't look in Tori's direction. "That's just the way life is."

"Your life, maybe," Tori said.

Jedediah hooked his thumbs into his gunbelt. "Let me sleep on this one. Maybe I will take it on, and maybe I won't. Either way, I won't be pushed for or against by either one of you two. The offer is real generous, and I'll keep that in mind."

"When can I have your answer?" Jeremy asked. At that moment he was so furious with Tori he could have slapped her to the ground, then put a boot to her—but for Jedediah and his deadly skills.

"Soon. Tomorrow, maybe. I've got some celebrating to do. I just returned after being gone better than a month, and I want to find out what it's like to sleep in my own bed again."

After Jeremy had ridden away, Tori started in again on why her brother should turn the job down, even though it promised a substantial amount of money. Jedediah, though, was more interested in getting to Santa Fe and in seeing the pleasure in a certain young woman's eyes when he gave her the necklace he'd bought.

Tori waited until Jedediah had ridden away before heading for the Randolph ranch to warn Mack. Unfortunately, Daisy had been killed, which forced her to make the twelve-mile walk on foot. It was not something she looked forward to. The desert was filled with dangers during daylight, even more at night.

But what choice did she have? She couldn't consider doing anything else until she had warned Mack of the possibility of being Jedediah's prey.

If she kept up a brisk pace, she could arrive at the Randolph ranch in three to four hours. With a large canteen of fresh water slung over her shoulder, Tori headed out, Jeremy's words and the threat in them playing over and over in her mind.

"What do you mean he's not here? He's *got* to be here!" Tori said to Juan, the butler, who flatly refused to allow her through the gargantuan front doors of the Randolph ranch house.

"Perhaps I can be of some assistance," a male voice said from inside.

The butler stepped away, after giving Tori one last disdainful look. Apparently, he was unaccustomed to women who wore Levi's arriving at the ranch long after sundown and requesting a private meeting with Señor Randolph, the younger. The butler's incredulity only served to heighten Tori's awareness of the differences between her world and the one Mack lived in.

Paul Randolph, Mack's older brother, opened the door wide and stepped aside for Tori to enter. "I'm sure whatever the problem is, it isn't nearly as bad as it now seems."

His smile was polite and politic—not friendly, to be sure, but at least polite—and that was about as much as Tori could expect.

"Thank you for letting me in. I've got to speak with

Mack immediately. It's terribly, terribly, terribly important that I do."

"Three terriblys in one problem!" Paul's eyebrows did a little dance of amusement. "Let's step into the library and we can discuss this terrible problem. You look exhausted, if I may be so bold as to say so."

"I had to walk here."

Her answer brought Paul up short. "From your house?" he asked, knowing how far away it was. Tori nodded, and suddenly Paul Randolph was taking this "terrible" problem much more seriously. "You can take your gunbelt off. You won't need your pistol while you're here, I can assure you."

Tori had never before given up her guns for anyone. However, now it seemed the proper thing to do. Though wealthy, the Randolphs were entirely different from the Kreys. After a second or two of doubt, she removed her pistol and holster and handed them to Juan, who took them, his only visible response the faintest wrinkling of his nose.

In the library, Paul chased out the maid, Gretchen, who was busy dusting the books. Then, alone with Tori, he poured a glass of wine for her and a small glass of brandy for himself. What little he did know of her made him think a love match between her and his brother wouldn't be made in heaven. Mack was the height of propriety—from all that training as a lawyer, Paul suspected—and Tori was not considered "proper" by those fashionable in Santa Fe. Besides, her anger toward wealthy people was something many in and around Santa Fe were familiar with.

"Now why exactly must you see my brother immediately?" Paul asked.

It occurred to him that Mack might have gotten Tori pregnant. Such an event would cause more than just a ripple in his brother's political plans. Though Mack's career wouldn't get completely derailed by such a scandal, it was something to worry about.

Tori looked at Paul, wondering exactly how much she could tell him, fighting her own prejudices against men from his world. Until she'd met Mack, Tori had never had any respect for a wealthy, highly educated man. Paul, as patriarch of the Randolph cattle empire, was wealthy, but he did not have the advanced formal education Mack did.

Could she trust him? Had Mack confided to his brother that he was the Midnight Bandit?

"I'm waiting for some kind of answer," Paul said, his patience wearing thin even though he knew politeness was in order.

"I'm sorry. It's really nothing that critical, I suppose. Just something between my brother and your brother." This was partly true, partly a lie; and though Tori didn't like deceiving Paul, she realized that for now it was necessary.

"Jedediah and Mack? I thought that problem with the reward money from Taos was straightened out," Paul said.

Paul wondered why Jedediah would send his sister marching through the desert at night for such a petty reason, then admitted to himself that he did not know either Tori or her brother very well.

"Apparently not," she said, not at all certain where her story was headed. She felt she was being sucked into a whirlpool, unable to stop her own destruction.

"Is there anything I can do to help?" Paul asked. Something was not as it should be, though what that something was, he couldn't say. His brother had been acting strangely lately, and he hadn't found out what had been bothering him.

"You're sure Mack's not here?" Tori asked softly, a plaintive quality to her voice that she barely recognized. She didn't really believe Mack was simply trying to avoid her.

"I'm afraid not. A problem came up, and he had to leave for Fort Richmond. We sell some of our cattle directly to the government through Fort Richmond."

"Yes, I know." Everyone had heard of the magnificent contract Mack had negotiated for his family with the U.S. Government for the sale of cattle to feed the cavalrymen.

"Some general or captain in charge of purchasing sent a frantic telegram, and Mack left as soon as he read it. It's not a big problem. Sometimes these men just want to rattle their sabers to make us Randolphs jump. I think it makes them feel important."

Tori found it odd that the Randolphs, the powerful Randolphs, could be inconvenienced by anyone or anything. She was just beginning to understand that she didn't know nearly as much about the world of the wealthy as she thought she did.

"Why are you on foot?" Paul asked.

Tori shrugged. What could she tell him? That her horse had been shot out from under her while she was riding away from Krey's men after stealing the payroll money?

"Miss Singer, I'm willing to help you if I can, but in order for me to do that you're going to have to be more honest with me than you have been. Now please, why are you here, what involvement has my brother with your considerable anxiety, and what has happened to your horse?"

Paul was surprised that both his words and his attitude

reminded him of Mack interrogating a witness who was committing perjury.

Tori breathed in deeply, looking at Paul. She could rise and simply walk out of the ranch house. He wouldn't stop her. He was much too civilized to hold her hostage until she gave him the information he wanted. But if she left she would certainly be making life extremely difficult for Mack, since Paul would demand answers from him.

Though lying wasn't something Tori did naturally or well, she sensed that in this particular circumstance, a lie was less damaging to everyone involved than the truth.

"My horse got spooked by a rattlesnake. She started jumping and broke her leg. I had to shoot her. As for the business between Jedediah and your brother, I don't know exactly what that's about. It has something to do with some fancy lawyer from Taos. He sent a letter to Jedediah. My brother . . . he gets real spooked by lawyers, so he wanted your brother on it right away."

Paul nodded his head slowly, and Tori achieved a modicum of confidence.

"Now you know as much as I know, Mr. Randolph—"

"Please, call me Paul. My brother's the formal one, not me. I'm just a cowboy."

Tori looked away. She didn't like Paul being so friendly, so warm and decent with her. His courtesy was playing havoc with her previous conceptions of Paul and men like him. She wondered how many of her beliefs concerning the wealthy were absurdly unfounded?

"It's late," Paul said. "Mack won't be home for a week. Maybe more. Why don't you spend the night here, and tomorrow you can take one of our horses home with you."

Tori shot him a fiercely suspicious look.

"You can keep the horse until you get another, or you can buy a horse from us. We have quite a number of fine mounts that we sell at reasonable prices." Paul smiled at Tori as though to say he was harmless as a kitten, which she didn't believe. "And you can rest assured that Gretchen will keep a careful eye on you while you're here."

"Gretchen?" Tori asked.

"She is the patron saint of propriety at this ranch. She's been here forever."

"What does she do?"

"Pretty much whatever she wants to. She's been cook, nanny, nurse, mother hen. You name it, Gretchen does it. Everything, including the cleaning."

Having a servant in the house had seemed to Tori like a form of slavery, a type of bondage that shouldn't be allowed. But the way Paul talked about Gretchen made her presence seem natural. Telling herself that she was curious and nothing more, Tori asked to meet the woman.

Twenty minutes later the blankets of a guest bed had been pulled back, and Gretchen was insisting—demanding was more like it—that Tori go immediately to bed after taking a nice warm bath. However, before she slept she would surely need a bite to eat, just a little something to bring the rose color to her cheeks, Gretchen insisted.

Tori was thunderstruck when Gretchen later returned with an enormous tray laden with food.

"It was a long walk, and young ladies such as yourself mustn't get too famished. It's not good for the bones," Gretchen explained as she laid out a nightgown on the foot of the bed. "And don't you worry about the boys around here. They're good boys, every one. Besides, even if they weren't, they wouldn't get past me. My room's right next door, and I hear every footstep in this house. Sleep in peace. I'll see you early in the morning."

Tori positively adored the elderly woman. Once again her attitude toward something she'd thought she understood—having a live-in servant—shifted in the direction of uncertainty.

# Sixteen

Tori awoke the next morning, first in panic, then with a wonderful sense of well-being.

When she opened her eyes, she did not recognize the room she was in, or the bed. Then she remembered the events of the previous evening—the long walk, the conversation with Paul Randolph, and Gretchen's loving, maternal attention.

Though the problem of Jedediah's considering hunting the Midnight Bandit still existed, Tori realized that as long as Mack was at Fort Richmond, he was safe.

Sitting up in bed, she stretched, raising her hands high above her head. The bed was huge, magnificently comfortable. The nightgown she had been given was also huge, made of cotton. It was, she suspected, Gretchen's. It hung on Tori in flowing waves of cotton. Tori had learned that Gretchen would never serve any food she hadn't tasted herself, and since the kind woman was nearly always cooking, she was also nearly always eating . . . and it showed on her in a grandmotherly, loving way.

A soft knock on the bedroom door was followed by Gretchen entering with yet another large silver serving tray covered with an assortment of breakfast foods giving off mouthwatering aromas. Tori tried to rise—she'd never before been served breakfast in bed, a decidedly decadent thing—but Gretchen would have none of it.

"You just stay there 'til that's all gone, and I'll come back later to see to you," she said as she left the room.

Alone again, Tori smiled. She'd hardly been able to say a word to the fast-talking older woman. Gretchen had proved again that she was an independent force at the Randolph ranch, just as Paul had claimed.

Tori ate scrambled eggs, warm, fresh-baked bread—sliced thick, toasted with care, and slathered liberally with sweet, rich butter—two peach halves in sauce, and four strips of bacon. With this, she drank a small glass of tomato juice and a cup of coffee. And all before she'd gotten out of bed.

*I could get used to living like this,* she absently thought as she rose and walked to a large bay window facing west.

The thought surprised her. Live like a pampered debutante—and like it? Unthinkable! Only it *wasn't!*

Tori sensed that she would have to be very careful or she might get swallowed up by this world; she might enjoy living in luxury so much that she would sacrifice anything—herself, her principles—to attain that.

In her mind's eye she saw the Kreys waking up and receiving exactly the same type of treatment from the hired help. Tori tried to cling to this thought, but it was virtually impossible. She simply couldn't imagine anyone like Gretchen working for Jonathon Krey for any length of time, just as she couldn't envision the Kreys treating their servants with respect.

Sipping her coffee, looking out to the west, Tori surveyed the Randolph range, a vast spread. At one time she'd heard the Randolphs had about a hundred cowboys on their payroll, and when driving a herd from one range to another, or to the stockyards or northward to Port Richmond, that figure could nearly double. She tried to imagine the responsibility entailed in employing so many men, but she couldn't.

*If Mack and I married, I'd look out at a scene like this every morning.*

Where had that thought come from? It shocked her so she spilled some of her coffee and very nearly dropped the fine china cup.

She and Mack married?

A bitter smile spread across Tori's mouth. She and he could be lovers—correction, she and the Midnight Bandit could be lovers—but they could never be husband and wife. Their worlds were too far apart to be bridged with matrimony. The most she could hope for was to be a secret lover, to share passion in the dark; keeping whatever feelings they shared—lust or perhaps an even deeper and more lasting emotion—to themselves.

"I'll have to be content with that," Tori said aloud.

She could hear the sadness, the frustration, in her tone. Mack Randolph would one day be mayor of Santa Fe and, after that, the territorial governor. Even the newspapers had speculated on it, and everyone agreed that Mack would get the votes necessary. Such a man could not have a common wife, a woman whose family name meant nothing to the people in power.

"Damn," she murmured, sadness and anger tightening once again around her heart. "Damn, damn, damn!"

Tori pulled the nightgown over her head and tossed it aside angrily. She had her old and faded clothes to put on—manly clothes, to be sure, but they were her own, and she'd bought them with her hard-earned money—before she returned to her small cabin. Jedediah might be there, and if he was, she was going to do everything she possibly could to convince him to refuse Jeremy Krey's profitable proposition.

The following days were difficult ones for Tori. Jedediah had been spending virtually all his time with some woman in Santa Fe—a woman whose name he was not inclined to reveal, no matter how much she pried. And Mack was still at Fort Richmond, according to Paul, seeing to the demands of a U.S. Army lieutenant colonel who thought the way to become a general was to make everyone doing business with the government as miserable as possible.

Though gone, Mack would be safe, for he would not be acting as the Midnight Bandit, Tori reminded herself.

Mack Randolph, the Midnight Bandit! Now that she knew the truth of it, she realized the physical similarities should have given him away. But he appeared so formal as a lawyer, always dressed in beautiful suits; and he hadn't been seen with a holster around his hips since he was a teenager.

How many other secrets did Mack have, secrets that would be positively delicious to discover?

Fortunately, he did not yet know she'd discovered his identity. If he hadn't kissed her, his secret would have remained intact. But he couldn't disguise his kiss, or the way it made her feel, and that had exposed the Midnight Bandit.

The horse Paul had "loaned" her was a young, strong

mare with a beautiful reddish coat and mane, and white "socks" to the knee. Tori had promised herself she would return the animal quickly, but once she had ridden into the desert to retrieve her saddle, left there when Daisy had been put down, she had decided there was really no need to hurry. The horse would give her an excuse for going to the Randolph ranch as soon as Mack returned.

As the days passed, memories of her passion-filled moments at the oasis did not diminish as Tori had thought they would. In fact, with each passing day the dull ache within her grew just a little stronger.

Each time she remembered how she had behaved, she blushed. So passionate! Never had she dreamed she'd be so lustful, so greedy for the loving the Midnight Bandit dispensed with skilled ease.

The Midnight Bandit . . . Mack Randolph . . . one and the same.

A slow smile curled Tori's mouth. She might be able to have a little fun with that bit of knowledge. For once *she* would have the upper hand on Bandit, and not the other way around.

When she looked out over the valley, she saw a flatbed wagon approaching. It was drawn by an old horse determined to go at its own pace, and the woman holding the reins didn't seem to be in any hurry, either. When the wagon drew nearer, Tori recognized the plump form of Gretchen.

By the time the wagon reached the cabin, Tori had water on for fresh coffee and she'd heated up the rich cinnamon rolls she'd baked early that morning.

"Good afternoon," she said brightly, reaching up to help

the older woman step down from the wagon. "What brings you all the way out here?"

"Master Mack sent me," Gretchen answered with a smile.

Tori did not at all like the title "Master" affixed to Mack's name, but she kept her opinion on the matter to herself. "Mack's back?" she asked, trying not to sound overly excited by the prospect. "I would have ridden to you if he . . ." She didn't know what to say, so her words trailed slowly off.

"He sent a wire. Besides, what we've got to do is best done here, away from the prying eyes of those boys." Gretchen waved to a number of packages in the bed of the wagon, and Tori went around to retrieve them. "Now let's see what we can do with these, shall we?"

Tori looked at the packages, all beautifully wrapped and bowed. Some were from stores in Santa Fe, and one, a hat box, was from a store in faraway San Francisco.

"Mack wanted you to have the very best. He said to spare no expense," Gretchen explained. When she saw the look of confusion on Tori's face, she smiled. "The dance, child! Surely, you haven't forgotten that the dance is tonight!"

Tori had no idea what response she should give the woman. The fact was, she *had* forgotten about the dance, but only because she'd already told Mack that she couldn't go. She didn't approve of the people who would attend, and she hadn't had the clothes for it.

Until now. Every package was from a fine store, the kind Tori had never even walked into.

After coffee was served and the cinnamon rolls were sampled and complimented, Gretchen suggested a slight alteration in the recipe for them, and Tori appreciated the tip. Next, the packages were opened.

"I didn't say I would go to the dance with him," Tori informed Gretchen, who seemed determined to stay in the cabin until she was absolutely confident that every article of clothing fit to perfection, no matter how much Tori complained.

"Yes, Master Mack said that." Gretchen pulled from the largest box a satin and velvet gown of blue and turquoise. It was trimmed with gold braid at the décolletage, the skirt's hem, and the wrists. "He thought you might be of a different mind once you saw the clothes."

Tori's stubbornness came to the fore. She didn't want Mack to think he could buy her affections with a gown, even if it did come from the finest clothier in Santa Fe.

"Really, there's no need to go to all this trouble," she said as Gretchen continued opening packages and pulling the contents out.

"No trouble at all," Gretchen replied distractedly, her concentration on a handbag that she was certain should have had just a shade more green in its blue-green coloring.

"I'm sorry, but I really must stop you here and now," Tori said with finality. "I'm not going to the dance. Quite frankly, I don't much care for the people attending—or for the things they stand for. I find them all—"

"Even Mack?" Gretchen cut in, looking at Tori over the tops of the gold-rimmed spectacles perched delicately at the tip of her nose.

The comment caught Tori off guard. "Well . . . well, no, of course not Mack, but—"

"It's Mack you'll be with. The rest will just be bystanders. Don't worry your head about anyone but you and

Mack, and you'll be doing yourself a favor." Gretchen said sternly. A lifetime of getting big, strapping, decidedly spoiled young men to do what they *should* do instead of what they *wanted* to do had afforded Gretchen ample experience in dealing with a reticent child, and in her eyes, anyone under thirty-five was still a child. "Now off with those infernal trousers, and let's see what alterations I have to make on this gown! We've only got a little time before Master Mack shows up."

Silently, Tori stood her ground. She would not be bullied by anyone, not even Gretchen.

The older woman would not be denied, however. She was determined, she was infinitely patient, and she knew that sooner or later Tori would give in. She was correct.

Three hours later, Gretchen was saying, "I'd have been here sooner, but some of the packages weren't ready." She put another stitch into the gold braid trim around Tori's wrist. "Master Mack's coming home today, and he wired that a bath should be waiting for him. He wants to be out of the ranch by three. If he takes it easy, he'll get here by five, and you and he will arrive at the dance by seven."

"It sounds like *Master*"—Tori drawled the word out slowly and sarcastically—"Mack has made plenty of plans for my life."

"He sure has. Got all of us at the ranch buzzing, too. Mack just doesn't do this, we always thought."

Tori wanted to protest, but she enjoyed the fact that she could make Mack do something he normally didn't do with women. And when Gretchen turned her so she might see her reflection in the mirror, her reluctance about going to the dance vanished completely.

"It is beautiful, isn't it?" she whispered, running her hands over the satin skirt.

"I thought the color would suit you," Gretchen replied, enormously pleased with her own handiwork. "Now do you want me to do your hair?"

"Gretchen, that really won't be necessary." Tori was about to say she still wasn't going to the dance. Instead, the words that came from her lips were, "Can I change my mind?"

"It's a woman's right," Gretchen said, already opening a small purse filled with the ribbons and combs that might be necessary.

Mack experienced a surge of excitement when he spotted Gretchen's old flatbed wagon at Tori's cabin. He tapped the reins against the horse's back, and picked up the pace a bit, anxious to see what clothes Gretchen had chosen for her.

He felt boyishly giddy, and he didn't care. After a week of hard negotiations with a pig-headed Army officer he had no respect for, it would be pure heaven to spend time with Tori again.

As he neared the cabin, he looked over the seat of his carriage one more time to see that it was immaculate. Then he checked his own clothes, straightened his tie one more time even though it was already straight, and thumbed a smudge off the toe of his boot with his thumb.

As his carriage came to a halt, Gretchen stepped out of the little cabin, a subdued smile on her face. A moment later, she was followed by an uncertain Tori, who nevertheless looked ravishing in a velvet gown.

She should not have been fearful of what Mack would think upon seeing her, for he was stopped dead by the sight.

"My God, just look at you," he whispercd, frozen in the carriage seat.

Gretchen, ever the soul of discretion when it came to the Randolph children, whom she had cared for since they were both in diapers, murmured something, then climbed into her wagon and headed back toward the Randolph ranch, a serene smile of accomplishment on her face.

The gown was V-necked, showing a suggestion of cleavage, gold braid touching flawless flesh. Tori fidgeted, shifting her weight from one foot to the other, and twice tugged at the modest décolletage. She was not used to the V-neckline, even though it was nowhere near as revealing as some of the more flamboyant fashions that would be worn at the dance.

Mack jumped down from the carriage, astonished at the difference in the woman before him. She had been transformed from a tomboy with a Colt revolver at her hip to a princess in satin and velvet. Even her coiffure was exactly as he had hoped it would be. Pulled away from her face and held loosely back with a blue-green ribbon, curling tendrils of golden blond hair slipped from her temples to caress her cheeks.

"Do you like it?" Tori asked softly, her confidence shaky at such close scrutiny.

"Beautiful," Mack said.

He stepped forward to take Tori into his arms when he remembered that to her, he was just a lawyer who really didn't know her very well. He stopped himself abruptly, and forced all memories of the lovemaking they'd shared when he was the Midnight Bandit from his thoughts.

Tonight, he was starting all over with her. He would be as honest with Tori as he possibly could, this time keeping his alter ego in the shadows of his life.

"I really hadn't intended on going to the dance with you," she said in a voice that was barely a whisper.

For reasons she did not completely understand, she felt it important to tell Mack that. She suspected that too many women had altered their lives to fit more easily into Mack's plans. She didn't want him to think that she was just like all the others from his libidinous past.

"Gretchen talked you into it, didn't she?"

Tori arched a brow above an amused green eye. "I'd have thought you would be counting on the expensive satin gown to do the trick."

Mack shook his head. "Not with you. I knew it would take Gretchen to change your mind. She has a way of getting what she wants."

A smile toyed with the corners of Tori's mouth. "You behave as if you know me very well, Mack, yet that can't be the case. We've only spoken to each other a few times."

She looked straight into his eyes, waiting for his next statement, knowing he wouldn't dare tell her the whole truth.

"I've got strong intuition about you," Mack said.

He looked away. Breaking the eye contact was the unconscious gesture of a man uncomfortable with the lie he'd told. Tori was certain then that Mack didn't have a clue about her knowing he was the Midnight Bandit.

"Yes, of course, a lawyer's intuition," Tori replied at last.

A feline smile stretched her lips and brightened her eyes as she allowed Mack to help her up into the elaborate carriage. Perhaps, with her knowledge and Mack's ignorance of the current situation, she could have some fun with him on this special evening . . . if she felt inclined to be the teasing kind.

"Shall we leave now? I don't want to draw more attention to myself by being late," she said, as a myriad of impish games to play on the lawyer came into her thoughts.

"You'll draw attention to yourself no matter what time we get there."

"Flatterer," Tori said with mild censure as she settled back into the plush leather seat cushion of the carriage.

She wondered exactly how comfortable it would be to make love with Mack in the carriage, and whether it would be better to enjoy his loving on the way to the dance or better to wait and tell him during the dance that she intended to seduce him on the way home. The waiting, from the time of her invitation until they were far from the spying eyes of Santa Fe society, would drive Mack out of his mind!

Such a delicious question to ponder! And the pleasure even greater because as long as Tori was with Mack, the Midnight Bandit was safe from her bounty-hunting brother.

# Seventeen

During the ride to the dance, Tori and Mack sampled a bottle of very fine Chablis from Mack's personal cellar. Tori very rarely drank, but she accepted the first glass of wine, and even though it had gone straight to her head, when Mack offered more, she did not refuse.

Three times Tori let her knee bump against Mack's, and on the third time she left her knee touching his. But the moment he moved his arm as though to put his hand on her knee, she moved away quickly.

"Please, Mack, let's do behave in a civilized manner tonight," Tori said, sounding hurt that he would even think she'd allow such an intimacy. Before the evening was over, before she let him touch her, she intended to have him gnashing his teeth in frustration.

Mack talked, telling stories that Tori found amusing and interesting. His natural voice, which had a cultured quality to it, indicated a man trained in public speaking and arguing points of law before a judge and a jury. His pitch was melodic, so different from the hard-as-flint tone he adopted for the Midnight Bandit.

On their journey into Santa Fe, they were lovers—at least they had made love twice on a single night a week earlier—yet now they treated each other as near-strangers on an uncomfortable first date. Tori considered this odd.

She knew Mack wanted her. From that first stolen kiss at the cabin when she'd realized he was the Midnight Bandit who had helped her to discover her own passionate nature, she had known he was not the type of man to be satisfied with just one night of passion upon a hard rock near a desert oasis.

As Mack's carriage moved down the streets of Santa Fe, Tori saw some people stop and look at them. The carriage was grand, she told herself, but even as she thought this, she knew it hadn't turned any heads. No, the fine people of Santa Fe who gawked so openly did so because one of its occupants, the popular Mack Randolph—everyone knew he was destined for an enormously successful career—was dressed to the nines and attending a formal dance with Tori Singer . . . tomboy, troublemaker, and sister of a bounty hunter.

"Judging from some of the looks I've received so far, I'd say my original guess was correct," Tori said, wishing she could get out of going to the dance without appearing a coward.

"And what was your original guess?" Mack asked.

He had noticed the disbelieving stares, but he'd also noticed something that Tori had not. Along with the condescending looks from many of the men and all of the women, there were also the shocked expressions of men who, like Mack, had never before seen a more attractive woman than Tori.

"That I don't belong here. These people will never accept me, and they'll never forgive you for bringing me among them."

Mack chuckled. He absolutely refused to feel anything but joyful on this evening.

Tori placed a hand on Mack's forearm and squeezed. It was hard as steel, and she wondered what regimen the lawyer set for himself to keep in such magnificent condition.

"I don't want to be the cause of your getting into any trouble," Tori whispered. Suddenly, it seemed all the condemning eyes of all of Santa Fe's elite were upon her.

"Trouble? What trouble? We're just two people going to a dance," Mack said with such feigned innocence that for a moment Tori wondered if he really didn't understand the situation.

"I read in the newspaper how folks are urging you to run for mayor. You know, I'm really not the right woman for you to be seen with."

Mack twisted a little more toward Tori in the carriage seat. His eyes were dark brown and resolute. "Listen to me, Tori . . . the only person in the world to say who is right for me is me. My life is not a democracy. Every damn fool in Santa Fe doesn't get a vote on what I can and can't do or who I'll see. I'll make those decisions for myself—and I couldn't possibly be happier than having you with me tonight."

If it were not for all the stares, Tori would have kissed him then and there. He had said exactly what she needed to hear exactly when she needed to hear it.

As uniformed coachmen took the carriage, Mack offered his elbow to Tori and escorted her along the pebbled walkway to the white mansion's enormous front doors, where a small army of servants awaited the guests' every wish.

From his jacket pocket Mack extracted a card, on which

was written in a florid hand, "Mack Randolph and Guest."
Who in all of Santa Fe would have dreamed that he would
choose Tori Singer as his guest?

The people of Santa Fe would understand that Mack
Randolph was not and never would be a politician like
Andy Fields, for sale to the highest bidder, a man with
no real views or opinions of his own.

Inside the mansion, once they were through the foyer,
a low murmur went through the assembled crowd. Though
Tori had not heard a single distinct word, she knew she
was the topic of conversation.

"I knew I shouldn't have come," she whispered out of
the corner of her mouth as they slipped past another
squadron of servants and stepped immediately into the
ornate ballroom.

Some of the guests standing about looked sympatheti-
cally at her, as if she were a displaced person who had
gotten lost and stumbled into the dance; others looked on
in shock. If Mack had walked into the ballroom with a
naked young woman of their class on his arm, he would
have caused less of a commotion than he had by arriving
with Tori.

"Don't be silly," Mack said, exerting the full force of
his charm.

He understood his environment, and how savage it
could be. What those in the ballroom did not yet know
was exactly how savage he could be in return if his protective instincts were put to the test.

"This is exactly where you should be," Mack added
reassuringly. "It's high time you made your entrance into
society."

Though he gazed upon her as though she were the only

woman in the world, as though he were completely oblivious to everyone but her, Tori could barely meet his eyes. Still, she felt warmed, albeit uncomfortably, by his scrutiny. Was he really informing his friends and all his enemies from the very beginning that he was going to flout convention and propriety, and that anyone who thought he should do otherwise could be damned?

Looking around at the other ladies in the room, Tori discovered that her décolletage wasn't nearly as revealing as most others. Silently, she thanked Gretchen for having the sense to pick out an elegant gown showing a modest amount of her ample bosom, rather than a daring or dramatic one. Tori had made more than enough of a splash by being at Mack's side; she didn't need to create a tidal wave by being showy.

Momentarily easing away from Tori, Mack deftly plucked two champagne glasses off the tray of a passing servant, spinning about as he accomplished his task. Smiling, he handed Tori a glass.

"Didn't even spill a drop," he said, clinking his glass lightly against hers.

She sipped the champagne. It started out being deliciously cold, but was soon heating her veins, giving her a glowing warmth and heightening the intimidating sensation of being surrounded by so much wealth.

When a young man stepped up to Mack to make some innocuous comment, Tori stepped away to give them privacy. But Mack immediately reached for her, taking her hand in his and returning her to his side.

When the young fellow had left, Tori whispered, "Please, Mack, everyone is watching," as she slipped her hand from his.

"I know," he replied, slipping his arm lightly around her waist.

Another gentleman approached Mack, and this time Tori was close enough to hear what was said.

"I know you can help me," the man said sincerely, his palms facing toward the ceiling as though ready to catch whatever words of wisdom might come from Mack's lips. "I sent the governor three letters explaining that the land has been in my family for three generations, and still he doesn't respond. All he says is, I've got to vacate the land immediately or I'll be arrested and remain in jail until I can prove my innocence."

"Listen, in this country nobody has to prove his innocence," Mack said, an annoyed look on his face. "Tomorrow, stop by around noon with the letters. I'll read them over, and we'll figure out what to do from there."

The gentleman sighed heavily, as though a great burden had just been lifted from his shoulders. "Thank you," he said as they shook hands, a bit too vigorously for this blasé crowd. "Thank you so very much. I just knew I could count on you." Then the gentleman turned to Tori and offered a short, very formal bow. "You have a good evening, miss. Sorry to take up so much of your time with Mack."

"No need to apologize," Tori replied, flattered suddenly that the gentleman should have felt obligated to apologize to her.

Moments later, several more men, ranging in age from the early twenties to the late fifties, began coming forward. Tori was always aware of the heat of Mack's hand at the small of her back, and of the eyes that stared at her from all corners of the ballroom.

"Mack, it is important that I speak privately with you," a youthful-looking man with prematurely graying hair said. He glanced sideways at Tori. It was not a disrespectful look, merely that of a man who has gotten himself into some sort of trouble and needs rather urgently to speak to an attorney.

"I need to walk about anyway," Tori said, easing out of Mack's grasp.

Since they'd stepped into the ballroom, there hadn't been a moment when he hadn't been touching her somewhere, on the forearm or at the small of the back, or lightly holding her hand in his much larger one. Tori had not been consciously aware of his reassuring touch until she stepped away from it. Now she felt she'd just let go of a lifeline and was drifting in a sea that could turn dangerously stormy without any forewarning.

She walked through cliques of guests without really having any goal in mind. Expensive scents, a highfalutin snatch of conversation here and there, flashing diamonds—all brought her insecurity about being socially inferior to the fore. Tori tried hard not to make direct eye contact with anyone, but to do this she had to gaze sightlessly ahead and not look down, since she didn't want to appear subservient.

For one second she found herself trapped in a dead-end hallway, with several quietly talking couples. Almost everyone turned at precisely the same moment to look at her. Though no words were spoken, Tori could imagine each person asking her why she was at the dance.

Didn't she realize that she didn't belong?

Her nerves getting increasingly edgy, Tori spun about in her new slippers—those, too, were courtesy of

Gretchen's foresight and Mack's generosity—and headed
in the opposite direction. From behind, a woman's soft
titter of laughter followed her. Frustrated and embarrassed,
Tori picked a glass of champagne off the tray of a passing
waiter, just as she had seen Mack do, though some of the
contents sloshed over the rim and down her hand.

"Damn!" she muttered, drawing the critical attention
of an elderly woman with diamond earrings that glittered
in the light from the crystal chandeliers overhead.

Tori walked on, sipping the champagne more quickly
than was wise, wanting to rush back to Mack's side, but
refusing to give in to her fears. Deciding that fresh air
was just what she needed most, Tori stepped out of the
ballroom into the mansion's courtyard.

She finished her champagne and set the glass down on
a marble bird feeder. One of the army of passing servants
could pick it up later, she decided.

Breathing in deeply, she inhaled the fragrance of the
familiar desert night, and her confidence began returning.
Inside the ballroom, where the smells of cigar smoke min-
gling with those of perfume, she had been constantly reminded that she was someplace she shouldn't be. Here in
the courtyard, though she was surrounded on all sides by
high walls, she was more at ease.

From the shadows to her right, she heard a soft, feminine moan. Tori squinted to see better. Her eyes still adjusting to the darkness, she recognized Jena Krey's pale
white flesh and stark black hair. Jena was in the arms of
a well-dressed man not much taller than she was, though
old enough to be her father. They were kissing, and the
man's hand was upon her breast, touching her through her
gown.

Tori's startled gasp drew their attention. The man glowered at Tori, but Jena merely smiled her peculiar cryptic smile.

"Go inside, and I'll speak with you later," she instructed the man, slipping out of his embrace. Her companion started to protest, but Jena silenced him with a glaring look from her piercing blue eyes. Then, just before he walked away—and clearly as much for Tori's benefit as for the man's—Jena kissed him hard on the lips with an open mouth.

The man stumbled off, clearly shocked by Jena's behavior yet wanting more of her passionate attentions. Jena smiled at Tori.

"He's a sweet man, really. Quite harmless. He's been so lonely since his wife died last winter," Jena explained, moving closer to Tori.

"I'm sorry. I didn't mean to disturb you or chase him away."

Tori's ears and cheeks were getting warm. She was embarrassed by what she'd seen, especially since Jena seemed so at ease with her own sexuality and Tori had yet to put hers into perspective. Also, she was becoming aware that she'd drank more than she should have.

"No need to apologize. It was nothing important." Jena's blue gaze appraised Tori. She'd already heard that Mack Randolph had arrived with the bounty hunter's sister, whatever her name was.

"Not important?"

Tori imagined being in Mack's arms, kissing him deeply while he touched her breast. She'd always believed it important. She valued Mack, herself, and the passion they shared much too much to think little of it.

Jena shrugged her slender shoulders. "I was only trying to cheer him up. He's been so sad lately." She made a pushing gesture with her hand, as though to push aside the invisible presence of the wealthy old widower. The man meant absolutely nothing to Jena, and the things she'd just been doing with him had already been forgotten. "I'm surprised to see you here."

Tori blushed a little, but held Jena's eyes. "Mack brought me. Mack Randolph."

"Yes, I'm well aware of who he is," Jena said. The faintest hint of contempt came into her voice as she sized up Tori, whom she'd looked upon as an enemy from the very beginning. She wondered exactly how great a threat Tori represented. "I'm just surprised that he brought you here. He is going to be governor, you know."

She heard the challenge, and she would not back down from it. "I'm aware of that. He's a good man. The people will vote for him."

Jena smirked as though Tori's words were either terribly funny or terribly naive. "The people will vote for whomever they're told to vote for. Money and power win elections, not the votes of every little jackass who takes the time to ride into Santa Fe to scrawl his pathetic 'X' by some damned fool's name."

Jena's bitterness, her hatred of ordinary people, caused Tori to take a step backward. Was that really the way elections were won or lost? She didn't want to believe the political process was so devious, or that Mack could be a part of that, but if he was so honest and aboveboard about everything, why had he become the Midnight Bandit . . . and why hadn't he confessed his identity to her?

"Do I shock you?" Jena continued, enjoying the horrified look on Tori's face. "I really don't mean to. I just think it's important to shed some silly notions of the way things get done in this world." Jena grinned, studying Tori's face. "Consider me your teacher, and this dance your first day at school."

"Maybe I'd better just step back inside." Tori was trying not to sound annoyed.

But her tone of voice revealed a lack of confidence, and for Jena Krey, that was like a signal to attack.

"Let me come with you," she said quickly, getting into step with the much taller blonde. "I'll continue your education."

"Really, that's not necessary."

"It's no trouble at all." Jena scooped two glasses of champagne from a passing tray, handing one to Tori without spilling a drop.

"How long does it take you people to learn to do that?" Tori asked, shocked to see the same inane feat performed again.

Why did it bother her? It was just one of a thousand different indicators that let Tori know Mack and Jena came from the same social circle, a circle that wouldn't willingly let her in. She was at the dance only because Mack had brought her, and everyone knew that.

"You don't learn it," Jena said, sipping her champagne and weaving her way effortlessly through the crowd. "You're born with it, or you're not."

Tori's head was spinning. She finished her champagne, hoping it would soothe her fevered brain and help her organize her thoughts, too inexperienced to realize that what she needed most just then was solid food and hot coffee.

Jena stayed at Tori's side, refusing to be shrugged off. As Tori walked, stopping and starting as one does when not accustomed to moving in crowds, she wondered whether Jena and Mack were sleeping together. If not, why was Jena, looking like she'd been slapped in the face, still by her side?

*Of course they are sleeping together,* a voice whispered in Tori's head. *Mack sleeps with all the women he escorts around town!*

Jena studied Tori's unstable walk and glassy eyes. The mountain lion had spotted a limping whitetail doe, and she was stalking it, waiting to go in for the kill at the moment she had the largest audience possible.

Jena intended to crush Tori, to destroy her in front of all these people. When it was over, this upstart would know that she could share her body with Mack, if that was what she really wanted to do, but she couldn't have the hubris to attend dances of this caliber with him without suffering greatly for her error.

Jena Krey wanted to live in the governor's mansion, and if she was to do that, she had to be at Mack's side when he got there. Consequently, any other woman accompanying him was an enemy whose destruction would be an example to all who might think about crossing Jena Krey.

"Wait a minute, Tori," Jena said, taking her prey's wrist to stop her. "Let's talk. There's no reason for you to run from me."

Tori, knowing the Krey mentality, sensed a trap was being set. But what was it? In a blinding flash of understanding, she realized that she and Mack had been behaving as though they were lovers, though she hadn't yet confessed to him that she knew he was the Midnight Bandit. And everyone knew—because Jena had made no secret of it— that she intended to be Mack's wife when he accepted the responsibility of life as a prominent politician.

Tori also realized with horror, that because of the wine she'd had in the carriage and the champagne she'd drunk at the dance, she no longer had complete control of her thoughts and feelings.

She looked into Jena's eyes and saw the anger bubbling in the wealthy young heiress's soul. All around her the guests gathered to watch the lioness devour her prey.

"Stay away from me, Jena. I'm warning you," Tori whispered, sensing the impending attack and deciding to go on the offensive rather than wait for it.

"You're warning me?" Jena stepped back. In all her life, she'd only been threatened twice, both times privately, and she had made both men suffer greatly for their threats. "You silly tramp, do you really think I'm going to bother with you? I don't care if you're sleeping with Mack." She spoke loud enough for the first row of onlookers to hear. "That doesn't matter. He's slept with a dozen women at this party, and I'm not in the least bit jealous of them. It's not who he sleeps with now that matters, it's who he's going to be sleeping with when he goes on the campaign for territorial governor that counts—and that's going to be me." Jena glanced around, then blushed a little, as though she were just now aware of how loudly she'd been speaking. "I'm not angry with you, Tori. I know he's got to get this wenching out of his system before he can settle down with me. Go ahead, sleep with him if you want. God knows, he's handsome as the devil and absolute heaven in bed." Her tone became hushed and ludicrously conspiratorial. "But frankly, it wasn't necessary for you to come to this dance. Mack told me he'd been most generous with you."

Tori heard the sounds men make when they're struggling to hold back laughter, and she knew that everyone who'd heard Jena thought she'd been sleeping with Mack to get into Santa Fe society.

"You bitch," Tori hissed, about to reach for the revolver at her hip . . . only it wasn't there. She wasn't wearing her Levi's, she was wearing the beautiful gown Mack had bought for her.

At that moment she was so embarrassed and so enraged that she would have gladly walked all the way back to her cabin so as not to spend another moment in the company of these treacherous, self-righteous animals.

She closed her eyes and breathed in deeply. Someone muttered, "My God, I think she's going to pass out standing up!" But she wasn't even close to doing that. The wine had taken the critical edge off her intellect, but it had also rounded the sharp edges off her inhibitions and had lessened her sense of intimidation. If Jena could be so open about her sexuality and still be accepted by this elite group, then surely Tori, who would never be or want to be a part of it, had a free hand in what she could and couldn't do on this evening.

When Tori at last opened her eyes, there were still a dozen people surrounding her, but now she looked upon them with the contempt they had previously shown her.

*Fine,* she thought, *if Mack can't take me with him to the governor's mansion, if all I can have is this night with him, then I'm going to make the most of it—starting right now!*

She turned and began walking back to the ballroom where she'd left him. The look in her eyes and the forcefulness of her stride encouraged people to step out of the way as she approached them. When a group of four men saw her coming, they snickered and turned collectively to face her so that she would need to walk around them. Tori would have none of it, and she shoved her way through their ranks.

"Pushy wench, isn't she?" one of them muttered.

Tori, her green eyes fierce and defiant, wheeled on the man and pointed a finger in his face. "Damn right, little man! Don't ever get in my way!"

The man's eyes got wide as saucers, and though he wanted to come back with a snappy response, he remained silent, unable to think of a single word to say.

As she approached Mack, Tori detected pain in his eyes. She knew then that he had heard about her embarrassment. People standing near him, no doubt relating every hideous detail of her ordeal, moved away quickly.

At that moment, Tori hated everyone in the ballroom, everyone at the dance. Everyone . . . but Mack, the high society lawyer whose life path was already predetermined for him, planned in such minute detail that it could never be altered sufficiently to allow Tori Singer to join him on it.

"Tori, I just heard and—"

She raised her hands, placing the pads of her fingers lightly upon his lips to silence him. Looking up into his eyes, she smiled as best she could, summoning from a place deep within her the courage and strength to hide the pain she now felt. She was determined to press forward with allowing her desires to blossom. The wine would be her ally against the inhibitions that had previously held her back.

"Mack, my Mack," she whispered, stifling a hiccup. She slipped her hand around the back of his neck, pulling him down so that she could whisper into his ear. "I know you're the Midnight Bandit. I knew the moment you kissed me, my darling. And unless we leave this minute, you and I are going to be making love in the middle of this ballroom, though quite frankly I'd rather not have an audience."

She turned and began walking, not sure where she was going in the huge mansion, only knowing that every second she spent without Mack's arms around her was wasted.

A sultry smile curled Tori's mouth. She'd heard that champagne was an aphrodisiac, and now she knew it was true.

# *Eighteen*

Mack was a jumble of chaotic emotions. Tori knew? From the first moment he'd kissed her?

Not only had he been unsuccessful in hiding his identity as the Midnight Bandit from Tori, but having her attacked by Jena Krey added to his upset state. How was Tori taking the cursed comments?

He followed her as she hurried through the crowd of people, her blue-green skirts rustling, her strides long and powerful. As Mack increased his speed to catch up to her, she increased hers accordingly, and when she looked over her shoulder at him, there was a smile on her face, a brilliant green light shining in her eyes, a glow to her that was at once exciting and mystifying.

What had Jena said to put Tori in such a good mood? Mack wondered as he picked up speed once again trying to catch her. Any faster and he'd be proceeding at an absolutely undignified jog, and though he already had much to explain, he didn't want to have to add tackling her to stop her.

Maybe she wasn't *really* in a good mood. Maybe it was feigned for his benefit, a brave front put forward for him.

She had said she wanted to make love. Though Mack was reluctant to take advantage of a painful situation, the opportunity to make love to the beautiful Tori was something he simply couldn't resist.

He reached out, his fingertips almost touching the puffed sleeve of her gown. Tori looked at him once again over her shoulder, and a giggle of delight escaped her moist, lightly rouged, kissable lips. She raised her skirts just a little, striding even faster than before, almost running now.

"Damn it, Tori, wait!" Mack said, much more loudly than he'd wanted to.

The expressions on the guests he passed had ranged from sympathetic to confused. The dance was buzzing with the news of what Jena had done and said to Tori. But only Mack realized that Jena's cruelty had been the motivating force behind Tori's decision to flaunt convention and seduce the Midnight Bandit, as quickly as possible.

An inebriated Andy Fields, was standing in the foyer, near the base of the long, winding stairway leading up to the second floor. When he saw Mack approaching so quickly, he grabbed his arm and held on tight. Mack's strength nearly toppled Fields over.

"What's the rush old boy?" Fields asked, weaving just a little, rather pleased with himself that he'd managed to stop Mack, whom he saw as a political rival.

Mack knocked Fields's hand away, furious with the damn fool. Tori was already ascending the stairs, providing a flash of white stocking and calf beneath the skirt she raised to make it easier for her to take the stairs quickly.

"There's no need to be testy," Fields continued, oblivious to all that was happening around him. "I just wanted to have a word with you."

With every step, Tori felt as though she had been freed

from a gigantic spiderweb. Once ensnared, she'd tried to fit into that web, and the more she struggled to fit, the more entangled she'd become. She had tried to fit into Mack's world, and had been insulted for her efforts. By not trying, by no longer caring what anyone thought of her behavior except herself and Mack, she had at last freed herself to be the woman she truly was.

Tori had just reached the top of the stairs when Mack finally pushed Andy Fields aside. She smiled down at him, as another laugh worked its way through her. Then she rushed down the hallway, having no idea of where she was going, her body at a fever pitch of excitement.

From behind, Mack called out to her, demanding that she stop immediately.

"Try and catch me!" she challenged, not caring at all who heard what she had to say.

She reached the end of the hall and followed it left. A man and woman, stood in the dimly lit corridor, their lips pressed tightly together in a passionate kiss. They stopped and looked at her.

"Don't stop for me," Tori said to them as she whisked past with a rustle of velvet.

The echoing of boot heels hitting the floor told Tori that Mack had decided to put an end to the chase. He was running now, and there was a predatorial gleam in his eye as he rounded the corner and closed in on her.

If she did not decide now which room to choose, she would be making love to the impatient Mack there in the hallway!

She turned a doorknob and stepped into a dark room, illuminated only by moonlight streaming through a narrow window on the far side. It was not, as she had hoped, a bedroom. Rather, it was a linen closet of some sort, with towels and sheets stacked up high on the shelves along the walls.

She hadn't been in the small room five seconds before the door burst open and Mack stepped in. He kicked the door shut as he reached for her. Tori offered no resistance when he pulled her into his arms, crushing her body against his own, kissing her fiercely, passionately.

"I want you, Mack!" she whispered, her head reeling with excitement. She was painfully aware of her own inexperience in such matters, and she could only hope that he would know what to do. "I want you now! Right now!"

She was turned, moved backward. Then she hit the hard surface of the door by which she'd just entered. Mack held her face in his hands, keeping her head at the most advantageous angle for his kisses. His tongue pressed between her lips, deeply entering her mouth, and Tori welcomed the intimacy of it.

"Mack! Mack!" she cried out, pushing her hands inside his jacket to feel the solid, sinewy muscles beneath the smooth silkiness of his white shirt.

"This is madness!" he replied, his own passion blazing out of control.

He'd spent virtually all his adult life doing everything he possibly could to maintain an appearance, even while endlessly pursuing women. In the back of his mind, he was aware that at that very moment downstairs tongues were wagging, telling version after distorted version of how he had chased after Tori. No one, with the exception of the man and woman now completely lost in a kiss, had seen him enter the closet.

He pressed Tori harder against the door, then darted his

tongue between her lips, playing it against hers. He was aware of her fingers against his chest, pressing against his pectorals and ribs. He'd been touched a hundred times before, but no hands pleased him quite so much as these.

"I need you, Mack!" she whispered hotly.

The passion in her voice fired Mack's blood. He filled his hands with her breasts, squeezing them hard, enjoying their fullness while Tori writhed in bliss. He wanted to free her breasts, to feel their silky luxuriance without the encumbrance of the gown's bodice, but there were far too many buttons and his blood was much too hot to allow for such patience.

Tori shivered, arching her back to thrust her breasts even more firmly into Mack's hands. When he released her, she sighed loudly, about to complain. Words were impossible because Mack's mouth was over hers once again, taking away her breath, kissing away any complaint she even considered. And when she felt her skirts being raised high, her sigh of anticipation sounded much more worldly than Tori was.

His lips were wet and warm against her throat as his hands brushed aside layers of velvet and cotton. Tori wrapped her arms around Mack's shoulders, holding onto him for support yet not wanting to impede him. She leaned back against the door, her shoulders pressed hard against the solid surface, her feet moving forward and spreading just a little further apart. When Mack's hand came up, brushing against her silk-sheathed inner thigh, moving over the stocking top until the length of his strong fingers were pressed against her femininity, the pressure was firm and exhilarating even through the overwashed cotton barrier of her pantalets.

The startled cry of ecstasy that was ripped from Tori's throat was one of uninhibited passion. She tossed her head back as the pressing fingers found the bud of her desire, tantalizing that small, excitable place with consummate skill. In an oddly disconnected way, she thought about her pantalets, and how incongruous they were with the rest of her ensemble. Gretchen had remembered to bring all new clothes for her, with the exception of pantalets. Would Mack be disappointed in them, since they were not made of fine quality silk but were old and slightly frayed from having been washed so many times?

Why think of that now? It couldn't possibly matter to him . . . But it mattered to Tori, and she promised herself that one day she would have beautiful lingerie, which she would wear for Mack's pleasure.

"This is insane." His whispered words came out muffled, his face buried in Tori's cleavage.

His hands were beneath her skirt, his fingers trembling with need as he sought the drawstring of her pantalets. When he found it at last, he pulled loose the knot, and dropped to his knees before her, his fingers curling into the waistband to pull the drawers down her tapering thighs and strong legs.

Tori was as frantic as Mack, perhaps more so. With his help, she pulled one slippered foot out of her cotton pantalets. The ache within her was overpowering, its intensity frightening. Her hands were still on Mack's shoulders, her fingers clutching at the collar of his jacket. She expected him to stand, though she still was unsure of exactly what he intended to do. She knew only that she wanted him inside her, that she wanted to feel his great strength, his power, his passion for life and for her.

"You'll be the death of me, but I must have you," she heard Mack say. He sounded helpless against the power of his desire for her, and the knowledge of her influence over this pragmatic man excited Tori even more.

When she looked down in the darkness of the closet, she saw Mack's face in shadows, caught the brilliant, wet gleam of his dark eyes. There was a quality to him now, a look kept hidden as a lawyer. The Midnight Bandit knelt before her, a man who knew exactly what he wanted and who was willing to break any rule to get it. In that instant Tori realized the duality of Mack's personality, and though it was a bit frightening that one man could have two sides so distinctly different, it was also wildly stimulating that such a man hungered for her.

She felt his hands at her buttocks, squeezing firmly, and she sighed, closing her eyes, not knowing what was to happen next but secure in his experience in such matters.

When he kissed her, his tongue flicking out to touch her intimately, Tori cried out in shock. She tried to move away, fearful of the intensity of the feelings that were so new, so unexpected, but Mack held her firmly, his large, strong hands overpowering her resistance.

Her warbling cry of ecstasy surprised Tori. She couldn't help but respond to his efforts. When strong hands roughly restrained her wrists, only then did she realize that she had grabbed Mack by the hair.

Her eyes glazed with passion, she looked down at Mack, not knowing whether to apologize for her uninhibited behavior or not. She ran the tip of her tongue over her lips in an effort to moisten them, but her rapid, ragged breathing had made even her tongue completely dry.

Once Mack had freed his hair from Tori's clenched fin-

gers, he slipped his hand behind her right leg and raised
her knee. Tori allowed him to move her however he liked,
and did not resist when he positioned her leg so that the
back of her thigh rested against his broad shoulder. His
hands, strong and decisive, ran over her legs and thighs,
adding fuel to the rapidly escalating fire of her passion.

He kissed her again, only this time the sensation did
not shock Tori. She was prepared for it, and knowing what
was going to happen and what she would feel heightened
her pleasure.

"Ohhh!" she sighed, tossing her head back until her
skull thumped loudly against the door, any discomfort inconsequential in comparison to the pleasure sizzling
through her.

Balancing precariously on one foot, Tori was only
faintly aware of anything other than herself and her body.
She heard a sound, a voice, and after a moment she realized that it was her own and she was chanting softly a
breathy, lusty, whispered litany, "Oh, Mack! Oh, Mack!"

The tightening began quickly, a clenching within herself as pleasure built upon pleasure. Had Tori been able
to see herself, she would have been stunned by the sensual
smile that curled the corners of her wide mouth, the smile
of a passionate young woman who knew exactly what she
was doing.

Each passing second caused the tension to increase.
Tori's mouth opened a little wider, and her breathing
stopped altogether as she waited for the powerful, wrench-
ing series of contractions that came upon reaching the
pinnacle of ecstasy.

And then, just when she was certain that reaching the
summit was inevitable, just a second or two away, Mack

moved away from her, pushing her leg off his shoulder. He rose to his feet ominously.

"What? Why?" Tori stammered, reaching out to take the lapels of his jacket into her hands, clutching onto him, frantic to have him continue.

Mack's eyes had never been more brilliant, nor had his astonishing passion ever been more focused. Without giving her any explanation, he put a hand to Tori's shoulder and once again pushed her so her back was against the door. The fear that what they had started would end here and now, without that release of passionate tension she was so near, vanished when she looked into his eyes.

Mack leaned into her, kissing her mouth as his hands once more raised her skirt. Only then did she feel the velvety heat of Mack's throbbing arousal touching her, sliding against her thigh, touching her just above the top of her stocking.

"Yes, Mack! Yes!" Tori cried out, twisting her arm around his neck to hold tightly onto him, raising her knee to bring her right foot around behind him.

She had been so close to the summit of ecstasy, and as Mack kissed her, his tongue dancing with her own, she realized that he had known exactly what he was doing all along, had known she had been at the edge of that sweet chasm she wanted to leap into.

"Be still," Mack whispered, his lips warm and wet against Tori's throat, his hands cupping her buttocks, squeezing tightly.

Only then did she realize she had been unconsciously moving her hips from side to side. The moment she stopped and balanced on one foot, Mack's strong hands at her behind to support her, she felt the heat of his passion touching her moist entrance.

In one breathtaking lunge, he buried himself in her, filling her with his desire. A cry of ecstasy was forced from her as he became fully engulfed within her. The sensation of having Mack within her was all that she needed to reach the peak of pleasure.

"Yes-s-s!" he hissed, Tori's cry ringing in his ears as he began his own relentless drive toward fulfillment.

She shivered, holding tightly onto him, feeling oddly powerless and mighty at the same time. The release of her passion had been stronger than she'd expected, so gripping that it was nearly painful when the contractions shuddered through her. And now, though her own passion had been satisfied, Mack was still deep within her, driving into her with steadily increasing fury. Her hips repeatedly struck the smooth, hard surface of the door as she was forced backward by his jolting thrusts. His hands held her buttocks tightly, making it impossible for her to move away from the onslaught of his desire. She felt his chest, heaving with the mighty exertion of his lovemaking, against her tingling breasts, his pounding heart beating so close to her own, in unity with hers.

"Mack! Mack!" Tori whispered, her cheek against his, her lips near his ear.

She stroked his silky hair, its softness in direct contrast to the lean, charging hips that propelled his arousal deep within her, reawakening her passion to soar with his.

She wanted his excitement to reach hers, wanted him to scale the heights he'd taken her to. Bringing her hand down, she cupped his taut buttocks, feeling his muscles flexing as he drove himself harder and faster into her. And then, when she was certain that she could take no more, Mack's low, passionate groan of ecstasy rumbled through him as he had his release.

Tori had not realized how close she was to the summit until, hearing Mack's ecstasy and feeling him driving and swelling deep within her, she again shivered through a climax that, while lighter and less intense than the first, was extremely satisfying.

Though a powerful man, once his passion had been spent, Mack sagged against Tori, gulping in air, his muscular body perspiring beneath the expensive clothing. Never in his life had he desired a woman so completely; never had he felt as though his entire body had turned inside-out during his climax.

And this time it was Tori who started to laugh. Softly at first, then a little louder as she became more aware of the world around her—and of what she'd just done. Mack, too, began to laugh, as he kissed Tori lightly on mouth, cheeks, eyelids, and forehead.

"I think I owe the host and hostess an apology," Tori whispered. Though she had both feet on the floor, her knees were shaking badly and every muscle in her body had relaxed to such an extent that she could barely stand.

"I think we both do." Mack cupped Tori's face lightly in his hand. He looked into her eyes, and a peaceful smile played with his lips. "You'll be the death of me, Tori. But even if you are, I'm more alive now, with you, than I've ever been in my life."

"That's how I feel when I'm with you," she replied.

He stepped away from her, and only then did she see how he had opened his trousers and pushed them down just to the tops of his thickly-muscled thighs. Her own skirt fell once again to her ankles, and though she was covered, the heat and feel of Mack's presence never left her.

On the floor near her feet were her old cotton pantalets. With the toe of her slipper, she kicked the undergarment across the floor with disdain.

Once he'd properly rearranged his clothes, Mack took her hand in his and peered out carefully into the hallway. Seeing no one, he tried to calculate exactly how much time he and Tori had spent in the linen closet making love. He couldn't even hazard a guess.

"Let's get out of here," he said, leading Tori into the hallway. "I need some fresh air . . . and you . . . again . . . soon."

"You're greedy," Tori retorted, pleased that he wanted her so much.

"You inspire that response in me."

Before they reached the end of the hall, she stopped to pull up her stockings. Mack watched her as she raised her skirts, then smoothed her stockings up high, near the tops of her thighs, where she adjusted her lacy garters. *He likes looking at me,* she thought with feminine pride. *Even though we just made love, it still excites him to look at me.*

They made their way through the crowd downstairs. Rumors had been going around that Mack and Tori had run off to some far corner of the mansion for a lustful tryst. More charitable folks said that he had only followed her upstairs to calm her because she'd become upset as a result of Jena Krey's cruel remarks. However, some of the guests who saw Mack and Tori exiting the dance took note of their flushed looks and faintly disheveled appearances.

According to their preferences, the witnesses concluded Tori's flushed skin tone was the result of a crying jag or a quick dose of Mack Randolph's passion.

# Nineteen

Jena Krey was angry enough to kill—and not cleanly. In her frame of mind, the killing would be slow and bloody.

Mack had gone upstairs during the dance and had made love with Tori. This infuriated Jena.

There were people who said Mack had only gone upstairs to calm Tori down, that the poor girl had clearly been crying. But Jena didn't believe that story for a second, not after seeing the well-loved look on Tori's face when she and Mack, hand in hand, had come down the long stairway and gone straight out to Mack's carriage.

Jena had seen that look on herself, in a mirror, back in those brief, exhilarating days when she and Mack had been lovers. Not for a second did she believe that Mack had only offered Tori a strong shoulder to shed tears upon!

Most infuriating of all was that Jena had actually ridden all the way out to the Randolph ranch and had blatantly propositioned Mack. But he'd turned her down! Now he was chasing after the sister of a bounty hunter like a stallion after a filly, not caring a whit that all of Santa Fe's elite was downstairs dancing and drinking.

Mack Randolph, always so concerned about appearances, about doing the right thing, the proper thing, the correct thing . . .

Jena tried to force the irritation from her mind, but she could not. As she saw it, Mack had embarrassed her by choosing Tori over her. Everyone knew Jena wanted Mack and intended to be his wife when he moved into the territorial governor's mansion, just as everyone knew she was more than ready to be with Mack *under any circumstances*.

Wasn't she the one with the reputation for being too sexually adventurous? The one who caused scandals by cavorting about?

Most galling of all to Jena was her belief that Tori was having fun with Mack. It should be Jena with whom Mack behaved so shockingly.

Jena took another glass of cold champagne, hoping it would calm her anger, but when she tasted it, she sniffed. The events of the evening had robbed her of her thirst.

Promising herself that she would get even with Tori, and that she would soon have Mack under her thumb and in her bed again, Jena left the dance early, knowing in her heart that it was time to take drastic measures.

Exactly what measures she wasn't certain.

They were four miles from Tori's cabin. The trip by carriage from the dance had been slow, filled with laughter and more lovemaking. Another bottle of wine had been opened, and Tori sipped from her glass slowly, not sure whether Mack's intoxicating lovemaking or the heady wine was making her skin tingle. They had discussed briefly why Mack had become the Midnight Bandit, but the topic was a bit too serious for her taste, so she had set her questions aside for a later time.

"They'll never forgive me," Tori said, sprawled across the carriage seat with her head against its padded side and her legs tossed over Mack's lap.

Mack held the reins loosely in his hands, and his long legs were stretched in her direction. Tori had never seen him look so relaxed—or so disheveled. His tie was askew, though not completely undone, and his shirt, unbuttoned to the navel, revealed an expanse of heavily muscled chest glistening with the perspiration brought forth by energetic loving. His hair, usually neatly brushed back from his forehead, was now a little damp at the temples, and had been roughly combed back with his fingers into some semblance of order.

"Who is 'they'?" Mack asked, glancing over at Tori. He ran his palm lightly up her leg beneath the skirt of her blue-green velvet gown. He thought her legs were perfect. He touched her through her stockings, then ran his finger along the narrow patch of flesh above her stocking top.

"The monied folks of Santa Fe. They'll say I corrupted you." The thought brought a laugh from Tori. "Imagine that, me corrupting you!"

Even Mack had to laugh at the absurdity of that notion.

"Do you really care what those people think of you?"

Tori studied him for a moment before answering. "Not really. They're important to me only because they are important to you. They're your people."

"No they're not," Mack said quietly.

There was little conviction in his voice because he knew she had spoken the painful truth. Those people were his people—with their gossiping, their back-stabbing, machinations and manipulations, double-dealing and blatant lies—and he knew how to play their games with the best of them.

"Not all of them are bad," Tori said, propping herself up on an elbow, until the effort became too great and she reclined again on the seat. Besides, she liked having her legs over Mack's lap and his hand running lightly, casually over her. "I did meet a few people who were kind to me."

"Money doesn't necessarily make a person evil, you know."

"Yes, I know that," Tori replied, aware of her own prejudices, though not confident of overcoming them.

Unspoken questions faced her and Mack. Difficult questions that could not be avoided forever. But she wasn't going to be concerned with forever—just with this night.

What would happen next? she wondered. Individually and together, they were dedicated to bringing Jonathon Krey to justice, dedicated to seeing that he did not continue to profit from his criminality. But how long could they continue to fight him? Krey was too powerful. He was, after all, trying to hire her brother to kill the Midnight Bandit. And Mack had said that he would not allow Tori to continue her crusade against Krey. Nonetheless, she would not stop—not for Mack, not for anyone. She refused to allow any man to make such an important decision about her life for her.

Mack began to button his shirt, and Tori raised her foot, stopping his progress with a stocking'd toe.

"Don't," she ordered. "I enjoy looking at your chest." She thrust her foot inside Mack's shirt to rub his chest and ribs with it. He smiled at her, clearly finding her openness surprising but not in the least bit unladylike. "Why don't you take your shirt off instead? Take it off for me," she said, mimicking an earlier order to her from the Midnight Bandit.

"Just my shirt?" Mack asked, a single eyebrow raised mockingly.

"That will do for starters."

Mack grinned, but he continued buttoning his shirt, pushing Tori's feet out of his lap when she continued to thwart his efforts.

"Stop it now," he said, his grin widening. "The last thing I need is a discussion with your brother on the sanctity of your virtue. He's got a reputation with guns that—"

"Is as renowned as your reputation with women?" Tori cut in. There was a hint of anger beneath the lightness of her tone. She could not forget that Mack was her first and only lover, but she was not his first, second, or even third.

"My reputation is inflated; your brother has the corpses to prove his."

Feeling just a little threatened, as though her family honor had somehow been put on trial by this lawyer, Tori said a bit softly, defensively, "He's never killed an honest man. You should know that."

Mack patted Tori's leg, looking at her for a beat without saying anything. "Yes, I know that. He's a good and honest man, and the things he does—the men he goes after and brings in—they deserve whatever happens to them. It's because he's an honest man that I agreed to represent him awhile back. He was being cheated by politicians in Taos, and that just didn't seem right to me."

"Justice is important to you, isn't it? It's why you became the Midnight Bandit."

Mack nodded. "I didn't actually become the Midnight

Bandit," he said, grinning just a little at the feebleness of his excuse. "I sort of adopted the role, as an actor does."

"What made you think of it? Anything specific?"

"I've been fighting with Jonathon Krey for years—since I became a lawyer. Maybe even longer than that. Some of the battles he's won, and some I've won. But it wasn't until I started working on the hospital, and saw that bastard worming his way into the project, that I realized how truly dangerous he is. He puts on a pretty face, like stage makeup, and then people don't realize how sadistic and dangerous he is. I've seen how he's been able to manipulate the entire legal system, twisting it upside down until even I don't have any faith in it, and it's what I've dedicated my life to. That's why I became the Midnight Bandit."

Mack shook his shoulders and looked toward the heavens, taking in a single deep breath, holding it for a second, then exhaling slowly. It wasn't until he was relaxed, had released his anger toward Jonathon Krey, that he looked to Tori again.

"Why did you decide Jonathon Krey needed to be taken down a notch or two?" he asked.

"First, I should tell you that Jeremy Krey has put a ten thousand dollar bounty on your head. He's tried to hire Jedediah to go after you, but Jedediah hasn't given him an answer yet."

"Ten thousand dollars? That's a lot of money."

"If Jedediah takes the job—"

"Don't think of that now," Mack cut in, feigning indifference to the information he'd just heard. He patted Tori's leg and asked, "Tell me, why are you out to take Krey down?"

Tori closed her eyes. She had a much more personal reason for hating Jonathon Krey, though she wasn't at all certain she could tell her story without breaking into tears.

"Come on, I've been honest with you," Mack prodded, not expecting the answer to be painful.

"It's nothing that he did to me personally," Tori began, speaking slowly and clearly, looking at the stars overhead as the carriage rolled slowly down the narrow road toward her house. "The thing about Krey that's so dangerous is his money, and what he does with it. Many years ago, I had a cousin who never could quite match up with the rest of the Singer family. He wasn't a bad child, really, just a little slow. One of Krey's hired men offered him money to take part in a bank robbery. Jonathon Krey was behind the whole thing, of course. He was the one who had planned it all. He needed this particular bank destroyed so that he could take over. Anyway, the robbery didn't exactly go as planned. My cousin was caught, and he made a deal with the sheriff. He gave him the names of the men who had robbed the bank with him. Those men were eventually caught and put in jail. Vigilantes dragged them out of their cells on the very first night and hung them all in the town square."

Mack experienced an emptiness in the pit of his stomach. "And then what happened," he asked, though he wasn't at all certain he wanted to know the answer.

"Stupid, sadistic pride. The brothers of the hanged men came after my cousin's family, looking for revenge. My mother, father, a brother, and a sister were visiting them at the time. Jedediah and I were in town buying provisions."

"And the mob got its revenge," Mack said, hoping to finish the story so that Tori wouldn't have to.

"Yes, they did. They set fire to the house, shooting everyone who rushed out. My entire family was killed."

"And that's why Jedediah became a bounty hunter," Mack said. In his mind he silently added, *And why you hate rich people as much as you do.*

They traveled the remainder of the way back to Tori's cabin in silence, each mulling over private thoughts and fears. Mack had rearranged his clothing so that he looked nearly as impeccable as he had when he'd come to pick her up, Tori noted, with a smile. It wasn't really himself he was worried about, but her reputation with Jedediah.

"My brother really isn't the cold-blooded killer the townsfolk say he is," Tori said, keeping her voice down as Mack reined in the carriage horse. She didn't want to awaken Jedediah, and it rather surprised her that he wasn't standing at the doorway already.

"I know he's not," Mack replied, though he couldn't forget that he was unarmed.

"Stay here. I'll be right back," Tori said, rushing into the cabin to tell Jedediah that she had returned home safe and sound . . . and that she wanted a few minutes of privacy with Mack if her over protective older brother would be so kind.

She lit the candle on the small kitchen table and carried it around the cabin with her, looking for her brother. He was nowhere to be found. On her pillow was a single sheet of paper. In Jedediah's sloppy handwriting the note said, he had decided to accept Jonathon Krey's offer to hunt the Midnight Bandit. It added that he was leaving immediately for San Martinez, where the Bandit was rumored to have a hideout, and would return in two or three days.

Tori felt she had been struck in the stomach. She could

hardly breathe. She placed a hand against the bedroom wall to support herself.

Her worst fears had come true. Her brother—her deadly, dangerous brother—was hunting her lover. There was nothing she could do to stop Jedediah now.

"Tori, are you all right in there?" Mack called out, standing in the doorway.

For an instant, she thought of burning her brother's letter, as if by destroying it, she would also destroy the meaning and intent in the words. But this wasn't a problem that would go away if she simply didn't look at it. What Mack Randolph did not know, in this instance, could very likely get him killed . . . and then where would she be? What would she have besides anger if something happened to Mack, her precious and passionate Bandit?

"Tori?"

She could hear the worry in his voice this time. "Come in, Mack. There's something I've got to show you," she said, thinking that the Fates must surely be very angry with her to treat her so cruelly, doing this to her at the end of an evening in which she and Mack—not she and the Bandit—had finally become lovers, and he'd taken her to yet another level of ecstasy.

"You've got to promise me that you'll never again become the Midnight Bandit," Tori demanded.

She was pacing the cabin while Mack, sitting at the kitchen table, read and reread Jedediah's letter.

"You're beginning to sound exactly like me—or like a nagging wife," he scolded with a smile. He accepted Jedediah as a threat, though he saw no need to alarm Tori.

"It isn't me Jedediah's been hired to hunt. You may be his lawyer, but Jonathon Krey has put ten thousand dollars on your head. Do you expect my brother to turn that much money down?"

"Money really scares you, doesn't it?"

"No, just the wrong people with money." She stepped up to the table, her soft green eyes wide and sincere. "Promise me the Bandit goes into retirement as of this moment."

Mack did not answer immediately, and a new world of fears sprang up fully formed within Tori's heart. "You don't know my brother as I do," she said. "Once he gets started on something, he doesn't stop until it's over and done with. He's like a bulldog that way. If he's on the hunt, I won't see him until its over. I don't even know how to let him know that you're the Bandit, so that he'll stop."

"Don't tell him anything. You must know I'm just as determined and single-minded as your brother," Mack said, not wanting to speak the painful truth, but not wanting to lie to her, either. "I can't give up now. Jonathon Krey must be stopped, and I'm just beginning to make him look into shadows to see if I'm there. Pretty soon, he'll really be feeling the effects of what I'm doing. And sooner or later, I'll find something—something solid that will stand up in court—that will enable me to put the bastard behind bars, or up on a gallows where he belongs."

Tori bit her lip to keep more words from spilling out. It would do no good to argue with Mack tonight. Later she would calmly and rationally explain to him why continuing to be the Midnight Bandit was foolishness. Right now was not a time for them to argue . . . not when they had just enjoyed such blissful harmony of mind and body.

Mack was staring at the handwritten letter, but he was no longer reading the words. There was no need for that. He'd memorized each one, and though he'd tried to convince himself the threat wasn't so serious, he was not a man who had ever been able to delude himself for very long.

"If Jedediah's after me, he's after you, too," he whispered, this sudden awareness causing a tightening in his guts. He was brave, but only a fool would casually disregard the danger Jedediah represented. "Jonathon Krey thinks he's only been dealing with the Midnight Bandit, but if your brother gets involved in this, he might figure the Bandit is really two people."

"He's *already* involved," Tori said testily, continuing to pace the floor.

She did not harbor the fears for herself that Mack did. She knew Jedediah would walk through fire for her, and would never do anything to hurt her. It was just the way her brother was, especially after the killings of their family and relatives. He was quietly, intractably dedicated to protecting her, and in seeing that violent criminals received the justice they so richly deserved.

Mack grabbed Tori's wrist as she passed him. Tired, he wondered how many hours ago he had left Fort Richmond upon having concluded his business negotiations. He didn't want to argue with her anymore.

"Whatever happens," he said softly, "it's not going to happen tonight. Jedediah's on his way to San Martinez."

"We do have tonight," Tori said quietly.

She pushed a strand of honey-blond hair behind her

ear. The frantic lovemaking, first in the linen closet, then in the plush, slowly rolling carriage, had made a shambles of the coiffure she'd created for Mack. She took his hand in both of hers, moving just a little closer to him so that she stood between his knees.

"And since my brother is so far away, I see no reason at all why you shouldn't stay here tonight. It's an awfully long ride back to your ranch," she continued, as though the distance somehow validated her reason for wanting him to stay.

For a moment, Mack didn't know what to say. He knew what asking him to stay meant to Tori. It was a bold move. Should anyone discover that he'd spent the night, she would be branded a trollop, or worse. *His* reputation wouldn't suffer at all, and this sexual double standard, though working in Mack's favor, rankled him nevertheless.

He brought Tori's hands to his mouth and kissed them. She was the most exciting, unique combination of strength and independence, femininity and courage, that he'd ever come across; and he silently cursed whatever powers on earth and in the heavens had created such impossible odds against their ever being happy together.

"I will stay with you tonight," Mack whispered as he rose to his feet, now looming over her.

Looking down into her lovely, pale green eyes, he wished that he could tell her he'd stay with her always. He suspected she wanted to hear those words, but to say them would mean lying to her, and he was determined to avoid doing that. Perhaps one day it might be necessary— Mack had been a lawyer long enough to have developed a cynical attitude toward absolutes, especially when words like "forever" and "love" and "truth" were involved—but that time wasn't now.

Holding Mack's hand, Tori led him to her small bedroom, and her even smaller bed. For the two of them to sleep together on it, they'd have to remain in each other's arms the entire night . . . which was exactly what Tori had intended, even if her bed was an acre across.

Mack removed his jacket and tossed it on the foot of the bed. Tori picked it up quickly and placed it on a wooden hanger, then hung it on a peg in the wall. She had been poor too long to be cavalier about expensive clothes.

"Your clothes are much too beautiful to be treated like that," she said.

She turned and watched him remove his tie, then his shirt. Their eyes met and held for a moment; then he unbuckled his belt.

"Is it all right not to make love?" she asked in a tremulous little voice. "Tonight, I just want you to hold me."

Mack nodded, and in his eyes was the understanding that Tori had so needed.

She took his clothes from him, neatly hanging them up. When he was completely naked, she came to him, raised up on her tiptoe, and kissed his mouth lightly.

"Sit down now, and I'll be with you in a moment," she said, her hands on Mack's chest.

Tori felt there must surely be something terribly wrong with her. She loved looking at Mack. The sight of his naked body touched her deeply, making her feel warm, inciting the very first stages of passion. But a man's body wasn't supposed to be beautiful, was it? She knew that men enjoyed looking at women, but the reverse was something she'd never heard of.

*I don't care what other women think or do,* she decided, with a hint of angry defiance against what passed for proper behavior. *It excites me to look at Mack, and that's all I care about.*

She undressed slowly, for Mack's benefit, feeling his eyes upon her as she rolled the white stockings down her legs, then slowly removed her gown and petticoats and chemise. A naughty smile curled her lips as she thought about her old pantalets, and how she'd deliberately left them in the linen closet.

"Come to bed," Mack said, his broad back leaning against the wall where a headboard would have been. He was beneath the light blanket, raising it for her.

Tori thought of putting on her pretty nightgown, the one Jedediah had bought her, but she didn't want anything separating her from Mack—physically or emotionally.

She got into bed, snuggling up to him as his arms went around her, pressing her nose up close to his neck, inhaling to catch the special, comforting scent of him. To feel his body, for once completely naked, pressed against her own completely bare flesh while sharing a comfortable bed was an experience she'd never had with him before.

"Good night, Tori," he whispered, stroking her silken hair. "Sleep well."

"Good night, Mack," she responded sleepily. "I love you."

She did not see his eyes burst open wide with shock.

Jena Krey sat on the edge of her bed, smoking a cigarette. Never in her life had she felt so acutely the sting of being slighted, overlooked in favor of another woman.

She should have taken Tori as a serious threat to her plans to begin with. Apparently this was not just one more poor girl from a nothing family who thought she could sleep her way into becoming a member of the cream of Santa Fe society. She was someone capable of ruining Jena's plans.

*So what am I going to do about her?*

Jena rose to her feet and reached for her robe, then decided against it. She had long ago learned that if she wanted to get a favor from her brothers, it helped to show a little skin, and her nightgown certainly did that. They were always much more amenable to giving her the time she needed to plead for their help when she was scantily clad.

What time was it? Two A.M.? Three? Jena didn't know, and she didn't care. The problems she faced were too critical to her happiness for her to wait until a reasonable hour.

She went down the hall to her brother Michael's room. He was the more intelligent of her brothers, his mind quick and devious, much like hers. Pressing her ear against the door, she listened carefully, and when she heard no sound from inside, she opened the door without knocking.

"Michael, are you awake?" she asked, walking into the room, barely able to see where she was going.

She sat on the edge of his bed, placing her hand upon the blankets. Then she heard the startled exclamation of a woman, and when the blankets were shifted, Jena saw the frightened face of the attractive young woman who'd been with her brother at the dance.

"Don't worry, I'm Michael's sister," she said to her, quickly pulling the blanket back over her nakedness.

The woman started to get out of bed, but Jena stopped her by placing a hand on her bare shoulder.

"Don't go," she whispered. "This won't take long."

She pushed gently but insistently until the woman was lying down in the bed again, her head on the pillow beside Michael's. The woman pulled the blankets up to her chin as Jena walked around the bed to the other side.

"Michael, wake up," Jena said, shaking her brother's shoulder.

Michael was only slightly surprised to see his sister in the room with him. He had learned that she was capable of anything, her behavior often so outrageous that it would seem impossible for her to top herself.

"What are you doing here at this time of night?" he groaned, blinking his eyes.

When Jena leaned down to whisper in his ear, her breasts, so thoroughly revealed in the sheer, low-cut nightgown, were very near his face. He didn't for a second believe that she was unaware of what she was doing.

Whispering, Jena told him that she needed to make Mack dependent upon her. But how could she do that? She had tried gaining power over him through sex, and that hadn't worked. The notion that he might reach the territorial governor's mansion without her at his side—with some other woman—was too painful for her to think about for long.

"What you need to do is beat the hell out of him," Michael whispered after a moment of deliberation.

"What good's that going to do me? I want Mack intact and in one piece," Jena replied, confused, though the idea of having Tori beaten instead was decidedly pleasant.

"Don't have him killed, just beaten up. Then, when he's

recovering, you can be there for him. He's strong and confident now. He won't be that way if he's got busted ribs and every breath he takes hurts like hell. That's when he's going to need someone to lean on, and if you're there when he needs you, you'll own him."

Jena's face broke into a beaming smile. "You're a genius," she said, much too loudly. She kissed her brother, got up, and went around the bed. "You treat Michael right," she said to the woman who stared at her over the satin trim of the blanket. "He's a good man, and he deserves to be treated right."

Next, Jena went to Jeremy's bedroom. Unlike Michael, who liked to look but wouldn't dream of touching, Jeremy reached out for Jena, who deftly avoided his outstretched hands.

"Listen to me now. There's something I need you to arrange for me," she said, positioning herself near the foot of her brother's bed. She told him she wanted Mack beaten, though she did not mention that the idea had originally come from Michael.

"I can hire men to do that," Jeremy said, rubbing his face sleepily. It seemed entirely unfair to him that Jena should be so close yet be forbidden him. "What's in it for me?"

His sister smiled as she rose smoothly from his bed. "Big brother, you get me into Mack Randolph's bed, and you can name whatever you want," she said as she left his bedroom, fully aware of what he wanted from her, though she had no intention of satisfying his wishes.

# *Twenty*

Mack awoke as Tori was easing out of bed. He held onto her, not wanting the naked warmth of her body to be away from his flesh.

"Go back to sleep," Tori whispered, kissing Mack's cheek and smoothing his sleep-mussed hair. "I'll be back in just a little bit."

"Hurry," he murmured sleepily, his brief moment of concern leaving him. "The bed's too big without you in it." Then he buried his face in the pillow he'd shared all night with Tori.

She looked down at him, letting her sleepy smile widen. In her little bed he was an even bigger man, thick in the chest, with muscles that displayed their strength even when he was completely at rest. Yes, he dominated her small cot; and Tori was amazed that she'd managed to stay in it with him all night . . . amazed until she recalled how they'd held each other all night, arms around each other even in sleep.

Tori slipped the pretty nightgown over her head, easing the garment down over her curves, smoothing the fabric with her palms. Before Mack, before the Midnight Bandit, this gift from Jedediah had only reminded her that she had no one to look attractive for. At last, with Mack sleeping peacefully in her bed and her heart filled with tender emotions for him, she had a reason to wear the delicate nightgown.

She went to the stove and got a fire going, then put water on for coffee. How did Mack's mornings usually start? she wondered.

The simple truth of it was that she had no idea at all how a wealthy lawyer began his day. All she'd learned so far was how he spent some of his nights.

Sitting down at the table, waiting for the water to boil, Tori closed her eyes and inhaled deeply. Yes, she could tell that Mack was in her house! His presence hung in the air like the sweet smell of new-saddle leather, clean and magnificently masculine.

Was she just being silly? Tori didn't care. She'd spent far too much of her young life being serious about everything. Now nothing really mattered except her happiness, Mack's happiness, and their love for each other.

The thought brought her up short, and her eyes burst open. Love. Yes, she couldn't deny it. She was *in love* with Mack Randolph. She was certain of it. Whether he loved her or not was another question entirely. He had feelings for her, strong and tender feelings. Tori was certain of that. Hadn't he held her in his arms all night without trying to make love with her, which was exactly the kind of interlude she'd needed?

But did he love her?

Tori couldn't say. Not with any degree of certainty. Loving someone, and being willing to make love with someone, could mean two entirely different things, especially for a man.

*Stop thinking about love,* Tori chided herself.

There was nothing she could do about it, one way or another. Mack's emotions and feelings were his own, and unless he chose to involve her in them, she would continue to be an outsider to him. Instinctively, she knew that if she tried to force her way into Mack's heart, made him put to words exactly what his feelings were, she would drive him away, not draw him closer to her.

The water was boiling, and her attention turned to making coffee. She was glad that something, no matter how mundane, occupied her thoughts for a few moments.

When she heard Mack move on the bed, Tori rushed to the closed bedroom door. "Don't you dare get up yet!" she called through it.

The squeak of the bed springs beneath his weight told Tori that he was still in bed. "Wouldn't dream of moving," he murmured.

It wouldn't be much of a breakfast in bed, but it was the best Tori could do under the circumstances. She arranged four oatmeal cookies in a semicircle on a dinner plate, around the tin cups she had stacked one inside the other.

She brought the plate into the bedroom. Mack was sitting up in bed, a pillow between his back and the wall. The blankets were pulled up to his waist, leaving his beautiful chest bare to her appreciative eyes.

"Breakfast in bed," Mack noted with a smile that brought the dimple to his cheek. The four cookies on the dinner plate were more precious to him than any breakfast he'd ever had, and he'd been served breakfast in bed for most of his life, often in some fine hotel in the United States, Europe, or Mexico.

"It's not really much," Tori apologized, suddenly painfully certain that her simple fare was paltry compared to what Mack was accustomed to.

He touched her lips with the tips of his fingers to silence her words. For a moment their eyes locked, Tori's wide and guileless, a little insecure; Mack's dark, soft, and tender.

"Don't denigrate what you've done. I think it's wonderful," he said softly.

Mack took the plate from her and set it on his lap, then picked up a cookie.

"Wait, let me get the coffee first," Tori said, dancing quickly out of the bedroom on bare feet.

A surge of emotion went through Mack as he watched her hurry off. Her body, so lush with feminine curves, moved fluidly beneath the sheer fabric of her white nightgown. And she was quick on her feet, agile and graceful, which impressed Mack. When she returned, holding the coffeepot, he picked up his cup and held it out for her to fill. She bent low to pour, affording Mack an unhindered view down the décolletage of her nightgown.

It was ridiculous to get such a thrill from a glimpse of pale, firm bosom, Mack told himself. It was especially absurd considering he'd held Tori all night, her breasts pressed firmly against his chest the entire time.

It didn't matter. Logic and reason held little influence with Mack where Tori Singer was concerned.

He waited until she had poured coffee for herself and set the pot on the floor.

"Delicious," he murmured, munching happily on a cookie.

Tori smiled, pleased that he seemed genuinely happy. For a second she pondered the fact that she was serving Mack even though she'd previously promised herself never to be in a subservient position to a wealthy man. How could she feel demeaned when his appreciation of her kindness showed so plainly in the chocolaty depths of his beautiful eyes?

Tori sat near the foot of the bed, crossed her legs, and smoothed her nightgown over them. She could feel Mack's eyes upon her, touching her, caressing her, making her feel warm inside.

"What's today got in store for us?" she asked.

Leaning back against the wall, sipping his coffee— which he thought the finest he'd ever tasted, though he knew the circumstances and current companionship had everything to do with the perception—Mack shrugged his shoulders. Thinking about anything other than Tori wasn't easy to do, particularly when she was in a sheer white nightgown that both concealed and revealed, tempting the imagination.

Tori looked away, trying to cope with Mack's beauty. When she did look back at him, she couldn't keep her gaze where it should be, someplace innocent—like his face! Instead, her eyes kept going down to the blankets, as though imagining what lay just beneath. And what her eyes could not see, her mind remembered with such clarity that a warmth seeped into her veins and moved through her limbs. Even her fingertips now itched to touch Mack in all the ways and in all the places that she had earlier lacked the courage to explore.

Mack restrained his smile. He had seen the influence he had over a woman's self-control before—many times, in fact—and he accepted it as a matter of fact, something in which he should not take too much pride. Just the same, he did nothing to hide his body, the sight of which he could tell was affecting Tori more and more profoundly.

As they made small talk, exchanging banalities, Mack watched a pink blush work its way slowly up Tori's chest and shoulders to her neck, cheeks, and ears. He saw, too, the blunt rise of her nipples become visible through the fabric of her nightgown.

When he finished his coffee, Tori poured him a second cup, and this time the sight of her breasts moving tautly inside the décolletage hit him with staggering force. Mack felt himself becoming erect, and though he tried to ignore the burgeoning of desire, he could not, nor could he hide the impact Tori had upon his senses. Holding her in his arms all night without making love to her had taxed his self-restraint terribly; and his strength of will, his ability to control his desires were rapidly deserting him.

"Tori, I don't know if you're aware of what you're doing to me," he said.

He paused to moisten his lips. He could not tell whether she was the most skilled seductress the world had ever known or it was her seeming innocence that was affecting him so profoundly.

She turned her face to him. Her eyes, jade-green, were wet, shiny, holding in them more than a hint of mischief.

"Maybe I do know," she said, her voice soft, sultry. "Maybe I don't. You have so much more experience in this than I do." She bent over at the waist to set her coffee cup on the wood-plank floor, then took Mack's cup from him. It was empty, and she nonchalantly flipped it to the floor, where it clanged in tinny protest. "What I do know is that you're not nearly as in control of yourself as you want me to think." She touched the tented blanket with a fingertip. "As witnessed by this."

Mack swallowed drily. He had wanted Tori to touch him more when they'd made love, to be more active rather than simply reactive. She had received his passion, and though she'd blossomed beautifully for him, she had yet to become the equal partner he was certain she would be. Now, as she played the innocent coquette while she squeezed him through the blankets, the reality of her passion stunned him.

"I fully understand," Tori continued, looking straight into Mack's eyes as she spoke, feeling his manhood pulsing through the blankets, "that you must return home. No doubt, your spending the night with me has caused quite a scandal among the Randolph clan."

Mack brought his right hand to Tori's face, running the pad of his thumb lightly over her lips. He slipped his hand beneath her heavy, silken hair at the back of her neck, pulling her just a little closer, his heart hammering in his chest, his passion doubling in intensity with each second.

Tori pulled the blankets down enough to expose him, and when she took his engorged manhood into her hand, the heat of it shocked her. Squeezing, she watched as Mack's eyelids fluttered briefly, passion soaring through him. She inched closer, her gaze locked with his, her small hand moving over the length of him as her desire escalated.

"Last night, I needed you to hold me close," Tori whispered. "This morning, I need more than that."

*Such wanton behavior,* a small voice inside her head whispered, somewhat critical, as though it wasn't really her own. Another voice, more insistent, replied, *Tori is a wanton woman . . . but only with Mack!*

She kissed him and, with the meeting of their lips, experienced the sweetest helplessness she'd ever known. She hungered for him and all that he could make her feel in every fiber of her body. She didn't *want* him; she needed him; she didn't want to make love with him, she *had to* if she was to maintain whatever sanity she still possessed.

Suppressing passion had never been a skill Mack had needed to nurture. After wanting Tori all night long, and now having her in his arms and feeling her trembling fingers circling around and gliding over the length of his arousal, he felt he was burning up with passion.

His hands were strong and unyielding when he took Tori by the shoulders, pulling her close, twisting and turning upon the undersized bed to position her beneath him.

"Wait, I want to kiss you," she said after he had pulled her nightgown over her head.

She had wanted to kiss Mack down low, as he had done to her. But he had not fully understood her intention, or he was much too aroused to allow for such a diversion. He thrust his knee between her thighs to separate them, stretching out above her, the velvety heat of her nakedness fueling the flames of his passion.

"I can't wait," he said a bit breathlessly, keeping his weight on his elbows so he could look down into her face.

His expression was one of confusion, for he considered this wild desire of his more befitting in a sexually awakening youngster than a grown man whose prowess was whispered about by the fashionable ladies of Santa Fe.

He reached between their bodies to touch her low, feeling the honey of her excitement, thankful that she was as ready as he.

"Let me," Tori said, a gentle command in her voice.

She was just a little distressed that Mack had not allowed her to experiment with his body, as she had wanted. So now she took his passion between her hands to guide him to her entrance. The heat of him touching her shot through her like a lightning bolt, and she raised her knees higher to form a valley for Mack's hips.

When Mack entered her in a single, thick thrust, she gasped, "Deep!" on a breathy sigh that might either be a request or a blissful exclamation of fact.

Mack was a man possessed, and Tori accepted his ardent passion with a shocking abandonment of inhibition. Beneath them, the ancient springs of her bed creaked raucously, protesting the thrashing of their bodies.

Tori hooked her ankles together at the small of Mack's back, squeezing his lean, undulating hips with her thighs. She heard him gasp as though in pain, tossing his head up and arching his back as he thrust deeply into her. Only then did she realize that she had raked her fingernails over his back, leaving long red marks as a reminder of the heady heights to which his passion had taken her.

They reached the summit simultaneously and quickly, a fact which embarrassed Mack slightly, though he did not comment on it. Tori was oblivious to any sense of brevity, so complete and unrestrained was her satisfaction.

Lying beneath him, her whole body tingling as she relaxed, she stroked his back lightly with her fingertips, feeling the welts she'd made on his pale, flawless flesh with her fingernails.

"I'm sorry," she said between panting gasps of breath. "Did I hurt you?"

"It doesn't matter," Mack replied, breathing deeply to recover his equilibrium.

A tiny corner of his mind, competitive and primordially male, took pride in knowing that his sensual skills had driven Tori to uncharacteristic levels of desire. Her passion for him had erupted, causing her to rake his back frantically with her nails.

She poured more coffee for both of them, and they drank and chatted softly. The sensation that she was enjoying a morning in the way she could almost daily if she were his wife came to Tori. Was this what it was like to be married? She was suddenly painfully aware that these moments with Mack were stolen. If Jedediah were to come home, he'd surely call him out and insist that guns be drawn. Furthermore, Mack hadn't returned to his own home yet, and though Tori couldn't be sure, she highly suspected that he would have some questions to answer when he got to the ranch. He had been born and raised a Randolph, and as such, he knew what his place was in society. Tori Singer had no place in his world, as far as his family and his obligations were concerned.

"As much as I hate to say it, I really must be going," Mack said, his arm still around Tori. His fingertips traced light circles on her bare back. "It must be after nine by now."

"Don't go," she quickly replied, leaning into him so that he would need to push her off to leave the tiny bed. "You don't have to."

"I do. Much as I hate to say it, I do," Mack repeated, turning beneath her. He kissed the top of her head, loving the feel of her silky blond hair against his lips, inhaling the fragrance of her to store in his memory.

Tori again complained, but Mack extricated himself. He put his clothes on even though she halfheartedly tried to stop him, making a game of her efforts. As he balled his necktie and shoved it into the pocket of his jacket, Tori jokingly accused him of leaving her to go to another woman. Oddly, Mack enjoyed her outrageous flirting, her display of nudity; and he suspected that if she really insisted upon it, she could get him to stay the morning, possibly into the afternoon.

"Really, I must leave," he said, cupping Tori's face to stop her movements. He looked into her eyes, hoping that she would understand and not feel abandoned. "I'll see you as soon as I can."

He kissed her softly, knowing he should say something more tender, perhaps address the vow of love she'd uttered just before falling asleep on the previous night. Did she even remember saying she loved him? She had been very tired, and she'd fallen asleep immediately after saying the words. Maybe it had just been the wine talking, Mack told himself. But he knew she hadn't been that intoxicated.

With a pretty pout on her lips, Tori wrapped herself in a blanket from the bed and walked Mack to the door.

"What do we do next to Jonathon Krey?" she asked, standing before the open door. It was a beautiful, sunny day, and she felt a pang of sadness that she couldn't spend every such day with Mack.

"We?" Mack asked with raised eyebrows. *"We* won't be doing anything. I thought we already discussed this."

"We did. We just didn't come to an agreement," Tori replied, her eyes narrowing. This was a conflict she really did not want to face.

"Yes, we did. You're going to stop fighting Jonathon Krey. It's as simple as that."

"No, it's not. *You're* in no position to tell me what to do."

Tori squared her shoulders. She had started fighting Jonathon Krey and his pernicious influence on her own, without asking for any man's acceptance of what she was trying to do, and she would continue on her own, if necessary.

Mack looked away, grinning sardonically. He knew the grin would infuriate Tori, because she always thought it meant he wasn't taking her seriously. But it was absurd for her to continue her lawlessness when she knew that Krey was on his guard. Mack also realized that the main reason he needed Tori to follow a safer course was that she had become a part of his life—how important a part he didn't yet know—but now he couldn't imagine what life would be like without her.

"Let's not argue," he said crisply, adopting the flinty tone he'd used when he was the Midnight Bandit.

He knew he was being unreasonable, even dictatorial, but he simply couldn't understand why Tori just once couldn't behave like any other woman he'd known.

"Just leave fighting Jonathon Krey up to me, and there'll be nothing for us to argue about," he added.

"Why not leave it up to me?" Tori shot back, crossing her arms over her chest, her stance and expression as intractable as her mood. *"I've* never had a gun pointed square at my back; that's something *you* can't say."

"We're not going to argue about this," Mack said after a long pause. Couldn't she just keep her mouth shut and simply do what she was told?

"You're right, we're not," Tori replied, kicking the door shut.

Alone in her house, she gritted her teeth, angry that Mack should suddenly find it impossible to think of her as a competent person able to take care of herself. Why couldn't he see how much he needed her, when it was so obvious?

Their argument had cast a dark pall over the day which had begun so spectacularly.


Jedediah knelt beside the carcass, feeling a cold, dead emptiness inside himself that he could not explain. The horse had been Tori's mare, Daisy. Though little more than the skeleton was left now that the coyotes and buzzards had picked the bones clean, Jedediah recognized the oddly stripped hooves that had been peculiar to Tori's mare. Then, too, he recognized the renailed, left hind shoe, which Tori had fixed herself in a marginally successful effort to save money rather than take Daisy to a blacksmith in Santa Fe.

The surprise wasn't in finding the carcass. Tori had told him roughly where the mare had gone down. The awful wound from the heavy-caliber bullet ending the noble mare's suffering was plain enough to see, despite the predation of scavengers.

What made no sense at all, what put the first tickle of surprise and doubt in Jedediah's mind, was the condition of the mare's legs. Not one of them was broken. The animal had obviously needed to be put out of its misery, but *not* because of a broken leg, which had been Tori's explanation for the tragic incident . . . or was that her excuse?

Jedediah looked in all directions, seeing the endless desert in all its splendor. A beautiful sight, certainly, if one had an appreciation for such beauty. Tori did . . . but was that reason enough for her to ride way out here?

He had the eerie sense that he'd been lied to. What skewed the equation for Jedediah was the belief that someone who *should* be telling the truth—someone with everything to gain and nothing to lose by the truth—was the one telling the lies.

But why?

He eased into the saddle and rode away slowly, in no hurry to return home to Tori or to ride into Santa Fe to report to Jeremy Krey.

## Twenty-one

Tori didn't trust anything anymore. Jedediah had been looking very strangely at her, and occasionally she wondered what his thoughts were. Did he suspect Mack was the Midnight Bandit? No evidence had been left behind anywhere to lead her brother to Randolph, the respected attorney. . . . Still, Tori was uneasy.

Perhaps Jedediah suspected she and Mack had become lovers, but usually if he had questions regarding her relationship with a man, he confronted her with them. His style was to attack problems head-on and work toward an immediate answer. Now, instead of being direct, he was even more silent than usual, and in the two days that had passed since his return from San Martinez, he hadn't once gone to see his sweetheart in Santa Fe.

Thoughts of Mack flooded Tori's waking hours. She tried to banish them from her thoughts, but she could not. The tender times, when she was in his arms and they were talking quietly, she remembered first; then vividly clear images of their lovemaking followed. Frequently, she would find herself blushing crimson, and though she was certain it was wicked of her, she let herself replay these passionate scenes repeatedly in her mind.

She wanted Mack. She loved him with all her heart and

soul, though there were things about him that she did not like very much. Such as his attitude toward her effectiveness against Jonathon Krey. When had Mack become so certain that she was a hindrance to their cause?

Could his attitude have changed because they'd become lovers?

Tori dismissed this notion. They had very nearly become lovers on that very first night when the Midnight Bandit had saved her from capture. And later, when the two of them had attacked Krey Cattle #3, he hadn't found her presence at his side so terribly disconcerting.

Unless, of course, his attitude toward her had changed. Perhaps she was something more than just another lover now.

This thought brought a smile to Tori's lips as she continued brushing down the mare "loaned" to her by Paul Randolph and not yet returned because Mack had insisted that she keep the animal.

Was Mack falling in love with her? He hadn't said as much, but then, he seldom said everything that was on his mind. As a result, Tori had learned to prod and pry in her attempts to find out what it was he was thinking, what was in his heart.

But if he loved her, as she hoped he did, then why hadn't he come to her? Two days ago she'd kicked the door shut on him, but two days was plenty of time for a man to realize that he was being a pigheaded fool! Now Mack should apologize so that he and Tori could again make love and then get on with their lives and their private war against Jonathon Krey!

Tori played the fantasy over and over in her mind. She pictured clearly the look on Mack's face as he swung out of the saddle. His grin was sheepish, boyish; it devastated Tori's anger, melting the ice in her heart. He would apologize, saying he'd finally realized what a damned fool he was being, and she would take him by the hand, tell him she forgave him, then lead him into her bedroom where they would make tender, glorious love all night long.

Except Mack never rode up, never grinned sheepishly, never said he'd realized the error of his ways.

"You're a damned stubborn fool, Bandit," she whispered, running the curry comb along the gelding's hind flanks.

She remembered the exciting times, when she hadn't yet learned who the man behind the mask was, yet was making love to him. He'd been so patient with her then, at that oasis, concerned for her comfort, for her pleasure, aware that she was a virgin and needed much tenderness. And, oh . . . how he had made her senses sing!

Far off, she heard a horse neighing. Her heart leaped in the hope that Mack had at last come to her. But emerging from the trees in the distance was Jedediah, and Tori's heart sank. There were times when she wished her brother wasn't around. If she couldn't have Mack with her, then she wanted to be alone with her thoughts, her dreams and memories.

*It's time to stop feeling sorry for myself,* Tori decided with determination. *I'm taking charge of my own life. I can't change Mack any more than I can become the rich society woman he wants me to be.*

Jonathon Krey leaned back on the sofa in his office and stared out the window. He puffed slowly, contemplatively, on his pipe. The rich, fragrant Virginia tobacco never failed to soothe him, and his lips curled into a smile, both cruel and cunning,

He had put all his energy into thinking about how to apprehend the Midnight Bandit. His other business enterprises were now neglected so he might concentrate on that man who prevented him from sleeping at night.

The seeds of a solution had grown slowly. He'd even considered one thought lunacy when it had first hit him.

*Who is my worst enemy?* he asked himself. The answer to that one was simple: Mack Randolph. But would Mack, a lawyer and outspoken advocate for increased law enforcement in the territory, actually break the law?

Randolph had certainly worked to the benefit of the downtrodden, but Krey knew something else about him, something kept from the journalists who so often devoted space and ink to praising him.

Mack Randolph was a man who enjoyed the ladies, and every politician knew that indiscretion—even a man's— was a death sentence to a political career. The fact that Mack had continued with his affairs proved to Jonathon Krey, as he sat in the dark puffing slowly at his pipe, that certain human factors drove him. Mack was not the political machine he presented himself as. He had a darker, hidden side that flaunted convention.

Would he go so far as to become the Midnight Bandit?

Jonathon had no doubt that Mack matched him, hatred for hatred. In fact, Jonathon highly suspected that Mack's hatred burned hotter than his own, primarily because Mack had more often than not failed to stop Krey whenever they'd clashed in a courtroom over one of Jonathon's business ventures. Could Mack's frustration be driving him to acts of criminality?

A crooked smile played over Jonathon Krey's lips as he bit down on the stem of his pipe.

Randolph could be the Midnight Bandit. He hoped he was. If he was operating outside the law, then he had the potential for being *way* outside it. This dent in the "knight's" armor could be helpful since Jonathon Krey desperately wanted Mack in his pocket, accepting bribes and taking orders.

He closed his eyes and tried to calm his thinking. He was jumping to conclusions, assuming immediately that a single errant thought was the truth, when in fact it might be nothing more substantial than wishful thinking.

Just the same, if Mack was the Midnight Bandit, that might explain a few things, like how the Bandit always seemed to know exactly where to be and how to strike with the most damage at Krey's enterprises.

"What you need two horses for, Mr. Randolph?" the ranch hand asked, saddling up Mack's mount and placing a bridle on the second one.

"I want to test their stamina," Mack replied, his voice low, his explanation lame.

"Never seen you show any interest in either of these horses before, Mr. Randolph. Geez, we got plenty of fine riding stock on this ranch without you having to ride horses that haven't been—"

"I'm really in quite a hurry," Mack said, wishing now that he'd simply saddled his own horse.

The ranch hand, though an excellent man with the

horses, was much too talkative, insisting on many more answers than Mack was willing to give.

Beneath his left arm was the blanket roll, bulging slightly with the things he'd placed in it earlier. He consciously forced himself to relax his grip on the roll, not wanting to draw any more attention to it than he already had.

"You're sure there ain't nothin' I can do for you, Mr. Randolph?" the ranch hand asked. "Any man that needs two horses with him probably needs a second man riding at his side."

"I appreciate the offer, but that really won't be necessary. I want to ride hard, to get my thoughts clear," Mack explained.

Completely confused, the ranch hand squinted his eyes. Mack suspected that never in his life had this cowboy needed time alone to think through a business proposition.

From the corner of his eye, Mack saw Juan stepping out of the ranch house. Mack stuck his boot in the stirrup and swung up into the saddle. With night coming on, he didn't want Juan, or anyone else, slowing him down or giving him more work to do before he could leave.

"Keep the boys close to home," Mack told the ranch hand as he accepted the reins for the trailing horse. "I don't want the Midnight Bandit thinking he can steal *our* payroll."

The cowboy's eyes grew big and round. "Do you really think he would come here?" The idea of losing his monthly salary was a frightening one.

"Never can tell. You just never can tell," Mack said, tapping his boot heels to the horse's ribs.

He felt a little guilty for putting fear in the cowboy's

heart. He had no doubt that, on his early morning return, he would see men with rifles standing guard at the gate and on the rooftops of the bunkhouses.

Tori peered out the window, careful not to move the curtain. She was watching Jedediah ride away. When he disappeared into the distant trees, a great weight was lifted from her shoulders.

Her brother had been acting strangely lately, asking peculiar questions, coming and going at the oddest times and for the strangest intervals. There was no one in the world she knew as well as Jedediah, but he had become a stranger to her.

For the first time in her life, his presence had begun to get on her nerves, and Tori knew exactly what had brought about this change in her: she wanted to ride. She had tasted the excitement of attacking the evil of Jonathon Krey, and she wanted to know that sense of accomplishment again. She would be *acting;* she would be taking steps toward a goal, rather than simply staying at the cabin, lamenting the fact that Mack Randolph wasn't the man she wanted him to be. Doing *something* was better than doing *nothing.*

From beneath the bed, Tori removed the items she had recently purchased at the dry-goods store in town. The cotton shirt, cut for a man, was the deepest shade of navy blue. Tori had told the clerk the gift was a present for her brother, though the man didn't care much one way or another. At the same time, using her meager funds, Tori had purchased a large kerchief, also in a dark blue color. The scarf would hide her golden hair. She couldn't ever *be* the Midnight Bandit, but she had learned lessons from him, lessons she would not forget. She would never again be noticed because her blond hair reflected the moonlight.

Tori went back to the kitchen table, where her revolver and holster waited. She'd already cleaned the revolver twice, just to give herself something to do while waiting for Jedediah to leave. All was ready to strike out at Jonathon Krey once again.

She was just tucking the overlong tails of the man's shirt into the waistband of her Levi's when she heard the pounding of a horse's hooves outside. Tori's heart leaped in her chest; her first thought was that Jedediah had returned. Somehow, he had figured out what she was up to, and rather than riding off to see his secret sweetheart in Santa Fe, he'd been waiting in the trees, hiding until this very moment so that he could catch her red-handed.

She began unbuttoning the shirt, not wanting to lie to her brother about it. She was just about to rush to her bedroom when something struck her as distinctly out of the ordinary. Stopping in her tracks, she could not fully realize what was wrong.

She listened to the sounds outside her door, and recognized that more than one horse had come to a stop in front of her cabin. She rushed to the table, pulled the Colt from its holster, and went back to the window.

"I don't believe it," she whispered, spying Mack dressed in black trousers and a black jacket. Though his shirt was white, Tori knew that in his saddlebags was a black shirt, cape, and mask, plus the holster and revolver which would complete his transformation into the Midnight Bandit.

"Tori, damn it, get out here!" Mack called out, even before he'd dismounted.

She waited just long enough to complete buttoning her shirt before rushing outside. The anger she heard in his voice, she knew was for theatrical purposes only. If anything, he was angry with himself for being unable to stay away from her, and this knowledge made her tingle inside.

"Good evening, Bandit," she said, her face shining with love and triumph.

"That's pretty funny. The one person in the world who knows I'm the Midnight Bandit is the very person I would have not know."

"At least I'm in exclusive company," Tori said, stifling the urge to throw herself into Mack's arms. "What brings you here this evening?"

"You know very well what it is," Mack said, turning his back on Tori to unstrap the blanket roll from the back of his saddle.

"Actually, I don't. I thought you weren't talking to me anymore."

"I'm not talking *sense* to you anymore . . . because you're too daft and headstrong to listen," Mack said, his back still turned to her.

Tori clenched inside at the insult, but fought against the urge to respond. After all, she had dished out her fair share of insults to Mack; she had to be strong enough to take a few herself.

"I've got something for you," Mack stated as he walked past her, onto the porch and into her home.

Tori rushed quickly in behind him, no different from any other woman in the world expecting a gift from her lover, enormously pleased that he'd been thinking of her even when they were apart. Mack still hadn't kissed her since his arrival, though, so she forced the smile from her lips. Gifts be damned, she wanted his kisses.

"Whatever you're bringing, it isn't what I want," she said as he stepped up to the small table. She placed his hands on her hips defiantly as Mack looked at her, clearly shocked by her declaration.

"How do you know? You haven't even seen it yet."

"I don't care. It's not what I want."

Mack glared at her. "Has anyone ever told you how frustrating you are?"

"Yes. You have. Several times, in fact." She stepped forward slowly, closing the distance that separated them. The look in her soft green eyes turning from feigned anger to burgeoning passion. "But I don't always leave you feeling frustrated, do I?"

Mack couldn't keep the grin from his lips. "No, not always. Just most of the time. Now tell me what it is you really want," he said, though he had a pretty good idea of what it might be.

"A kiss, for starters. Then a pleasant howdy-do would be nice." Tori touched the tip of Mack's chin with her forefinger, and let her fingertip glide slowly down his throat. She could feel his pulse, and she could almost guarantee that it was racing faster than he would have liked under the circumstances. "Aren't lovers supposed to kiss when they've been apart?"

Fleetingly, across the surface of her mind, she questioned her description of their relationship. She was in love with him, and she'd shared her body and her passion with him. Whether Mack was in love with her was still unanswered. Did she really dare find out? If he was not, it would be devastating.

"You're absolutely right," Mack replied.

The kiss was soft initially, until after a second or two of tenderness their passions heightened. Mack's arms went around Tori, pulling her in close, forcing her curvaceous body to conform to his solidly muscular one.

She waited for the tip of his tongue to touch her lips before parting them. Then, accepting his tongue into her mouth, she purred contentedly. Whenever she kissed Mack this way, so deeply and intimately, her passion sky-rocketed, turning spontaneously from warm to super-heated, from hot to volcanic. She raised a knee to slide it along the outside of his thigh, her upward progress stopped only when her knee bumped against the underside of Mack's holster. She thrilled when his hand slid down her backside to squeeze her firmly, forcing her to him.

"L-let's . . . let's go inside," Tori stammered when the kiss had finally ended.

The interior of the cabin was quite dark. She had every intention of leading Mack straight to her bedroom, but he went to the kitchen table.

"You were going out tonight, weren't you?" he said, lighting the lamp which illuminated her holster and revolver.

Tori hesitated. She wanted to lie about her preparations for another raid on Jonathon Krey's overstuffed coffers.

"Well?" he asked, setting his blanket roll on the table.

Tori squared her shoulders. She resented having to defend her actions to Mack. "Yes," she said steadily. "I was just getting ready when I heard you riding up."

He turned to face her. "I figured as much," he said as a slow smile spread across his face, making his dark eyes shine in the way Tori liked so much. "That's why I brought this with me." He tapped the blanket roll with a finger.

"What is it?"

"Find out for yourself."

Tori walked past him to the table, perplexed and just a little worried. Oblivious of her evaporated passion, she unrolled the blanket carefully to reveal a cylindrical roll of black silk. When she picked it up, the silk unrolled farther, allowing a smaller piece of silk to fall to the wooden floor.

"What is it?" she asked.

"You can't tell? Granted, I'm not much of a seamstress, but I thought I did a reasonable job of it, under the circumstances."

On closer inspection, Tori noticed the rough stitches along the edge of the cloth, which was accompanied by a tie and collar. And on the floor lay, not a black silk kerchief but a mask.

"My own mask and cape!" Tori exclaimed with delight.

It wasn't so much the gifts that pleased her as Mack's intent. He was assuring her that she could be her own woman, make decisions for herself. However stubborn he might be initially, he did see the light eventually!

The most beautiful gown in the world would not have pleased Tori as much as the simple, primitively constructed cape and mask.

"I had to guess at the length," Mack explained as she brought the cape over her shoulders. "I had mine made in San Francisco by a Chinese tailor who knew enough not to ask too many questions. Naturally he was paid well for his silence."

Tori tried on the mask, fitting it over her eyes and nose,

then tying the ends into a knot at the back of her head. Her vision was absolutely unobstructed, and after only a second or two, she hardly noticed the silk against her face. Now she understood how Mack had made love to her while wearing the mask without being distracted by it.

She turned to him. "How do I look? Like the Midnight Bandit?"

The words made Mack tighten up inside. The last thing he'd wanted was for Tori to be mistaken for the Midnight Bandit. Still, he wanted her identity concealed should anyone see them. He managed a smile, a pretense that her comment had not in any way caused him concern.

"No, you look much better than the Midnight Bandit ever did," he joked.

Beaming, she took off the mask. Her green eyes sparkled with excitement.

"What were you going to do tonight?" she asked.

Mack noticed that she was eager to try out her new persona in cape and mask; her old persona seemed to have forgotten about making love. Though he would have loved nothing more than to taste the sweetness of her charms once more, he let the moment pass.

"What were *you* going to do?" he replied.

"The General Store over at Tula Valley. As you know, Krey owns it, and he's extending credit to every family in the area—more than folks can handle. Of course, he keeps increasing the interest charged, and now some of the people can't even pay the interest, much less the balance. Even worse, some families are so far in debt to Krey they're unable to buy anything else from him."

Her observations surprised Mack. He'd thought he kept up with all of Krey's moneymaking schemes, but he hadn't even heard of this one. Though he prided himself on being a man of the people and a defender of the downtrodden, Mack realized now just how isolated his wealth had kept him from the harsh realities of life. He'd been a protector of people less fortunate than himself, yes. Of the common man, no.

Tori didn't know what to make of the expression on Mack's face, and uncertainties she'd thought deeply buried suddenly surfaced.

"Isn't that a good idea? If you have a better one, I'll do whatever you think is right."

"What were you going to do at the General Store?"

"All the records of what's owed are kept there. Once a month, Michael Krey comes by and picks up the money from Billy Quinn. I thought I'd just burn the records."

Seeing Mack's bright, approving smile, Tori grinned with pleasure.

"What are we waiting for?" he asked.

When they were outside, she looked at the trailing horse. "Why this one?" she asked. "You're already letting me use one horse I still haven't paid for."

"Yes. And your brother knows that. But what he doesn't know, and what no one except us knows, is that these horses will be sold tomorrow, and will be on their way to Fort Richmond on the day after. Should anyone spot us, it'll be awfully difficult to trace these horses back to the Randolph Ranch. By the day after tomorrow, it'll be impossible."

Tori was thoroughly impressed. "You think of everything, don't you?"

"Not always, but I try. Believe me, Tori, I try."

## Twenty-two

Mack looked at the thick, gold pocket watch, angling it so he could read the hands in the moonlight.

"It's only a little after eleven," he said, smiling sardonically. "If we break in now, the newspapers will have to stop calling me the Midnight Bandit."

"Don't worry, darling, I won't tell anyone you were an hour early," Tori replied in a whisper.

She had tried to remind herself a dozen times that what they were doing was dangerous, and that she shouldn't be in such buoyant spirits, but being other than joyous when she was with Mack was impossible. He had come to her, complete with cape, mask, and horse, and he'd even agreed to follow through with her plan to strike out at Krey.

Mack smiled in return. What should he think when Tori used a word like "darling"? Though she didn't seem to need much reassurance, he rarely used endearments with her. And never far from his thoughts was the sleepy sentence uttered by Tori moments before she'd fallen asleep in his arms. Those three words had played holy hell on his peace of mind ever since. "I love you," she had said, and the words had seemed quite natural to her.

And maybe they were for Tori, but not for Mack. Even

when women had asked him to say them, he had always refused.

Instinctively, he knew that real love was uncharted territory, and that if he cherished the future, he would not cheapen the words by blithely using them with every woman who shared his bed and took pleasure in his passion.

Was Tori waiting for a declaration of love? And if he gave it, would he be telling the truth or giving in to avoid another testy confrontation with her?

"Do you see any guards?" she whispered. "I don't."

Mack brought his mind back to the problems at hand, wondering how he could have let his thoughts wander. Kneeling in the darkness near the small group of buildings that Jonathon Krey had erected in Tula Valley, he scanned the shadows once more for sentries.

"I think the way is clear," he decided. "We want to stay as far from the saloon as possible. It sounds pretty dead in there, but you never know when someone might stagger out."

Tori looked at the buildings once more, squinting to see the structures better in the darkness. Krey had built a small saloon, where the liquor served was of poor quality, often watered down, and always overpriced; a general store in which customers paid way too much for a sack of flour for the benefit of not having to travel all the way into Santa Fe; another shack occasionally used as a bordello, whenever Jeremy Krey convinced some hard-up prostitute to give him half her profits, and to bestow sexual favors upon him; a blacksmith shop usually without a smith; and a dentist's office that doubled as a veterinarian's and undertaker's office. All three jobs were now done by a man who'd been a fine doctor until a nose for laudanum had dulled his intellect and his skills, causing a woman to die needlessly in childbirth. He had made a hasty departure from St. Louis only minutes before an enraged mob had decided to lynch him in the town square. Not much was expected of him anymore, and that was the way the doctor liked it.

The saloon was the only building in which lamps burned, and the night breeze carried from it the sounds of a card game in progress.

Mack got to his feet and started the final approach to the General Store. Tori adjusted her mask one more time, made sure that her bandanna—she'd opted to do without the old hat—was in place to hide her blond hair, then wrapped her cape around herself as she followed Mack.

As they moved swiftly and silently through the night, Tori sensed an unidentifiable change in herself, a change she was later shocked to understand.

By putting on the cape and mask, she was hiding her identity, not only from those people who might recognize her, but also from herself. Yes, behind the mask she was no longer Tori Singer. The Midnight Bandit? No, that was Mack. But she *wasn't* Tori. She felt different, bolder somehow, freed by the anonymity the mask gave her.

As they crept closer and closer to the General Store, a part of her seemed to be expanding, her courage and confidence building with each step. She was hiding, to be sure, but by hiding behind the mask she was also setting free something within herself that she'd always kept hidden, even from herself.

The two masked lovers stalked past quarters built for Krey's low-paid hands before arriving at the darkened rear doors of the General Store.

"Where does Billy Quinn live?" Mack asked.

"I think upstairs," Tori whispered, standing close beside him and leaning against the drafty, poorly made, two-story building. "Sometimes, after he closes the store, he goes to the saloon. If he drinks enough to pass out, then he stays there and Krey takes a night's wages from his pay."

"Wages?"

"The saloon is also a hotel, sort of. If you drink enough to pass out, you can sleep on a cot. Krey charges dearly for the privilege."

With each passing minute, Mack was discovering just exactly how far removed he was from the real victims of Jonathon Krey, the people with whom he'd always felt such an affinity. The idea of sleeping on a cot in a saloon was so foreign to him as to be unimaginable.

The doors and windows of the store were locked and barred and there was no exterior stairway for escape should the ramshackle building catch fire. Poor Billy Quinn, Mack decided, in the event of a late-night fire.

"How did you plan on getting in?" Mack asked.

Tori grinned beneath the mask. "I hadn't thought it through that far. I figured I'd think of something once I got here."

Mack shook his head, though he couldn't help smiling. For most of his life he'd calculated every move, every step necessary to achieve his goals successfully. Then along came Tori! With her, he was an entirely different person, more spontaneous, quicker to smile, more inclined to live his life rather than run it like a carefully monitored business enterprise.

"Well, you're here, so start thinking, unless you want

to wait until morning for Quinn to unlock the doors for us."

Tori stepped away from Mack and began inspecting the doors and windows.

In the near-total silence of the night, she was thinking of ways to enter the building, and discarding every idea almost as quickly as it came to mind, when the off-key singing of an Irish ballad drifted along on the night air, getting slowly and steadily louder.

Tori rushed to Mack, and together they moved away from the General Store and into the shadows. She saw the singing came from Billy Quinn, who was weaving and stumbling his way down the single dusty street, holding a whiskey bottle in his right hand. Occasionally, he paused to swig deeply. They could see that he was on the very edge of falling into an alcoholic stupor.

"And to think that we were afraid he'd see us," Mack muttered in disgust after Tori had identified Quinn. "He couldn't see his own shoes much less us."

Mack and Tori crouched behind the horse trough, even though it didn't seem likely Billy Quinn would notice them.

Quinn staggered to the rear door of the General Store, then fished around in his pocket for the key. A full minute later, he stuck the key into the lock, and after nearly another minute, he figured out which way to turn it. Mack, meanwhile, was muttering disgustedly that a man like Billy Quinn should never have so much influence and power over the lives of good men and women trying to make a decent living for themselves and their families.

Mack's unflagging contempt for violence—except in rare desperate circumstances—kept him from rushing forward and clubbing Quinn from behind. A hard jab to the back of the head and the sot would be sleeping on the floor of his store with only a lump and a headache to show for it in the morning.

"Look at that idiot," Mack growled under his breath.

Quinn, in a simultaneous attempt to put his key in his pocket, drink from his whiskey bottle, and enter the store, dropped his key in the dirt. When he bent over to pick it up, he hit his head against the door, staggered back several steps, then dropped the whiskey. Prioritizing his desires, Quinn went immediately for the bottle, groping in the moonlight for it. By the time he'd recovered the whiskey and had it to his lips, he'd completely forgotten about the key.

Quinn stumbled through the door and closed it behind him. Mack heard confused grunting as he staggered through the store. Eventually, a lamp was lit upstairs in Quinn's small living quarters.

"I'll give you two to one odds that he didn't lock the door," Mack whispered.

"I thought you weren't a gambling man."

"I'm not. But I like to guess the odds against me just the same."

Tori got to her feet and slipped quickly through the night to the door. Her heart was pounding in her chest as she wrapped the cape around her and then turned the doorknob slowly. The door, on poorly aligned hinges, creaked but opened rather easily with little pressure.

When Mack had joined her, he took her hand and together they entered the General Store. They closed the door behind them in case someone came to check on whether Quinn had made it back or not.

Taking Tori by the shoulders, Mack brought her close to lean down and whisper in her ear. "We'd better wait a couple minutes until we're certain he's sleeping it off."

Tori nodded, saying nothing, feeling the heady exhilaration of once again being where she shouldn't be. The element of risk always heightened her awareness of her surroundings and herself. It accented the heat of Mack's hands upon her shoulders, his nearness, his limitless allure. Suddenly, a week's separation and celibacy brought an ache to the marrow of her bones.

"As long as we've got time to kill," she whispered, slipping her hands inside Mack's jacket, circling his waist. She ran her fingertips lightly up and down his spine, lovingly massaging the muscles on either side, feeling them pulse as she touched them.

As he looked at Tori, desire surged through Mack, like a lightning bolt. Through the mask, he could see the green fire in her eyes, the excitement and enthusiasm for life glowing in them. An awareness of Tori's vitality—he could think of no other word for it—sparked his own energies.

"You're a very wicked woman," Mack whispered, a moment before his lips closed down over hers.

Tori closed her eyes, luxuriating in the highly sensual kiss. She pressed her breasts insistently against his chest, which never failed to heighten her excitement.

This time, it was she who first explored his mouth with her tongue, insisting that he open his lips wider. The mask and cape which would hide her identity from others, now hid her inhibitions from herself, leaving her free to do whatever she wanted, to be bold and demanding in her sexual appetites.

She grasped the hand Mack rested on her hip. "I love

the way you kiss," she whispered. Then she moved his hand to her breast, her fingers forcing his to tighten over the taut mound. Though she repressed all sounds of pleasure, reminding herself to remain as silent as possible, her excitement was growing stronger and more insistent with each passing second.

She kissed Mack again, her tongue dancing against his, as she continued to hold her hand over his so that she could revel in the heat and strength of his palm against her breast. She took pleasure in her own forcefulness, in her newfound willingness to be demanding when it came to having Mack satisfy the sensual cravings he'd first aroused in her.

In the middle of this delicious kiss, feeling her passion building, Tori fully experienced her own desire for perhaps the very first time. A heat was rising within her, the petals of her womanhood were becoming moist and swollen with excitement, and the pulse of her heartbeat throbbed in that sensitive spot concealed beneath the folds of her femininity. She was an experienced woman now, knowledgeable as to what was happening with her body, no longer confused or frightened by her excitement, by the passion that before had mystified her.

Would she dare make love with Mack right then and there? The danger of exposure, of being caught by Billy Quinn, would add to the excitement. But as Tori kissed Mack's throat, nipping lightly at his flesh with her teeth, she had to admit that the chances of Quinn waking from his alcoholic stupor were remote, at best. There really wasn't much danger there.

And if she didn't stop kissing Mack very soon, she

would not *allow* him to *stop* kissing her until he had quenched her passion.

She took a half-step away from him, looking up into his face. Her skin felt as though he were touching her everywhere, running a thousand feathery fingers over her from head to toe. Even her scalp tingled with the building passion.

"Bandit, when we get home . . ." Tori said, leaving the sentence unfinished.

"When we get home . . . what then?" he replied, a self-assured half-smile curling his lips and making Tori want to kiss him once again.

"Do you have to make a game out of everything?" she asked.

"I like to play. Now tell me, what's going to happen when we get home?"

This was a small play for power on Mack's part, and Tori rather enjoyed it. They were *both* powerful people. With Mack, there was always something going on just beneath the surface of every conversation, and in this moment she sensed that his desire equalled her own.

Emboldened by the anonymity that mask and cape gave her, Tori decided to find out exactly how far this new, dynamic persona could take her.

"Let me give you a hint," she said, taking his hand by the wrist.

She moved even closer to him once again, bringing his hand to the juncture of her thighs. The pressure of his fingers and palm against her brought a floodtide of heat through her senses, and her eyelids fluttered briefly as delicious feelings shuddered through her.

With little effort, and without shedding even a single

article of clothing, Tori was quite certain that she could reach the summit of passion from Mack's caresses, just as she had that first night when she'd attempted to break into Jonathon Krey's mansion.

When Mack began to move his hand, Tori tightened her fingers around his wrist. The simple pressure of his hand against her, even through her pantalets and Levi's, was about as much as she could sanely accept.

"That . . . should give you . . . something to think about," she said after a moment, finding it difficult to speak clearly. Her heart was racing.

She pushed Mack's hand away, fully aware of how she had teased him. She also anticipated the delicious thrills that would be hers once the evening had come to a close and she and Mack were safely ensconced in her cozy, little cabin.

Mack took a moment or two to compose himself. Every time he was with Tori, every time he kissed her or touched her, and she responded just a little differently from the last time, he craved her that much more. Even now he wondered what new and delicious surprises she had in store for him when they returned to her home.

*Back to business,* he thought with equal measures of determination and despair, since business wasn't at all what he was in the mood for.

They checked the ground floor of the General Store first. Scraps of paper lay scattered around an empty cash drawer at the front. One slip read Sack of Flour. Beside that was a set of initials. Mack crumpled the paper up and tucked it into his shirt pocket.

It became apparent from notes they found that Billy Quinn was at best marginally literate, and that his book-keeping was appalling. He had no filing system, per se. Apparently people came to the store when they needed something and charged it when they didn't have the cash to buy what they needed. So they went into debt to Krey's General Store, and once they'd gotten in, they never got out. Ironically, this moneymaking operation, while having a devastating effect upon the people living near Tula Valley was, Mack knew from his experience with Krey's business matters, quite an insignificant contributor to Krey's wealth.

"We've got to go upstairs," Mack said after some time spent on unproductive searching. "There are only fragments of information down here, not what we really need."

He found the way to the stairs, and took each step slowly and carefully, annoyed by the creaking beneath his weight. With every breath he hoped that Billy Quinn was still drunk and dead to the world. Though Mack did not draw the revolver from its holster, he kept his right hand on the butt.

The door to Billy's living quarters was ajar. They consisted of a tiny room, crowded with supplies to be brought down to the General Store as needed. Also crammed in this little room was a wash basin, pitcher, clothes rack— though judging from the looks of the clothes he was sleeping in, he'd been wearing them quite some time without the benefit of laundering—and a flat-topped desk. Upon closer inspection, Mack discovered that the desk was simply a door placed on two sawhorses. Upon this were a single kerosene lamp, a pen and ink set, a stack of slips of paper weighted down with a large stone, and a leather-bound ledger.

Even from across the room, Mack determined this last to be a book of quality, the kind printed in San Francisco. He used several ledgers just like this to record the operations of the Randolph Ranch and its various business enterprises.

"Look at that," Mack muttered.

Tori followed the direction of his disgusted glare to Billy Quinn lying on a cot, his shirt mostly unbuttoned, his trousers half open, one suspender strap on and one off, one boot on and one off, his mouth gaping open, his arms flayed out. He was passed out cold as a man could be and still be alive.

"To think that we were worried he might hear us," Mack growled in an almost conversational tone.

"Well, it isn't exactly like we wasted our time," Tori replied a little defensively. She didn't want anything negative said about her bold behavior with him earlier. Her confidence was rising steadily with each passing day—and with each time she and Mack shared their sensuality. Still, fear was never far from the surface.

Mack heard the ragged edge to her tone and smiled reassuringly. "No, it wasn't wasted at all." Much as he wanted to reassure Tori, he also wanted to do the deed they'd set out to do, then get out of the General Store. Even if Billy Quinn was dead drunk, neither Mack nor Tori knew enough about the way business was done at the store to have any assurances that someone else wouldn't show up at any minute.

Mack took the thick ledger book out of the room, then knelt near the head of the stairs. From a shirt pocket he withdrew several stick matches. With his thumbnail, he struck one.

"This is what we've been looking for," Mack said, running his finger down a column of figures to point to the name "Matthews."

He briefly studied the ledger. Judging from the legibility of the handwriting and from the misspellings, Billy Quinn simply stood behind the counter at the General Store during the day, scribbling down customers' purchases. And then, at regular intervals, Michael Krey would show up at the store and transfer all the information from the slips to the master ledger.

The Kreys weren't making a fortune off this, but they were making too much profit from unfortunate people.

"Did you get all the slips you could find?" Mack asked Tori as they knelt at the head of the stairway.

"Everything that had anything written on it. I didn't really pay much attention to what was on them."

"Just as well," Mack said, a slow burning anger building inside him. He shook out the match.

Tossing all the slips of paper they'd found into the ledger, he closed it and tucked the book under his arm. "Let's get out of here. It smells of fresh drink and old sweat."

Tori followed him, keeping her distance for she felt his anger. What she couldn't know was that it was directed primarily at himself for not knowing how best to attack Jonathon Krey—and for his previous ignorance of this credit situation.

Silently, they made their way to the tethered horses, and once Mack was certain that nobody would see the flames, he put a match to the ledger.

"This is going to make a lot of people happy," he said as he watched the flames devouring the pages, destroying the records of ruinous debt. "Now all we have to do is get word out that this has happened, and make sure nobody confesses to what is really owed. Then there won't be any way in the world Jonathon Krey can prove in court these people owe him anything."

Mack took his mask off and looked at Tori. "Have you any idea how proud I am of you? I'd never have thought of this. I was so damned blind I didn't even know Jonathon Krey had this scheme going."

Tori took off her own mask, untying it and folding it to tuck it into the back pocket of her Levi's for later use. "It isn't that you were blind," she explained softly, tenderly, able to feel Mack's discomfort and sense of inadequacy, even if she didn't agree with it. "Your money just isolates you from this kind of madness, that's all. You shouldn't hold yourself accountable."

"But you knew what was happening," Mack replied, his ravaged soul only partially assuaged by the words Tori had spoken.

"But I'm not a rich woman."

For several seconds they knelt there, looking into each other's eyes, each distinctly aware of the differences in their social stations.

"I don't know if I'll ever understand you," Mack said quietly.

Tori smiled broadly then, her white teeth flashing in the moonlight. "Your problem is that you're trying, my darling! You'll never understand me in a thousand years!"

She bolted to her feet then and leaped into the saddle of the mare Mack had brought for her. "Come on, I'll race you home."

He cast aside his personal demons in an instant.

"What does the winner get?" he asked.

"Ask me when we get there and I'll tell you!" Tori replied without a moment's hesitation. She put her boots to the mare's ribs and, at a full gallop, headed for her ranch where she could once again feast her senses on the excitement and stimulation Mack Randolph was so willing to dispense.

# Twenty-three

"You don't really have to leave," Tori said, lacing her fingers together behind Mack's neck, leaning into him so that as much as was possible of her naked body was pressed against his clothed form.

"I have to," Mack replied.

He placed his hands on Tori's hips to push her pelvis away. Her passion was intoxicating, addictive, and just a little greedy at times. Although his desire had been satisfied, he knew he'd stay if she persisted. When Tori was near, it was hard to remember that he was a man with many responsibilities.

And much as he didn't want to leave her, Mack knew that to stay the entire night would cause trouble for Tori. Then, too, if he arrived in the morning at the gates of the Randolph Ranch, at least one of the ranch hands would see him. Other than tending horses and cattle, ranch hands were good at drinking, playing cards, wenching, and gossiping about what the Randolphs were doing.

"I've got to go," Mack said, his voice a husky whisper. He cupped Tori's face in his palms, knowing that to touch her anywhere else was dangerous in the extreme. "I'll be back though, I promise. Just as soon as I possibly can."

Tori pouted, pushing out her full lower lip, her hands

resting lightly on Mack's trim hips. She knew why he had to leave. Though she would not be sharing her bed this night with him, she accepted that—at least for now—they could not live idyllically.

"When will you come back?" she asked, standing at the open doorway, strangely unselfconscious about not having a stitch of clothing on.

"Soon."

A little voice inside Tori warned her that she should leave it at that, that she shouldn't try to pin Mack down to anything more definite. But another voice, the one of that less secure woman who had just shared her passion in a most uninhibited manner with Mack, spoke up and demanded, "When, Mack. Don't just say 'soon.' I deserve more than that."

He bent to plant a light kiss on her forehead. "You deserve everything. I'll be back very soon. Tomorrow. If not tomorrow, then the day after. And if I'm not back by then, I want you to ride to the Randolph Ranch and demand to see me. Make a scene. Shout and scream. Threaten to burn the place down."

Under normal circumstances, Mack was not a man given to hyperbole, so his statement had special meaning for Tori. She could not help but smile.

"And won't you be surprised if I do just that!" she said at last.

"Not at all," Mack replied.

She pushed his hands away from her face and stepped into the circle of his arms once again to press her cheek against his chest. "Tonight was special for me," she said softly.

"It was special for me, too."

Tori wanted to say she was in love with him, but she just didn't dare. Not when he was about to leave. And despite the words he'd just spoken, there really was no guarantee he would ever return. In fact, if he wanted to bar her from the Randolph Ranch, she'd never get past the high, arched, stone gates.

"Yes, special," Tori said at last, her cheek against the fine fabric of Mack's shirt, her ear picking up the smooth, even beating of his heart.

Mack wondered if his feelings for her were what love really was. If so, what could he do about it? Despite the contempt he occasionally professed for politics, he could not ignore Tori's family history; that would get dragged through the newspapers. He couldn't protect her from those headlines. And he couldn't pretend he wasn't bothered because she wasn't the type of woman the voters expected at the side of their next mayor—or territorial governor.

He thought of many good reasons why this affair with Tori wasn't fundamentally different from any other he'd had, with the exception of Tori's lower social status.

But the others *had* been different. *Tori* wasn't fatuous and frivolous. She was vibrant, forceful, a little angry, wildly passionate, daring to a fault.

"I have to leave now," Mack said firmly, as much to himself as to Tori, extricating himself from her arms. He turned away from her. "I'll see you as soon as I can."

"Turn around and you can see me one last time," she said.

The impish quality in her tone, the flirtatiousness she was beginning to master, made it impossible for Mack to do anything other than what she said.

He turned slowly, standing just outside on the narrow porch. Tori was leaning against the doorjamb in what, had she been dressed, would have been a most casual pose. Legs crossed at the ankles and arms folded just beneath her breasts, her hair disheveled from hours of lovemaking that at times had been frantic, at times tender, she looked miraculously innocent.

Except that she was naked. Had she been a wildly insatiable princess from some obscure country, a woman with countless virile young slaves to see to her every desire, she would have looked perfectly natural.

Mack admired those magnificent, pink-tipped breasts, the sweeping curve of her hips, the smallish triangular thatch of hair, and those long, strong legs that could hold so tightly onto him.

"I just wanted to give you one last reminder as to why you shouldn't stay away too long," Tori said, a kittenish curl to her lips.

*I'm much too experienced with women to be so dumbfounded,* Mack thought, entranced by her beauty, unable to find a snappy rebuttal.

Closing the door, Tori had no idea that she'd managed to do what no other woman had—she'd had the last word. For her it had been a little teasing; for him, it was the breakdown of resistance. What difference did background and status make?

"I've *got* to leave," Mack said as he walked toward his horse, assuring himself. As he slipped the toe of his boot into the stirrup, he added, "And I've *got* to come back to her as *soon* as possible!"

\* \* \*

Exhausted from lack of sleep, from lovemaking, from the emotional turnaround of believing she'd lost Mack and then having had him invite her to attack the business of Jonathon Krey, Tori nonetheless knew that she wouldn't soon be able to sleep.

Thank goodness Jedediah was gone. What would have happened if her brother, still employed by Jonathon Krey, had been around?

She wasn't as frightened as she originally had been. Though Jedediah was an extraordinarily skilled bounty hunter, Mack now knew he was after him; fortunately, Jedediah didn't know who the Midnight Bandit was. This was an advantage that Mack could use to the maximum.

A pleased smile curled Tori's lips. She and Mack had shared that tiny bed, and if either had been uncomfortable, neither had complained about it. The feel of his warm, naked body against her had made the little bed just right.

Remembering her chores put a momentary frown on her face. At night, she'd been riding with mask and cape to thwart Jonathon Krey; but during the day, she still had to feed the cattle and the six hogs. There was time for everything . . . except sleep, it seemed.

About to go to her bedroom, she heard a horse approaching. The hoofbeats were slow and uneven. In her mind, Tori pictured Mack tapping his heels to his horse's ribs, then reining back to turn around. He didn't *want* to return to her, but he had to.

"I knew you couldn't leave me," she said, her grin broadening triumphantly.

Still completely naked, she wondered how to appear for Mack at the door. Perhaps the nice white nightgown? No, he'd already seen her in that. Her meager wardrobe provided her with limited options, so she would greet him exactly as he'd left her—with a smile on her face end open arms.

She went to the door and took off the locking bar so Mack could let himself into the cabin. For at least a little while, she would pretend to be surprised that he'd returned to her. Outside, the horses—Mack's horse and the trail horse he'd brought for her to use—had stopped.

Tori waited, standing near the door. The seconds ticked by, and still no knock came, no Mack burst into her cabin to sweep her into his arms and carry her to the bedroom.

What was taking him so long?

Perhaps he lingered outside, angry with himself for lacking the willpower to leave yet wanting to kick the door down.

Then, at last, boots thumped across the porch, the crude latch on the door was raised, and without a knock the door was opened.

"I knew you couldn't leave me," Tori said, victory ringing in her tone.

But victory was not in the cards, for when Mack stepped into the cabin, clutching onto the door for support, she saw that his face and shirt were soaked red with blood. Blood streamed from a cut over his eye, and his lips were cut and swelling.

When he collapsed in her arms, she was too frightened even to scream.

Regarding the three men, Jeremy kept the smile from his face, though he was overjoyed with their work. These hands—illiterate hired thugs who two days earlier had been paid to watch cattle—were making no effort to hide their pleasure, however.

"We did just like you said." Jack, the leader of the three spoke. "We beat him bad, but we didn't kill him. He won't be going nowhere soon."

"You're sure you didn't leave him to die?" Jeremy inquired. Personally, it wouldn't have bothered him if Mack Randolph had been killed, but for now that wasn't the plan. Besides, it wasn't what he'd hired these three men to do.

"No, sir. We got him back up on his horse and headed back for his whore's house," Jack answered.

Jeremy reached into his inside jacket pocket and brought out his wallet. He extracted a stack of ten-dollar bills and peeled them off slowly, handing each man three, one at a time. Then he paused, smiled at the men, indicating he was a leader and realized that capable talent was sometimes hard to find, and gave each man an additional twenty dollars.

"The extra twenty is to see you out of town," Jeremy explained.

"Out of town? You didn't say nothin' 'bout us having to hightail it," Jack said.

"That's right, I didn't. But you should know that a man as powerful as Mack Randolph might well hire someone like Jedediah Singer to track down the men who beat him. Now do you really want to be around when Jedediah rides up and tries to arrest you?"

One of the younger men unacquainted with Jedediah Singer's lethal reputation, grumbled, "Let him come. I'll have him runnin' with his tail between his legs in two seconds."

Jack looked at him and said quietly, "You'd be dead in one second." He then turned to Jeremy. "How long you want us gone?"

"A month should do fine," Jeremy answered. "You'll still have a job here when you return. Do yourselves a favor and don't spend all that money in the first week."

When the men left him, Jeremy's spirits were so exuberant he could hardly contain himself. Mack Randolph had been beaten bloody! It had cost Jeremy just a hundred and fifty dollars to have it done. Looking back, Jeremy wondered why he'd never had it done before. Mack had certainly been a thorn in his side for a number of years, yet Jeremy had never openly struck back. Not until now.

He checked his pocket watch. A little past eight o'clock in the morning. He wanted to rush to Jena's bedroom to tell her the news, but she'd crucify him if he did that. There was a standing order at the ranch that Jena Krey simply wasn't to be disturbed for any reason whatsoever before noon.

Too restless to stay in one place, Jeremy decided a quick trip to Lulu's was in order. One of her girls could smooth the rough edges off his desire. Then later, around noon, he'd go to Jena and tell her what had been done. She would be overjoyed, he was certain of it.

Jeremy wondered which revealing nightgown Jena had worn when she'd gone to bed, and he quickened his pace on the way to the stables. Yes, Lulu's was definitely the place for him to be.

"You idiot! You moron! You stupid, fat slob!" Jena screamed, flying about her bedroom, completely unmindful of how her breasts were bouncing beneath the sheer nightgown.

Jeremy stood with his back to the door, not quite knowing what to say or do. Of all the reactions he'd thought his sister might have to the news that he'd had Mack beaten, this wasn't it. He had anticipated her sashaying around her bedroom in just her nightgown. Hell, that was half the reason he'd waited until the downstairs grandfather clock chimed noon before rushing to her room—but he hadn't figured she'd be so angry.

And how could he concentrate on what she was saying when she paced back and forth so scantily dressed? Jeremy wanted to reach out and touch her, but she was obviously not in the mood for any of that.

"How could you have done such a thing?" Jena demanded, stabbing his chest with a forefinger. "Don't you ever think?"

Jeremy swallowed his anger. "You were the one who came to me and said you wanted him beaten up. I only did what you asked. I thought you'd be grateful. You *said* you'd be grateful."

Jena shot Jeremy a scathing look. "Don't remind me of what I said." She inhaled deeply, forcing herself to be more composed. There was no undoing what had been done, she told herself. "Tell me the whole story once again."

Jeremy explained that he'd hired Jack and two other cowboys, giving them explicit orders to beat Mack soundly but not kill or maim him. Since Mack and Tori had become lovers, the men had waited for him at the Singer cabin lying in ambush amid the trees. At sunrise, when Mack had headed for his home, Jack and the other two had jumped him, punching him in the face and kicking him in the ribs repeatedly. Finally, they had tossed him back onto his saddle and headed his horse back toward the cabin.

Jena, completely unmindful of the way Jeremy kept looking at her in the nightgown, shook her head slowly, astonished at her brother's stupidity.

"Now Mack's face is all bruised, and he's in some goddamn woman's bed!" Jena hissed through clenched teeth. "I didn't want his face damaged, damn it! And, more than that, I didn't want him in some whore's bed! What good's that going to do me?"

"But I thought you wanted him beaten up so that he had to stay in bed," Jeremy said softly, still not quite understanding that what he had done was so wrong.

"Yes, but I didn't want his face hurt!" she screamed. "And the only whore's bed that man should be in is mine! Mine, damn it, mine!" The red glint in Jena's eyes was homicidal. "Get out of here. Get out of my sight, damn you!"

Softly, Jeremy said, "You promised you'd be nice to me if I did this for you."

"Nice? To you? I'd rather sleep with every unwashed cowboy in the bunkhouse than let you touch me!"

Jeremy left his sister's bedroom then, making a straight line back to Lulu's. The only way to get this kind of frustration and anger out of his system was through a woman. One of the prostitutes at the bordello was in serious trouble! She didn't know it yet, but she would the moment Jeremy walked through the door.

# Twenty-four

Two full days had passed since Mack had collapsed into her arms; actually it had been fifty-four hours since she'd thought her entire world had suddenly come crashing to an end.

He was sleeping now in her bed, his face cleaned of blood, a bandage over the left eye. His cut upper and lower lip were still swollen where a fist or a boot had connected savagely.

Tori leaned against the doorjamb of her bedroom. Mack's arms rested at his sides, the light blanket pulled up under them.

For hours she had watched his chest rise and fall as he breathed shallowly, and many times her heart had leaped in her chest when she'd thought he'd stopped breathing.

Who had done this to him? she wondered, consumed with anger. Nothing had been taken from Mack—not even his heavy gold watch, which would certainly be worth the better part of two hundred dollars, its Swiss craftsmanship and intricate engraving testimony to its excellence even to the most untrained eye.

It was a good thing the men hadn't robbed him. Had they bothered to go through his saddlebags, they would have found the cape and mask of the Midnight Bandit.

Tori's first inclination was to blame Jonathon Krey; she tended to blame him for everything that went bad. But she realized she was biased. Besides, Krey, from what Tori had learned, was more inclined to make his problems disappear entirely. If he'd suspected Mack was the Midnight Bandit, Mack would be dead now.

And why would he have done this to Mack, anyway? Though the two were enemies, they had been able to maintain an appearance of civility, as witnessed by the work they'd done jointly on behalf of the charity hospital. Besides, Mack's identity as the Midnight Bandit was still a secret . . . or was it?

Tori thought long on this. Finally she decided that Jonathon Krey couldn't possibly know Mack was the Midnight Bandit. If he did, he wouldn't have hired men to give Mack a beating, he would have hired assassins to put an end to him.

So what was she to do now?

Take care of Mack and protect him from the human vultures ready to pick his bones.

Vivid memories came back to Tori then, of her recent confrontation with Jena Krey. Yesterday, Jena had arrived in a carriage with several men to take Mack to her mansion in Santa Fe. There, she assured Tori, the finest physicians would tend to his wounds.

"He's staying with me." Standing in the doorway of her home, Tori had refused to budge, even in the face of Jena and the gunmen she'd brought, and she was unimpressed by the ornately appointed carriage intended to take Mack into town.

"Why should he stay in this drafty shack?" Jena demanded derisively. "I can give him everything he could want. What can you provide for him?"

Clearly, Jena would offer more than medical services to Mack; the look in her eyes told Tori that.

"Just get away from here," Tori whispered. "Get off my land. I can take care of Mack."

Jena tossed back her head, her eyes flashing with anger and condescension. "Sure you can. At least, you think so. But I know Mack; I know the kind of man he is. You'd better learn some fancy tricks pretty quick if you want to keep his attention for very long."

Those words and Jena's look of scorn had been burned into Tori's mind, and no amount of time would erase them.

Damn Jena Krey! Damn her to hell!

Tori turned away from the bedroom. She didn't want to be so close to Mack when such anger was in her heart, afraid that somehow her emotions might affect him adversely even as he slept.

She went to the kitchen area. Mack would be waking soon, and he'd be hungry. When Paul Randolph had ridden over to check on his brother, he'd brought with him enough food to sustain ten people for several weeks.

"If there's anything you need, just ask," Paul had said. "Don't hesitate for a second. I want him to have everything he could possibly desire."

Tori had smiled her thanks. She liked Mack's brother. Though Paul's inclination had been to take his brother home, he'd acquiesced to Tori's wish to take care of Mack. However, so that Mack's presence wouldn't be "any great financial burden," Paul had sent a wagon loaded with supplies over.

What would it be this morning? Ham and eggs, with

fried potatoes on the side? Yes, Mack enjoyed that. But perhaps before eating he'd want to wash up a bit. He'd complained of needing a bath the last time he'd awakened.

Tori set about putting water on to heat. As she went about this simple task, she thought about what the future held. Not much, she sadly concluded. However much she hated Jena Krey, the fact of the matter was, that woman was dead on the mark about her superior standing in Mack's world. Tori had been granted this time alone with Mack to tend to his cracked ribs and his battered body, but these circumstances would never be repeated.

*Don't think about it,* Tori told herself. Since she could not change the past, and had little control over the future, she would make the most of these days with Mack. And watching his extraordinarily rapid recovery, she knew she had best savor every second because soon her time with him would run out. The voters demanded a mayor, and they wouldn't accept one without a wife, but that wife had to be from the right family, from the right class.

Tori filled a large kettle with the heated water, tossed a wash towel in along with a cake of soap, placed a drying towel over her shoulder, then returned to the bedroom. Mack was still on his back, a hand now resting lightly on his ribs.

"Good morning," Tori whispered, not entirely certain whether he was awake.

"'Morning. I'm not so sure how good it is," Mack groaned. Then, as his feelings for Tori surfaced through the pain, he opened his eyes and smiled. "The ribs are throbbing a little, that's all. Doc Jamison said that would happen when they started to mend. It's a good sign."

"Yes, a good sign." Tori tried to cover the sadness she

felt. How criminal it was that Mack's body, so beautiful, so powerful, so magnificently sculpted, should be so senselessly damaged! Why?

She set the kettle down on the floor, then sat very cautiously at the edge of the bed. With Mack's broken ribs, any unnecessary movement had to be avoided.

"I'll be able to get up today," Mack said.

"No, you won't. Not for at least a week. Doctor's orders."

Mack growled his disapproval. "What do doctors know?"

"About broken ribs? More than a lawyer, I'm afraid. Besides, I promised your brother I wouldn't let you out of bed. Now, you don't want to make me a liar to your brother, do you?"

"Paul can be a bit on the dictatorial side can't he?"

Tori squeezed out the wash cloth, then worked in a rich, soapy lather with the bar of soap Paul had provided. "Let's get you cleaned up a bit."

"I can do that myself," Mack replied, his independence suddenly being challenged.

He reached for the cloth, but when Tori pulled away from him, he moved his arms too quickly. Stabbing pain from the broken ribs on his left side shot through him, and he gritted his teeth to keep from crying out in pain. He was recovering quickly, but not so quickly that he was ready to be up and about.

"Don't fight me," she said sternly, her green eyes boring angrily into Mack's brown ones. "Now just lie back and, for once in your life, do as you're told."

"Yes, Nurse Tori," Mack said with thick sarcasm as she

began soaping up his right arm, then wiping the soap away with the warm, wet wash cloth.

She washed his face, neck, chest, and arms, enjoying herself immensely as she chatted with Mack about inconsequential things. She adjusted the bandage near his left eye so that it no longer interfered with his vision, then she leaned away. What remained to be washed was beneath the blankets, and Tori wasn't at all certain how he would react to that.

"I think I can do the rest myself. I've been bathing myself without the help of a nanny for a couple of months now."

"I'm not listening to you," Tori replied as she brought the blanket down to the foot of the bed.

For an instant, her breath caught in her throat. Mack was completely naked. She had known this, so it shouldn't have struck so sharply. But seeing him now, awake and in control of himself—that enthusiasm for life shining in his eyes—was different from looking at his naked body while he was sleeping or unconscious.

"This is silly," Mack said.

He started to sit up, but the moment his shoulders got more than a few inches off the mattress, fresh pain knifed through him from the damaged ribs. He lay down again, his breathing ragged, his features showing the strain of self-control.

"It's silly pretending you're not in pain." Tori pursed her lips into an angry, tight line. "Now stop hurting yourself. I hate seeing you do that."

Mack closed his eyes, breathing softly, evenly, waiting for the pain to subside. "It's not the pain that bothers me so much, it's the feeling of uselessness, of needing your help just to wash myself."

Tori began washing Mack's feet. Now that he'd reclined and was motionless once again, she could enjoy the domesticity of what she was doing. Still, she remained aware of Mack's richly sensual nakedness.

"You should just accept my help," she said as she lathered Mack's right thigh. "Often people have needed your aid against Jonathon Krey, but you've not taken a cent for it. Now it's time for you to let someone do something nice for you. Don't fight me. It's only fair. You have to learn to receive as well as give."

Mack closed his eyes, letting the impact of Tori's words sink in. On only a few times in his life had he ever felt quite this helpless, once during a severe case of influenza when he was a young man, and another time when he'd had what the doctor suspected was a case of food poisoning and was wretchedly sick for eighteen hours.

*Yes,* he thought, *time to relax and let my body heal.*

This realization would have been considerably easier to accept if he were not so conscious of where Tori was about to wash him. Despite the modicum of sensual anticipation he felt, he knew embarrassment at seeing himself as an infant needing care.

He felt her hands on his phallus, soft and warm, slippery with water and soap. Nothing sexual about it, Mack told himself. Nothing sexual at all. No reason at all to be embarrassed—and no reason to respond. No reason at all to respond like a man when one of the world's truly vivacious, earthy women was working her hands along him in a manner that in other circumstances could only be considered blatantly, openly, even aggressively, sexual.

He toyed with opening his eyes, then banished that thought. Any hope he had of not responding to Tori's touch was predicated on his ability to not look at her. If he did open his eyes, if he saw her, examined her beauty, perhaps even watched her soapy hands working over him . . . all hope of calm detachment would be lost.

*There are words that can be spoken,* he thought then. *Perhaps some light, teasing banter to shatter the tension that now seems to have taken all the air from this small room. Yes, some silly little joke that Tori would be mildly annoyed at. That'll stop her cold.*

If Mack was trying to control himself, Tori intended that he fail. She wanted to destroy whatever calm he sought. With the wash cloth, she wiped away the soap suds she had worked over him. Very slowly and with infinite care, she cleaned Mack, then curled her fingers around him, squeezing lightly, gently. She felt him move in her hand, very subtly at first, almost imperceptibly, then with increasing force. His lifeblood coursed into him, making him stretch and grow, thicken, pulse with virility. A deep, throaty sigh escaped her as she watched his burgeoning manhood expand under her touch, responding to her even though it was apparent that he had not wanted to do so.

With the towel, she patted Mack dry, but by this time his manhood had reached full dimensions, and all pretense on his part that he was passively being washed had been abandoned.

"Tori, as much as I would like to, I don't really think I can make love with you, at least not with the energy that is necessary," he said quietly, his eyes still closed. There was an edge of anger in his tone, as though he was blaming himself for not being able to satisfy her.

"I know that, darling," Tori whispered in response, her voice husky with escalating passion. Still, she was apprehensive, uncertain of what she was going to do next. "This time, you must not think of my pleasure."

"But—"

She put a finger to his lips. "Shhh!" she whispered. "There's nothing for you to say."

But there was much for Mack to say. He was a man of more than considerable experience with women, and though he'd certainly allowed himself to be pleased by a woman before, he had always been a man who believed in reciprocity. A *quid pro quo* approach to sexuality, made him determined to satisfy his partner, while demanding satisfaction for himself. Now, his broken ribs howling in protest with each breath he took, the slightest movements of his arms reminding him of where boots had struck or ham-sized fists had battered him, Mack knew he could not give as good as he would receive—certainly not with his split and swollen lips.

"You're fighting it," Tori whispered, her hand moving slowly over his manhood, her eyes lidded as though she were sleepy, though in fact she was completely aware of everything she was doing. "Don't fight it . . . relax . . . and enjoy." Her voice was a soft, sultry purr as she shifted her position on the bed so that she was sitting a little lower now, closer to his knees. "You don't always have to be the one in charge."

Mack's hands were at his sides, and he had to consciously loosen his fingers to release the blankets that he'd balled up in his fists. Was this really Tori, his Tori, touching him this way?

He opened his eyes just a little to look at her. She smiled softly at him, her every movement, every gesture, languid, indolent, natural, as though she'd done this a thousand times, as though the questions plaguing her didn't really exist.

"There now," Tori whispered, smiling but in command. "I can see in your eyes that you're a little more relaxed, more at ease." She leaned forward slowly, her gaze locked with Mack's, and kissed his chest. "You've had a difficult time. Let me take care of you."

She flicked the tip of her tongue against his flat nipple, and his sudden intake of breath pleased her. He bunched the blankets at his sides again in his fists. Tori released her hold on his manhood, then took his forearm in both hands and began kneading the tension-knotted muscles firmly.

"What did I tell you?" she asked in a scolding tone. "I told you to relax, didn't I?"

"Yes," Mack replied, his voice a thin, hoarse, croaking sound.

He watched as Tori massaged his arm until it was relaxed, then did the same for his other arm. He wondered if this was some bizarre, absurdly pleasurable form of torture. Never in his life had he felt less capable of satisfying a woman, nor more desirous of doing so.

"So, will you relax?" Tori asked, leaning over him, one hand on his naked chest, the other on his flat abdomen just above his thrusting manhood, which, despite being ignored for the past few minutes, had lost none of its rigidity.

"I'll try," Mack replied.

Tori reached low, curling her fingers around his shaft once again. "I suppose I'm making it hard for you," she said, the double entendre accidental. She smiled almost wickedly when she realized exactly what she'd said, and how it could be interpreted.

Mack could not reply with words at first. He swallowed, struggled to moisten his lips, then finally whispered, "Quite so, I'm afraid."

She kissed his chest, letting the tip of her tongue follow a line from one nipple to the other, moving just above the tight bandage wrapped around his battered ribs. For only an instant, Tori squeezed her eyes tightly shut as she thought about the pain and fear Mack must have known when the men attacked him, clubbing him to the ground and then brutally kicking him.

*Don't think about his pain,* she thought then. *Think about his pleasure. Think about what you can do to make him happy now.*

She moved lower on the bed again, sitting near his knees. He filled her hand with his strength, and as she touched him, she felt an odd sense of power. Mack, even though battered and in pain, could not resist the temptation of her feminine charms. Ironically, by pretending that she was completely confident, she was slowly making herself so. She felt sure now of her ability to arouse Mack, strengthened by his response to her.

It didn't matter then that he had known many women, most of them probably more skilled in the art of lovemaking than she. What did matter was that he was in her bed—and was responding to her caresses even though he was in pain.

"You are such an exciting man," Tori whispered, her breath warm over the inflamed tip of his arousal.

She kissed him then, softly, quickly, tentatively. With her right hand resting lightly upon his stomach, she felt him suck in his breath and unconsciously hold it. For a single instant a myriad of conflicting emotions went through her as she wondered whether she was doing something wrong. She simply didn't know, and there wasn't anyone other than Mack to ask, though putting such a question to him was completely out of the question.

She inhaled deeply. He smelled of fresh soap and clean water, despite the faintly disquieting odor of the disinfectant she'd gently patted on the cut over his eye.

She tasted his manhood then, putting her tongue to him, and again his body tightened up, all those finely honed muscles in his legs, arms, and chest knotting with excitement. This time, however, the flinching was accompanied by a soft, rather strangled sigh of pleasure, and Tori's confidence was heightened.

In a playfully scientific manner, she went about calmly experimenting with him to find out exactly what he enjoyed the most, and what he didn't care for as much, judging his satisfaction by how he breathed or held his breath, by how he held his body, tense or easy, and by the myriad little reactions that he displayed.

She discovered that rational, coherent thought and observation were infinitely easier to sustain when one was doing the pleasing. Memories of her own wild, incoherent thrills when Mack had kissed her down low spurred her on.

A warm flush of excitement shuddered through her as she recalled the spine-tingling excitement she'd known as the joyous recipient of Mack's exquisite skill, and this fueled her desire to satisfy Mack more than he'd dreamed possible.

She took him in deeply, feeling his passion pulsing through him, taking delight in the way his arousal throbbed with tension.

Tori looked up into Mack's face, and when her eyes met his, he looked away, closing his eyes.

After a moment of deliberation, Tori leaned away from him slightly. "Do you like to watch me?" she asked.

Mack looked at her. His tongue went around his mouth to moisten lips now dry from his ragged breathing. "Yes," he admitted finally, his gaze darting from Tori's smoky green eyes down to the small hand which continued to move over the length of his now-moist arousal.

"I like it when you look at me," she replied, her words more confident than her emotions. Actually, she'd felt scrutinized, but she wanted whatever Mack wanted.

She leaned down to kiss him once more, then sat upright at the edge of the bed. In a calm, matter-of-fact fashion, with no haste at all, she began unbuttoning her shirt. Once she'd stripped it off, she neatly folded it and placed it at the foot of the bed. Then, with calculated languor, Tori unfastened the ties of her chemise and stripped it off to reveal her breasts, the nipples aroused and erect, to Mack's hungry gaze.

"I like it when you touch me with your eyes," she explained in a whisper. "It makes me feel pretty, womanly. Sometimes I don't feel very womanly, I guess, because of the clothes I wear and the way I'm built. When you're a tomboy people don't think of you as womanly."

A thousand thoughts were racing through Mack's mind,

each one more disjointed and inchoate than the last. Tori's naiveté when he'd first seduced her must have been a charade, he decided. She hadn't been as inexperienced as she had pretended, or she could not turn him inside-out with the consummate skill she was now displaying.

Only his battered, broken body prevented him from taking her in his arms and throwing himself upon her—and she knew it. And that was why, with calculated calm, she was taking her sweet time about everything she did— whether it was removing her shirt and chemise to reveal the pink-tipped breasts that had piqued Mack's desire— had, in fact, become something of an obsession of his—or turning her attention back to his manhood, swollen and aching for the caresses of one young woman.

His voice a hoarse whisper, he said, "You're going to kill me."

Tori smiled at Mack as she finished carefully folding her chemise and placing it neatly upon the foot of the bed. "No, my darling, I'm not going to kill you. I'm going to show you just exactly how alive you really are." She took him in her hands again, loving the heated pulse of his passion against her palms. "I'm going to teach you many things," she continued, her gaze locked with his as she leaned forward once more, her breasts firm and warm against his legs. "And for starters, I'm going to teach you that you must never underestimate me."

The warm wetness that surrounded him forced Mack to close his eyes. Tori chastised him quickly, telling him he must keep them open so that she would be sure he wasn't thinking of another woman. Mack could not force his throat to work sufficiently to tell her that thinking of another at the moment was impossible.

"Just relax," he heard her say, but he could not.

No matter how much he wanted to, no matter how determined he was to at least break even in this bizarre battle of wills with Tori, he could not remain calm, could not relax, could not, in fact, do anything but surrender himself to her—completely, passionately, irrevocably.

# Twenty-five

Jena Krey wanted to kill, and she very likely would have if her father hadn't been in a similarly lethal frame of mind. Since the death of her mother, Jena had realized it was her job to make sure the elder Krey's deadly impulses were kept somewhat in check. She didn't have to be told this, she simply understood it, so whenever her father was savagely angry, she forced herself to remain calm in order to put a damper upon his foul temper.

"It can't be as bad as all that," she now said, leaning against Jonathon Krey's heavy desk and looking down at him as he sat in his enormous, leather-covered swivel chair.

"It damn sure is! The point isn't that I can't collect on the money that's owed to me. The amount's small change, any way you look at it." He looked up at his beloved daughter, but there was no compassion in his eyes whatsoever. "The problem is that the people no longer fear me. The Midnight Bandit broke into the Tula Valley General Store and stole the debt ledger. It's not the money I'm worried about, it's that people now know I can be defied without their suffering for it."

Jonathon balled his hand into a fist and raised it high

above his head, about to smash it into his desk. Jena moved quickly, grabbing his fist with both of her hands.

"That's enough, Papa," she said, her dark eyes flashing with excitement and concern. A man out of control always excited and touched something responsive within her. "You can't undo what has already been done, and hurting your hand isn't going to fix anything."

Jena kissed her father's hand, then set it gently upon his desk.

"You're right, of course. You're always right, Jena," he said quietly. "What would I do without you?"

"Probably break your fist."

He laughed then, because he knew she was right. Once his anger had abated, he began rationally and calmly to dissect the problems that had been plaguing him lately.

"Stealing the General Store ledger was a slap in the face but, in reality, nothing more than that. An insult, not really a threat." Jonathon was speaking more to himself than to his daughter.

"That's absolutely right."

Jena was pleased. Her father's color and disposition had at last returned to normal, and he sounded pleased with her for calming his temper. She wanted him to owe her.

"And now that I've got Jedediah on the Bandit's tail, it's only a matter of time before he's hanging from the end of a rope."

"Any man Jedediah Singer captures doesn't hang from the end of a rope, he just gets buried," Jena said as she crossed the room to pour herself a cup of coffee. "But the Midnight Bandit isn't the only problem we've got."

"Oh?" Jonathon replied, unaware of how solidly Jena was inserting herself into the situation.

"There's also Jeremy," she said. As she turned to her father, her expression indicated that she didn't like having to tell the painful truth, but it simply had to be put out in the open. "He's been . . . I don't exactly know how to say this, and in fact it might be completely in my imagination . . . but he's been bothering me lately, Papa. Often."

"If you didn't run around in just your lingerie, maybe he wouldn't bother you."

"Would you say the same thing to Jeremy?" Jena asked. There was no hesitation because she had this all well rehearsed. "Of course you wouldn't comment on what little he wears, not even when his robe is open and his belly is hanging out." She looked away as though terribly offended. "What you just said makes me feel I'm somehow to blame."

Jena went to the office window and looked out, pleased with her performance thus far.

"It's my house just as much as it is his," she continued, after a suitably theatrical pause. "I shouldn't feel as though . . . as though I need a lock on my bedroom door just to keep my own brother out." She turned eyes that begged for understanding to her father. "He even hired some of the boys to beat up Mack Randolph. He did this because he knows I want to be with Mack when he moves into the governor's mansion."

Jonathon's brows furrowed with confusion. "But Jeremy's known all along that you intend to marry Mack. Everyone in Santa Fe knows that."

"Yes, Papa, that's true. Only now it's something more than that, and you know it. Mack's a shoo-in for mayor, but that's just a stepping stone."

"What's your point?"

Apprehension tightened Jena's innards. She hadn't anticipated that her father would question her reasoning. That worried her, since she'd always believed she could exercise more control over him than now appeared possible.

"You know how much money could be made by having me inside the governor's mans—"

"What's your point, Jena? I'm the one who taught you the profitability of family political connections," Jonathon said a bit testily.

"I think Jeremy wants me. Maybe he was trying to impress me by having Mack beaten—you know Mack went sniffing after that little whore, Tori Singer—or maybe he had it done because he knows I want to be with Mack, and he's jealous."

"I don't know. . . ." Jonathon looked away from his daughter so that he could think a bit more clearly. "That just doesn't seem much like Jeremy. He's not a bright man, but he's never really been attached to anyone or anything . . . other than himself, that is."

Icy fear stabbed through Jena. Her teasing and tormenting of Jeremy had produced his insistence that she follow through with her end of their agreement, but she had always assumed that her father would unquestioningly take her side and then give Jeremy a stern talk or, even better, kick him out of the mansion, sending him to New York or San Francisco or anyplace where he could drink beer and indulge himself with the prostitutes he so enjoyed. Either way, Jena hadn't anticipated Jonathon questioning the validity of what she claimed.

"Whatever you think is best, Papa," she said meekly, her heart racing. "I just thought I'd bring it up to you. You know I tell you everything."

She left the room before Jonathon could ask her any more questions.


Tori was sitting on the porch of her home, sipping a cup of coffee, leaning back and feeling good about life. In the three days that had passed since Mack had been attacked, his recovery had been astonishingly swift and very soon would be nearly complete. Earlier in the day, Doc Jamison had stopped by, and his professional assessment of Mack's recovery confirmed Tori's. Mack's own assessment was that there was no reason in the world for him to stay in bed when there was so much for him to do, but every time he'd tried to get up, Tori pushed him back into bed. When he still resisted, she reissued Paul's threat of putting him into Doc Jamison's private clinic in Santa Fe until he completely recovered from his wounds.

Tori knew Mack wasn't yet the man she'd known. Not by any means, no matter what he said. His strength and stamina hadn't returned, though he was now getting up for his meals and was walking around a bit now and then. His appetite was nearly normal, though after eating he was always tired.

Still, Tori was comforted to see the twinkle of mischief return to his eyes, to have to dance out of his reach as she passed by, to feel a naughty hand on her backside or brushing her breasts. He even teasingly promised that it would never happen again—as he was reaching for her!

Once having learned she could satisfy his desires without forcing him to strain his already damaged body, Tori had become positively insatiable. Despite Mack's protests, always variations of I'm too weak to fight you, she en-

joyed her newfound sensual skills. And Mack found them
delightful. Though the point of it all wasn't to keep score,
he was looking forward to the day when his body was
strong enough to satisfy Tori as thoroughly as she did him.

Out of the corner of her eye Tori saw movement. In the
distance, riding on horseback over the crest of the hill and
through the tree line was Jena Krey.

Tori's anger flared at first. Jena was an outrageously
determined woman, and this time, without carriage or
bodyguards, she seemed prepared for a fight. Tori wondered whether Jena's change in mode of transportation
had to do with her suspicions concerning what kind of
woman Mack found most beguiling.

As Jena approached, the long, white plume in her small
hat became visible. Tori smiled. How fitting for a preening
peahen to have a feather in her cap. But then, how ridiculous she looked in her gray wool jacket, frilly white
blouse, and matching oversized skirt, made especially vo-
luminous to accommodate riding a horse. Unlike Tori,
who preferred straddling a horse, Jena had chosen the
more socially acceptable sidesaddle posture.

Tori rose to her feet. This kind of confrontation would
be met standing.

"I see you've come alone this time," she called out, as
Jena reined in her gelding, stopping aggressively close so
that dust swirled around the porch and Tori.

"I've come to talk to Mack," Jena stated sharply. The
implication was clear; she did not wish to speak with Tori.

"He's sleeping." Tori's pulse quickened, but she ignored
that. For some reason, Jena didn't seem quite the threat
she had earlier. "Come back another time."

Jena Krey scowled at her, dismounting despite Tori's

instructions. She was a little surprised that Tori's posture wasn't nearly as defensive as it had been the first time they'd clashed over where Mack spent his recovery and who should be his personal nurse.

"You've had your fun," Jena said, standing very close to her foe, secure in her superior breeding and in her ability to intimidate. She'd made stronger people than Tori cower in fear. "It's time for Mack to get back to his own kind."

A smile crooked Tori's lips. *"His own kind?"* She enunciated each word as though it were unintelligible and foreign. "Let me guess, you're included in that select group, but I'm not."

Jena rolled her eyes. "Look, you know the way life is just as well as I do. Frankly, I don't resent Mack for stepping out of his own circle for a while. I understand that men like him need to . . . experiment. It's in their blood, and women of my class simply have to accept and understand that."

Jena put her foot on the porch, and Tori took a step sideways to block her path. For an instant, when their eyes locked, unrestrained hatred was transmitted by both women.

"Know your place," Jena whispered malevolently, clearly indicating she meant violence if her demand wasn't accepted.

"This is *my* place," Tori replied, refusing to back down an inch. When she saw the shock in Jena's eyes, her confidence soared. Then, to prove that she had teeth and claws of her own, she added, "And Mack's in *my* bed."

Though Jena took two steps backward, she quickly regained her composure. Still, she'd been staggered by Tori's blunt declaration.

"Mack's been in many beds," she returned, theatrically drawling out the words. "So that hardly puts you in exclusive company."

Tori would not take the bait. Defiance shone in her clear green eyes as she said, "Yes, I'm aware of the past. The difference is, I know something you don't."

Jena's mouth twisted into a sneer, which distorted her cultivated beauty. "What could that possibly be?"

"I know what Mack's future is."

Jena laughed bitterly. "Not likely, darling. You're an amusement to him, a temporary diversion. You lack the staying power he will need. You lack the experience."

That first time Jena had intimated Tori lacked the sexual skills necessary to truly satisfy Mack, and the words had struck an open nerve then. Now Jena's claim appeared absurd. Too many times in the recent past Tori had seen a look of astonishment and absolute satisfaction in Mack's eyes for her to believe the accusation.

"You're right if you think I haven't slept with as many men as you have, but you're wrong about something."

"And what might that be?"

"I don't doubt for a second that you know how to satisfy a dozen different men night after night after night. Even a dozen times in one night."

Jena stared into Tori's eyes, expecting her to back down. When she didn't, her fear—an apprehension like her father's, that people were beginning to lose their fear of her—became stronger. She didn't know what to say to Tori, or what to do about her. She just wanted the impoverished sister of the dangerous bounty hunter to disappear without a trace and, once gone, to evaporate from Mack's memory.

Suddenly Mack stepped into the open doorway. He was barefooted and shirtless, wearing only his trousers. The bandage around his ribs had been put there fresh that morning by Tori.

"She's right about that, though she's exaggerating," he said quietly, looking straight through Jena. "A dozen times in a single night would kill me."

Mack had been standing near the doorway long enough to hear Jena's comments, which sent his contempt for her to dangerous levels.

Jena was so stunned by Mack's bald admission that she couldn't even react. Did he really prefer the company of an inexperienced tramp like Tori?

"You must have gotten kicked in the head harder than you first thought," she said, struggling for some version of a smile. "Mack, surely you must realize—"

"That I wish you hadn't come here? Yes, I realize that, Jena," he said, cutting her off. "Now if you don't mind, I'd like to return to my bed. I'm not one hundred percent recovered yet, but I'm getting there . . . with Tori's help."

He turned then and disappeared into the cabin, leaving Tori smiling like the cat who'd just ate the Krey family's canary.

"I'll get you for this," Jena whispered, positioning herself sideways on the horse. "Trust me, Tori, you'll wish to God you'd never done this to me."

"I didn't do anything. You've brought this all upon yourself," Tori replied, but Jena didn't hear because she was already riding away.

\* \* \*

Jena was grateful for the long trip back to Santa Fe. She had so much to think about. Sitting easy in the saddle she allowed both her horse and her mind their own easy pace.

There was just no way around it: Tori Singer had to die. But if it were discovered that she had put a bullet in Tori's back, Mack would despise her. If he hated her, how could she be comfortably ensconced in the governor's mansion? She'd mistakenly planned to draw nearer to Mack by having him assaulted, and that plan had backfired, thanks in great measure to Tori.

Jena realized that however Tori was dealt with, the plan must be well conceived to avoid another failure.

As she rode along, memories of Tori's defiance so enraged her that she actually trembled. The woman had changed, become strong in a way that Jena had never dreamed was possible for the common-born. Worst of all, Mack found her strength admirable, yes, even pleasurable. Why was he, of all people, willing to spend so much time in that miserable little shack? Why not have Tori stay at the Randolph Ranch?

Jena knew she didn't understand any of this, but she did know the wife of the territorial governor had limitless power within the territory—and she would be the woman who held that power. Anyone who stood between her and that power would be eliminated.

And there was Jeremy to think about. Jena had pandered shamelessly to his lust in order to get Mack beaten up, but then she'd given her brother nothing for his efforts. Not that he really deserved anything; he'd injured Mack's face. Even if she'd forgotten to mention avoiding damage to it, Jeremy, dim though he was, should have figured out that she didn't want Mack's good looks marred.

What was she to do about Jeremy? About Tori?

Jena sighed wearily, thinking that her father had become obsessed with the Midnight Bandit. Well, she had worries that were much more pressing than having some silly ledger stolen.

And then it hit her. In a single moment of brilliance, she realized that she could get rid of her two most pressing problems—Jeremy and Tori—at the same time and, in the process, probably earn Mack's esteem.

Mack was sleeping, and would until morning. He'd overdone it when he'd tried to playfully wrestle with Tori, then had required laudanum against the pain from his broken ribs. The laudanum always knocked him out for hours.

"Sleep well, my darling," Tori had whispered, looking down at his large form, which dominated the bed and, in fact, the entire cabin.

She bent to gently kiss his forehead, then straightened and tiptoed toward the door.

With the sun down and her black cape around her shoulders, the silk mask ready to be placed over her eyes, Tori was about to strike. At Jena, who'd thought she could intimidate Tori into walking away from Mack without a fight!

Before leaving the cabin, she had checked the load in her revolver, then had returned the gun to its holster. She hoped it wouldn't be necessary to use the weapon, but she didn't want to be caught unprepared.

She walked outside into the desert night.

*Let's see, where should I strike tonight?* she mused. *The Krey mansion in Santa Fe? No, much too risky, and it has already been done once. Krey Cattle #3?* Tori discarded that thought, too, as she grabbed the horse's reins. To do that would punish cowboys who might not want to work for Krey, but who simply had no other option.

Tori mounted up and headed out into the darkness. She felt confident. The Krey empire had many tentacles. By sunrise, she intended to have inflicted damage to one more of those, and with any luck, some of the people who had been most injured by Krey would benefit from her actions.

## Twenty-six

Jonathon Krey sipped his morning coffee. The Midnight Bandit was a very clever fellow, he admitted to himself, but nothing would be more rewarding than to personally castrate him.

Most vexing to Krey was the realization that the Bandit could not possibly be Mack Randolph. Jonathon had been thoroughly convinced that Randolph was the Midnight Bandit, until last night's raid on Krey Cattle #2. Randolph, who was still in bed recovering from his wounds, couldn't be the Bandit.

Jonathon Krey had wanted to be able to tie up all the loose ends quickly and easily so that he could go on with the business of making money. Now, since Randolph wasn't the Midnight Bandit, he was still the odds-on favorite to end up being elected territorial governor. And Jonathon had no doubt that when Mack took the oath of office, Jena would be standing proudly at his side as his loving wife.

He shook his head slowly, his vision distant and unfocused as he thought about his daughter. Much as he loved her, there were times when she frightened him. He had never met a more ruthless individual in his life, and that included himself. There was simply no doubt in Jena's mind that when Mack took up residence in the governor's mansion, she would move in with him. Even as a very young girl, Jena's intractable determination to have everything that her eyes lit upon had astonished him.

Whether she or Michael was the brightest of his children was difficult to tell. Michael had the discipline and the foresight to see beyond a horizon that Jena never even noticed. But for sheer cunning, Jonathon wouldn't want to wager his fortune on which of the two exercised it better.

Poor Jeremy. Even as a child, he'd always been on the portly side. Now his beer consumption had given him an enormous, sloppy stomach, and though he was not truly stupid, he'd never had the discipline to master anything completely. His personality inclined him toward gambling and wenching. The fact that he had never been of any true value to Jonathon was occasionally disquieting, but Michael had always been his resource, there to lean on—stable Michael to pass the reins of command to when the time was right.

Jonathon dismissed thoughts of his children. The Midnight Bandit needed his full attention.

The Bandit, at least, had been seen. He wore a black cape and mask to hide his identity, and moved like a shadow in the night. But who was it?

Jonathon's anger began to burn once again inside him, so he set his coffee aside. Lately, his stomach had been giving him problems, making it difficult for him to sleep at night, causing him to avoid some of the foods he most enjoyed.

The Midnight Bandit was making it difficult for him to enjoy his life! Jonathon Krey just couldn't imagine what he'd done to be treated so badly, so unjustly. To

put everything in his life back on course, he had to crush
the Bandit . . .

But how?

He belched softly, and this time the burning sensation
went all the way up to his throat. Jonathon Krey grimaced
in pain.

Again he determined that when he caught the Bandit,
he'd carry out the only punishment equal to what the Bandit was doing to him—castration.


Jena wiped her hands on the skirt of her dress. She just
couldn't seem to keep them from feeling slick and sweaty.

Squinting against the sunlight, she scanned the horizon
again and still saw no rider. Then she looked to the south,
where the scrub trees were thick. No one.

Jeremy would come to her, wouldn't he? What if he'd
finally grown so tired of her excuses and lies that he simply no longer believed she would ever make him "happier
than a cat licking cream" as she'd promised?

*Stop thinking that way!* Jena thought irritably. *He'll
come! He's wanted me for years! He'll come!*

But her fears persisted. She knew she had been pushing
Jeremy for a long time, flaunting her body, teasing him,
hinting that she would satisfy his passion, though always
avoiding his groping hands. She couldn't help telling him
how repellent she found him, calling him an overweight
pig of a man, dim-witted and gluttonous.

Even Jeremy couldn't be pushed forever, Jena reasoned.

Pulling a white hanky from the small purse hanging
from the thin velvet cord encircling her left wrist, she
dabbed her forehead and temples once more. *God, but it's*

*hellishly hot!* she thought. She imagined herself at home on the veranda, being fanned by one of the servants, drinking cool lemonade, or maybe even a mint julep.

Jena closed her eyes, and for a few moments thought only of all the terrible, nasty things Jeremy had said to her over the years. She thought about all the times he'd "accidentally" opened her bedroom door while she was undressing, "accidentally" walked in on her when she was in the bathing chamber, of how he was always touching her back or shoulder or letting his knee rub against hers under the dinner table while they ate.

When she opened her eyes, she was smiling once again, and feeling confident. She hated Jeremy all over again, and this hate could not allow her to fail. He was a fat, evil man, stupid and vain, and he could not outwit her in a thousand years.

Suddenly, Jeremy approached on horseback. she considered waving to her brother, indicating she was happy he'd come out on the desert to be with her, but then she stopped herself. It would be too great a departure from her normal behavior to be thrilled to see Jeremy, and if ever she needed to appear as normal as possible, now was the time.

He tapped his heels to the horse's ribs, hurrying the last three hundred yards to her. When he reached Jena, she saw that his shirt was sticking to him, and perspiration was running in little rivers down his neck and temples.

"You just had to pick a place way the hell out here, didn't you?" he said irritably as he got down from his horse.

Jeremy's annoyed tone hid his surprise that Jena was actually waiting for him. He hadn't really thought she'd follow through with the plan to meet privately, even though the plan was hers. A dozen times, he had told himself that she was just toying with him one more time. He guessed if he saddled up and rode all the way out to the deserted Barlington Mine #4, he'd only end up wasting his time, and when he finally rode back home, he'd find her waiting, cool and poised, laughing softly to herself because she'd have put one more thing over on him.

But now Jena smiled softly, maintaining a ten-foot separation between them. "Well, we could hardly conclude our deal at home, and I certainly wasn't going to take a hotel room in Santa Fe, where every majordomo and doorman knows us."

Jeremy reached for her, but she skipped out of the way. "Now wait a minute, I want to get something straight first."

He grinned obscenely. "So do I. That's why I'm here." He pulled loose his tie and began unbuttoning his shirt.

"Wait, don't you want to talk first?"

"I've talked to you my whole life."

For an instant, Jena's mind went blank. She had planned this afternoon's events, but once again she was discovering that in real life unexpected things had a way of happening.

"Don't do that," she said with a tight voice.

Jeremy, his eyes dark and menacing, stopped unbuttoning his shirt. Way out here, too far for anyone to hear his sister's screams, he intended to collect on her debt to him—one way or another.

"Why not?" He shifted a little to his right, blocking any attempt Jena might make to rush for her horse.

She smiled with more confidence. Her plan might come together after all. She'd always prided herself on her ability to devise appropriate plans spontaneously. "How would you like me to do that?" Jena asked, feigning embarrassed shock at her own boldness.

Jeremy chuckled. "I would," he said, grinning, his eyes roaming over Jena. "I'd take that like I'd take a royal flush."

Jena made a motion with her hands. "Button your shirt again, then wait your turn."

"Wait my turn?" Jeremy snapped, preparing himself for another deception.

Jena crossed her arms under her small bosom and looked at her brother sternly. "I've been planning this for a long time. If you follow my plan, you're in for the time of your life, I promise."

For a few seconds, Jeremy regarded her, analyzing her intentions. She'd lied to him so many times. . . . Finally, with a wary expression, he rebuttoned his shirt.

Breathing a sigh of relief, Jena began unfastening the buttons of her blouse. For a moment she thought Jeremy's eyes would bulge right out of their sockets, and she managed a modest blush.

When he took a step closer, she stepped back quickly. "I'm not ready yet!" she said sharply. "And I don't like you looking at me that way. It's so . . . so. . . ."

"Vulgar?" Jeremy volunteered.

"Exactly!"

"What do you expect? I'm a vulgar man."

He reached for Jena, and once again she danced away. Her blouse was open enough to show her chemise beneath, and though she'd regularly shown more than that at home, it now wasn't enough to pacify Jeremy.

"Turn your back," Jena said, adopting her most spoiled, petulant tone. "I don't want you watching."

"What difference does it make!" Jeremy bellowed. "I'm going to see it all soon enough anyway!"

"It makes a difference to me," Jena explained. "Now do as I say or we can call this whole thing off right here and now."

Jeremy grinned then. If Jena thought she could stop him now, she had another think coming. Just the same, it would be better if she went along willingly, so that he wouldn't have to resort to violence.

Grinning crookedly, he turned his back on his sister. "Hurry up," he said. "I don't want to wait forever."

She moved closer to him, reaching into the purse hanging from her left wrist. "Trust me, this will be over before you know it."

The derringer was in her hand a moment later, pointed straight at Jeremy's back. He must have heard the metallic sound of the hammer being thumbed back, but Jena did not hesitate to pull the trigger.

Jeremy was dead before his body landed facedown in the desert heat, a single bullet through his heart. The fine wool of his jacket was singed with gunpowder.

For a moment, Jena stood over the corpse. What did she feel now that she had murdered her brother? Oddly, almost nothing. Though she'd always loathed Jeremy, his presence in the mansion had meant she had a fat pig to insult and belittle. She'd always felt superior to him. Now she wouldn't have Jeremy to berate anymore, but other than this minor loss, this sense of inconvenience, she felt nothing at all.

\* \* \*

The ride back to the ranch had been slow, in order to cater to Mack's broken ribs, but it had buoyed his spirits to be in the saddle. Once home, he heard the ranch hands declare themselves eager to take on whoever it was that had attacked him—and they didn't care if the fight required fists, guns, or knives. To a man, they reported vigilance for strangers—and attention to any rumors as to who the cowards were who had attacked their boss.

Later, dressed in freshly laundered clothes and sipping a cup of Gretchen's herbal tea, famous for soothing aches and pains—an old German recipe, she said, handed down from her sainted grandmother—Mack reclined on the sofa. He was feeling a strange sense of unease, though he couldn't say why.

"How are the ribs?" Paul asked from a rocking chair, eyeing his brother with the wary concern of a protective older brother.

He'd always been proud of and fiercely loyal to Mack. This cowardly assault—three against one, from ambush, at night—had to be avenged, and Paul would not rest until the attackers were brought to justice. As a believer in God—he wanted nothing less than Christian justice—an eye for an eye. Forgiveness was God's business, not his.

"Itching, mostly. What really bothers me is the cut over my eye." Mack touched the thin strip of a bandage over his left eyebrow. "Hard on the vanity, you know," he added with a self-deprecating grin.

Paul chuckled, though he really saw no humor in the situation. As far as he was concerned, this had been an attack on the Randolph family, not just one member of it. Mack spoke of putting his assailants behind bars; Paul preferred a more private justice, where one thug at a time would experience punishment both swift and sure.

"You're getting too old to be the fair-haired pretty boy anyway," Paul said. "Now how about explaining what you've got going with Tori. She doesn't exactly strike me as your type."

"What's that mean?" Mack retorted defensively.

Paul smiled at his brother's readiness to defend Tori.

"In the past, you always apologized for the women you . . . spent time with. Now you're defending one. That's a nice change. What does she mean to you?"

Mack stretched out a little more on the sofa, staring now at the library ceiling. "The damned truth of it is I really don't know. Sometimes I can't think of living without her. Other times I know the only way we'll ever get along is if I live according to *her* rules, *her* standards. I don't think she can change enough to fit in here."

Any notion that Mack might marry and move away from the Randolph Ranch was not even a possibility. Both Paul and Mack had known from earliest childhood that they were destined to live at the Randolph Ranch—until becoming territorial governor forced Mack to change residences.

Paul recalled the few conversations he'd had with Tori. She'd spoken like a man, he thought then, declaring what she would do rather than deferring to a man's judgment. He liked that about her, but he imagined it might be difficult to live with.

Then there was Mack's political career to consider. Tori's brusque forcefulness, her Levi's and the Colt at her hip put her so far outside Santa Fe society that the wealthiest of the city would surely mount a campaign against Mack if she were at his side.

"Does she make you happy?" Paul asked.

"Enormously. Why do you think I wanted to stay at her home rather than come here to recuperate?"

"Lots of women have made you happy, Mack. She's not the first one."

"She's the first one who makes me happy outside of bed. With the others, I did all the things I was supposed to do. I danced with them, lavished them with flowers and gifts, but I did that to get in bed with them. You've had your share of lovers and know how it goes."

"Yes, I know what you're talking about. But continue. There's something more you want to say."

"Oh? Hmmm. Yes, I think there is." Mack closed his eyes and a vision of Tori filled his mind. "What I mean is, yes, what we have when the candles are blown out is indescribable, but what we have the rest of the time—between two people, a man and a woman—that's wonderful, too. I really like the time I spend with her."

"Like it . . . or love it?" Paul asked. The difference was enormous. "If you like it, then she's your friend, and a woman you are having a very enjoyable affair with. But if you *love* the time with her when you're not making love . . . then you're in love with her, little brother. And you'd better ask yourself whether you can afford to be in love with a woman like Tori Singer." Paul paused for a moment to choose his words carefully, knowing the dangerous ground he was treading on. "You've made a lot of plans, set some very high goals for yourself and for the family name. Whether you like it or not, a time may come when you'll have to choose between Tori and all the projects you've put into motion prior to meeting her."

Mack rose gingerly from the sofa. "Damn," he whispered. "Damn . . . damn . . . damn!"


"Now mind you, I'm not one to speak ill of anyone," Jena said to Deputy Dylan McKenzie as she dabbed her neck with a hanky, "but she was riding as though the devil himself was chasing her." Sniffing in disgust, Jena looked around the sheriff's office, wondering how on earth anyone could willingly spend even a minute there. Not only was the deputy a model of the hygenically neglected lawman, but to make matters even worse, there was a drunk in one of the jail cells. The sound of his snoring was seriously getting on Jena's nerves.

"But you didn't say what she'd done," the deputy said. He was glad the sheriff wasn't around because that gave him a chance to speak with Jena Krey, a woman who normally wouldn't have looked twice at him.

"Well, I don't exactly know what she's done, Deputy Dylan, that's why I'm here talking with you now. I saw Tori Singer riding away from our old mine like she had the hangman chasing her, and it seems to me, if you were the good deputy I think you are, you'd do a little investigating on your own to see what she was riding so fast *from*."

Jena looked away, wishing to God that it wouldn't continue to be necessary for her to have to deal with mental inferiors. It galled her to explain to Dylan every move he was supposed to make.

"But you didn't see or hear nothin' else?" McKenzie

did not relish the thought of riding out in the afternoon heat to investigate anything, especially not on something as flimsy as a woman's hunch.

"You know the kind of blood she's got running through her veins." Jena's anger now could be heard in her voice. "Her brother is Jedediah Singer, the murdering bounty hunter. Nobody really knows how many men he's killed. What makes you think his sister is any different than he is?"

Dylan nodded his head slowly, wondering if the stories of Jena Krey's promiscuity were true, and if they were, whether they might extend to the deputy sheriff of Santa Fe.

"I see what you mean," he said agreeably. Maybe he could worm his way into Jena Krey's good graces.

Jena rose and finally offered the unwashed lawman a genuine smile. "I thought you would," she said, then left the smelly, Sheriff's office, promising herself she wouldn't ever step foot in there again, even if her life depended upon it.

Jena made three more stops before heading back home. She went to see Paula Nearing, who charged a small fortune for her services, but simply did wonders for a woman's hair. At Paula's salon, Jena reported to all the women there that she'd been out for her morning ride— she claimed, to the surprise of customers who'd never seen her out before noon, that she had been taking morning rides for months now—when she'd spotted Tori Singer "riding like she had the good Lord's wrath upon her."

"She's such a strange young woman," Jena said, keeping her voice down just enough so that the salon clientele leaned close to hear her. "You never know what she's capable of. Her brother's that bounty hunter that kills everybody."

Jena's next stop was at the seamstress's shop, where more rumors concerning Tori Singer's "erratic, suspicious behavior" were spread, came to life, then took on a life of their own.

Finally, Jena stopped at the Sundowner Hotel, where fashionable young women could sit on the north veranda out of the sun and enjoy cool drinks while their husbands or beaus drank beer and whiskey in the hotel's saloon. Once again, her tale of seeing Tori Singer in the vicinity of the old Krey mine was served up for consumption. She simply couldn't understand why the good people of Santa Fe didn't do something about women like Tori Singer. It was disgraceful, Jena insisted, verifying the reactions of her listeners.

As Jena left the veranda, confident that tongues would continue wagging about Tori Singer, she felt comfort, marrow-deep, knowing that she, in one afternoon, had disposed of two of the most troubling people in her life.

Deputy Dylan McKenzie hurried to ride into Santa Fe before sundown. He wanted the townspeople to see him, the corpse of Jeremy Krey thrown over the saddle of the trail horse he was leading.

He hoped his discovery of this corpse out in the desert would make him a hero. It couldn't hurt his reputation any. Generally he was considered lazy by the citizens of Santa Fe.

As he rode down Main Street, he worried that Jonathon Krey would somehow find him responsible for his son's death. After all, a deputy was supposed to prevent crimes—particularly murder, especially the murder of a prominent citizen—from occurring.

Despite the heat, Dylan shivered at the prospect of explaining to Jonathon Krey that his son had been shot in the back. But at least Dylan knew who the murderer was. Tori Singer had been spotted riding hard and fast away from the scene of the crime. Everyone in Santa Fe had long thought her dynamite just waiting to explode. Should Jonathon Krey want to take his anger out on Dylan, at least the deputy would be able to defend himself by saying that the killer would soon be in custody.

As Dylan continued walking his trophy through town, word traveled quickly.

Residents began lining the street to watch him leading the trail horse. The deputy authoritatively pulled his hat down over his eyes, hoping to give himself an appearance of mystery and of quiet competence.

"You know who killed him, Deputy?" someone from the gathering crowd shouted.

Dylan tried in vain to see who had asked the question. But it really didn't matter so long as he had the answer he knew the crowd wanted.

"I'll have the guilty party in custody by morning!" he replied, raising his voice enough to make it carry.

Receiving a cheer from the crowd, Deputy Dylan McKenzie never felt better about himself.

# Twenty-seven

In her small barn, brushing down the mare Paul Randolph had loaned her, Tori decided she'd need to figure out some kind of payment schedule so she could keep the horse. On two different occasions Mack had insisted that she not worry about paying for it, but Tori couldn't accept such a valuable gift. She didn't want even the slightest suspicion that the mare was a payment for sexual favors.

Finished brushing, feeding, and watering the horse, Tori returned to her other chores, finally returning the pitchfork to its proper place, hanging the water bucket up on the wall peg, and then walking out into the bright morning sunlight.

She was still squinting, when she felt the muzzle of a rifle jab her in the back.

"Just raise your hands nice and slow, and don't make a play for it 'cause I'll shoot a woman just as quick as I'll shoot a man," Deputy Dylan McKenzie said.

His excitement at arresting this particular woman was so intense he was shaking in his boots. But Tori was shocked. This deputy, renowned for laziness and cowardice, had caught her? In the blink of an eye she saw herself first in a courtroom, standing before a judge, then pacing a tiny prison cell.

"Just stay right where you are," Dylan continued, his nerves settling now that he believed himself to be in no danger.

Tori's composure had also returned. She knew better than to argue with the deputy—or put up any resistance. Dylan, the coward, could probably shoot a woman. When he twisted her wrists behind her back one at a time to lock on the handcuffs, Tori closed her eyes against a sinking feeling that her life was over.

Once her hands were securely cuffed, Dylan put his hands all over her body under the pretense of searching for hidden weapons. At first Tori twisted away from him, but then she realized how much he enjoyed overcoming her struggles. Finally, when he'd finished manhandling her, she glared at him. "First time you ever touch a woman, Deputy?"

Dylan just grinned and took her by the arm, leading her to the porch where he forced her to sit.

"Mind telling me what I've done?" Tori asked. Could she have been recognized during her thwarted attempt to steal from Krey Cattle #2? As she sat down, she again realized the wisdom of Mack's advice to plan every move out carefully well in advance.

"I'm arresting you for the back-shootin' murder of Jeremy Krey," Dylan said over his shoulder as he walked into the cabin.

Tori's head began to spin, so fast that it was hard to remain in place without falling.

Murder? There had to be some mistake. She was a thief. In court, she might even confess to that, and when she did, she'd tell the jury that she had stolen from Jonathon Krey to help those poor families—like the Dahlbergs, who had been so grievously hurt by Krey. She was no murderess. There had to be some mistake.

Tori shook her head and blinked her eyes to stop the spinning, but now there was a ringing in her ears. Panicking, she tested the strength of the handcuffs, but thick bands of iron bit into the tender flesh of her wrists.

Murder? Jeremy Krey?

"You're out of your mind." Tori had actually spoken the defiant words not just thought them. Dylan didn't hear her because he'd gone inside and was rummaging through her possessions. "I said, you're out of your mind!" she shouted. "When my brother finds out you've gone through our place and arrested me on this silly charge, he's going to skin your hide. He'll do it, Deputy, and don't think he won't."

The ringing in her ears had finally ended, and her confidence was returning. Despite everything, she was completely innocent of murder, and the facts would prove it.

"Well, well, well," Deputy McKenzie said smugly as he walked back onto the porch. There was a swagger to his step now that hadn't been there before. In his hands were the black silk cape and mask Mack had made for her. "You have been a busy young lady, haven't you? I haven't just arrested the murderer of Jeremy Krey, I've arrested the Midnight Bandit to boot!"

Rage roiled inside Mack. For this, someone was going to pay dearly.

Why had it taken so long—nearly four hours—for news to get to the Randolph Ranch of Tori Singer's arrest for the murder of Jeremy Krey? And now virtually everyone in Santa Fe was talking about how Tori had also been revealed as the Midnight Bandit?

"Don't go off half-cocked," Paul said, standing in the doorway to Mack's bedroom. He'd seen his brother angry plenty of times, but he'd never before seen him in such a worrisome state.

"Trust me. I'm not. I'm loaded for bear," Mack replied as he carefully, hiding the pain in his ribs, slipped his arm into a figure eight-shaped holster strap, then dropped a small revolver into the leather pouch. He seldom carried concealed weapons, but with his gray pinstriped jacket on, the revolver nestled under his left arm was all but invisible.

"Remember, you're a lawyer," Paul said quietly, knowing better than to stand in Mack's way.

Paul had earlier assembled some men as back-up should the situation take on extralegal dimensions. Now these men were getting their weapons readied, their horses saddled; and they were being given assignments with military precision.

"I won't forget," Mack stated with savage sarcasm, inspecting some papers before he shoved them into his briefcase. "With an honest-to-God lawman like Deputy Dylan McKenzie arresting Tori for murder—and such shining examples of integrity in our local government—how could I possibly forget that I'm a lawyer and must abide by the law?"

How unjust it all seemed! Why should he, Mack Randolph, be handcuffed by the law, by all its rules and statutes, when men like Jonathon Krey and Deputy Dylan did whatever they desired?

Had becoming the Midnight Bandit had any positive impact after all?

Paul excused himself, saying he had other things to do. Mack knew that meant looking in on the boys to see how their efforts were progressing. He himself had been on the organizing end when Paul's fiery temper and desire for immediate justice had had to be dealt with, so he knew that beyond the range of his vision, men were scurrying about and readying weapons, and Paul would be explaining that they must stay out of Mack's way while at the same time remaining close enough to help him if they were needed.

As Mack's ribs began to throb, he let out a laugh. The damn pain would provide a reminder of the ruthless enemy he faced. He embraced the pain, knowing it would keep his senses deadly sharp.

A horse was waiting for him when he got outside. As he strapped his briefcase onto the saddlebags, he could see men running past the nearby bunkhouses.

"I'll be going to the sheriff's office first," Mack said to the young ranch hand, taking the reins of his horse. He knew that whatever he said would be passed on to the appropriate men. "Once I get Tori out of jail, I'll figure out my next step. Tell the boys to stay out of range for a while. I don't want the townspeople thinking they're being bullied."

The boy, his eyes wide, said nothing. New to the Randolph Ranch, he'd never before seen the place mobilize against an enemy, and he clearly found it exciting.

As Mack raced toward town, his mind worked through possible strategies. Once he arrived, his horse lathered from the breakneck pace, he saw curtains moving as people posted at their windows tried to avoid being seen. The men lounging outside stores and shops stopped talking and watched silently as he rode past. Randolph's angry arrival had been nervously anticipated.

Mack hoped Sheriff Max Stryker was in town. Max was a good and decent man, hardworking and honest, reasonable. Deputy Dylan McKenzie, on the other hand, was the type to be bought, bribed, or bullied into submission.

Mack saw Dylan standing outside the sheriff's office, talking to three young women, likely telling them a fantastically exaggerated account of how he had bravely and heroically captured the dangerous Midnight Bandit. Then Dylan spotted Mack riding quickly toward him and hastily dismissed his female audience to rush into the sheriff's office. By the time Mack arrived, Dylan was standing in the doorway, holding a sawed-off double-barreled shotgun.

"Afternoon, Mr. Randolph," Dylan said, his cheek bulging with fresh chewing tobacco. He spit a long brown stream into the dirt, close enough to the highly polished toes of Mack's boots to be an insult, not so close that it couldn't be called an accident.

Mack tried to ignore the indirect confrontation, the swinish behavior.

"Better start packing your bags," Mack said, swinging down from his mount. It took all his willpower to keep from reaching for the small revolver hidden in the holster beneath his left arm. "You're not going to be working in Santa Fe much longer."

"Now how do you figure that?" the deputy said, a smirk on his face. With the shotgun, and with Mack's reputation as being an upstanding attorney constraining his actions, Dylan was feeling pretty confident. To aid in this respect, a small crowd had gathered and their presence would prevent Randolph from behaving foolishly.

"I want Tori out. Now!" Mack's voice was extremely calm, but his eyes burned with murderous rage. "I don't know who put you up to this, but you're going to pay for it, Deputy. Pay dearly."

"Mr. Lawyer Man, are you threatening me? Me, a sworn officer of the law?" Dylan demanded, moving to block Mack's entrance into the sheriff's office. He angled the twin barrels of the shotgun up just enough so that they were now pointed at Mack's knees as he approached. Only a few ounces of pressure on the triggers and Mack would be cut down.

"It's not a threat, it's a commitment," Mack said, walking forward slowly, his eyes on the deputy's face, not the shotgun aimed at him.

"You threaten me and I'll lock you up with the lady." The deputy chuckled then, glancing around to see who was watching his performance. "That is assumin' she's a lady," he added, before he laughed outright.

Mack walked past the deputy, not all that surprised he hadn't been stopped. After all, he had the legal right to visit a client in jail.

His heart seized up the second he saw Tori through the iron bars, sitting in her cell on the dirty cot provided for those people who got arrested. At least she had a cell to herself, and the other three cells were unoccupied. Mack had had too much experience with men behind bars for him to have any illusions about their character.

"Are you all right?" he asked.

On seeing him, Tori shot off the jail cot and rushed to the iron bars. She placed her hands over his on them and squeezed her eyes tightly shut for an instant, afraid that tears would start. She'd believed herself composed, but at looking into Mack's dark, painfully worried eyes, raw emotion filled her. Finally, when no words would come, she simply nodded her head.

For a long moment they stood in silence. A rage unlike anything Mack had ever known before was boiling inside him. But he knew he must keep his temper in control, for angry men were stupid men, and this was not a time when he could afford to behave stupidly.

"What happened?"

Tori looked down, finding it easier to speak when she didn't have to look into Mack's eyes.

"I was in the barn. When I walked out, the deputy put a gun to my back. I thought it was for trying to steal the Krey Cattle payroll, but I was being arrested for the murder of Jeremy Krey. Then he went through the cabin and found that cape and mask you made for me, so I'm also arrested for being the Midnight Bandit. Kind of ironic, don't you think?" She actually managed a philosophic smile. "I just can't believe this has happened to me."

"Don't worry. I'll get you out of this."

"I didn't kill him, Mack. I hated Jeremy, but then, everyone hated him."

Though he'd never believed her capable of cold-blooded murder, it reassured Mack to hear Tori's denial.

"I never should have made that cape and mask," he whispered, inwardly damning himself for his contribution to Tori's incarceration. "I did it as a lark. I thought you would enjoy it."

"Don't start blaming yourself," she cut in, her head snapping up. She fixed determined green eyes on Mack.

"Blame won't accomplish anything now. What's past is past." She reached through the bars to lightly place her hand against Mack's cheek. "And don't even think of confessing to being the Midnight Bandit. Even if you did that, I'd still have the murder charge to contend with. I need you as my lawyer, Mack, so don't do anything heroic like giving yourself up. That won't help me at all."

"Give myself up?" Mack asked, raising his eyebrows theatrically. "I never even thought of it." But his tone admitted this as a possibility for getting Tori freed.

Staying with her until confidence shone in her eyes once again, Mack made her promise never to lose faith that all would turn out right. Only then did he leave the sheriff's office.

He found the deputy talking with several women just outside the jail. Dylan McKenzie was making the most of his deed. From the bits of talk Mack overheard, capturing Tori alive was testament to the deputy's genius and courage, the likes of which Santa Fe had never seen before.

"Deputy, can I talk to you privately?" Mack asked evenly, recognizing that at present Dylan wielded much more power than he did. Humiliating the deputy in front of these young women wouldn't do anyone any good.

"Why certainly, Mack," the lawman replied with a smile. It was the first time he'd used Mack's first name, and he noticed the reaction it drew from the women. Deputy Dylan McKenzie was feeling more powerful at that moment than he ever had. He stepped away from his admirers, giving them a parting smile.

"If anything happens to her while she's in jail, I'll kill you," Mack promised quietly.

The statement caught Dylan off guard. For a moment

he stared at Mack in disbelief. Then he raised his shotgun, still holding it near his hip, until the barrels were pointed straight at Mack's chest.

"Are you threatening me? You dare to—"

"Shut up, you insignificant worm," Mack hissed, the words coming out through clenched teeth. "I'll tell you this just once. I'm holding you responsible for Tori's safety while she's in jail. That means if she hangs herself, I'm holding you responsible. And if she has a visitor at night— like you, for instance—who decides he wants to rape her, I'll take your skin off in strips, then kill you. No one's to touch her, and if someone does, I'll kill you."

Mack turned and walked away from the deputy. To stay any longer would tax his patience further than he could stand. Striding down the boardwalk, he took long strides, his eyes not really focusing on where he was walking, he paid just enough attention to his surroundings to keep from knocking anyone down.

"Mack, can I speak with you? It's important."

The civil voice came to him from behind. It took several seconds and several more strides before Mack realized someone was talking to him, and speaking politely. Mack stopped, not wanting to talk to anyone, but sensing that he had to.

"I've heard what happened," Gerald Washburn, a local businessman, said in the oh-so-serious tone he used to explain to employees that there would be no changes in the office rules.

Mack said nothing, sizing up the man. Washburn, unfortunately, was one of his most vocal supporters for mayor of Santa Fe. Everyone knew the man lived and breathed business, and would never let anything get in the way of making a profit.

"There's something you're not saying, Gerald. What is it?" Mack asked flatly, in no mood for Gerald's political double-talk.

Gerald looked away a moment, running his fingers through his salt-and-pepper hair. He pursed his lips, as if the next words were difficult for him.

"I'm awfully busy, Gerald," Mack pressed. "If you have something to say to me, do it."

Gerald reacted by stepping back from Mack. Nobody talked to him with such disrespect. Mack's demeanor, having changed somewhat lately, confirmed Gerald's worst suspicions.

"I'll be plain with you, Mack. Me and the boys have been talking. We've all heard about Tori, and we know she killed Jeremy Krey. We—"

"That's an allegation, nothing more," Mack cut in, annoyed by this ludicrous conversation.

"It's a fact as far as me and the boys are concerned," Gerald Washburn said sternly. "And if you're as smart as we've always thought you were, you'll sail clear of that young gal who's in jail right now. Me and the boys heard all about what you and her did at that dance a while back. We didn't say a word about that because we know a young man's blood flows mighty hot. But you defend that gal in court, you fight for her, and there's just no way we can support you for mayor."

Mack wondered how much longer he could hold his temper; his desire to strike out physically, violently, was becoming so strong. How unimportant it seemed now to worry over his political career and the impact Tori might have on it! Prior to her arrest, Mack had spent some time considering what various factions of the citizenry, his constituencies, would think of seeing Tori beside him on the political platform when he ran for mayor of Santa Fe, but now. . . .

"You can't be serious!" he replied, the heat of his anger escalating.

"You're damned right I'm serious. We can't afford a mayor that makes a goddamned fool of himself over a woman. That's what I'm saying. Hell, Mack, we don't begrudge you having your fun. All of us know what that little gal looks like, and there isn't a one of us who wouldn't hop in the haystack with her if we got the offer. But you've got to know that whoever we back for mayor and territorial governor—and by back I mean not just with money, but with considerable votes—that man's locked in."

Gerald Washburn was warming to the subject, particularly since it illustrated just exactly how much real power he held.

"Now if you're as smart as me and the boys have always thought you were," he continued, "you'd just go on a little vacation. Go to New York City and have yourself a good time while the trial takes place. There's nothing you can do to save her. She's guilty as hell, and you don't want to be anywhere around when she starts pointing the finger of blame at others, or when her pretty neck swings in a rope."

Calmly, Mack reached out and grabbed Gerald Washburn's tie. Then, choking the man, he pulled Washburn toward him until their faces were eye to eye.

"Her pretty little neck," Mack repeated, as he tightened

the tie which had become a noose, "will never be touched. Even if I have to burn all of Santa Fe to the ground, I'll see to it that Tori goes free."

When Mack finally released his hold on Washburn's tie, the plum-faced businessman stumbled backward several steps.

Clearly shaken by Mack's implied and explicit violence, he croaked, "I'm shocked, Mack. I expected . . . better of you." He swallowed and coughed. "But if you insist on behaving this way, then the boys and I will simply have to . . . find another man to support. You aren't the only man in Santa Fe with a future."

"Who else, Gerald?" Mack snapped, mildly curious as to who the well-heeled businessmen of Santa Fe had waiting in the wings to take his place. Maybe someone who'd be more the obedient, dim-witted public servant they'd clearly expected him to be.

"Andy Fields is a good man," Gerald threatened, though without much confidence. "We've talked to him and see him as a man who understands how the system works."

Mack sneered. "I see. That means you can buy him cheap, and he'll do what you tell him. I'm glad we had this conversation, Gerald. Much easier for me to tell you to go to hell right now rather than after the election, when you think you own me. I'm not for sale, Gerald. I never have been. Tell the boys that, and tell them if they try to stand in my way, I'll crush them."

Convinced he would have many men on his side in a battle against this single renegade lawyer, Washburn whispered venomously, "You Randolphs may not be as strong as you think you are." He turned and almost stumbled away. Could a war against the might of the Randolph

Ranch be won, and if so, would victory be too expensive in the long run?

Servants ran around nervously at the Krey mansion, but they were quiet as church mice, assuming the funereal attitude expected of them with a death in the family.

Ironically, the attitude of the "mourners"—Michael, Jena, and Jonathon Krey—was quite different.

Michael's chief concern was how many of Jeremy's menial tasks would now be his. While Jeremy had greatly enjoyed his extortionist role in the operation of Lulu's bordello, Michael had always found such business ventures, though highly profitable, distasteful.

Jena had no concerns whatsoever. She had successfully managed to get Jeremy to hire men to beat Mack up, had murdered Jeremy before he'd put his filthy hands on her, and had framed Tori. Virtually everyone in Santa Fe now believed that Tori Singer murdered Jeremy Krey. For Jena, life couldn't get much better.

Jonathon had reacted to his son's murder with surprise. Why had Tori murdered him? Had Jeremy found out that she was the Midnight Bandit, forcing her to kill him? It seemed unlikely. Jeremy was the last person on earth capable of discovering the identity of the Midnight Bandit. Still, stranger things had happened.

Jonathon, Jena, and Michael were gathered in the huge, nearly empty ballroom. A crystal decanter of brandy sat on the enormous table, and all three held snifters of this finest of French spirits.

Jonathon pushed himself far enough away from the table to stand. He raised his glass and said in a solemn voice, "To Jeremy."

Jena and Michael exchanged a glance. Neither sibling was much inclined to spoil the taste of the fine Napoleon brandy with a toast to a brother they had barely tolerated, had often berated, and had never liked, much less loved.

"Well . . . ?" Jonathon asked, still standing, though his brandy glass was now on the brightly polished oak table.

He looked at his children, waiting for them to show at least some sign of sorrow for the untimely death of their brother. Michael made a slight effort to appear sorrowful, but he simply couldn't find any appropriate words. Jena didn't even bother to appear regretful.

Several seconds of stony, questioning silence passed before she answered, "Well, what? He was a stupid, fat, hairy pervert, and the ugly truth is, no one is going to miss him."

Jonathon was too shocked to even speak. His daughter had voiced these sentiments when Jeremy was alive. Just the same, Jonathon found it abnormal that Jena and Michael had so little regard for their brother.

"He was your brother," he reminded them.

"He was a pig," Jena replied.

"Amen!" Michael added, supporting his sister's opinion, though he disliked sticking his neck out for anyone other than himself.

Jonathon looked at his son and daughter for a moment, then turned his back to them. Had he really created such heartless monsters? he asked himself. Then he realized that, in truth, he did not mourn the death of Jeremy any more than they did. Actually, even the familial obligation to defend his deceased son was leaving him.

"Fine. He's dead," Jonathon agreed. "The truth is, we don't miss him at all. Fine. It doesn't matter. What *does* matter is that the people of Santa Fe *think* we're sad."

"Papa, why worry about it?" Jena asked.

She sprawled now in her chair, the brandy glass held loosely in her hand. Looking at her father, she was making no effort to hide her disdain.

"He was your brother," Jonathon repeated, losing interest in the conversation. But suddenly, he paused to look at his children, really examine them, as a strange thought came to him.

"You killed Jeremy, didn't you?"

Spoken as a question, it wasn't a question at all, it was an observation.

Jena at last stood to face the accusation. She didn't appear in the least sorry about her brother's murder, but when her gaze met Jonathon's, it was distinctly guilty.

"My God, you did kill him." Jonathon was uncertain whether he was pleased or disgusted with his daughter.

Jena looked at her father, calculating the answer which would please him most. She struggled to find a lie that Jonathon might accept as the truth, could think of none, then smiled sheepishly.

"Papa, does it really matter?" she asked.

Jonathon wondered what a father was expected to say when he discovered that one of his children had killed another. Still, he had never considered Jeremy a true Krey, so it wasn't as though a member of his family had actually been murdered. In fact, Jeremy's death was something of a relief to him.

"I," Jonathon said after a long pause, "actually, I don't really know."

Jena smiled then, and her gaze went from her father to her brother. Now she could feel pleased about her audacity—and not in the least sorrowful over her role in the assassination of the thing misnamed Krey.

"You did it, didn't you?" Jonathon asked.

For several long seconds Jena merely matched her father's gaze, trying to figure out exactly what he wanted her to say. Finally she decided that the truth would come out eventually, and if she came forward with the facts, at least she could present them in her own fashion.

"What difference does it make?" she demanded, bursting to her feet. "He was an idiot! We're money ahead without him."

Had Jena not commented on the profitability of having Jeremy dead, Jonathon might not have suspected with such certainty that his daughter was the one responsible for Jeremy's death. But looking into her eyes, he saw no sorrow, no sense of loss.

"You murdered Jeremy! Sweet Jesus, Jena, you shot your own brother in the back," Jonathon said then, his absolute conviction stunning him. "It wasn't that girl Dylan arrested, was it?" Jonathon pursued. "It was you all along."

Jonathon looked at Jena, realizing how magnificently cold-blooded she was. He looked at her as though seeing her for the first time. Did she even possess a heart that beat like any other human being's?

He could see the various responses going through her mind as she weighed an appropriate response against the honest one. In that instant, as he realized that his youngest child—his only daughter—had murdered his second son, he didn't know whether to be appalled by her savagery or impressed with her efficiency. The fact was, everyone had wanted Jeremy to disappear from the scene, but no one else had had the courage or the determination to make it happen, until Jena had decided to simply put a bullet in his back.

"You are wicked," he whispered at last.

Jena's gaze flicked from her father to her brother. With neither man did she see the censure she had feared, and not seeing it, her grin broadened.

"Wickedness becomes me, don't you think?" she asked, making no effort to hide her pleasure in her murderous accomplishment. "And I'm brilliant. I hated Jeremy and I hated that little tramp, Tori, so in one move I was able to get both of them out of our lives permanently."

Michael, who had spent many hours at his father's side, uncertain of the outcome, suggested: "Let's not forget that Mack's defending Tori. And from what Jena's told us, there won't be any evidence to put the Singer woman at the scene of the crime."

Jena's smile twisted into a bitter frown. She did not like anyone questioning her skills.

"I'm going to have Mack," she said quietly, just a little fearfully. "I'm going to be his wife when he becomes the mayor, and I'm damn sure going to be at his side when he takes office as the territorial governor!"

"Don't worry, darling, you'll have everything you want." Jonathon, having already forgotten Jeremy, wanted once again to protect his daughter from any unhappiness. "Well, Michael, it's obvious that we've got to arrange evidence that will convict Tori Singer."

Jena smiled then, secure that her father and brother were protecting her. Whatever they would plan would provide such a rock-solid case against Tori that not even Mack's great skill as a defense lawyer would prevent her from a date with the gallows.

# Twenty-eight

Mack sighed heavily. He rubbed his eyes, burning with the strain of repeatedly examining the documents regarding Tori's arrest.

He pushed himself away from the desk and stretched his legs out in front of him. Should he order more coffee from the hotel's kitchen and get back to work, or simply close the files on Tori for a while and get some sleep? Pulling the watch from his pocket, he opened it at exactly the same time the grandfather clock in the hotel's hallway chimed softly. Midnight. Bitter memories came to him of his well-intentioned capers as the Midnight Bandit.

Midnight. He was in a hotel room in Santa Fe so that he could be close to Tori, who had already spent three nights in jail. Midnight. Damn.

Mack put the watch back into his pocket and tried to concentrate on how to convince a jury that Tori wasn't the Midnight Bandit. For the hundredth time, he cursed himself for having made the cape and mask for her. If he hadn't done that, there wouldn't be a shred of evidence to link her to being the Bandit.

A plan began to form in Mack's mind. At first, it seemed too absurd to consider; yet it wouldn't leave him alone.

Maybe it wasn't so absurd after all.

He got to his feet and walked to the windows overlooking the street. Even at midnight, there were still plenty of gamblers at the Cattleman's Paradise saloon and casino.

For a minute, Mack closed his eyes. He tried to decide whether this plan resulted from Fate smiling benevolently down upon him or whether he was about to make the biggest mistake of his life.

Fate? Why else would Mack now be looking at a casino owned by Jonathon Krey? Luckily he had stuffed his cape and mask into his briefcase before leaving the ranch.

He was grinning as he went to the large bed and stripped off his jacket and tie. He didn't have the dark shirt with him, the one he always wore when he'd adopted the persona of the Midnight Bandit, and he didn't have his black holster and Colt. He'd just have to do without.

The Bandit would strike a little late this time, he thought, but by morning the citizens of Santa Fe would be seriously reconsidering whether Tori was the Midnight Bandit.

Mack was kneeling at the edge of the roof, looking down at the street below. If he didn't manage the crossing, he'd never survive the four-story fall. He imagined the articles the journalists would write after his mask had been peeled from his dead or dying remains in the street below.

He forced such thoughts from his consciousness. The task he'd set for himself was difficult enough without adding fears.

He pulled the rope tight one last time and checked to be sure the grappling hook he'd tossed to the casino rooftop across the street remained secure. It had to hold as he made his way across the chasm, but in something like this, there could be no guarantees.

After pulling on tight-fitting leather gloves to protect his hands, Mack tossed a leg over the edge of the rooftop and gripped the rope tightly.

Inhaling deeply, he steeled his courage, then slipped off the edge. The rope sagged under his weight, but the grappling hook remained in place.

The instant his weight pulled on his arms, the pain in his ribs exploded, fresh and new, more acute than when he'd first broken them. He waited, his teeth clenched against his agony, until his vision cleared.

Slowly, hand over hand, Mack made his way along the rope, his black silk cape fluttering in the evening breeze. Four stories below, men were walking about, entering and leaving the casino, oblivious to what was happening high above them.

By the time he was halfway across the street, the strain on his hands, arms, and shoulders was almost unbearable. Perspiration stuck his shirt to his chest. His ribs were on fire, and he realized, too late, that he'd not regained all his strength since the beating.

He paused a moment to look down, aware immediately that such a move was a mistake, then continued on, hand over hand, trying to maintain a smooth, swinging rhythm to make the crossing easier on himself.

He couldn't get caught, yet all it would take would be one hotel guest looking out the window, or one person on the street looking up. The closer Mack got toward the rooftop of the casino, the more fearful he grew that he'd hear a shout, then a gunshot, then he'd feel the burning sensation of a bullet striking him. No longer able to hold onto the taut rope stretched across the buildings, he'd spend the hideous seconds falling, falling. And then blackness would envelop him when he hit the ground.

*Stop thinking that way!* he scolded himself.

He was only a few hand-over-hand swings away from the edge of the casino's roof. He paced himself so that he wouldn't have to continue holding onto the rope longer than necessary, then kicked his foot up on the roof.

Straining to raise himself, he was at last kneeling on the casino's roof. Mack paused a moment, flexing his hands slowly to bring sensitivity back into them, aware of blood pumping into his biceps and forearms.

He waited until his heart rate was nearly back to normal, then moved away from the edge of the roof, running in a crouch; certain only that when this evening had come to an end, the Midnight Bandit would go into permanent retirement.

Two doors led from the roof down into the casino. Both had enormous iron locks designed to be intimidating and functional. But while large, heavy locks are designed to withstand the force of a sledgehammer striking them without the locking mechanism opening, their very size makes them easier to open with the appropriate tools.

From the slender leather case he kept in the breast pocket of his jacket, Mack extracted a dentist's cleaning hook. Made of the hardest, finest steel available, it worked as well for lock pickers as it did for dentists. In less than a minute, he had eased open the lock and pulled at the resisting door, probably not opened in several years.

He climbed down a ladder into total darkness. Three sulphur-tipped matches later, Mack had navigated himself through the storage attic to an unlocked door. Pressing his ear to it, he held his breath to concentrate on the sounds he heard. With difficulty, he tried to distinguish the nearby sounds from those the gamblers made far below.

He opened the door slowly, as yet resisting the urge to pull the small revolver from the holster beneath his jacket and cape. In all his adventures as the Midnight Bandit, in every raid on the overstuffed coffers of his enemy, Jonathon Krey, Mack had managed to keep from having to fire a gun, and if all went well, on this night—his last performance as the Midnight Bandit—he would be as successful at that as he had been in the past.

Michael Krey stood at the railing of the second floor of the casino, looking down at the roulette players. The place was busy, which surprised him. He wondered if the excitement in town—the rumors of Mack and Tori, of Tori and Jeremy, and the countless variations on them—had heated the blood, making men feel like gambling.

Below him, he saw a man's world. The only women present were there to quench the thirst men had for liquor and commitment-free sex.

Yes, all was well in Michael Krey's world. Because this was *his* world, where he belonged, wearing the finest clothes that money could buy, associating with the wealthiest, best educated, most successful people of the territory, he was not like Jeremy, who had preferred Lulu's, with its garish decor and loud, bawdy atmosphere.

Jeremy was gone, murdered by his own sister, shot unceremoniously in the back. The grimness of it brought a pitiful smile to Michael's lips. When he'd been alone with Jena, he had asked her to tell him everything about the murder, all the little details that had caused the "tragedy." Jena, still enormously pleased with herself and not in the least bit embarrassed or saddened by what she'd done, had left nothing out, not even the promise she'd made to get Jeremy to do her bidding.

"Would you have let him?" Michael had asked his sister.

"Let him what?" Jena replied innocently, looking up at Michael.

"Do it to you. What do you think I'm talking about?"

Jena's lips pursed in thought, and a moment later she replied in all seriousness, "Probably not. He was fat, hairy, and always sweating. But I suppose if it had been necessary, I would have."

Jeremy's repulsiveness had bothered her, had held her back! Not the fact that he was her brother. Michael was speechless for several seconds.

Much as he wanted to hate his sister for what she had done, he just couldn't. She had told the truth when she said nobody ever really liked Jeremy. And now that he was dead, there was one less slice to the pie when the Krey fortune was divvied up.

Yes, all was well in Michael Krey's world. Someday soon, Jonathon would retire, and then he, Michael, would be in complete control of the funds.

His spirits rising, he looked at the gamblers below and began wondering which were losing more than they could afford. And, of those big-time losers, which had attractive wives who might be willing to show special consideration to Michael if he was considerate about a husband's gambling debts.

\* \* \*

A cunning smile tugged at the corners of Mack's mouth. And behind the black mask that hid his identity, there was a twinkle of amusement in his eyes. If he wasn't such an honest man, if, as the Midnight Bandit, he sought personal gain, he suspected that he could quickly, and with a minimum of effort and risk, make himself independently wealthy.

These thoughts were going through his mind as he spun the dial on the safe tucked away in the wall behind the flattering portrait of Michael Krey. He turned the dial slowly, the fingers of his left hand resting lightly upon the handle, waiting for the faint, telltale *click!* signifying the proper number on the dial had been reached.

He made a full revolution of the dial without finding the first number. He made another slow, complete turn, paying even closer attention to what he was doing, and still he couldn't feel the internal tumblers falling into place.

"Damn it," he whispered, taking a step away from the safe.

He let his hands rest at his sides and shook them gently, needing their sensitivity heightened if he was going to get the safe opened.

Just as he was about to try once again, something registered in his brain. He stopped and looked around, sure that instinct was warning him. But of what? He was alone in the office, and from all that he could tell, alone on the entire third floor of the casino. So what was wrong?

*There isn't anything wrong,* the inner voice whispered. But something was *different*.

The instant Mack's fingers again touched the rotating

dial on the safe, he realized the safe was not a Barns & Bradley. Instead, it was a Sears and Roebuck.

For nearly a minute, Mack stood quietly, staring at the safe, convincing himself that he had the skill to open it. This sudden twist of fate wasn't just the gods punishing him for hubris, the fact was, he wasn't much of a thief. There was only one brand of safe that he could open. There really *wasn't* much difference between his skill and Tori's after all.

Frustrated, he cursed, nearly muffling the footsteps in the hallway outside the office door.

He reached for the holstered revolver beneath his jacket and cape, at the same time blowing out the lamp he'd lit on Michael's desk. Mack hadn't quite knelt behind the desk when the door opened.

He raised the pistol, aiming it at the intruder's stomach. Down the hall there was wall lamp burning, but that was the only illumination, and it silhouetted the man who entered while keeping Mack hidden behind the desk. From the way the fellow moved—short, mincing steps, hands outstretched just a little, as if he was unable to see yet familiar with his surroundings—Mack could tell that the intruder's vision had not yet adjusted to the darkness.

"Close the door," Mack said, adopting without conscious thought the hard, flinty tone he'd always used when the Midnight Bandit.

The man froze in place, then slowly raised his hands to shoulder level. He gently kicked the door closed. His composure was impressive.

"No need for gunplay," Michael Krey said quietly. He had no intention of getting shot by a desperate, half-drunk cowboy who believed all he needed was a pocket full of gold coin to finally get his luck to change for the better.

Mack kept his revolver trained on Michael. Because Michael Krey was so composed, there was a real chance he was planning something, and whatever that something was, Mack wouldn't be happy about it.

"Turn around and walk backward to your desk," Mack said, already moving toward his right so that he stayed out of striking distance. "There're some matches near the lamp. Get it lit, then turn toward your safe."

"There's no lamp on my desk."

"There is now."

"How long have you been in here?"

All of Mack's warning signals were triggered. He couldn't hear a hint of fear in Michael Krey's voice. Annoyance at being inconvenienced was there and mild disdain at the break-in and being held at gunpoint . . . but not a hint of fear.

Mack waited until the lamp was lit and its pale yellow glow spread out across the room. Then, for maximum effect, he waited until Michael had blown out the match before he said, "If you think I won't kill you, you're dead wrong."

Michael's shoulders stiffened involuntarily.

"Turn around."

Michael turned slowly, his composure still intact, though frayed now at the edges. When he came face-to-face with the Midnight Bandit's frightening masked and caped form, he sucked his breath in sharply and held it. Mack raised his revolver just enough to draw Michael's eyes to it, then he slowly thumbed back the hammer. In the silent room, the sound was magnified countless times, and at last Michael Krey began to suspect that there were situations in his life from which neither his name nor his money could save him.

"The Midnight Bandit," he said finally, with an unsuccessful attempt at bravado.

"The one and only."

"But I thought . . ." Michael's sentence died away as irrefutable proof stared him in the face.

"That I had been arrested?" Mack made a bitter sound deep in his throat. "Did you really believe that girl was the same person who crept through your bedroom during the charity ball?" He made another angry, derisive sound, certain only that he wanted to get Tori out of jail as quickly as possible.

"I didn't know you'd gone through my bedroom," Michael said after a long pause.

"What you don't know could fill a library."

"Now listen here—"

Before he could say more, Mack had closed the distance that separated them, to touch the cold, hard muzzle of his revolver against Michael's temple.

"No, you listen," Mack said, his tone flinty, deadly. "Open the safe."

"But I'm not sure that—"

Mack added pressure to the revolver, so that it was forced against Michael's skull. "Be sure or be dead."

"Pull the trigger and there will be a dozen men in this room in thirty seconds."

Mack recognized the bluff and reminded, "You'll still be dead."

"What do you want?" Michael asked, now with a slightly tremulous quality to his voice.

"First off, open the safe."

Without argument, Michael went to the wall safe, spun the dial, and soon had it open. He reached inside with both hands and began removing stacks of money, piling them neatly upon his desk. The unwavering pistol, combined with the calm, deadly voice and the black mask and cape, all worked to make him more polite and agreeable than he'd ever been in his life.

When Michael had finished, eight wrapped bundles of paper money and one canvas sack of gold coin sat on the desk for Mack's inspection. There was also a very small notebook with several names in it, and a larger notebook, with many names, dates, and figures written inside.

Mack shoved both notebooks into the pocket of his jacket, noting Michael's quizzical look as the money was ignored.

"I don't like seeing innocent people hurt," Mack said quietly. "The girl in jail isn't the Midnight Bandit. I'd appreciate it if you'd see that she's set free by morning."

Michael cleared his throat, tried to speak and failed, moistened his lips and tried again. Nothing in his privileged past had prepared him for speaking while a small but deadly pistol was pointed squarely at his heart.

"I can't get her out," Michael said, raising his hands once more to shoulder level. "She murdered my brother. Shot him in the back."

"She didn't murder anyone!" Mack snapped. He began stuffing stacks of paper money into his pockets, again knowing the reward of injuring the Kreys financially, though there was less pleasure in it when not being able to share the moment with Tori. "I want her out of jail before noon tomorrow, or I'll hold you accountable."

Michael's tongue went around his mouth several times quickly. His emotional control was rapidly evaporating. "I can't get her out, I tell you!"

"She didn't kill anyone."

"I know she didn't, but that doesn't make any difference!"

Mack raised his weapon and aimed down the barrel, pointing it squarely at Michael's forehead, fully aware of how unnerving it was to stare down the muzzle of a gun.

"Who killed your brother?" Mack asked quietly, in a voice that sounded like death itself.

"I . . . don't know." Michael looked away, not knowing which was worse: looking down the muzzle of the Bandit's revolver or looking into the Bandit's impassive, emotionless masked countenance.

"Jeremy was my friend, and I intend to get my revenge," Mack said, not at all sure where he was going with the lie. "How else do you think I broke into your house during the celebration?"

"Jeremy let you in?"

"Like I told you, he was my friend. Now tell me who killed him. He never did like any of you, never trusted you, always knew you'd cut him out in the end if you ever had the chance. He and I split the take."

"It wasn't me," Michael whispered. His knees were shaking so hard now that he needed to sit but didn't dare. He couldn't imagine the Bandit wanting to be friends with Jeremy, but he wasn't going to ask questions of anyone holding a gun on him.

"Tell me who did it, Michael. If you won't I'll assume you're hiding the murderer, and as far as I'm concerned, that makes you just as guilty as the one who pulled the trigger and shot Jeremy in the back."

Michael's weakening courage snapped completely. The Bandit could kill him, and he wasn't about to die to protect his sister.

"Jena did it! She shot him, then made it look like Tori did it! That's the truth! I swear to God, that's the truth!"

The news hit Mack with such force that for a moment he took his finger away from the trigger so he wouldn't accidentally shoot Michael.

Jena a murderer? His first thought was that Michael was lying, protecting himself by pinning the blame on someone else. But on second thought, Jena murdering Jeremy—and in such a cold-blooded way—wasn't all that shocking. Jena had always considered the rules most people live by nothing more than an inconvenience.

"Turn around," Mack said then, disgusted with every member of the Krey family. He didn't even want to know why Jena killed Jeremy.

"I've given you everything you've asked for," Michael said, the high whine in his voice proof of how advanced his fear had become. "You have no reason to kill me."

"Turn," Mack whispered, moving closer. His contempt was reaching such a level that he couldn't bear listening to Michael say anything else.

The moment Krey's back was turned, Mack brought the butt of his revolver down on the back of his head, hitting him hard. Without making a sound, Michael crumpled, unconscious as his body struck the floor.

For a heartbeat, Mack looked down at him lying in a heap on an incalculably expensive Persian rug. It came to him that it would be so easy to permanently rid the world of another Krey. But doing that would put him in the same category as the Kreys. Mack just could not allow himself to become one of the very monsters that he hated, to be so Krey-like that he would single-handedly decide who would live and who would die.

It wasn't fair that he couldn't play by the same rules—or lack of rules—as the Kreys, but then, he had known all along that life wasn't fair.

He left the bag of gold coin on the desk. Crossing back on the rope would be difficult enough without all that additional weight.

Holstering his revolver, Mack opened the office door and came face-to-face with two blackjack dealers who were coming to get some money from their boss.

Mack's reflexes had always been superlative, and he had the advantage in knowing that anyone he saw was an enemy.

"What the—" was all the closest dealer could say before Mack hit him square in the chest with his shoulder, sending the man toppling backward onto his fellow dealer.

Mack took off then, moving like the wind down the darkened hallway. Every second was precious now, and he knew it. Though the dealers had been caught by surprise, their confusion wouldn't last long once they found their employer unconscious on the floor of his office.

He had nearly climbed the ladder when the pounding of boots against a wooden floor echoed off the walls. These sounds brought on a fresh burst of speed, and he ascended the remaining rungs with dispatch.

He hit the rooftop door with his shoulder, remembering how difficult it had been to move when he'd entered the casino. The door swung on rusty hinges, and when it could move no further, slammed against the supporting wall. Mack heard the heavy, old lock strike the rooftop and skid to a stop. For only a second or two, he searched the darkness for it. He couldn't find it in the darkness.

"The roof! He's going up to the damn roof!" one dealer shouted.

Mack rushed to the edge of the roof. The grappling hook was still in place, the rope still tautly stretched from the casino to the hotel. There was no time to make it easy on his broken ribs. He grabbed the rope and leaped over the edge, in agony once again when his arms took the full weight of his body, stretching the muscles in his abdomen.

With very little hesitation, Mack began swinging hand-over-hand toward the hotel.

He hadn't reached the halfway point when the dealers spotted him. Neither man was armed, so they reached over the roof and tried to shake the rope enough to make Mack lose his grip, but the line was much too tight from supporting Mack's weight for their efforts to have much of an effect.

"The hook!" Mack heard one of the men say. "Kick the hook loose!"

Mack felt the rope shake, and worse, he heard the grappling hook slide just a little way against the stone edge of the roof.

"Harder, damn it! Kick the hook harder!"

For Mack, it was as though the world had suddenly slowed down, while he continued to think in normal time. He heard the thud of a boot striking the grappling hook, kicking it toward the rim of the roof; he looked down at the street below, and in a split second calculated the odds of surviving such a fall as close to zero; he looked at the hotel, and figured he'd never reach it before the dealers kicked the grappling hook loose.

Damn.

It seemed absurd that he would die because of a couple of unarmed blackjack dealers. For an instant he thought of simply releasing his hold on the rope. He would end up just as dead as he would by having the grappling hook kicked free, and this way the decision would have been his. But that would be giving up. If Mack was to die, he preferred dying as he had lived, defying the odds and fighting to the bitter end.

He'd just come to this realization—that he would continue fighting, no matter what—when the blackjack dealers pooled their efforts and kicked simultaneously at the grappling hook.

Hanging onto the rope, Mack heard the hook scrape free, and immediately he felt the tension go from the rope. For an instant he remained suspended—weightless—in midair. Then he began to descend at an alarming speed. His hands tightened around the rope an instant before he reached the end of the slack. With one end of it still firmly fixed to the hotel rooftop, Mack began swinging toward the side of that building.

He looked at the side wall of the hotel and smiled, though racing toward it at a deadly pace.

Wasn't life magnificently absurd?

# Twenty-nine

It wasn't the brick side wall of the hotel that Mack hit. He crashed through a second-floor window, making a great deal of noise and ending up with more than just a few cuts, to land on a bed—much to the surprise and consternation of Mr. and Mrs. Ignatius Smyth, who weren't terribly excited about sharing the bed with each other, much less a stranger.

"Go back to sleep! This is all just a bad dream," Mack told them as he hastily climbed off the bed, trying not to step on either of the octogenarians.

Mrs. Smyth's reaction to the intrusion was to put a pillow over her head and babble incessantly, "Oh, God! Oh, God!"

Mr. Smyth's was to flay out blindly with his fists at the unseen intruder—unseen because the hotel room was very dark and because Mr. Smyth had no time to put his spectacles on before commencing the pugilistic defense of his marriage bed.

Mrs. Smyth might have been more proud of her eighty-four-year-old husband's courage had she not inexplicably pulled the pillow from her head and sat up, which put her face directly in the path of her husband's left fist. She never did entirely believe Ignatius's vow that he had not intended to give her a black eye.

Not quite believing his luck, Mack stood at the door and patted himself down quickly. Nothing seemed broken, and he had very few deep cuts and scrapes from breaking through the window. He stripped off his mask and cape, dropping them to the floor, then stepped out into the hallway just as Ignatius began apologizing for knocking his wife half out of bed with a roundhouse left.

The hallway was deserted. He hurried to the stairway and made his way to his third floor room. He could hear the commotion outside in the street and also in the hotel. Stripping off his clothes, Mack collected all the money he'd taken from Michael Krey's safe and stuffed it into his briefcase.

The sizable cut along his chin was bleeding considerably; several more cuts Mack considered inconsequential. From his traveling case, he took out his cup, shaving soap, and brush. He dipped the brush into a pitcher of water, quickly working up a thick lather, then dabbed the lather inconsistently on his face. Taking his straight razor in hand, barefoot and bare chested, he stepped out into the hallway.

"What's going on?" he asked as a bellhop, eyes wide with excitement, rushed down the hall.

"The Midnight Bandit robbed the Cattleman's Paradise, and he may be in the hotel right now!" the young man exclaimed. He saw the red staining the white lather on Mack's face. "Mister, it looks like you cut yourself pretty bad."

"I heard glass breaking. It startled me," Mack explained, pleased beyond words that his alibi was now rock-solid.

"No need to worry, mister. The Bandit don't hurt folks, he just robs them," the bellhop said, then continued on his way.

By morning, Ignatius Smyth was something of a hero to many people in Santa Fe. Of course, he was also considered a damned old fool and a liar by others, because when the Midnight Bandit's mask and cape were found in his hotel room, old Ignatius just couldn't resist confessing that he—a man of eighty-four, nearly blind and hard of hearing—was in fact the notorious Midnight Bandit.

When some journalists printed Ignatius's confession of guilt, Mrs. Smyth merely rolled her eyes, one swollen and black, heavenward.

While Deputy Dylan McKenzie was in favor of arresting Ignatius—there was the bounty to be considered, after all—Sheriff Max Stryker was the voice of reason. He administered two shots of whiskey to Ignatius, who promptly went to sleep on the sheriff's couch and did not awaken for four hours.

"Some bandit," the sheriff muttered disgustedly as old Ignatius snored noisily, a look of contentment upon his sleeping countenance.

Tori sat on the edge of the small cot in her jail cell, her hands folded neatly together in her lap, her eyes closed. She was daydreaming again. Lately, she'd been doing more and more of that in a conscious effort to keep depression at bay. And every time she retreated into her mind, into her memories and fantasies, she returned to the world she'd known when it seemed as though she and Mack were the only two people who existed.

A serene smile spread across her lips as she sat there, slowly and steadily blocking out all the sounds filtering in through the barred cell window. When she daydreamed of her times with Mack, sometimes she neither heard nor felt anything of the outside world.

But now she heard the rattle of keys, then a clanking as the outside door, the one separating the sheriff's office from the jail cells, was opened. For an instant, Tori squeezed her eyes more tightly shut, hoping she could block out Deputy McKenzie's comments. But, unhappily, she could not. If she had to think about the real world, she couldn't hold onto her imaginary one.

Tori inhaled deeply, then let her breath out on a single long sigh. Next, she knew, she would hear the deputy suggesting that if she showed him 'a good time' in her cell, he had the power to make her life more comfortable.

Tori had explained several times that exchanging her comfort for his groping hands was no deal.

She wondered if she should tell Mack about what McKenzie had been trying to do. But then, very quickly, she dismissed this idea. Mack had enough problems to deal with without having to worry about something as silly as her harassment by Deputy Dylan McKenzie.

Mack couldn't win the case. Tori was certain of it. The jury would have to decide between the word of a known troublemaker and that of a powerful family in the territory. To make matters worse, the presiding judge was Robert

Ringer, whom Tori herself had witnessed accepting a bribe from Jonathon Krey.

The future looked bleak, but at least Tori had her memories. . . .

"Got yerself a visitor," the deputy said, rattling the numerous keys on the big, round ring, which was just one of his many annoying habits.

Tori's eyes widened with gratitude, and she almost shouted out Mack's name. But she remained sitting and closed her eyes, very briefly this time. Mack hadn't been scheduled to see her. Apparently he had sensed that she needed him, so he'd come, drawn to her by forces neither of them thoroughly understood.

"Good afternoon." Tori kept her tone calm, though she was thanking God that Mack had come to her. "I wasn't expecting to see you until this evening."

"Some questions regarding your testimony yesterday need to be cleared up."

As Mack waited for the deputy to unlock the cell door, he narrowed his eyes at Tori to examine her carefully. Normally, when he arrived, she was excited to see him, but she controlled her excitement because he'd told her that Deputy McKenzie must never know the extent of their attachment, must never know that they'd been lovers. Now, sitting there with her hands folded in her lap, Tori appeared almost drugged, as though she didn't have a care in the world.

Mack stepped into the cell, waiting until the deputy relocked the door. He gave McKenzie an annoyed look. "I want privacy with my client." He hated to go through the same stupid games every time he saw Tori. "You don't need to stand outside the cell to protect me, so don't say that. And I won't let you listen in, so don't stick your ear just outside that door."

The deputy curled his lips derisively. "Ain't nobody in town can figure out why you're defending this gal. You ain't making no money for it, and everybody knows she murdered Jeremy as pretty as you please. Hell, there's plenty of women in town who look real close when you walk by. Why worry 'bout this one? When it comes time to vote for mayor and such, folks will remember this."

"It's for the jury to decide whether Tori is guilty or innocent, for the voters to decide whether they want me in public office." Mack pointed to the outside door. "Now I insist upon privacy with my client. Please leave."

Mack didn't turn to Tori until he was absolutely certain he was alone with her and they wouldn't be overheard.

"Hello, Mack," she said when he finally turned to her. Her voice was soft, distinctly sensual, a nighttime voice Mack had heard before, out of place here in a jail cell. A pleasant surprise to see you again."

"What's wrong, Tori?" Mack sat beside her on the small bed, slipping his arm around her shoulders. "Did the deputy say something to you again?"

"No, it's nothing like that." She smiled at him, touching his face gently with her gaze. Tori didn't know how many more times she would be able to look at him, so she wanted every feature, every line, every nuance of him, embedded in her memory.

Mack didn't like this drastic change in her. She wasn't angry. Every time he'd seen her at the jail before, he'd had to wait ten to fifteen minutes for her to calm down enough to discuss the case rationally. She'd needed that much time just to vent her anger over the way Deputy McKenzie was treating her.

"Tori, I'm worried, seeing you like this." Mack touched her cheek lightly with the backs of his fingers, feeling for a fever. This calm, passive, serene Tori was *not* the Tori Singer he'd fallen in love with.

"Now Mack, how many times have you told me I mustn't get too angry, that I accomplish nothing by letting men like Deputy McKenzie and Jonathon Krey rile me?"

Tori placed a hand lightly upon Mack's thigh. She loved the feel of the fine fabric of his trousers, and the solidity of the muscles beneath. For all the times she had touched Mack, she'd not lost even a little of the thrill of it.

"I didn't want you grinding your teeth in rage, but I don't want you so . . . accepting of your fate, either."

Tori leaned toward him to kiss him. At first he leaned away, still surprised and confused by this change in her. But she would not be denied, and leaned farther still until she kissed him, though he did not really kiss her back—at least not the way she wanted him to.

"Mack, darling, we don't have much time left together," Tori whispered. Her green eyes smoldered with sensuality. She moistened her lips, thirsty for the taste of his kisses. "Why waste it talking?"

He grinned then, looking away, shaking his head in amazement. "Tori, let's be serious here. We're in the Santa Fe jail, and you're on trial for murder. As irrational as it seems, there really is something more important to do right now than make love."

"Not as far as I'm concerned," Tori whispered, sliding over on the cot so that her thigh was pressed to Mack's.

"Be serious now," he repeated more sternly. "If we're going to win this case, we'll need to concentrate."

The logic would have been fine, except that Tori didn't believe the case could be won, not even with Mack's brilliant legal mind working full-time on her behalf. She had no future, but she did have the here and now, with Mack at her side, and if she closed her eyes, she might be able to forget that she was in a locked jail cell. She might be able to forget everything except how wonderful it was to taste his kisses upon her lips, to feel the passion he had for her.

"Mack, darling, I'm serious," Tori continued, tilting her head to the side to nuzzle his neck. She felt him try to move away, but she would not be dissuaded from her goal, neither would she allow him to push her away. "It isn't like you to resist."

Though just a little annoyed, Mack was grinning. "I know it's not like me, and I promise you, just as soon as we win this trial, I'll be more than happy to give you my undivided romantic attention for as long as you care to have it. But while the case is under way, I think—"

"You think all the time," Tori complained, slipping her fingers into his thick, coal-black hair, turning his face to kiss his mouth. "You taught me to not think so much, and now I'm going to teach you the very same lesson."

Mack groaned theatrically. He didn't have any idea of what had gotten into Tori, but he was certain that, though he was willing to walk through fire for her if that was what she asked of him, this wasn't the time to give their amorous inclinations free rein. He had—he was only now truly becoming aware of it—a long future to share with

Tori. The rest of his life, in fact. That future, not his immediate desires, most concerned him now.

"Mack, kiss me, will you?" Tori continued in that faintly disturbed tone she had adopted. "You've been so preoccupied from the moment you stepped foot in my cell."

"Of course I've been preoccupied," he said, pushing her away and getting to his feet. He needed to think clearly, though he still didn't have a clue as to why she was behaving so irrationally, as if she were without a care in the world. "How can I be anything *but* preoccupied when the woman I love is sitting in jail, being tried for a murder she didn't commit?"

Tori had been about to rise from her small cot, but upon hearing Mack's words, she couldn't move, other than to turn her face away. For a second or two, she was afraid tears would begin to flow. Mack had said "the woman I love . . ."

Had she ever heard such beautiful words?

Now it was too late for her to have many more tomorrows with Mack, Tori realized. She had fallen in love with a man who loved her back. At least she now knew Mack loved her.

Composure returned to Tori quickly, and when it did, she was more determined than ever to forget all about the trial, the depressing surroundings she was in, and to take pleasure in Mack.

"Have you any idea how much I've wanted to hear you say those words?" she asked quietly, looking up at him. "I love you, you know? More than you can imagine. More than I ever thought I could love anyone. And I've loved you for a long, long time, Mack Randolph."

Only then, with Tori repeating the words he'd spoken, did Mack fully realize what he'd said. The reality of it was as shocking for him as it had been for her. How many times had he gotten himself in trouble because he'd *refused* to give a vow of love to the woman he was seeing? How many times had he been consciously aware that he could avoid a fight if all he would do was say I love you to the woman in bed with him?

Too many times, to be sure. But Mack hadn't ever spoken the word "love" because he'd known all along that what he felt was many things, but love wasn't among them. Not, that is, until he'd found himself with a tomboy named Tori Singer, and come to the conclusion that he was willing to risk everything—money, reputation, happiness, freedom, even his life—to protect her and keep her with him, because a life spent *without* her would surely be a hollow, empty experience.

"Tell me again that you love me," she said. The impish green twinkle had returned to her eyes, and she nibbled teasingly on her lower lip.

"Now you're teasing me," Mack said with a grin, backing up until he felt the iron bars of the cell door against his shoulders. He knew the twinkle in Tori's eyes, knew what it meant. But for the life of him he couldn't figure out why she was in *that* kind of mood while in *this* kind of place.

"In a way, I suppose you could say that," she replied, and as she spoke she began unbuttoning her light blue denim shirt. "But Lord knows, you've teased with me in your time."

"Yes, Tori, but this isn't the time for—"

When she pulled her shirt off, the words caught in

Mack's throat. He watched, temporarily transfixed, as her fingers toyed tauntingly with the bows holding her chemise closed.

"Time for what, Mack?" Tori asked, her tone as innocent as a child's, her fingers tugging loose the top bow of her chemise to display a little more cleavage.

"For *that*," he replied, feeling ridiculous. A myriad of memories—what Tori had been like when he'd first met her, first kissed her—flashed across the surface of his mind, vividly impressing on him how much she had changed.

"That's where you're wrong," she said in a whisper, getting slowly to her feet. She pulled loose the second bow on her chemise, then the final one. With a slight shrug of her shoulders, she sent the chemise drifting down her arms to drop unceremoniously on the stone floor of the jail cell. "This is the perfect time."

"Tori—"

"Mack, you've just said you love me. Now if that is the truth, then I want you to prove it, right here, right now." Tori crossed her arms just beneath her breasts, fully aware of how her nakedness drew Mack's gaze and inhibited his thinking.

"Can't this wait until after the trial?" he asked, his voice a breathy whisper that lacked all conviction.

She shook her head, walking forward slowly, then took his hands in her own and began leading him to the small cot.

She did not trust in tomorrow. She didn't even believe she'd be happy an hour from this moment. Tori knew only that she loved Mack, that he loved her, and that at least for a little while, even though they were locked in her cell, they had each other.

About everything beyond that, she had grave doubts, but she had Mack, she had this moment . . . and she was going to make the most of both.

"Don't worry about a thing," Mack said as he finished adjusting his tie, casting a nervous glance in the direction of the cell door, wondering when Deputy McKenzie would show up to escort him out. "This trial will turn out just the way we want it to."

He was lying, trying to bolster Tori's confidence.

"No matter what happens, don't blame yourself," she said. She didn't believe for a second that the trial could be won, and she didn't want Mack holding himself responsible for something that, from the very beginning, was beyond his power to change.

"Don't talk like that," he said. He was just now hearing the undercurrent of defeat in Tori's tone, which he suspected explained her odd behavior earlier. She was accepting defeat . . . and that frightened him.

"It won't be your fault if we lose. We never really had a chance to begin with." Tori leaned back on the bed, propping herself up with an elbow. The lovemaking she'd just shared with Mack would have to last her the rest of her life, but that wasn't something she wanted to think on very long right now. "You never really had a chance to get me free, Mack. You're a good man—honest and decent. You've gone against a very bad man with a very bad family. The Kreys don't play by the same rules you do, and that's why there's nothing you can do to win this trial for me." She looked out beyond the bars at the window of her cell. "Don't blame yourself. I don't blame you. I love you."

# Thirty

It was the third day of the trial, and even though Mack had tried hard to keep his spirits up, he had not done so. Every time he looked into the eyes of the jury, the disbelief he saw reflected in their eyes, the suspicion and doubt he saw on their expressions, told him they believed Tori was guilty of the cold-blooded murder of Jeremy Krey.

The most damaging testimony came from Jena. She broke down in tears as she was testifying. When she broke down a second time, it required both her father and brother to be at her side to shore her up as she told her heart-wrenching account of seeing Tori riding away from "the scene of that awful, bloody crime!"

Mack waited for Jena to break, waited for her to at last look at the jury and tell them that she was lying. He knew she wouldn't, of course, but just the same, he kept hoping she would do something that would tip the jury to her duplicity.

But Jena never broke from her story, never revealed that she was lying, not in her face, in her eyes, in the way she held her shoulders as she sat in the witness chair. She was, Mack now realized, the consummate liar, and as such, she was perhaps more dangerous to society than her father.

Tori touched Mack's sleeve, and he turned toward her.

"I never did those things," she whispered, trying to neutralize the vehemence of Jena's lies.

"I know you didn't," Mack whispered, stifling the "darling" that very nearly had come from his lips. He dared not whisper such endearments to her now, in the courtroom, even though he desperately wanted to make her feel more confident, wanted her to know beyond a doubt that he believed in her.

What was he to do? The jury believed that Tori had killed Jeremy Krey. Mack knew that she hadn't committed the crime. If he put Michael Krey on the witness stand, Krey would only lie, as would Jonathon.

It was cruel, he now realized, how the law worked. Justice wasn't being played out in the courtroom; instead, power, deceit, and corruption thrived. The Kreys held all the keys to victory, using them at whim, destroying anyone who dared get in their way.

As Jena's gut-wrenching lies continued, Mack lowered his eyes and looked at a spot on the floor, letting his mind focus, going deeper and deeper into itself, to a place where nothing existed but pure thought. Somehow, some way, he must free Tori. Mack believed in the legal system, even when it was being perverted and abused by an ambitious prosecuting attorney—and by greedy scoundrels like Jonathon, Michael, and Jena Krey.

But how could an honest man fight such dishonesty, such corruption?

When Mack turned toward Tori, his eyes once again became sharp and focused. Nebulous ideas were forming. . . .

"Don't worry about a thing," he reassured her with a smile, as he patted the back of her hand.

Judge Robert Ringer looked at Mack and asked, "Have you any questions for this poor young woman?"

Mack looked at the judge and remembered seeing him accept a bribe from Jonathon Krey on that fateful night when the Midnight Bandit had first run across Tori inside the Krey mansion.

The judge was projecting sincerity and sympathy. Mack thought, *This guy's a master at deceiving people, too. If I didn't know better, I'd even think he was really sorry for all that Jena's supposed to have gone through.*

"No, Your Honor, I have no questions for her."

Mack rose from his chair, feeling as though Tori's freedom and his own personal happiness were slipping through his fingers. He looked into the jury box, and his gaze met Andy Fields's. Fury welled up in Mack's breast as he thought back to that night when, as the Midnight Bandit, he had crouched in the dark with Tori and watched Jonathon Krey give Fields a bribe. It seemed so unjust that Tori's guilt or innocence should be in the hands of venal men like Judge Ringer and Andy Fields.

The judge rapped his gavel hard, putting the court into adjournment until the following morning.

Mack leaned close to Tori and, giving way to an endearment, whispered to her, "Don't worry, darling, I think I know how we can put an end to this travesty."

It was late at night when Andy Fields kicked his feet up onto the foot stool, then leaned back on the sofa in his den. All was good in the world, as far as he was concerned. Tomorrow was the last day of the trial, and when it was over, there would be few serious obstacles standing in his way to becoming the next mayor of Santa Fe.

He took a sip of whiskey, washed it down with a heavy swallow of beer from a brewery in St. Louis, then issued a long, slow, satisfied sigh. Everything tasted better to Andy now that Mack Randolph seemed so willing to discredit himself in the eyes of the voters of Santa Fe by fighting for Tori Singer. Even Mrs. Fields's cooking seemed to have improved dramatically since the murder trial had begun, and the prostitutes at Lulu's appeared more energetic and more pleased to see him.

Andy closed his eyes, letting his mind wander aimlessly as the alcohol began to take effect. Yes, everything *was* perfect in his life. His wife, seeing his smooth road to being elected mayor of Santa Fe, had stopped nagging him about his drinking and wenching, and now concerned herself only with his appearance, always making sure that his shirts were free from wrinkles and immaculately clean. Nobody would ever accuse *her* of being a bad wife to the mayor of Santa Fe!

It was mildly disconcerting that his children still didn't like him—and they made no effort to hide their feelings, either. That was a disappointment to Andy Fields, since he would have preferred to parade them around come election time, but the fact of the matter was his contempt for his children was commensurate to their contempt for him, so, card player that he was, he figured he was even on that score and didn't give the matter more thought.

With his head resting on the plushly upholstered back of the sofa and his eyes closed, Andy was suddenly aware that a slightly cool breeze passed through the room. He smiled. It was a stiflingly hot evening, and the breeze felt good upon his skin.

Good, that is, until he sensed that he was no longer alone in his den, and that whoever had entered the room had not come through the door. . . .

"Don't move."

The two words were spoken calmly, in a conversational tone. Every muscle in Andy Fields's corpulent body tightened, and though he tried to remain calm, he couldn't even breathe. He opened his eyes, but did not turn his head, afraid that such movement might somehow anger the intruder. Out of the corner of his eye, stepping out of the shadows, he saw Mack Randolph approach from the veranda. At that moment, his heart almost stopped because in Mack's hand was a long-barreled Remington revolver, and absolutely everyone knew Randolph simply didn't carry guns.

Unless, of course, special circumstances forced him into a situation where he needed to use them—for instance, if he needed to kill a juror . . .

"Dear God, please don't hurt me," Fields whispered.

Mack approached slowly, the muzzle of his revolver never losing its deadly aim at Fields's nose.

"God? Hardly. Just me. I've come to offer you the deal of a lifetime."

Fields liked what he heard. He asked, "And what is that?"

"More money than you can imagine."

"And if I refuse?"

Mack leaned closer, looking Fields straight in the eyes, and said, "If you refuse, I'll kill you here and now and be done with it. This isn't a time when you can take the time to negotiate for the best deal."

For several seconds Fields simply looked at Mack, contemplating the veracity of his last statement. Then, slowly, he realized that while Mack Randolph might bluff in a courtroom, he'd never bluff in a situation like this.

"Don't even *think* about trying to trick me," Mack said, his voice barely above a whisper, yet still carrying an authority that other men could never achieve. He knew Fields's wife and children were asleep upstairs. "Just listen to what I have to tell you."

"Yes," Fields said. He swallowed drily, his Adam's apple bobbing up and down. "Yes, *sir*," he added, just in case a certain formality might prove favorable. He tried to take his eyes off the unwavering revolver, but couldn't. Unmindful of his words, he mumbled, "Sir, yes, sir . . . sir . . . sir . . ."

"Shut up, Fields."

"Yes, sir."

Mack looked at the man, astonished that Andy Fields was, in theory, what constituted his strongest political rival. Could the political arena really be so desperate for candidates that it would even accept men such as this?

It was a question Mack didn't want to ponder long, and he was almost thankful that he had more pressing matters to contend with.

"C-Can I off-offer you a drink?" Fields said, trying to be polite, to sound casual. He was not a man who was stable under pressure, and it showed.

"I'm particular about those I drink with," Mack said, disdainful of even the most casual suggestion that he and Andy Fields could ever be friends. "Now listen up, because the things I'm going to tell you, I'm only going to tell you once."

"Yes, sir," Fields whispered. "Whatever you say."

Mack looked around the room, a deadly hatred pooling within his breast. Andy Fields was just the type of man who would put Tori in prison, or even send her to the hangman, without ever giving his decision a second thought. Because of that, Mack wanted desperately to make him pay in such a way that he would remember this evening for the rest of his life.

"That's right. Whatever I say." Mack realized that he had little capacity for cruelty, as he had little capacity for revenge, but he was determined to do something—*anything!*—to make Andy Fields pay for the havoc his corruption had heaped upon the good people of Santa Fe. "Are you listening to me?"

"Yes! I told you I was!"

Mack smiled. He meant the expression to be intimidating, and it was.

"Tori Singer didn't kill Jeremy Krey," Mack said, leaning against a bookshelf. "In fact, she is about as far from the person responsible for the murder as she can be."

Time had allowed Andy to regain at least a little of his composure. He adopted what he hoped was a nonchalant posture, though his eyes still held sparks of primal fear.

"How can you be so sure? And why should I believe anything you've got to say, anyway? You're defending that Singer gal in court! I'm the head juror! For God's sake, man, I shouldn't even be talking to you!"

For several seconds, Mack simply looked at Andy Fields, hating the man, but at the same time not liking the path he himself had taken. He realized that he was about to cross over a line, to commit acts infinitely more corrupt—more *wrong*—than anything he'd done as the Midnight Bandit.

The men looked at each other, Fields fearful for his life, Mack fearful for his soul. Could he, a respected attorney with political aspirations, really follow through with the plan even he concluded had been poorly thought through?

"I need another drink," Fields said, beginning to rise from the sofa.

"Sit!" Mack snapped, and Fields dropped back onto the sofa as though he'd been shot. "Tori didn't kill Jeremy Krey. Jena Krey did."

Mack watched as Fields's expression evolved, first reflecting shock, then doubt, then a modicum of understanding. Anyone who knew Jena would not be overly surprised to discover that she was a murderess.

"I'm telling you this for a reason," Mack continued, after giving Andy Fields enough time to fully digest the information. "There aren't many people who know that Jena killed her brother. I know. You know. Jena knows, of course, and so do her father and brother."

"Why are you telling me this? If you know it, why haven't you brought it up in court?" Andy Fields was not an overly bright man, and the twists that had so recently taken place had thoroughly confused him. When he had accepted the five hundred dollars from Jonathon Krey to ensure a guilty verdict in Tori's trial, Fields had accepted the money without concern. The facts, at that time, all pointed to Tori.

"I'm the Midnight Bandit," Mack said quietly, just a hint of a smile now curling his mouth.

Andy Fields recoiled in his chair, wanting desperately to run from the room, knowing in his heart he didn't have a prayer of escape. How had everything gone so wrong, when all had just minutes ago seemed so right?

"I was on the balcony the night of the celebration of the hospital's opening, and I watched you take Jonathon Krey's bribe," Mack continued. "I know Judge Ringer is also taking money under the table from Krey. I know that Jena killed Jeremy because Michael told me."

"But . . . but—"

"Silence!" Mack watched as Fields began to shiver. It was a pathetic sight. "I'll be letting the Kreys know that you're aware of Jena's guilt. Of course, by doing this, I'll be putting you in jeopardy. If I were to hazard a guess, I'd say Jonathon Krey will probably hire a gunman to kill you. You and I both know how protective he is of his only daughter."

Andy Fields at last was able to tear his eyes away from Mack's revolver. He stared at the carpeted floor in front of him, his mind working feverishly. There had to be some way for him to get out of this mess! Perhaps Mack was lying about everything! Perhaps it was all just a bluff!

"I'll tell him I don't know anything!" Fields said suddenly, as though this was a great revelation.

Under other circumstances, Mack might have found the statement humorous. As it was, he said, "How can you convince Krey that you don't know his daughter is a murderer? By bringing the subject up, won't you be proving that you do know it? And we both know what Jonathon Krey is like. Just to be on the safe side, he'll have you killed. Face it, Fields, you're expendable, any way you look at it." Mack moved closer, so that he was standing over the seated man in a most intimidating manner. "How does it feel to be a dead man?"

"I'm not dead yet!" Fields said, suddenly looking around the room as though to determine what he would take with him when he rode away from Santa Fe without a backward glance.

"Going to leave town?" Mack asked, curious as to whether Fields would leave his wife and children so abruptly.

"Tomorrow," Fields answered, nodding his head vigorously. "Right after the bank opens."

Mack smiled bitterly. It took a cold man to abandon his wife and children, a thoroughly heartless one to leave them penniless. "You don't want to do that just yet," he said quietly.

When Fields started to fidget in his chair, Mack raised his revolver just a little more. Fields froze. "Listen carefully, because I'm only going to tell you once. You'll be leaving town, all right, but not tonight, and not tomorrow morning."

"That's what you think!" Fields hissed. He was infinitely more frightened of Jonathon Krey, whom he knew to be a murderer, than of Mack Randolph.

Mack stepped closer and very lightly touched the muzzle of his revolver to the tip of Fields's nose. Andy Fields's eyes crossed as he stared at the barrel. His Adam's apple bobbed up and down as he tried to remain calm, proving he couldn't.

"You're going to convince me that you'll do everything I'm about to tell you. You see, when I'm finished talking, I'm going to look into your eyes, and if I believe that you'll do what I tell you, I'm going to let you live. However . . . if I have my suspicions about whether you're able to follow my instructions, then I'm simply going to kill you right here and now, and be done with it."

"Yes, sir, yes . . . sir, sir, sir," Fields stammered.

"It's nearly three o'clock, damn it all! Can't we come to a conclusion? We've been sitting in this room for three hours, and there's not a breath of air in here."

Robert Simms was the juror who was doing the complaining, though he wasn't the only one to protest their frustrating inability to arrive at a verdict on the murder charge against Tori Singer.

All eyes in the room turned toward Andy Fields. He was staring at his own hands, which were folded before him on the table. A dribble of sweat ran down the back of his neck, to be soaked up by his collar. He'd very nearly sweated through his clothes, though it wasn't hot enough to warrant that.

"You're the only vote of dissent," Simms said, biting the words off, glaring at Fields. "Damn it all, you know she killed Jeremy Krey! All the facts point to her!"

Fields looked up, didn't like the accusing eyes staring back at him, then looked down again. Never in his life had he felt so trapped, so thoroughly caught by forces stronger than himself.

"Everybody in this room knew Jeremy Krey," Fields said, searching in vain for some way of justifying his argument that Tori was innocent. "Hell, at one time or another, we've all thought of putting a bullet in his back."

That comment drew a chuckle from several of the jurors. Jeremy had had friends only as long as he was buying the drinks or the women at Lulu's for his friends' enjoyment. The minute that stopped, nobody wanted to be in the same room with him.

"Maybe so," Simms said, not at all amused. As far as he was concerned, there was no doubt that Tori had pulled the trigger and put a bullet in Jeremy's back. The only thing he couldn't understand was why Andy Fields, the head juror, seemed so determined to resist accepting the truth like everyone else on the jury. "But none of us in this room killed him—Tori Singer did. Now why can't you see that?" Simms leaned across the table, glaring furiously at Fields. Simms had much better things to do with his day than argue with Andy Fields. "Unless, just maybe, you've got a *reason* for not seeing the facts the way the rest of us do?"

Andy Fields wanted to die when he heard those words. He had taken money from Jonathon Krey to guarantee a guilty verdict, and he'd taken money from Mack Randolph to guarantee a not-guilty verdict. Fields had sold his soul, and now, he suspected, someone was going to pull his heart right out of his chest.

He had always known that he wasn't a truly popular man, but he had become a successful businessman in Santa Fe, and he threw lavish parties that were attended widely and praised by all. Now he was being accused, perhaps in a roundabout fashion, of having a vested interest in seeing to it that Tori Singer was found not guilty. Most frightening for Andy Fields was that this accusation, put forward by Simms out of sheer frustration, was dead on the mark, and a serious investigation would probably reveal as much. If these men turned on him, they'd go for the jugular like a pack of hungry wolves, and Fields knew it.

"Well, say something!" Simms demanded.

Fields closed his eyes and tried to block out every voice so that he could hear his own thoughts. The previous night he'd been frightened right down to his boots when Mack Randolph had suddenly appeared out of the shadows, holding a revolver, threatening to kill him while his family slept upstairs. Mack's bargain—if that was what it could be called—was really quite simple. Andy Fields was to make sure that Tori Singer was to be found not guilty of the murder of Jeremy Krey. As soon as the trial was over, he was to take the money Mack had given him—money that had been stolen from Michael Krey, Fields had been informed—and ride out of town immediately, never to return.

It had seemed a pretty good deal last night. Easy enough to accomplish, and Fields would be many thousands of dollars richer when it was over.

Except every man in the jury believed that Tori was guilty, and no amount of arguing on her behalf could convince even one of them to agree with him.

So here he sat, trying to maintain his courage, having been told by Mack Randolph that he'd be killed if Tori was found guilty, for Jonathon Krey would soon be informed he knew Jena was the real killer, which ensured that a gunman would soon be looking for the would-be politician, who was accused—and accurately so—of accepting some kind of bribe on Tori's behalf.

"Well, Fields, what the hell have you got to say for yourself?" Simms demanded.

Andy Fields tilted his head up, looked Simms straight in the eyes, and said, "I say we vote again."

The men all sat down at the long table, and fresh white slips of paper were handed out. Each man, pencil in hand, scribbled upon one, folded it in half, then placed it in the hat handed around the table. The hat ended up with Andy Fields, the head juror.

Fields looked around the table one last time. These men would destroy him if he continued to oppose them on the verdict, and he knew it.

He reached into the hat and began pulling the slips out one at a time, unfolding each and reading off the vote, which he tallied on a piece of paper.

"Guilty . . . guilty . . . guilty," Fields read, saying the words slowly, as though he actually had to read them to know what the count would be.

This time the count was different. This time it was unanimous: Tori Singer was guilty of the murder of Jeremy Krey.

"At last!" Simms exclaimed, pushing back his chair, almost leaping to his feet. It had taken six votes to reach a unanimous decision. "Now I can get back to my office. I've wasted too much of my day here as it is! Hang the wench! That's what I say!"


The jurors entered the courtroom, and Mack unconsciously held his breath. How did they look? He studied the faces of the men. Were they pleased with the decision they'd come to?

Beneath the table, Mack reached over, placed his hand upon Tori's, and gave it a confident squeeze; then he smiled at her.

"Everything is going to be just fine," he said.

She closed her eyes.

Judge Ringer turned a grave face toward the jury. Mack looked at the judge, remembering how confident he'd appeared when he had accepted Jonathon Krey's bribe. It seemed so unjust that such a man should have power over so many honest people.

"Has the jury reached its verdict?" the judge asked.

Andy Fields rose to his feet. Mack noticed that his hair was sticking to his forehead, plastered there by perspiration. It was hot, but not that hot. And then Fields glanced from the judge over to Mack, and Mack's fear level soared. Fields looked absolutely lost.

"The jury has reached its decision," Fields said, his voice not loud enough to carry to the farthest reaches of the courtroom:

"Please speak up," Judge Ringer said.

"You bet, Judge," Fields replied.

There was a moment of laughter from the spectators in the audience at Andy Fields's disrespectful reply. The spectators were silenced instantly when the judge glared at them. He had the power to intimidate an entire room full of people with just a look.

"Ah, sorry, Your Honor," Fields replied. He pulled at the collar of his shirt to loosen it, then cleared his throat three times in succession. "The jury . . ." he began, then stopped. His gaze darted from Judge Ringer to Mack Randolph, then over to Jonathon Krey.

Mack's stomach tightened into a knot. He couldn't breathe.

"Well?" Judge Ringer prodded, leaning toward the jury box, clearly annoyed that Fields was taking so long.

"The jury finds the defendant . . . not guilty."

Robert Simms, sitting in the back row of the jury box, bolted to his feet, exclaiming, "What the hell?"

Jena Krey also rose swiftly at the verdict, shouting,

"She's guilty! Hang that bitch or I'll kill you all, you stupid bastards!"

Her father and brother moved to restrain her, but the jury was clearly stunned by her outburst. Jena's face turned crimson as she struggled to extricate herself from Jonathon and Michael. She was trying to get to Tori, and from the look in her eyes, one would conclude she intended to kill Tori Singer herself.

Mack guessed what had happened during the jury deliberations. Deception could be the only explanation for Robert Simms's exclamation. Mack knew that if Simms had a chance to explain, everything was lost.

All his life, Mack Randolph had loathed chaos, confusion, disorder. Now, he had to create what he hated to protect the woman he loved.

He exploded to his feet, intentionally striking the table he'd been using with his thigh, causing it to topple over and send all his notes and papers across the floor.

"This jury owes my client an apology!" Mack declared at high volume, rushing toward the judge's bench. He wanted Ringer paying attention to him, not to Robert Simms. "This trial has been a mockery of justice! A travesty! I want an apology for my client!"

Judge Ringer pounded with his gavel. "Order! This court will come to order immediately, or I'll find each and every one of you in contempt!"

Jena was trapped between her father and brother. Though she couldn't free herself from them, they couldn't silence her vindictive tongue, either.

"Judge, kill that tramp!" Jena shouted. "My father paid good money to you; goddamn it, earn some of it!"

Mack heard those words and thought, *Thank God she's a lunatic!*

Ringer reacted to Jena's words by pounding his gavel with all his might. He couldn't afford to have Jena saying such things. He shouted, "Bailiff, arrest that woman for slander! I want silence in this court this very instant! Court adjourned! The verdict is not guilty!"

Jena was still screaming. "Arrest me? You insignificant fool!" She turned to Jonathon and shouted, though his face was close to her own, and he was trying his level best to place his hand over her mouth. "Papa, kill that man! Have him killed right now!"

Amidst the confusion, Mack watched Andy Fields slip out the side door of the courtroom. Then he rushed to where Tori was seated, looking upon the chaos in stunned silence. He took her hand and literally jerked her to her feet.

"Time to go," he said above the rising din in the courtroom.

# Epilogue

*Two Years Later . . .*

Tori sat in her rocking chair, sipping tea sweetened with honey. She looked at her husband, wishing there was something she could say that would ease his mind, something she could do to turn the clock backward so that the past could not haunt Mack Randolph.

The burden of guilt, she knew, rested squarely upon her own shoulders, though Mack was the one who had to carry its weight. For a second, she closed her eyes, loving her husband more than life itself, wishing there was some way she could erase what had gone before so that his reputation would be as spotless as it had been when she'd fallen in love with this enigmatic man.

"Why don't you have a brandy, dear," she suggested softly. "It'll help soothe your nerves."

"I'm not nervous!" Mack replied, much too quickly, stopping his pacing of the library for the first time in the past three hours. "Besides, I need to keep my wits about me."

"Of course, darling," Tori replied softly.

It had been a difficult mayoral campaign. Mack's opponent had never let the voters forget that he had married a woman who had been tried for murder. Added to this were the varying accounts of what had truly transpired at the trial. The head juror, Andy Fields, had disappeared immediately after Tori had been found not guilty. Six months later Fields had broken his neck falling down a flight of stairs in a bordello in San Francisco. When the authorities had checked Fields's hotel room, they'd found almost three thousand dollars in currency and gold coin. There was no *official* explanation as to how a man like Andy Fields was in possession of that kind of money, though rumors suggested a link to Mack Randolph and his vast fortune.

When Mack's opponent had suggested that Tori be brought to trial again—after all, the conclusion of her first trial was not exactly by the book—Mack had pointed out that she *couldn't* be brought to trial again—that would be double jeopardy.

Tori thought about all the things that had happened to the Kreys since the trial, and even though she tried to hate the family, she could not wish what tragedies had befallen them upon anyone. Michael Krey was the first to fall victim. The once-proud and even arrogant young businessman who strutted through the streets and boudoirs of Santa Fe as though he owned the entire city and the people in it instead of just its largest casino was now pushed daily along the boardwalks in a wheelchair. A thief, the newspapers had reported, had broken into the Cattleman's Paradise to steal money from Michael's personal safe. A scuffle ensued, and then a shot rang out, striking a glancing blow to Michael's temple. At first the wound did not seem too serious. But though his eyes opened and closed, he had lost the use of his limbs. He could not speak or communicate in any way, though there were those people who said there was fear in his eyes whenever Jena was nearby.

Jena was the only person who'd heard the late-night gunshot ring out, and she was the one who had found Michael and supplied the "facts" of the break-in and shooting that had been given to the newspapers. She was, the newspapers had reported, "heart-sick" over the incident involving her brother, though after the tantrum she'd thrown in court, there were many people who doubted she could be heart-sick over anything.

Jonathon Krey, with his beloved son now in a vegetative state, slipped deeper and deeper into an all-pervasive depression. He was rarely seen in public now, and rumor had it that he now refused to see his daughter alone. He had a standing order among the servants that whenever she asked to see him, at least one servant was to be in the room with them at all times.

But that was another family, one that Tori no longer had much to worry about, though it did seem as though justice had been cheated because Jena was still dashing about the streets of Santa Fe, her heart as untroubled as it ever had been, still in search of excitement and adventure. Political scandals, murder, maiming . . . none of it had actually touched Jena deeply, and Tori suspected that nothing could.

Though Mack had tried to make sure that his life was free of scandals, during his first political campaign, many voters were questioning just exactly how honest a man he was.

Even Tori had asked him how he'd managed to get her set free, and he looked her straight in the eyes and said,

"I'll tell you this once, and then we'll never speak of it again. Once you told me we couldn't win the case because Jonathon Krey doesn't play by the rules, but I do. And the more I thought about that, the more I realized you were absolutely right. So for once in my life, I *didn't* play by the rules. I used Jonathon Krey's methods and Michael Krey's money to defeat Jena Krey's wishes."

Tori wanted to ask more, but she'd promised Mack she'd never again bring the subject up, and she had kept that promise.

Almost one year to the day after the trial, after a six-month engagement, Tori and Mack were married. Their life together had been blissful . . . until Mack had decided to run for mayor of Santa Fe. That was when the past, and all the rumors, came back to haunt them.

The clock chimed softly. Ten times. The voting booths had been closed for three hours. That meant the counters should have the total very soon.

Tori watched Mack pacing the length of the library, and she thought, *If I've destroyed his political career, I'll never forgive myself.*

The knock on the door was crisp. Paul Randolph entered the library without being invited. " I've got bad news for you, little brother."

Tori's heart sank, and she squeezed her eyes shut.

"What's that?" Mack asked in a grave voice.

"I'm going to have to fire you as attorney for the Randolph Ranch."

"Why? I've always done my job."

"Maybe so, but from now on you'll be too busy with your duties as mayor of Santa Fe."

Tori rushed across the library and threw herself into Mack's arms, and he twirled her around and around.

"You and me together," he whispered into her ear, "we're unbeatable."

Tori kissed him, knowing in her heart of hearts that he was right.

## YOU WON'T WANT TO READ
## JUST ONE—KATHERINE STONE

**ROOMMATES**                                    (3355-9, $4.95)
No one could have prepared Carrie for the monumental
changes she would face when she met her new circle of
friends at Stanford University. Once their lives intertwined
and became woven into the tapestry of the times, they would
never be the same.

**TWINS**                                        (3492-X, $4.95)
Brook and Melanie Chandler were so different, it was hard
to believe they were sisters. One was a dark, serious, ambitious New York attorney; the other, a golden, glamourous,
sophisticated supermodel. But they were more than sisters—they were twins and more alike than even they knew
. . .

**THE CARLTON CLUB**                             (3614-0, $4.95)
It was the place to see and be seen, the only place to be. And
for those who frequented the playground of the very rich, it
was a way of life. Mark, Kathleen, Leslie and Janet—they
worked together, played together, and loved together, all behind exclusive gates of the *Carlton Club.*

---

*Available wherever paperbacks are sold, or order direct from the
Publisher. Send cover price plus 50¢ per copy for mailing and handling to Penguin USA, P.O. Box 999, c/o Dept. 17109, Bergenfield, NJ 07621. Residents of New York and Tennessee must
include sales tax. DO NOT SEND CASH.*

## PASSIONATE NIGHTS FROM

## *PENELOPE NERI*

**DESERT CAPTIVE**                         (2447, $3.95/$4.95)
Kidnapped from her French Foreign Legion escort, indignant Alexandria had every reason to despise her nomad prince captor. But as they traveled to his isolated mountain kingdom, she found her hate melting into desire . . .

**FOREVER AND BEYOND**                    (3115, $4.95/$5.95)
Haunted by dreams of an Indian warrior, Kelly found his touch more than intimate—it was oddly familiar. He seemed to be calling her back to another time, to a place where they would find love again . . .

**FOREVER IN HIS ARMS**                   (3385, $4.95/$5.95)
Whispers of war between the North and South were riding the wind the summer Jenny Delaney fell in love with Tyler Mackenzie. Time was fast running out for secret trysts and lovers' dreams, and she would have to choose between the life she held so dear and the man whose passion made her burn as brightly as the evening star . . .

**MIDNIGHT CAPTIVE**                      (2593, $3.95/$4.95)
After a poor, ragged girlhood with her gypsy kinfolk, Krissoula knew that all she wanted from life was her share of riches. There was only one way for the penniless temptress to earn a cent: fake interest in a man, drug him, and pocket everything he had! Then the seductress met dashing Esteban and unquenchable passion seared her soul . . .

**SEA JEWEL**                             (3013, $4.50/$5.50)
Hot-tempered Alaric had long planned the humiliation of Freya, the daughter of the most hated foe. He'd make the wench from across the ocean his lowly bedchamber slave—but he never suspected she would become the mistress of his heart, his treasured sea jewel . . .

*Available wherever paperbacks are sold, or order direct from the Publisher. Send cover price plus 50¢ per copy for mailing and handling to Penguin USA, P.O. Box 999, c/o Dept. 17109, Bergenfield, NJ 07621. Residents of New York and Tennessee must include sales tax. DO NOT SEND CASH.*

## WHAT'S LOVE GOT TO DO WITH IT?

*Everything . . . Just ask Kathleen Drymon . . . and Zebra Books*

| | |
|---|---|
| *CASTAWAY ANGEL* | *(3569-1, $4.50/$5.50)* |
| *GENTLE SAVAGE* | *(3888-7, $4.50/$5.50)* |
| *MIDNIGHT BRIDE* | *(3265-X, $4.50/$5.50)* |
| *VELVET SAVAGE* | *(3886-0, $4.50/$5.50)* |
| *TEXAS BLOSSOM* | *(3887-9, $4.50/$5.50)* |
| *WARRIOR OF THE SUN* | *(3924-7, $4.99/$5.99)* |